WILL I SEE?

Story by Iskwé and Erin Leslie
Script by David Alexander Robertson
Art by GMB Chomichuk

**HIGHWATER
PRESS**

TRIGGER WARNING: VIOLENCE AGAINST WOMEN.

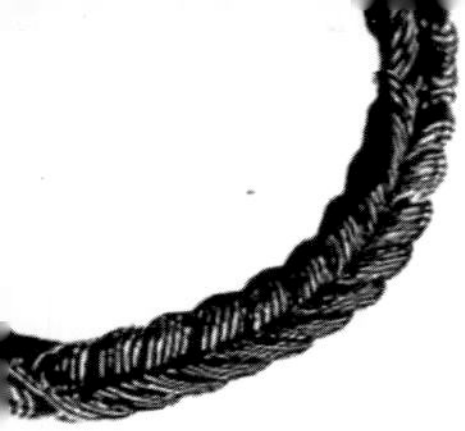
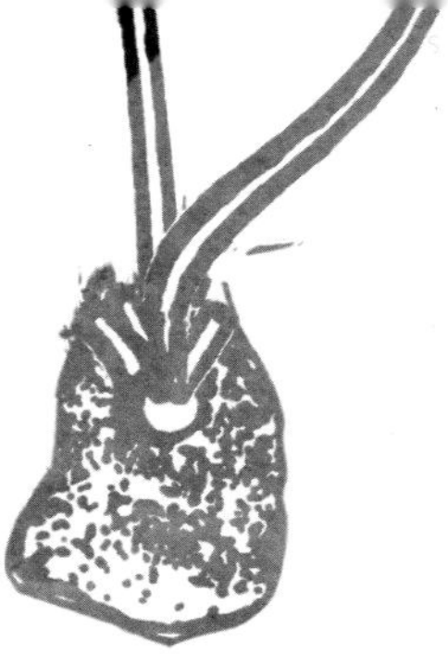
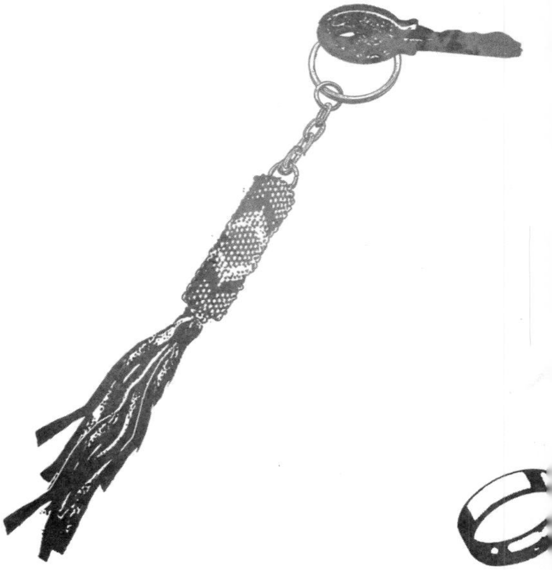
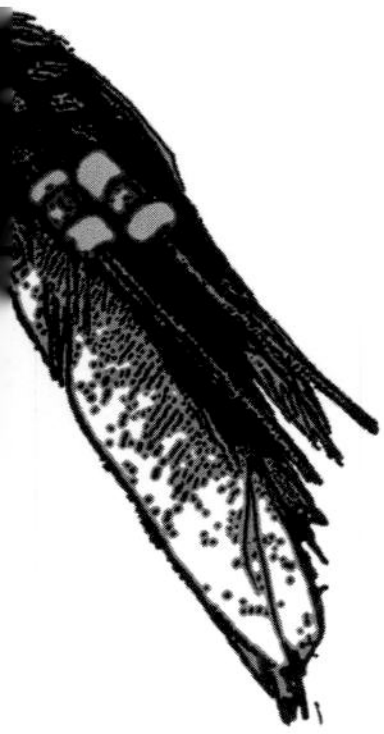

For each of the women we've lost, together, we stand as one.

— Iskwé

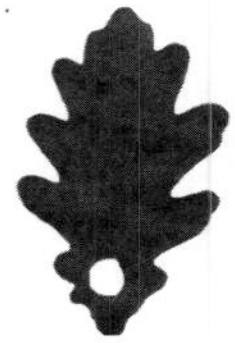

For the over four thousand Indigenous women and girls we have lost and for my daughters, that they grow up strong, and in a safer place.

— David Alexander Robertson

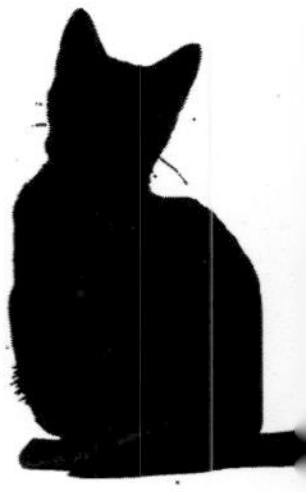

For the seen and the unseen. For the forgotten and the remembered.

— GMB Chomichuk

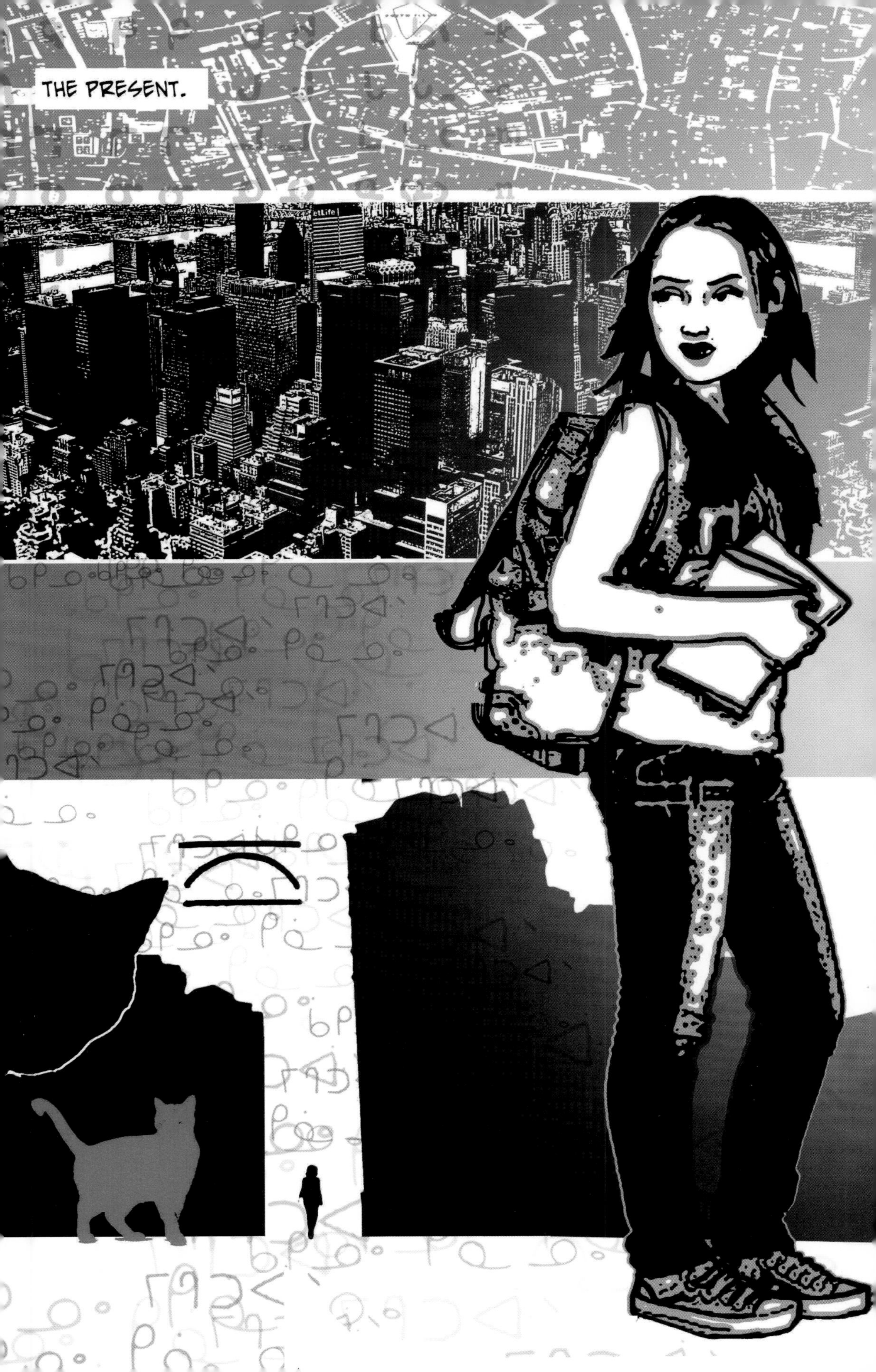
THE PRESENT.

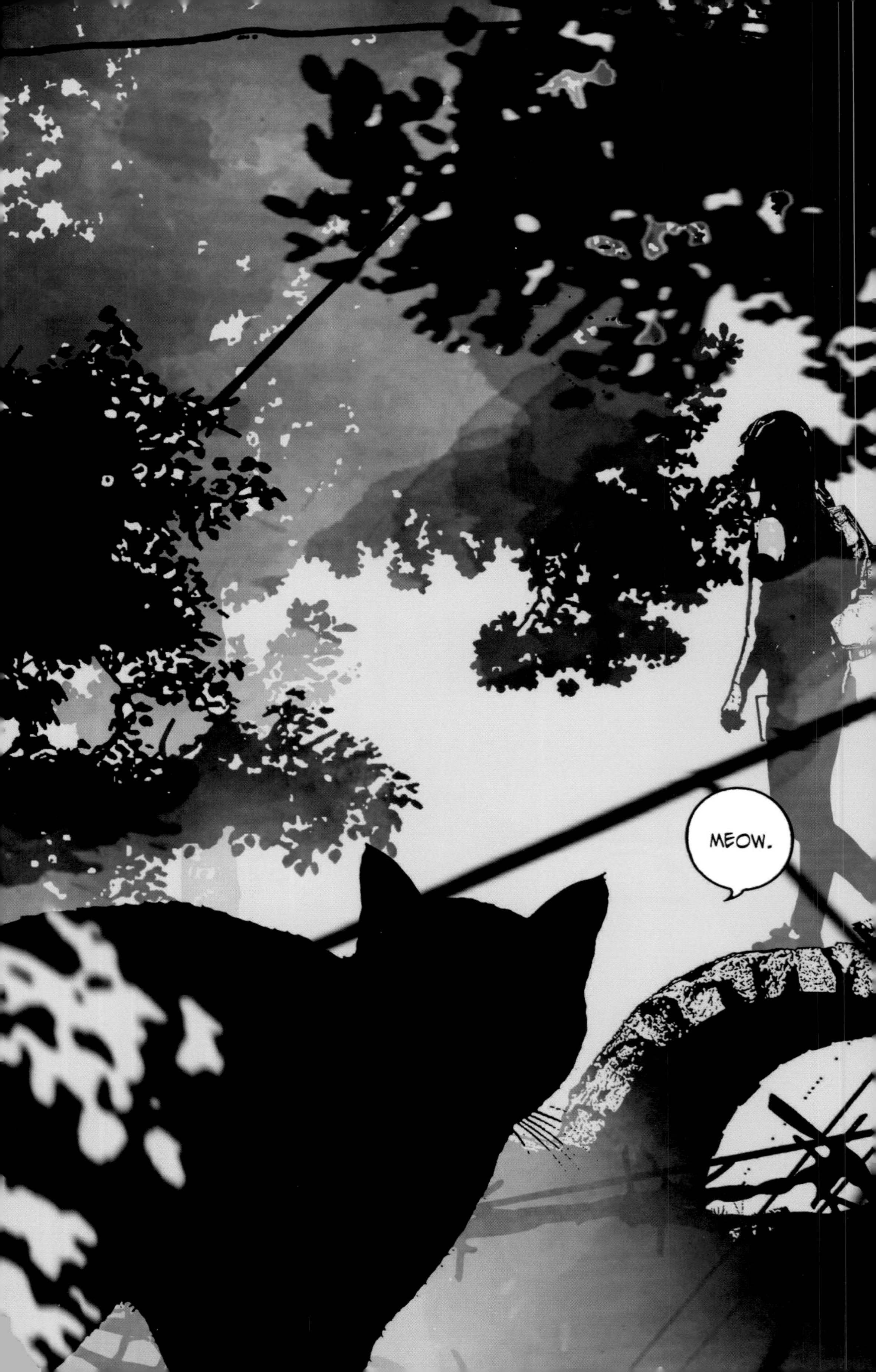
MEOW.

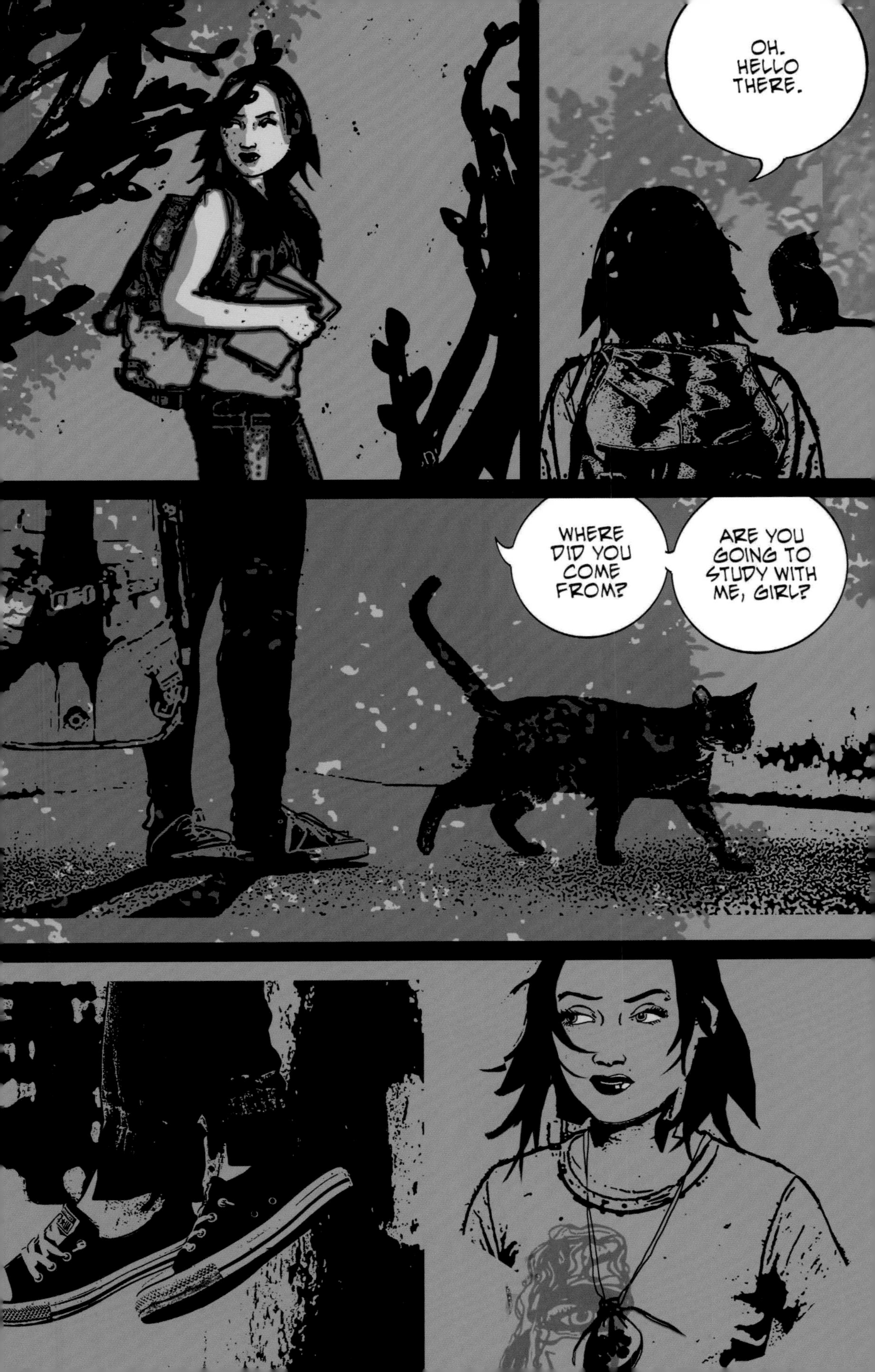
OH. HELLO THERE.
WHERE DID YOU COME FROM?
ARE YOU GOING TO STUDY WITH ME, GIRL?

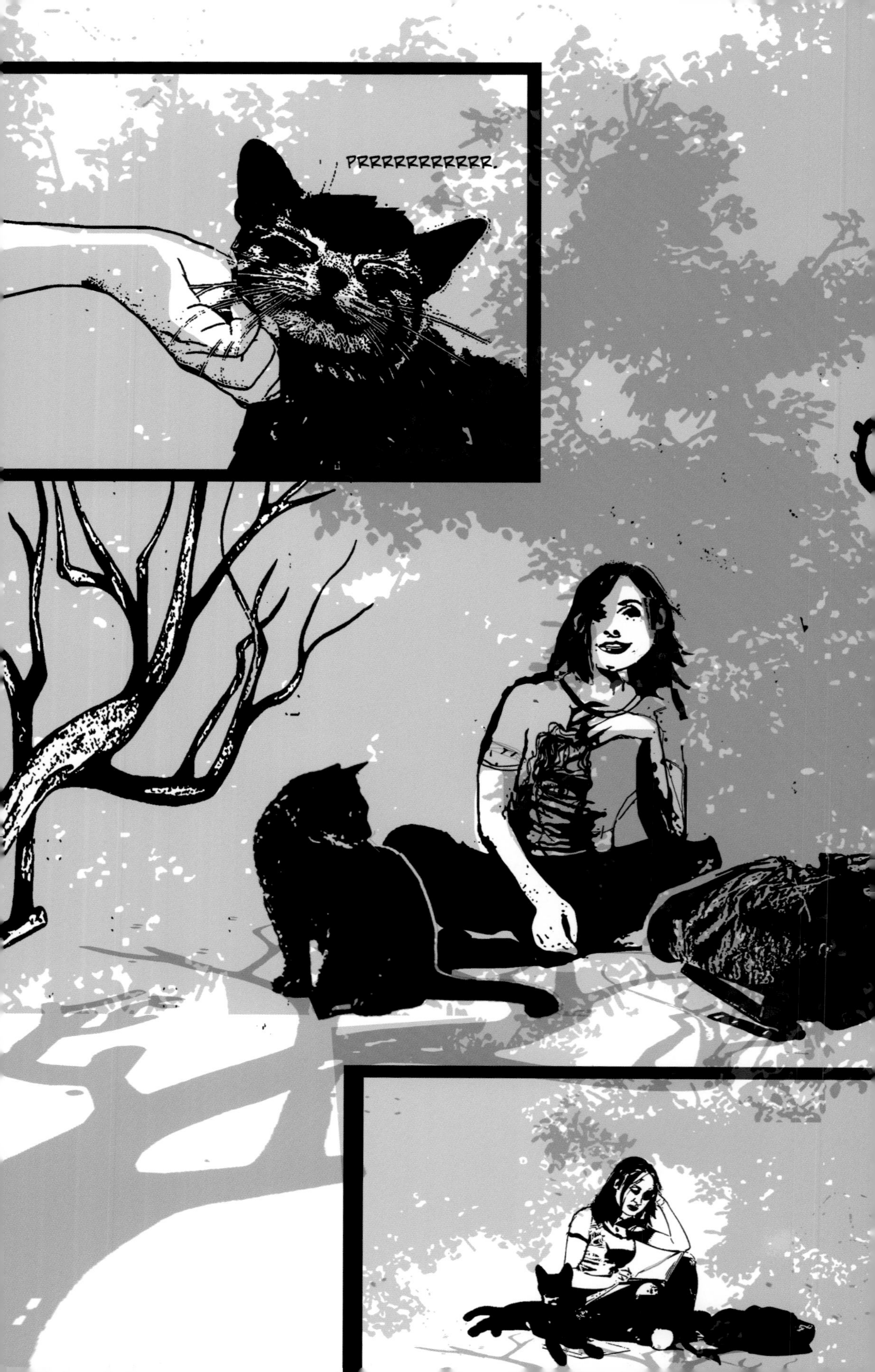
PRRRRRRRRRRR.

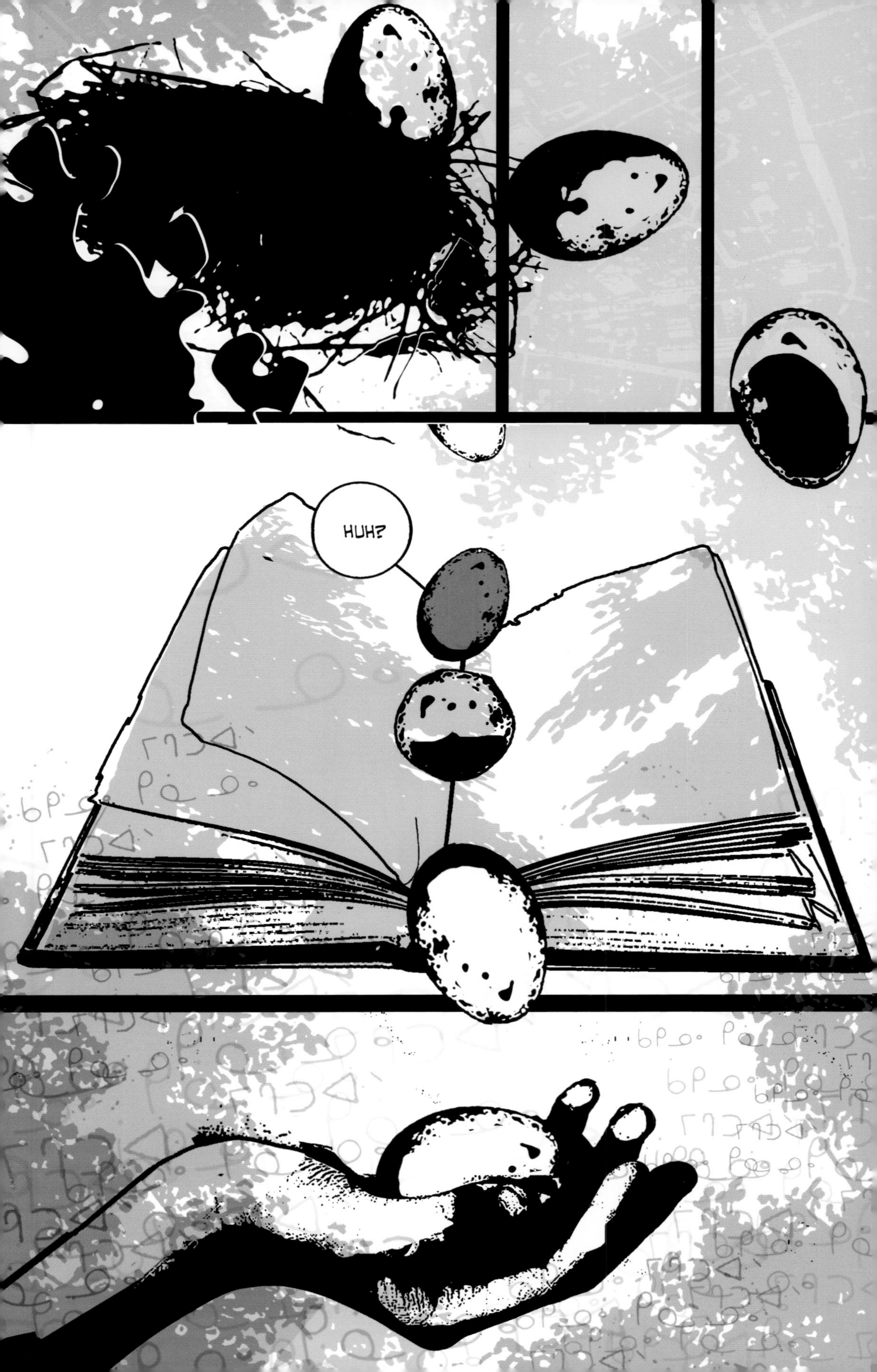
HUH?

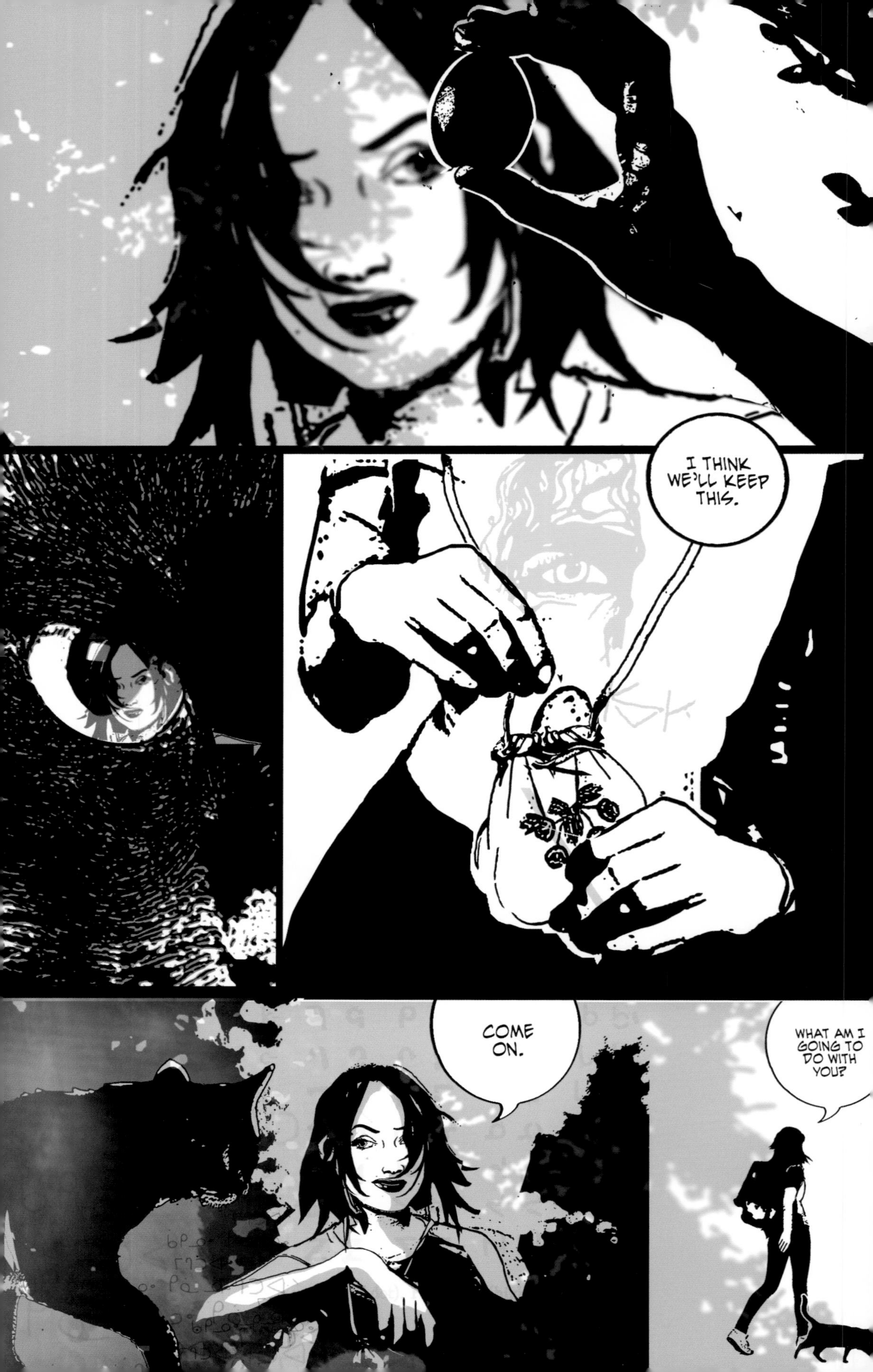
I THINK WE'LL KEEP THIS.
COME ON.
WHAT AM I GOING TO DO WITH YOU?

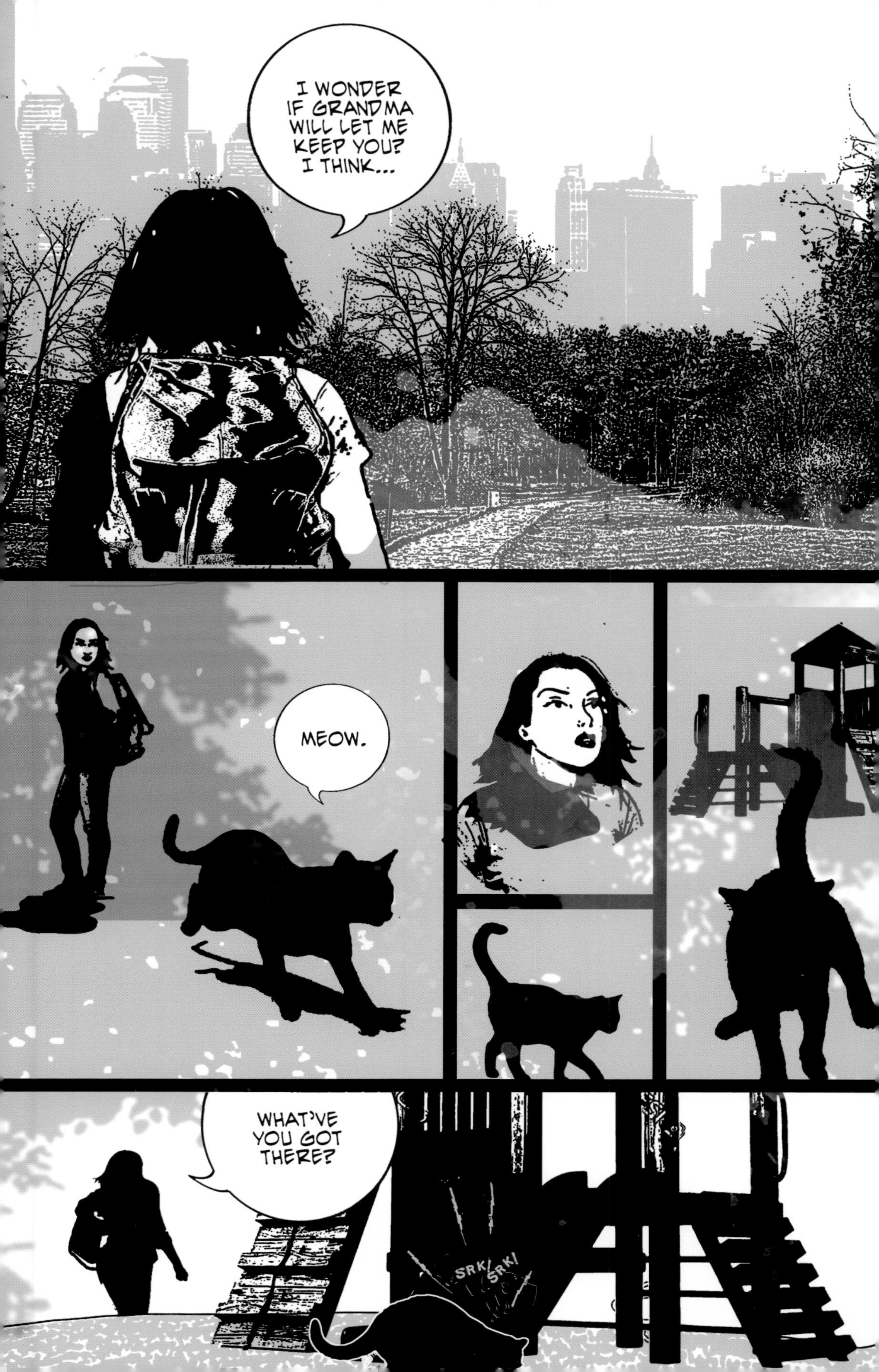
I WONDER IF GRANDMA WILL LET ME KEEP YOU? I THINK...
MEOW.
WHAT'VE YOU GOT THERE?
SRK! SRK!

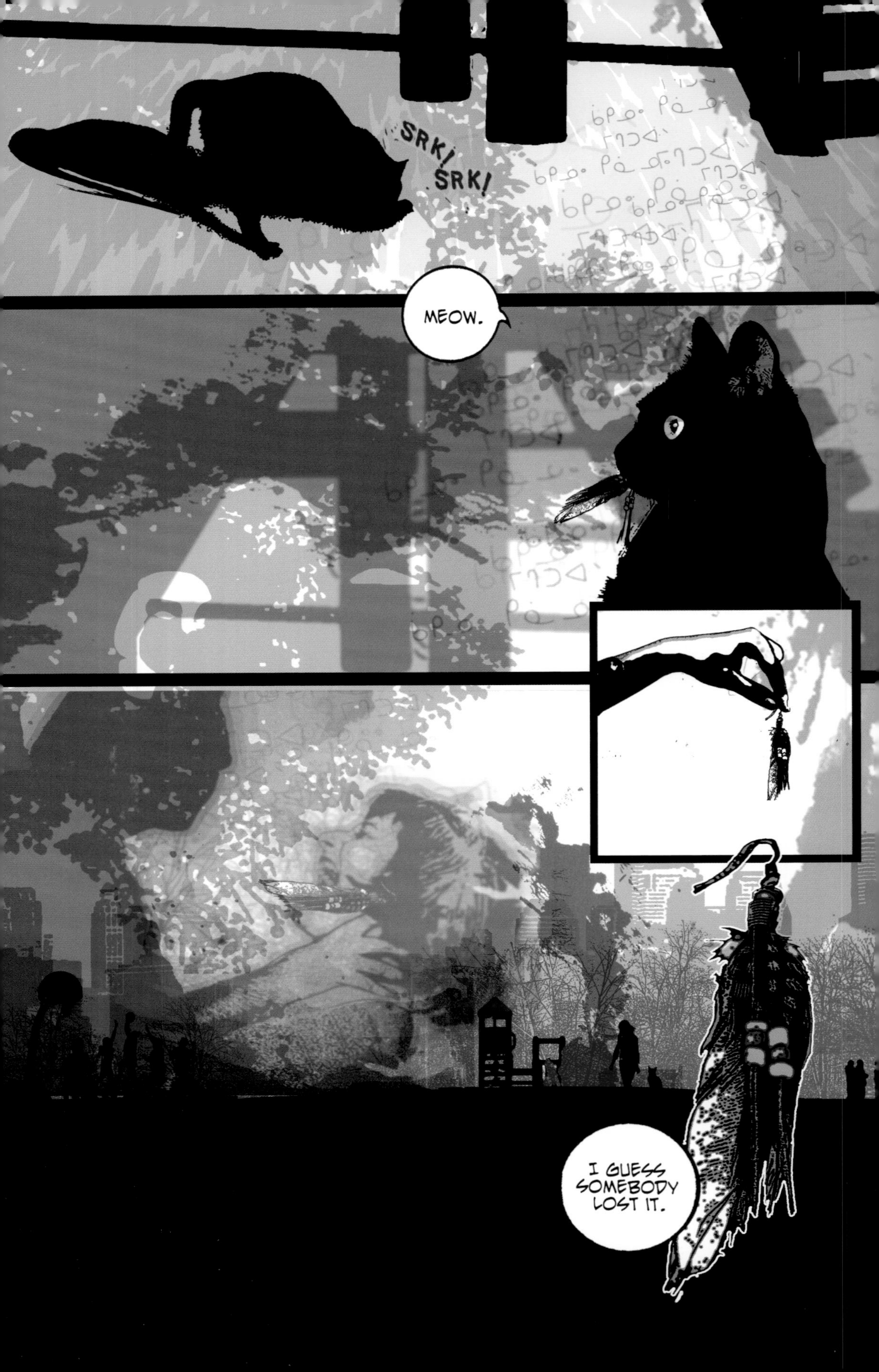
SRK!
SRK!
MEOW.
I GUESS SOMEBODY LOST IT.

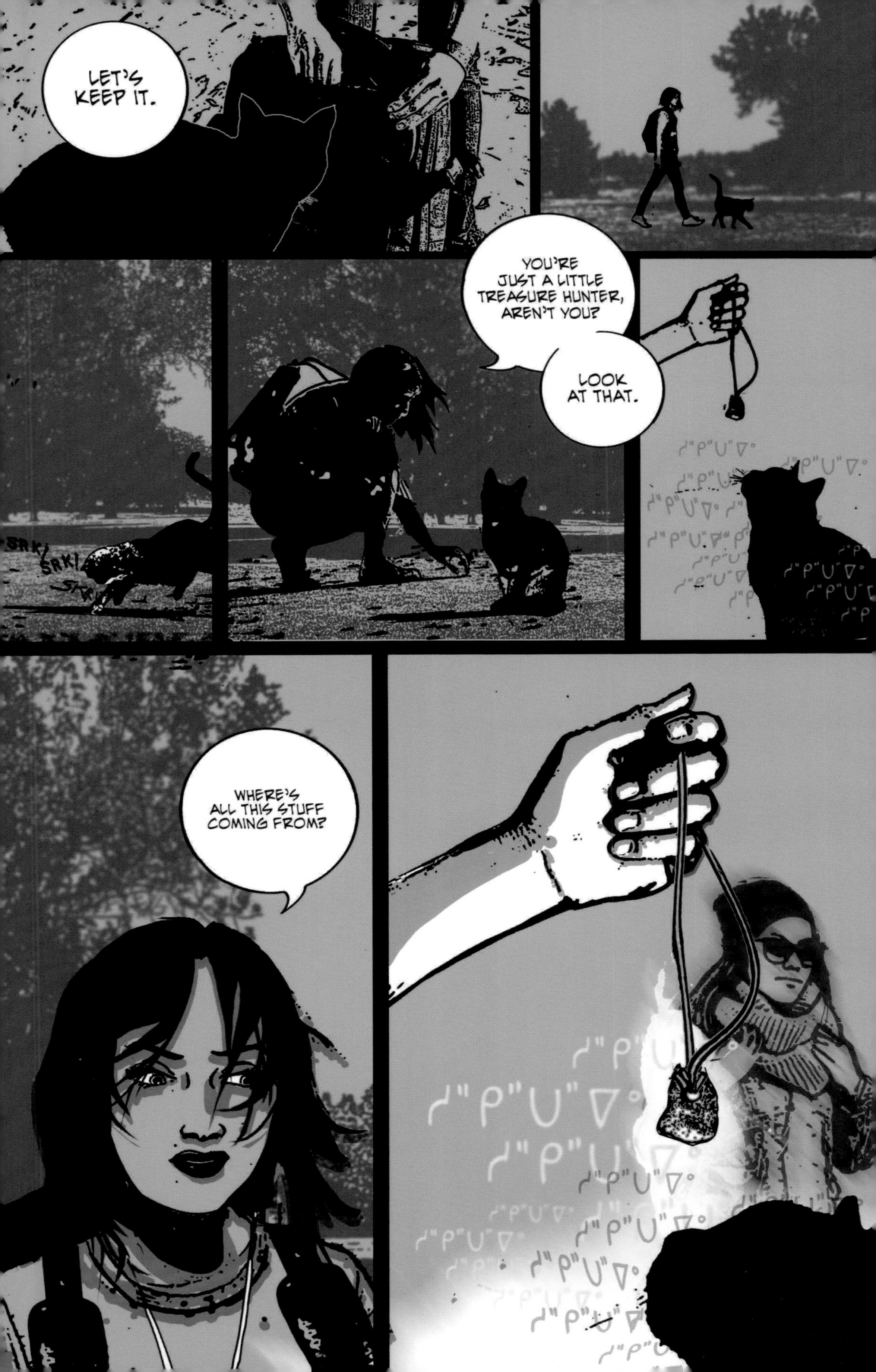
LET'S KEEP IT.
SRK! SRK!
YOU'RE JUST A LITTLE TREASURE HUNTER, AREN'T YOU?
LOOK AT THAT.
WHERE'S ALL THIS STUFF COMING FROM?

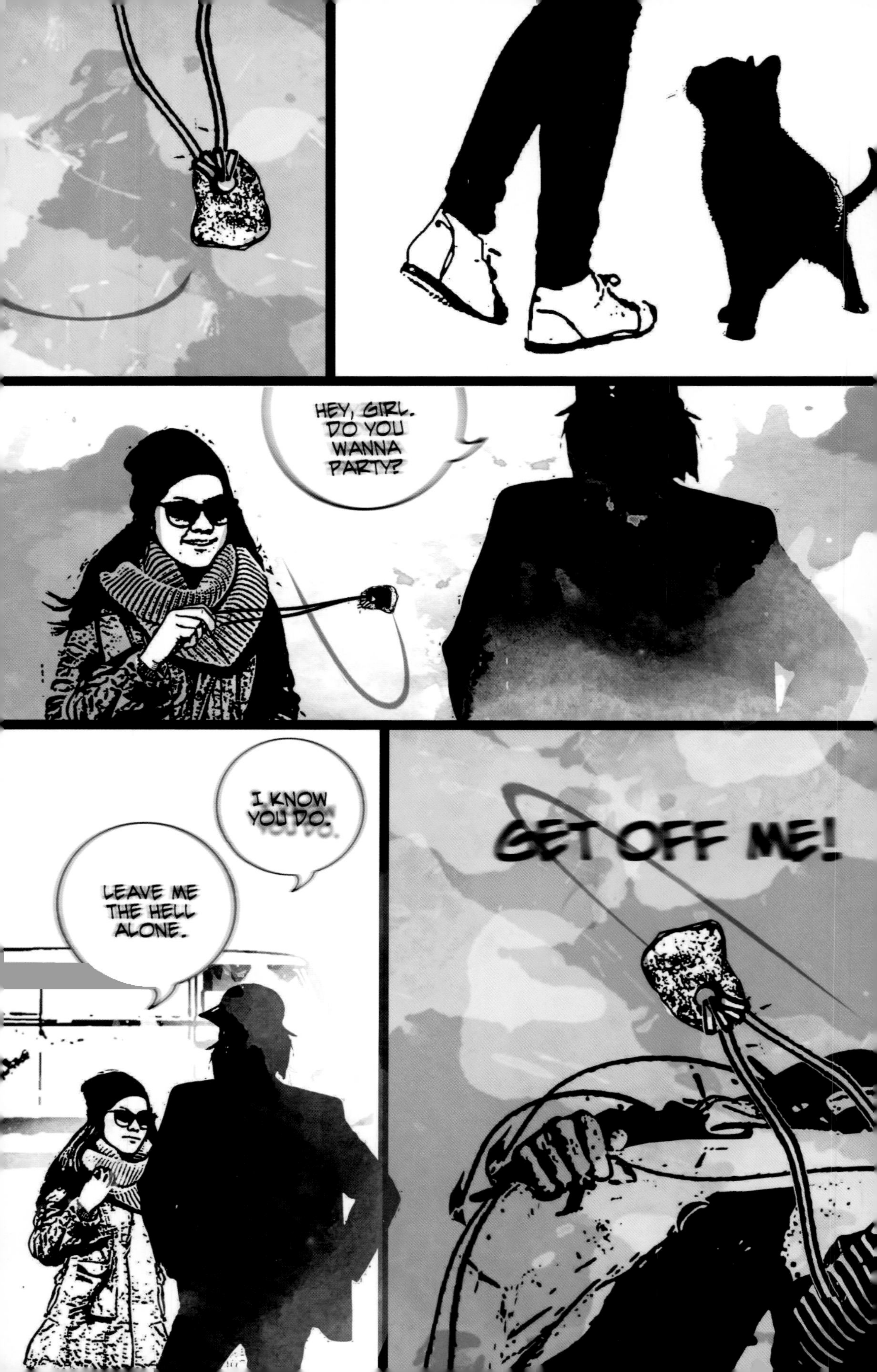
HEY, GIRL. DO YOU WANNA PARTY?
I KNOW YOU DO.
LEAVE ME THE HELL ALONE.
GET OFF ME!

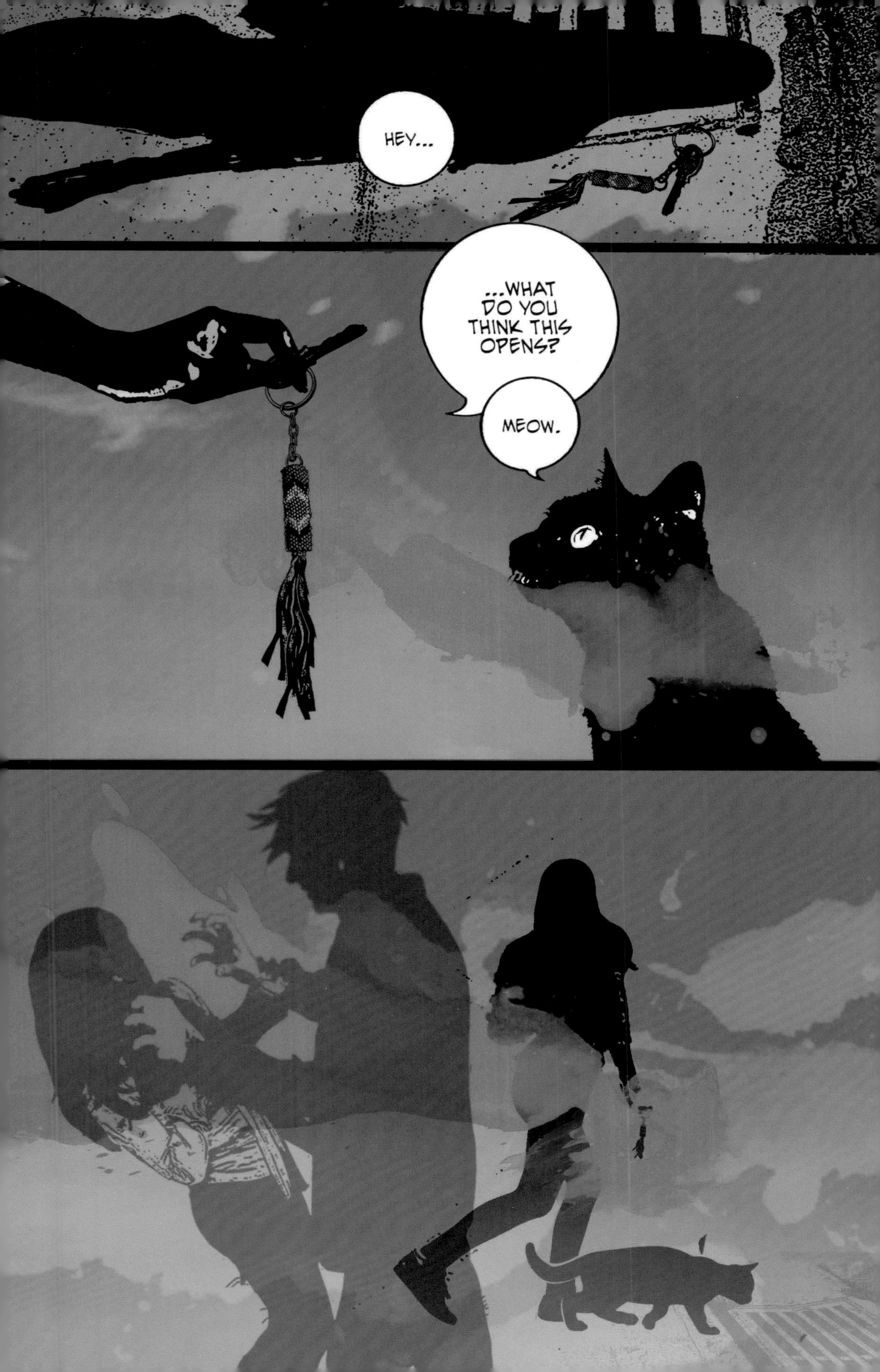
HEY...
...WHAT DO YOU THINK THIS OPENS?
MEOW.

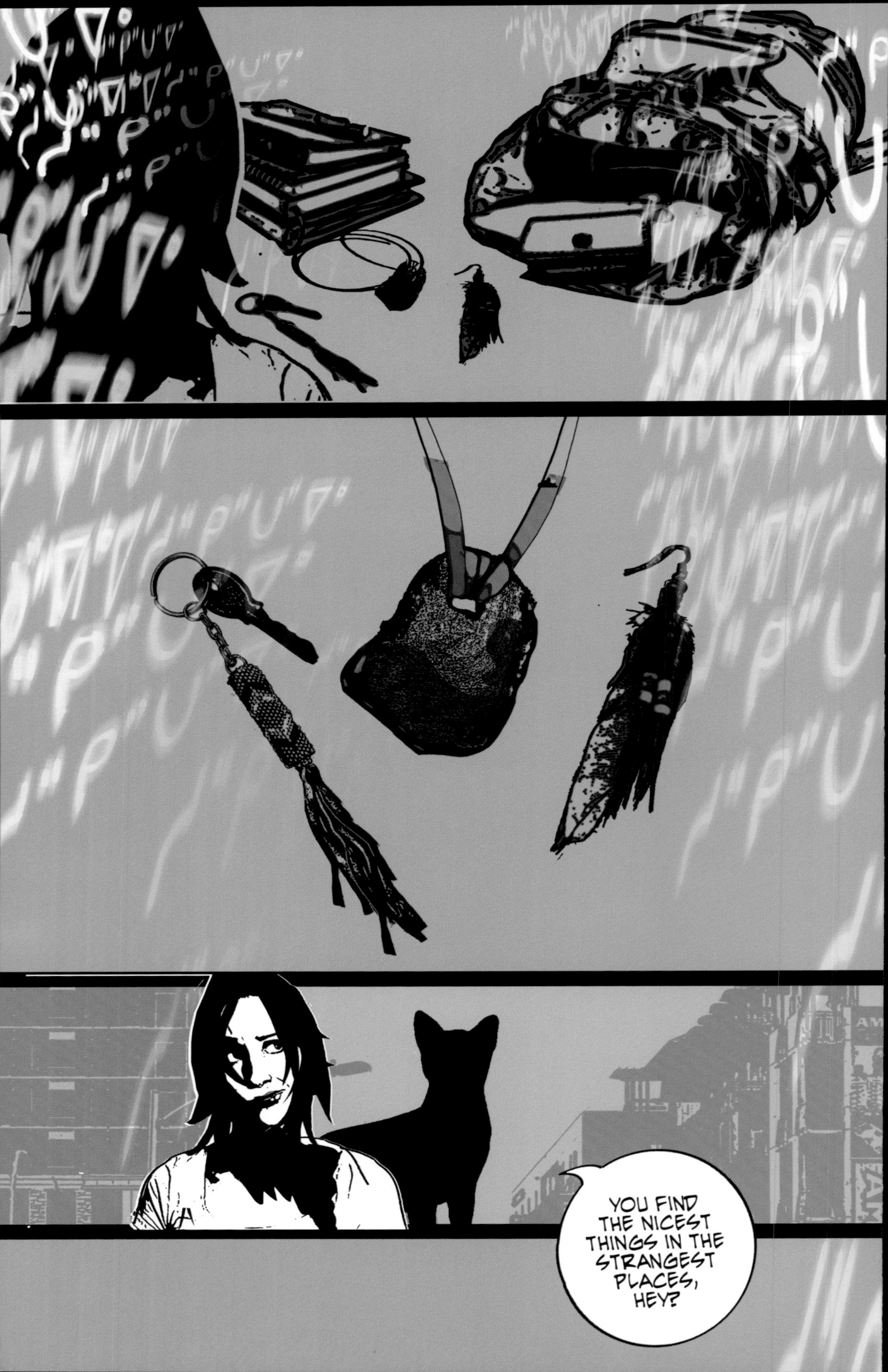
YOU FIND THE NICEST THINGS IN THE STRANGEST PLACES, HEY?

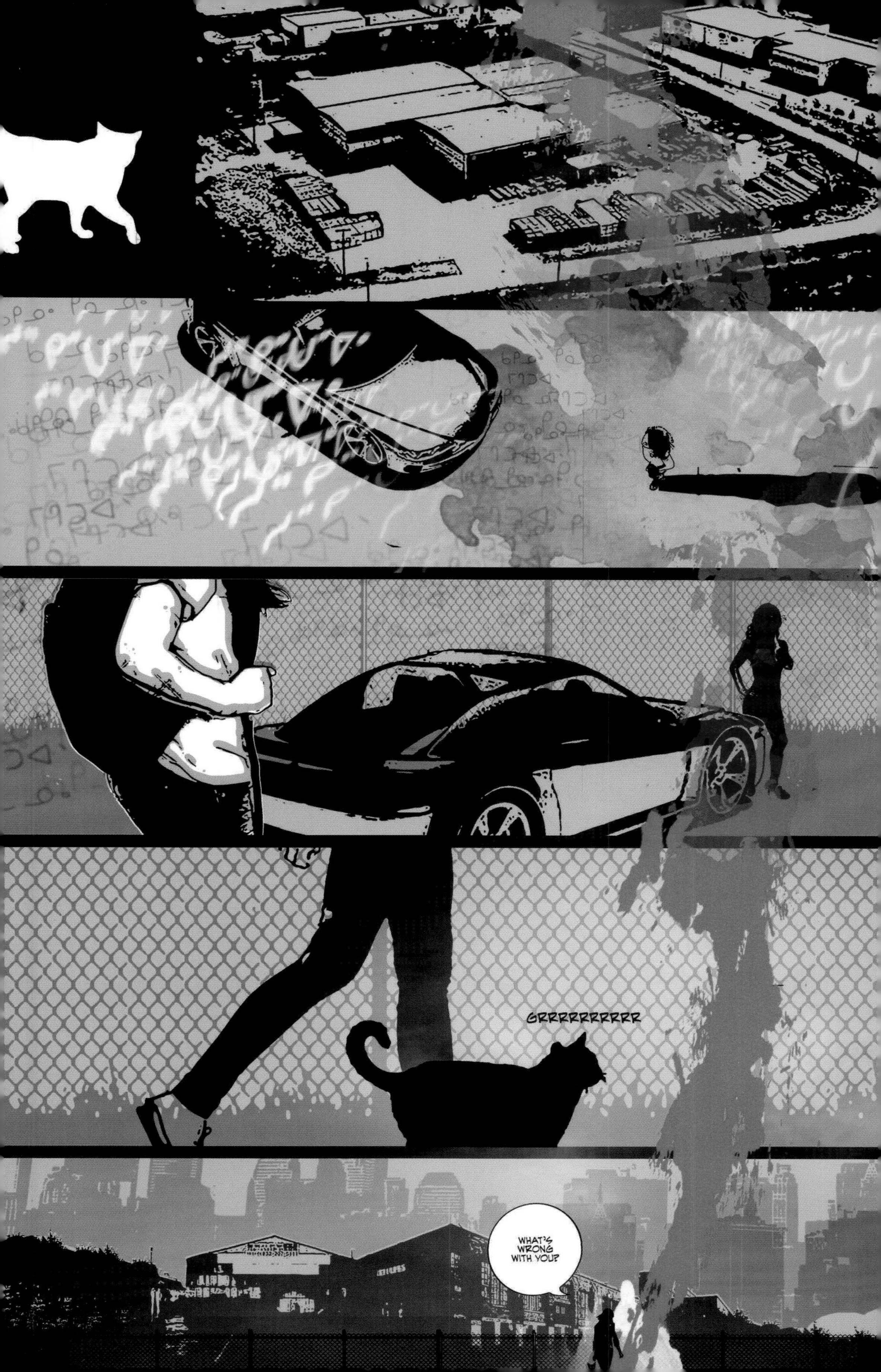
GRRRRRRRRRR
WHAT'S WRONG WITH YOU?

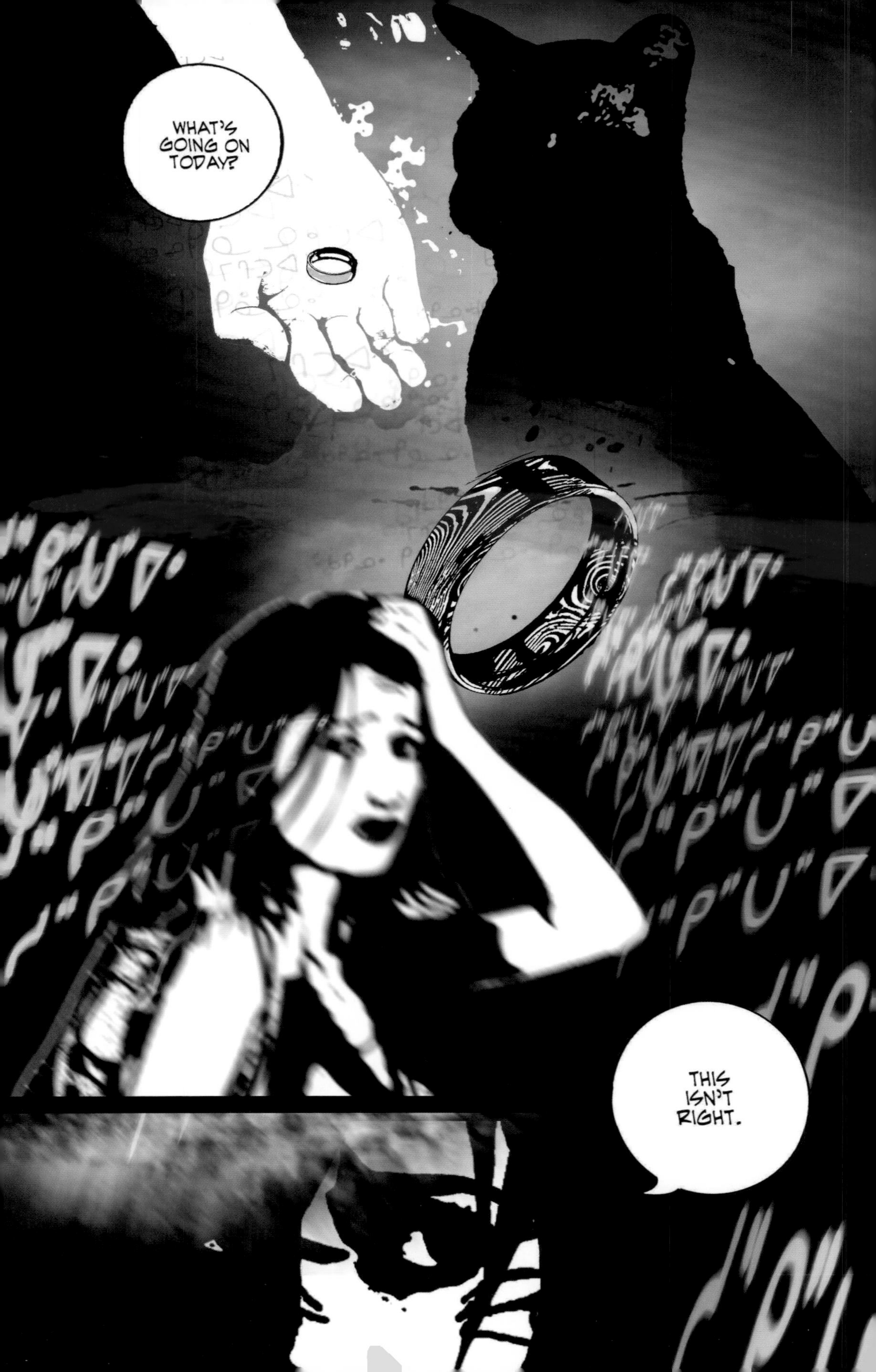
WHAT'S GOING ON TODAY?
THIS ISN'T RIGHT.

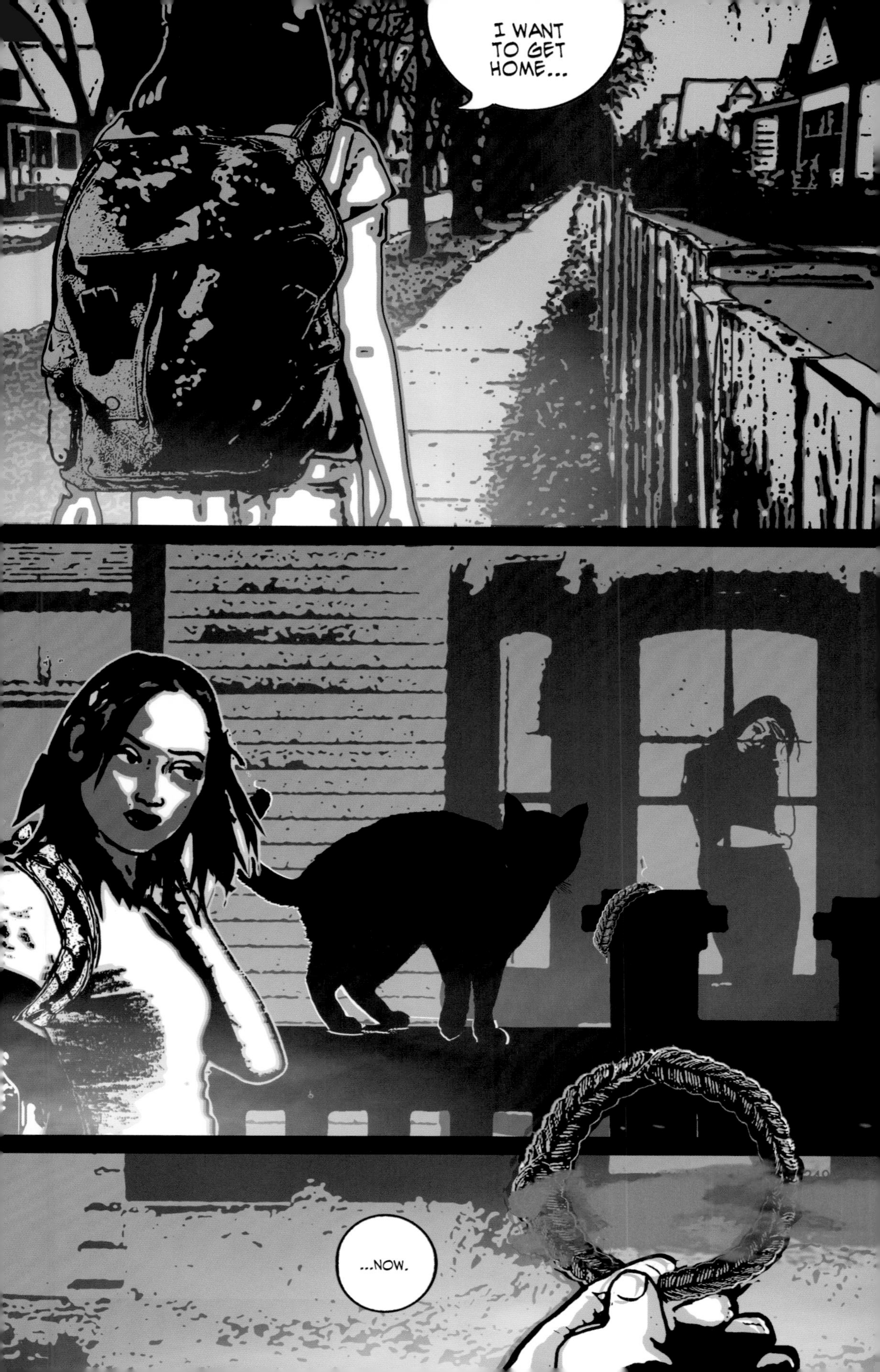
I WANT TO GET HOME...
...NOW.

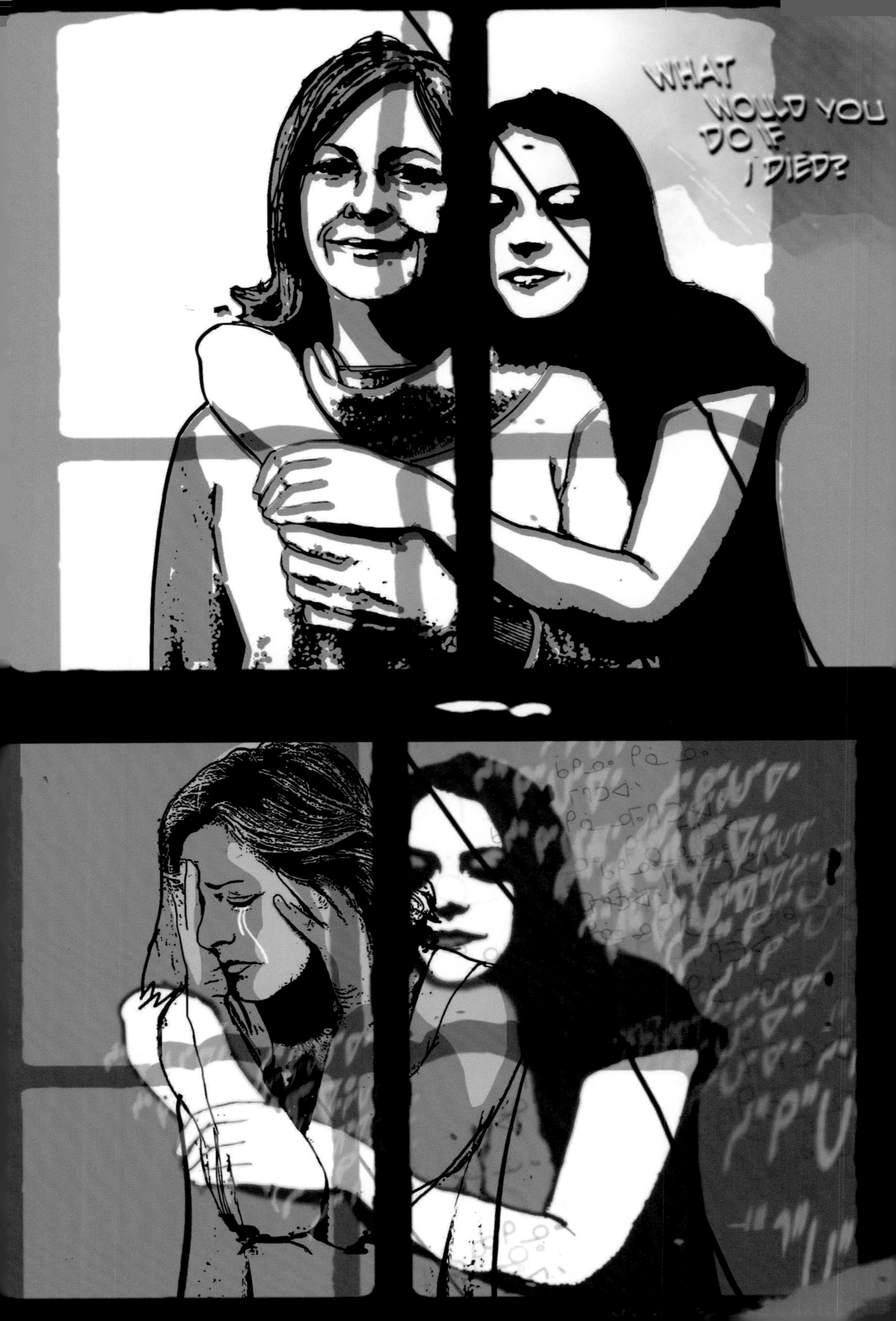
WHAT WOULD YOU DO IF I DIED?

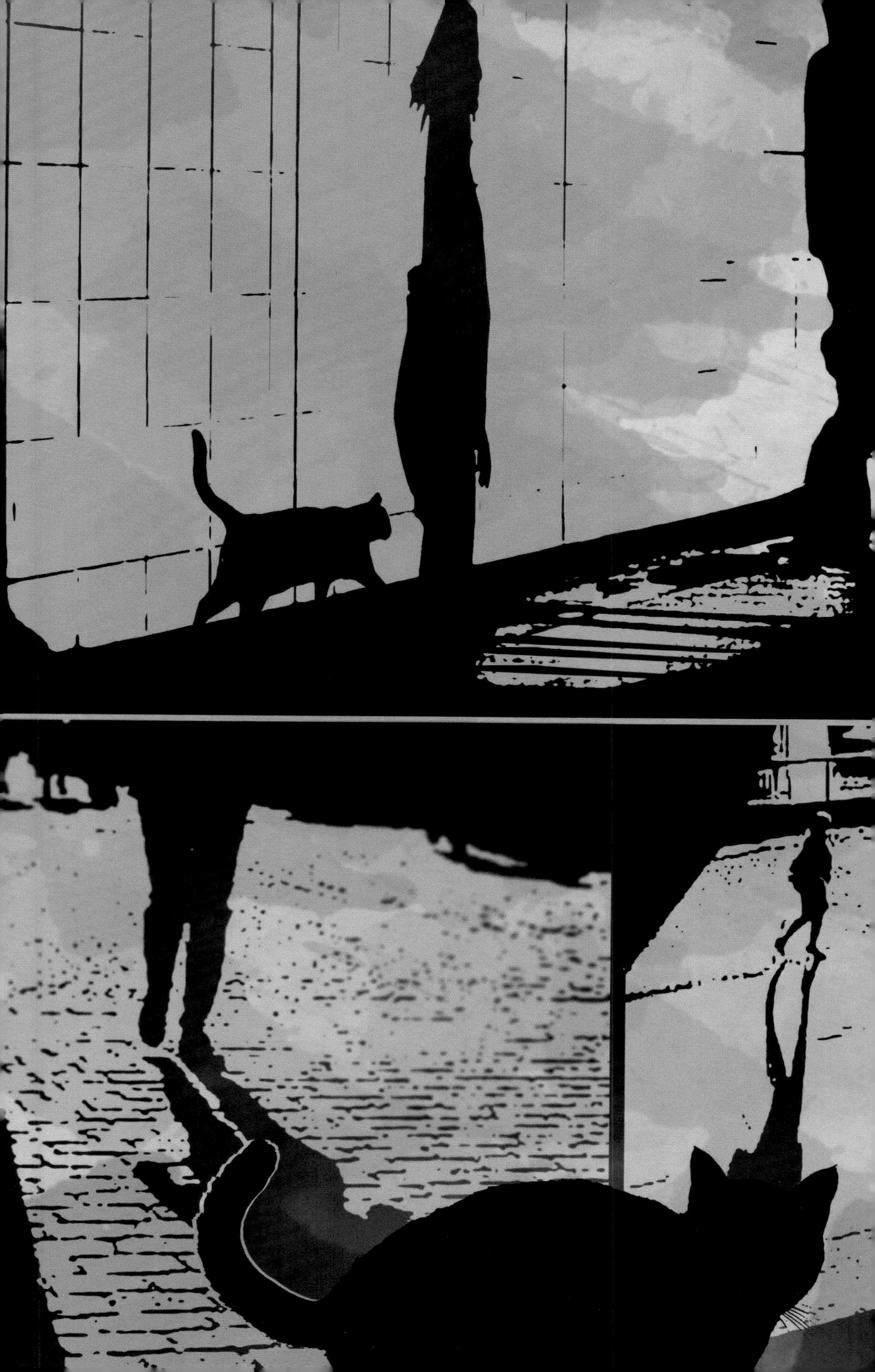

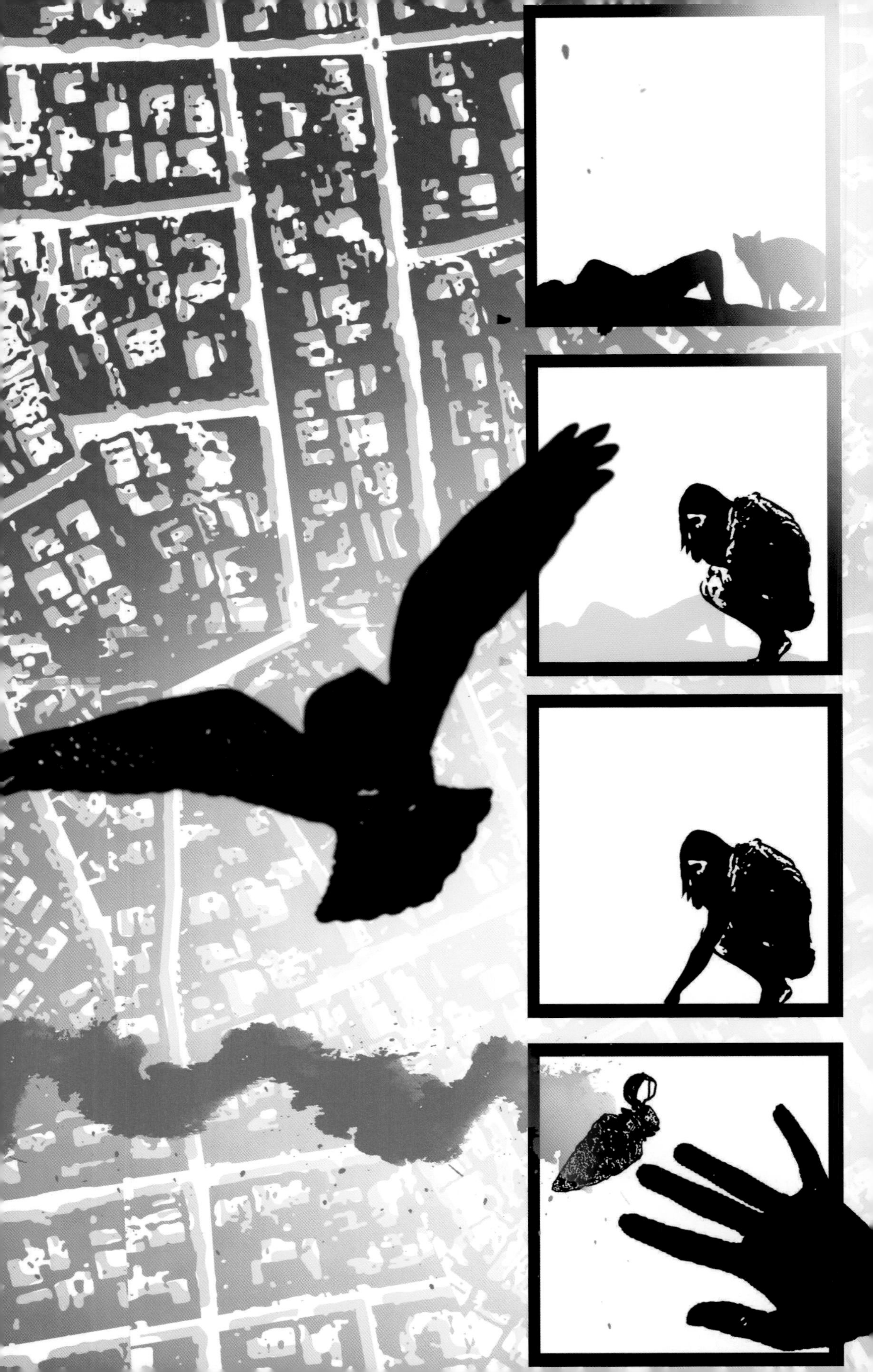

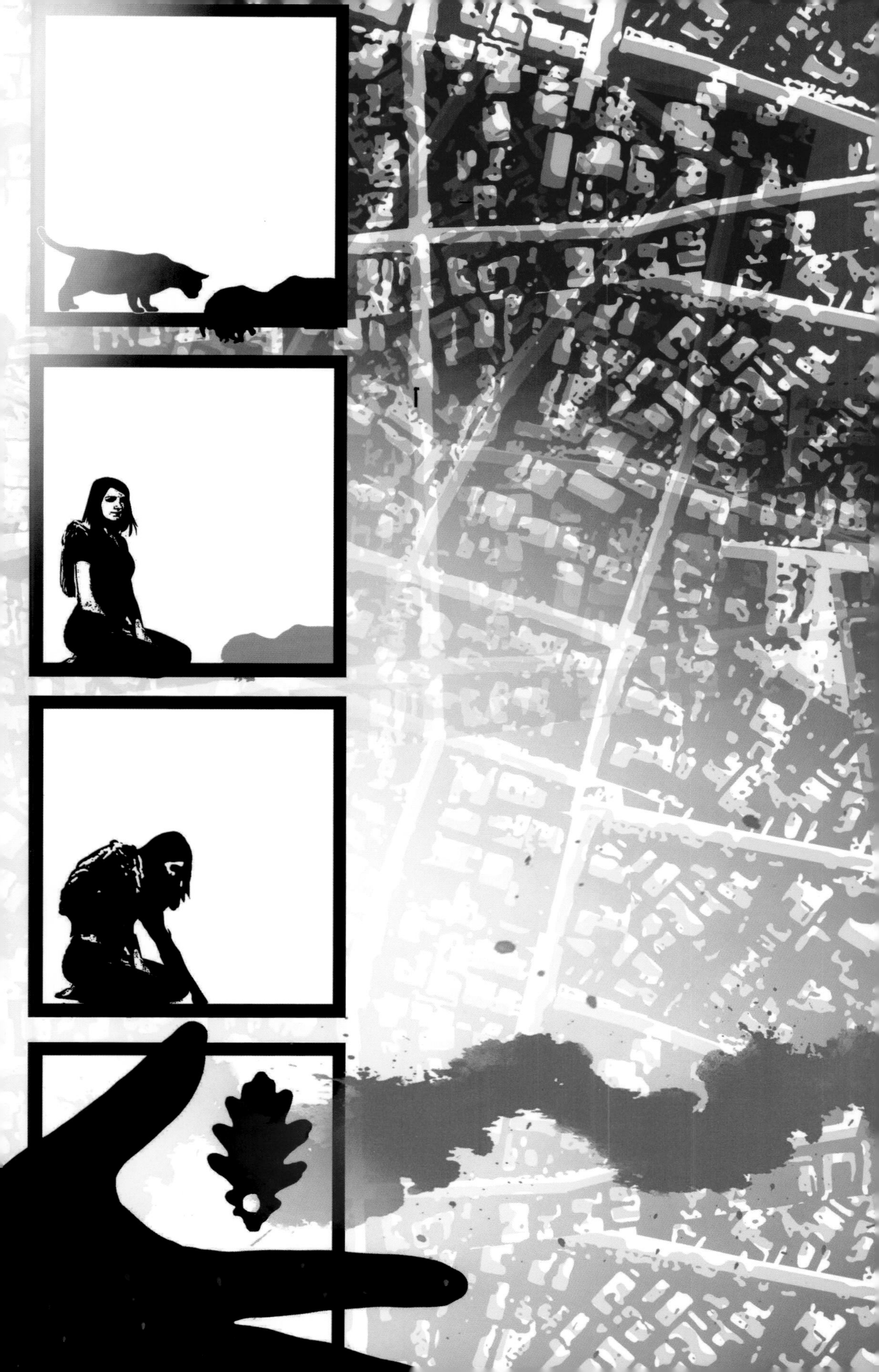

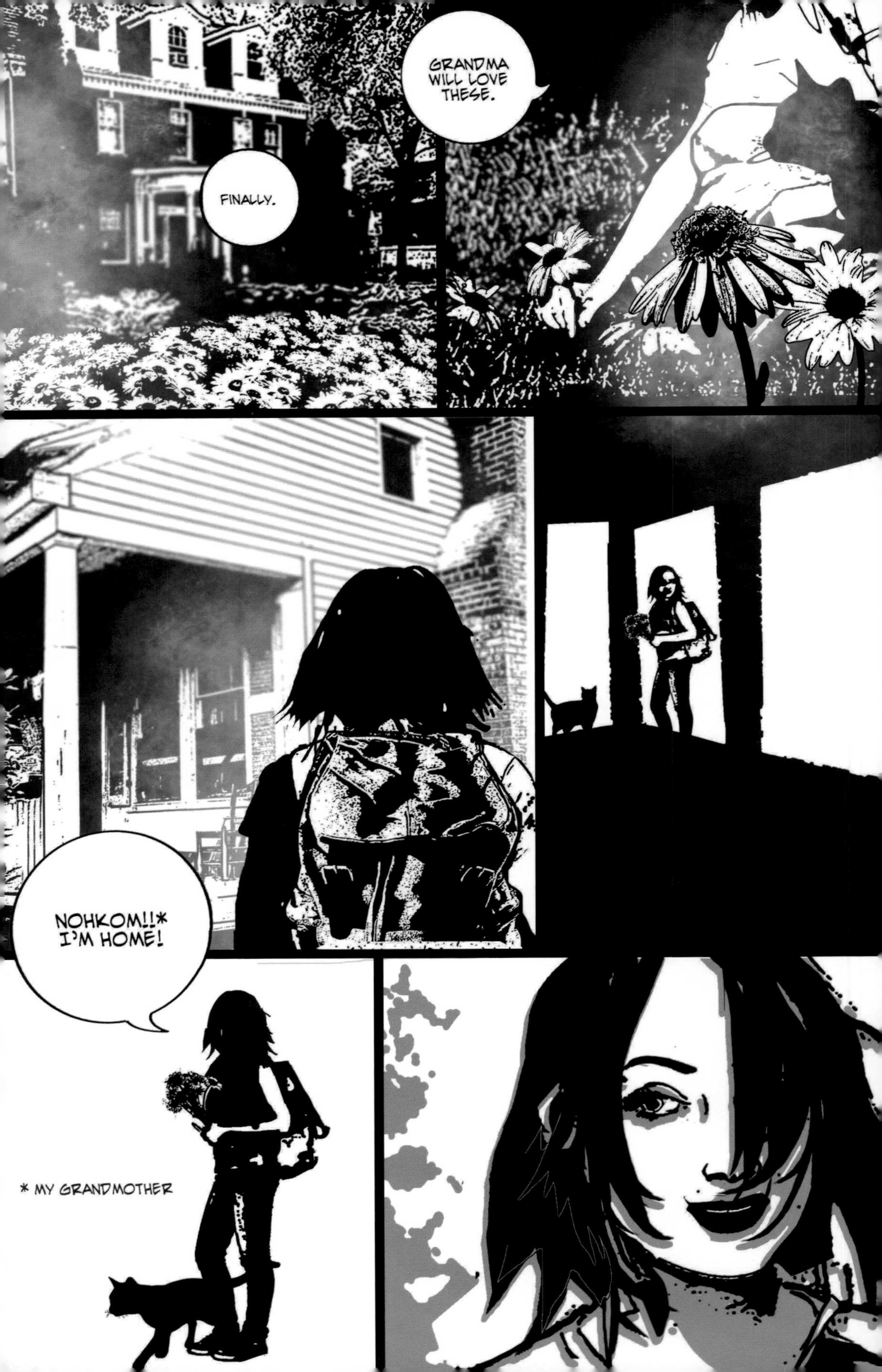
FINALLY.
GRANDMA WILL LOVE THESE.
NOHKOM!!* I'M HOME!
* MY GRANDMOTHER

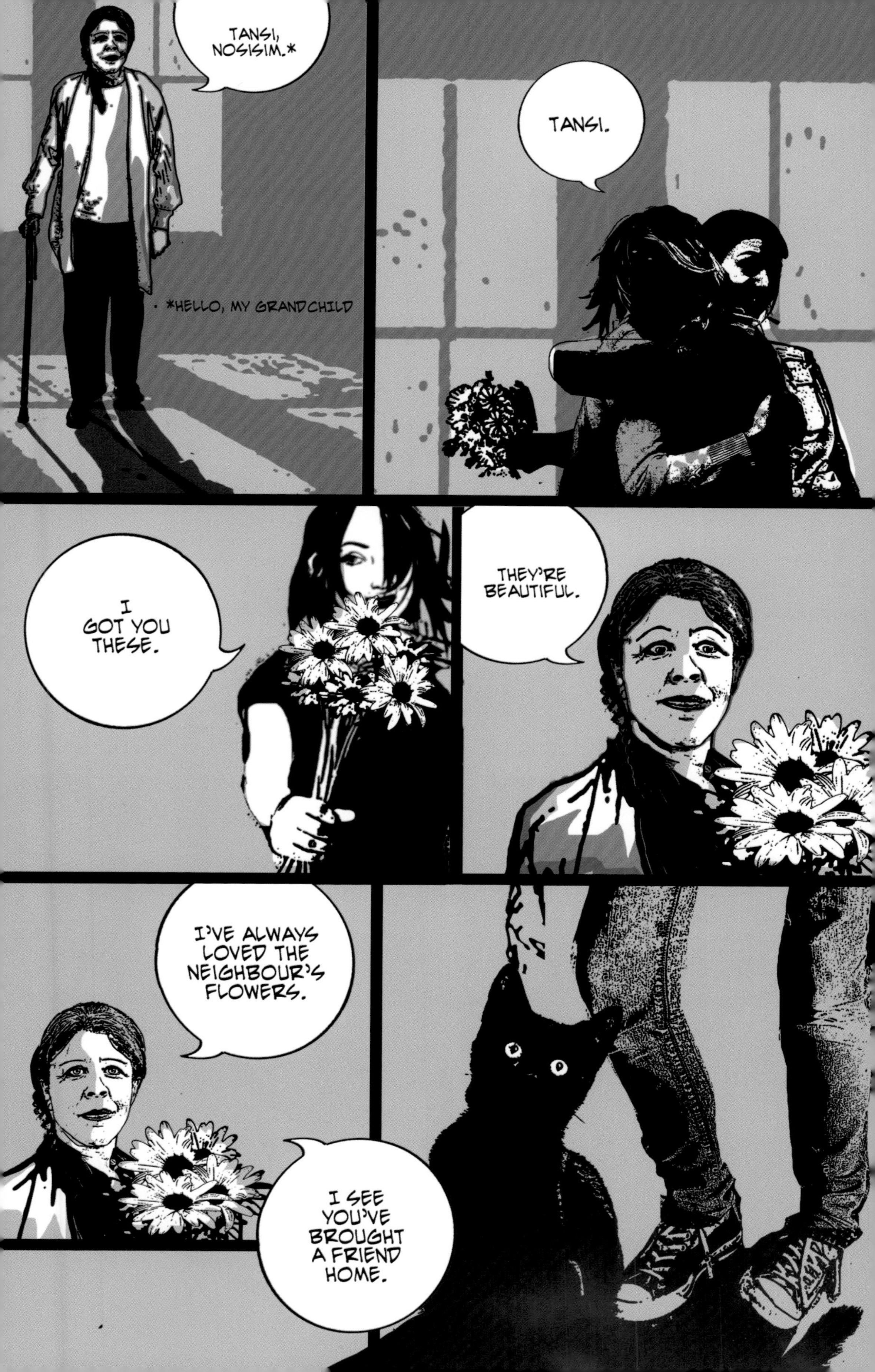
TANSI, NOSISIM.*
*HELLO, MY GRANDCHILD
TANSI.
I GOT YOU THESE.
THEY'RE BEAUTIFUL.
I'VE ALWAYS LOVED THE NEIGHBOUR'S FLOWERS.
I SEE YOU'VE BROUGHT A FRIEND HOME.

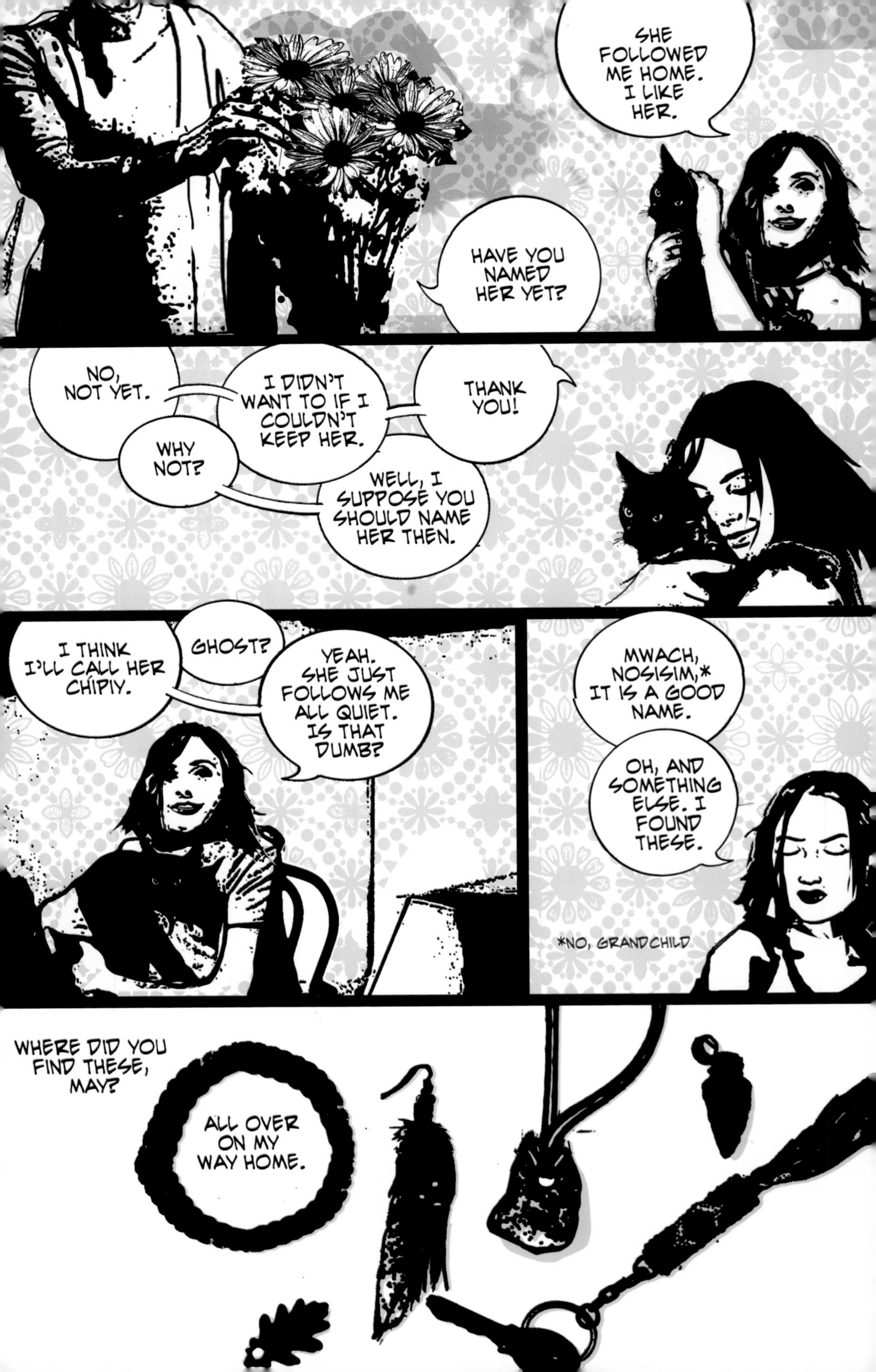
SHE FOLLOWED ME HOME. I LIKE HER.
HAVE YOU NAMED HER YET?
NO, NOT YET.
I DIDN'T WANT TO IF I COULDN'T KEEP HER.
THANK YOU!
WHY NOT?
WELL, I SUPPOSE YOU SHOULD NAME HER THEN.
I THINK I'LL CALL HER CHÍPIY.
GHOST?
YEAH. SHE JUST FOLLOWS ME ALL QUIET. IS THAT DUMB?
MWACH, NOSISIM,* IT IS A GOOD NAME.
OH, AND SOMETHING ELSE. I FOUND THESE.
*NO, GRANDCHILD
WHERE DID YOU FIND THESE, MAY?
ALL OVER ON MY WAY HOME.

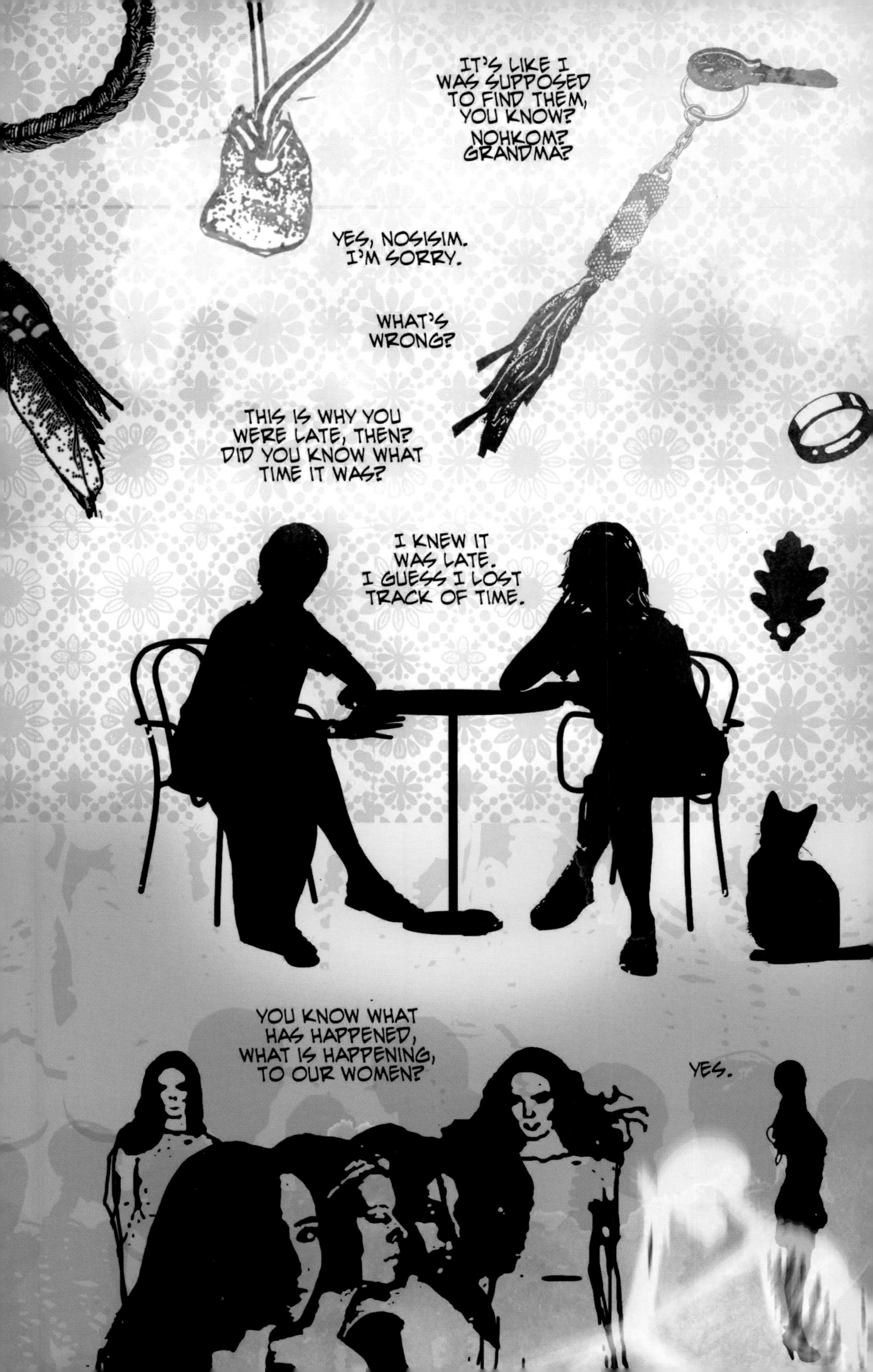
IT'S LIKE I WAS SUPPOSED TO FIND THEM, YOU KNOW?
NOHKOM? GRANDMA?
YES, NOSISIM. I'M SORRY.
WHAT'S WRONG?
THIS IS WHY YOU WERE LATE, THEN? DID YOU KNOW WHAT TIME IT WAS?
I KNEW IT WAS LATE. I GUESS I LOST TRACK OF TIME.
YOU KNOW WHAT HAS HAPPENED, WHAT IS HAPPENING, TO OUR WOMEN?
YES.

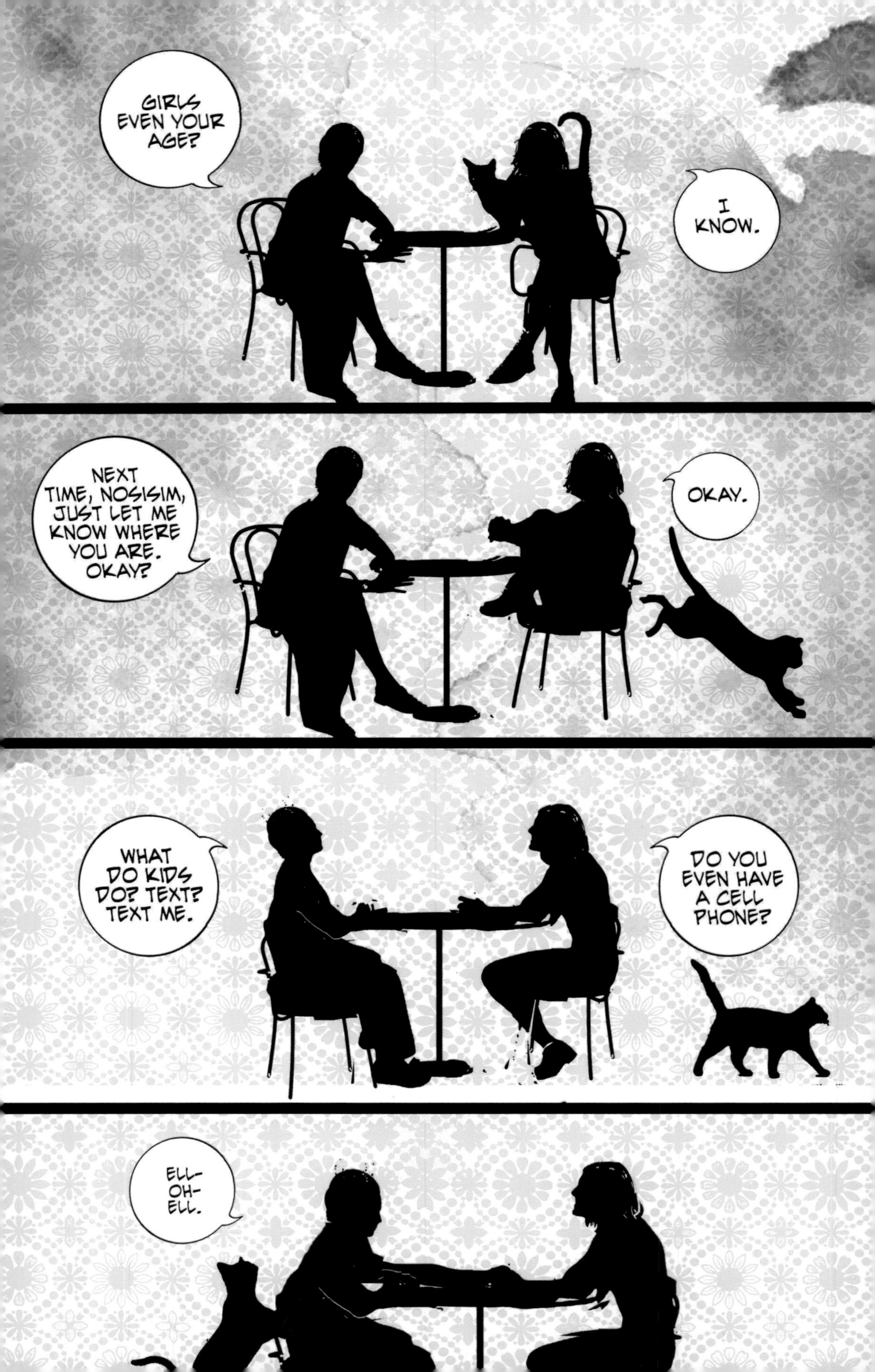
GIRLS EVEN YOUR AGE?
I KNOW.
NEXT TIME, NOSISIM, JUST LET ME KNOW WHERE YOU ARE. OKAY?
OKAY.
WHAT DO KIDS DO? TEXT? TEXT ME.
DO YOU EVEN HAVE A CELL PHONE?
ELL-OH-ELL.

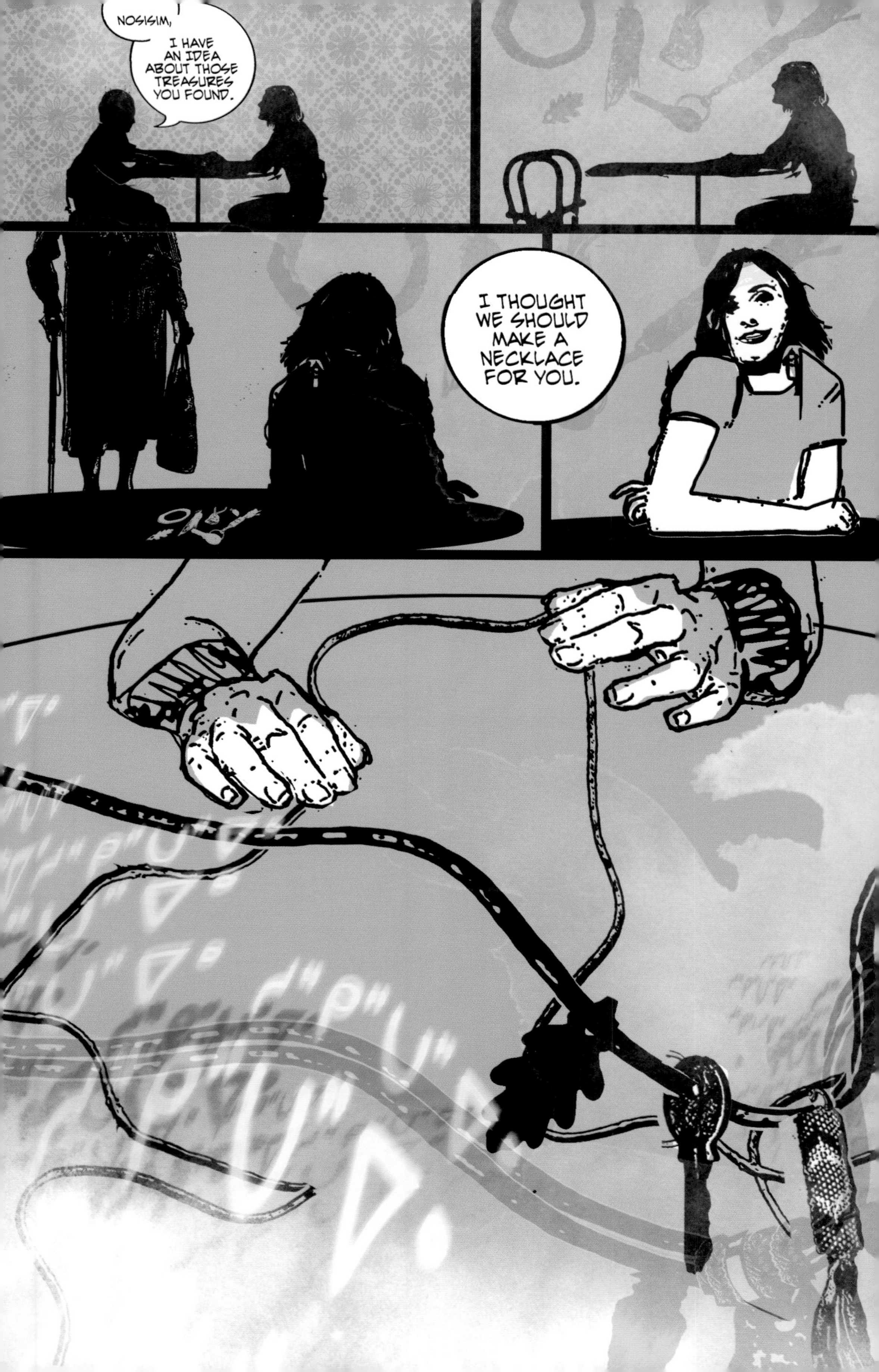
NOSISIM,
I HAVE AN IDEA ABOUT THOSE TREASURES YOU FOUND.
I THOUGHT WE SHOULD MAKE A NECKLACE FOR YOU.

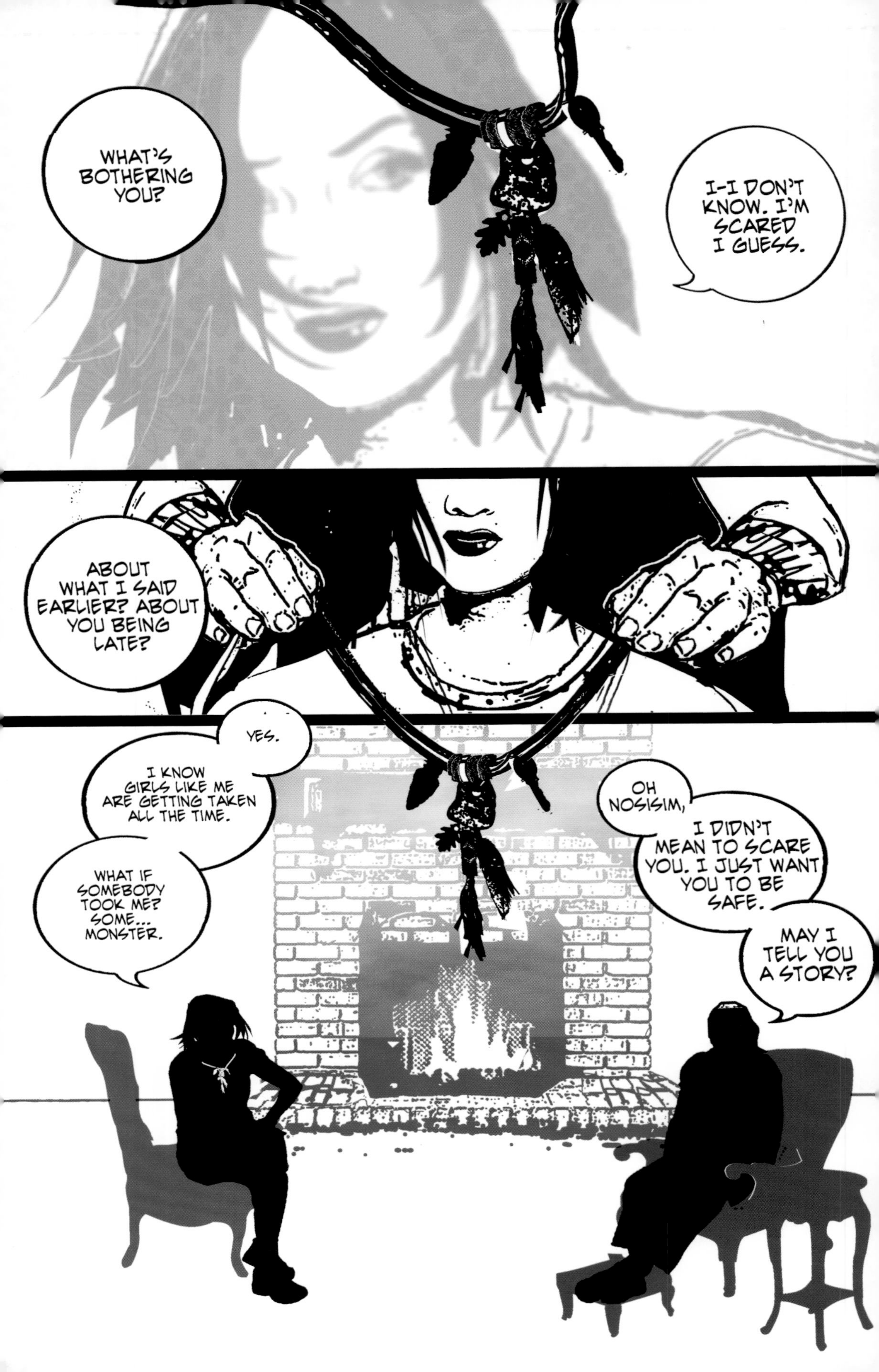
WHAT'S BOTHERING YOU?
I-I DON'T KNOW. I'M SCARED I GUESS.
ABOUT WHAT I SAID EARLIER? ABOUT YOU BEING LATE?
YES.
I KNOW GIRLS LIKE ME ARE GETTING TAKEN ALL THE TIME.
WHAT IF SOMEBODY TOOK ME? SOME... MONSTER.
OH NOSISIM,
I DIDN'T MEAN TO SCARE YOU. I JUST WANT YOU TO BE SAFE.
MAY I TELL YOU A STORY?

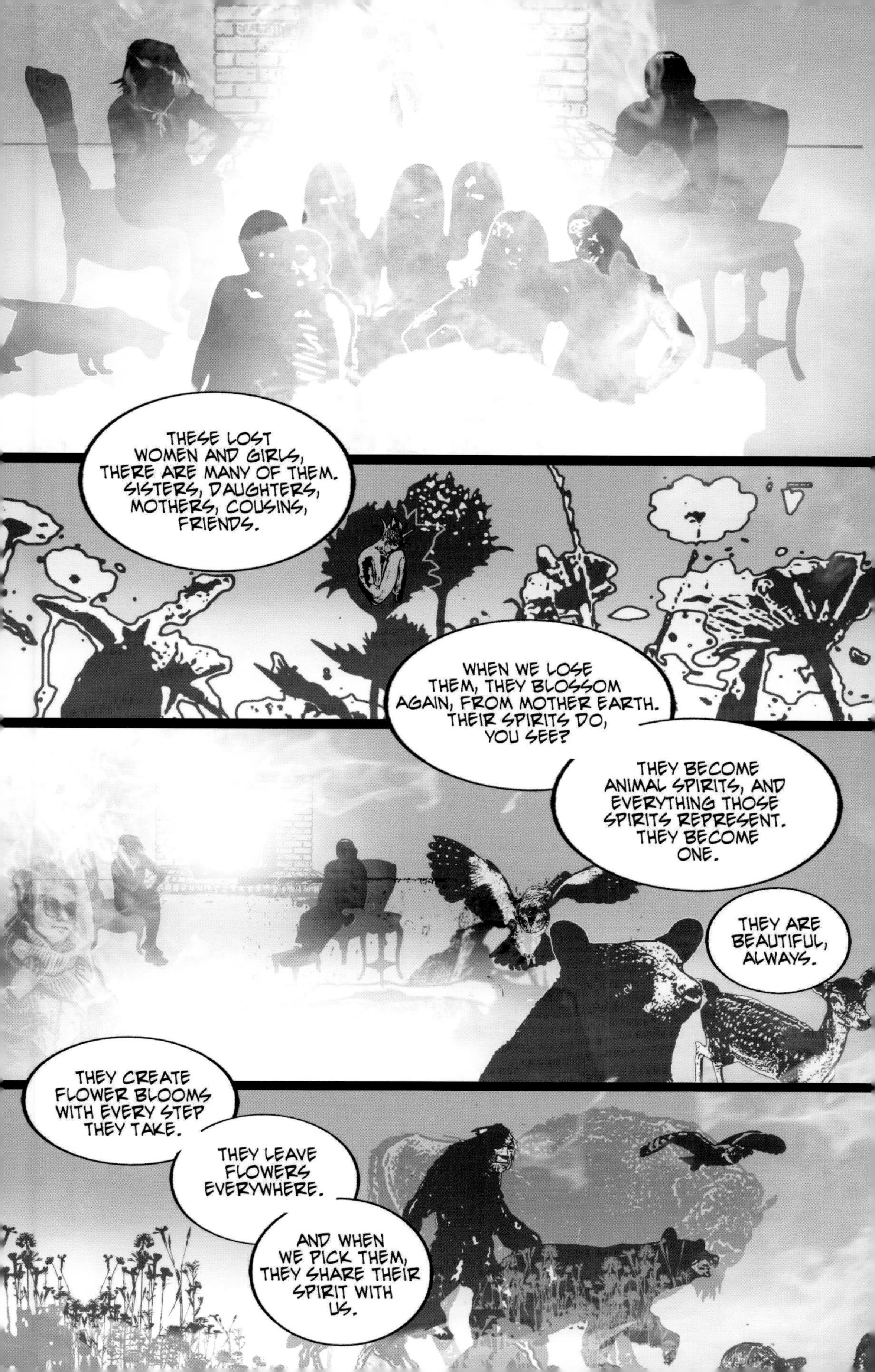
THESE LOST WOMEN AND GIRLS, THERE ARE MANY OF THEM. SISTERS, DAUGHTERS, MOTHERS, COUSINS, FRIENDS.
WHEN WE LOSE THEM, THEY BLOSSOM AGAIN, FROM MOTHER EARTH. THEIR SPIRITS DO, YOU SEE?
THEY BECOME ANIMAL SPIRITS, AND EVERYTHING THOSE SPIRITS REPRESENT. THEY BECOME ONE.
THEY ARE BEAUTIFUL, ALWAYS.
THEY CREATE FLOWER BLOOMS WITH EVERY STEP THEY TAKE.
THEY LEAVE FLOWERS EVERYWHERE.
AND WHEN WE PICK THEM, THEY SHARE THEIR SPIRIT WITH US.

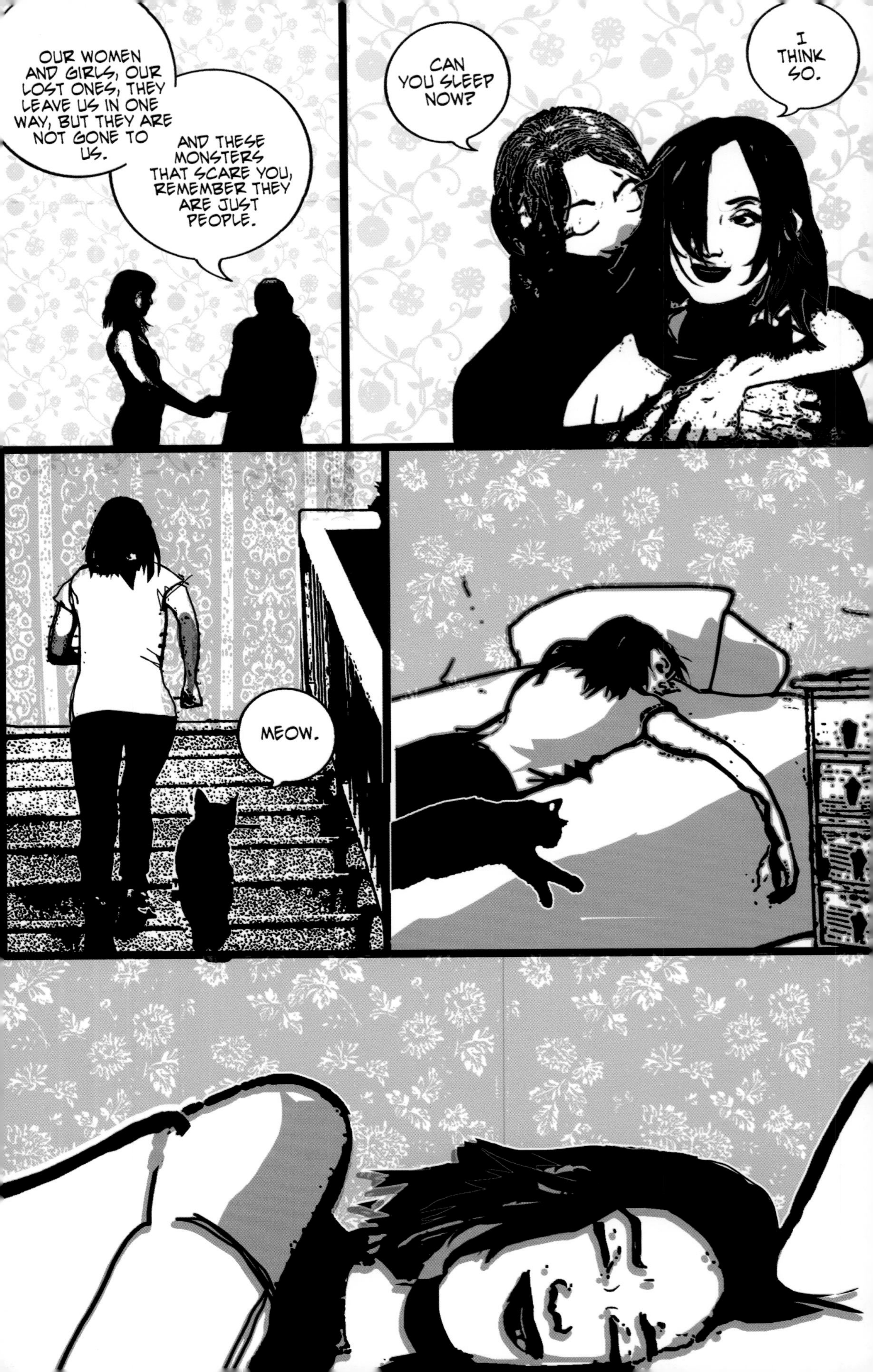
OUR WOMEN AND GIRLS, OUR LOST ONES, THEY LEAVE US IN ONE WAY, BUT THEY ARE NOT GONE TO US.
AND THESE MONSTERS THAT SCARE YOU, REMEMBER THEY ARE JUST PEOPLE.
CAN YOU SLEEP NOW?
I THINK SO.
MEOW.

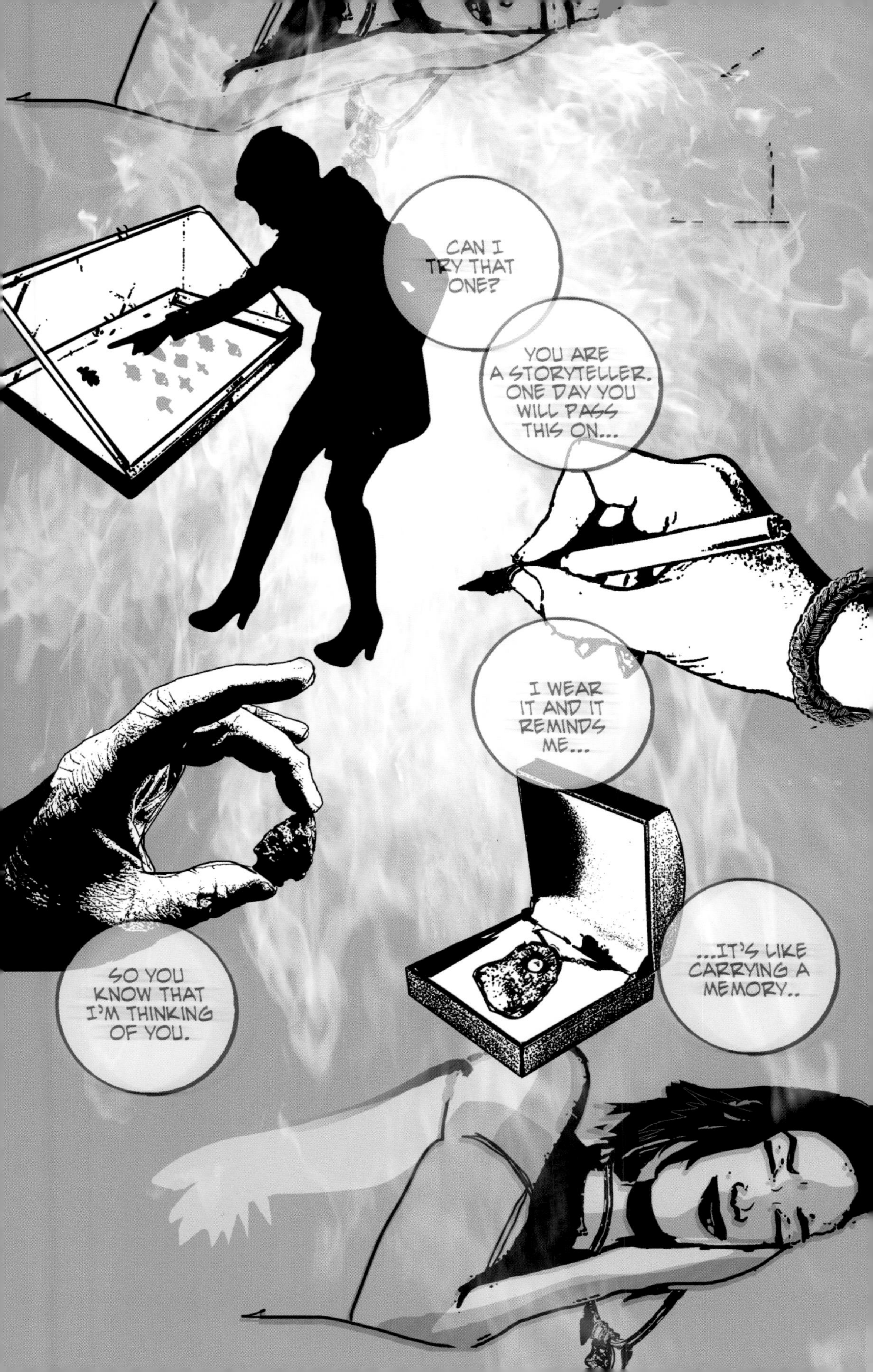
CAN I TRY THAT ONE?
YOU ARE A STORYTELLER. ONE DAY YOU WILL PASS THIS ON...
I WEAR IT AND IT REMINDS ME...
...IT'S LIKE CARRYING A MEMORY..
SO YOU KNOW THAT I'M THINKING OF YOU.

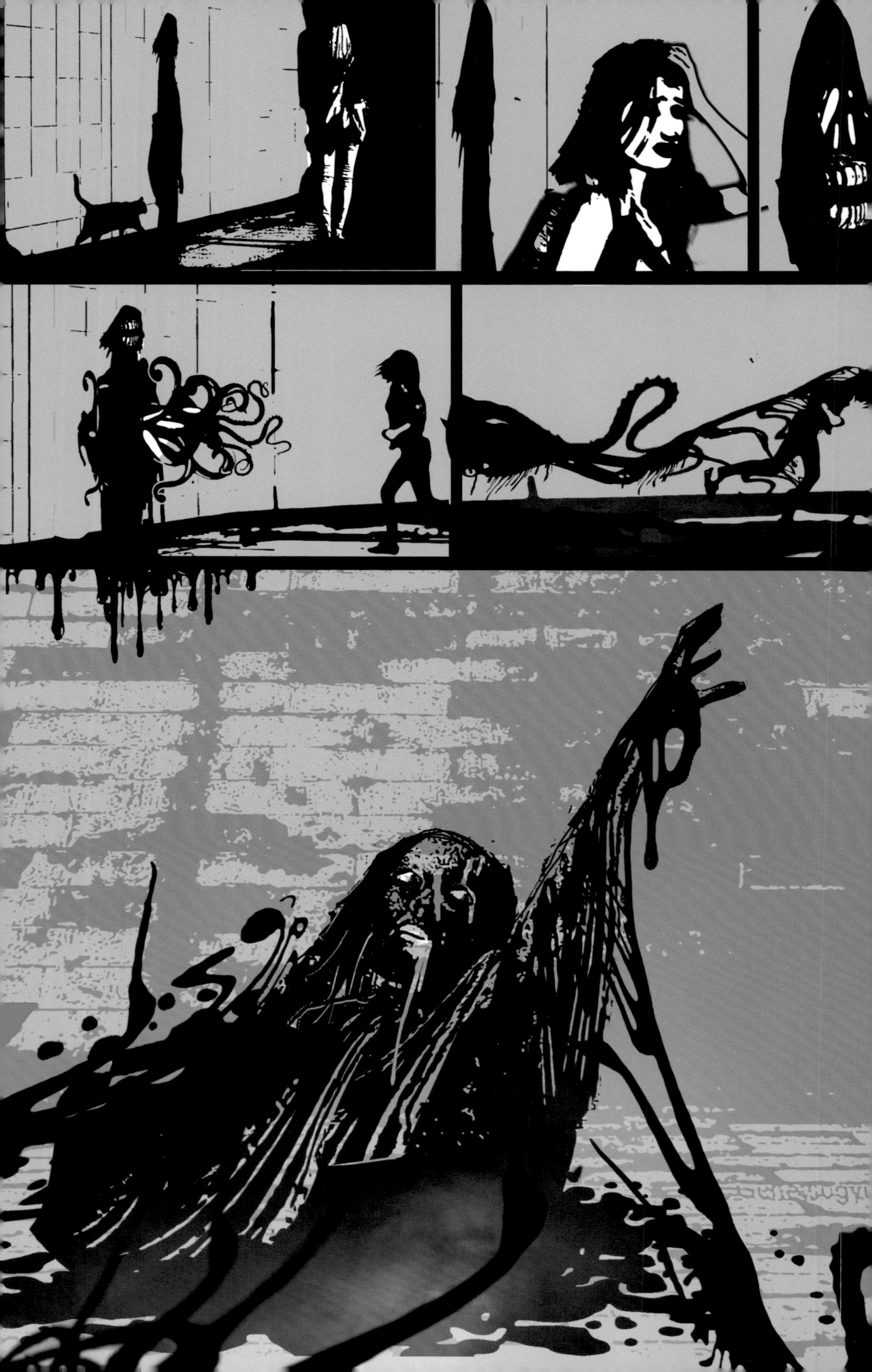

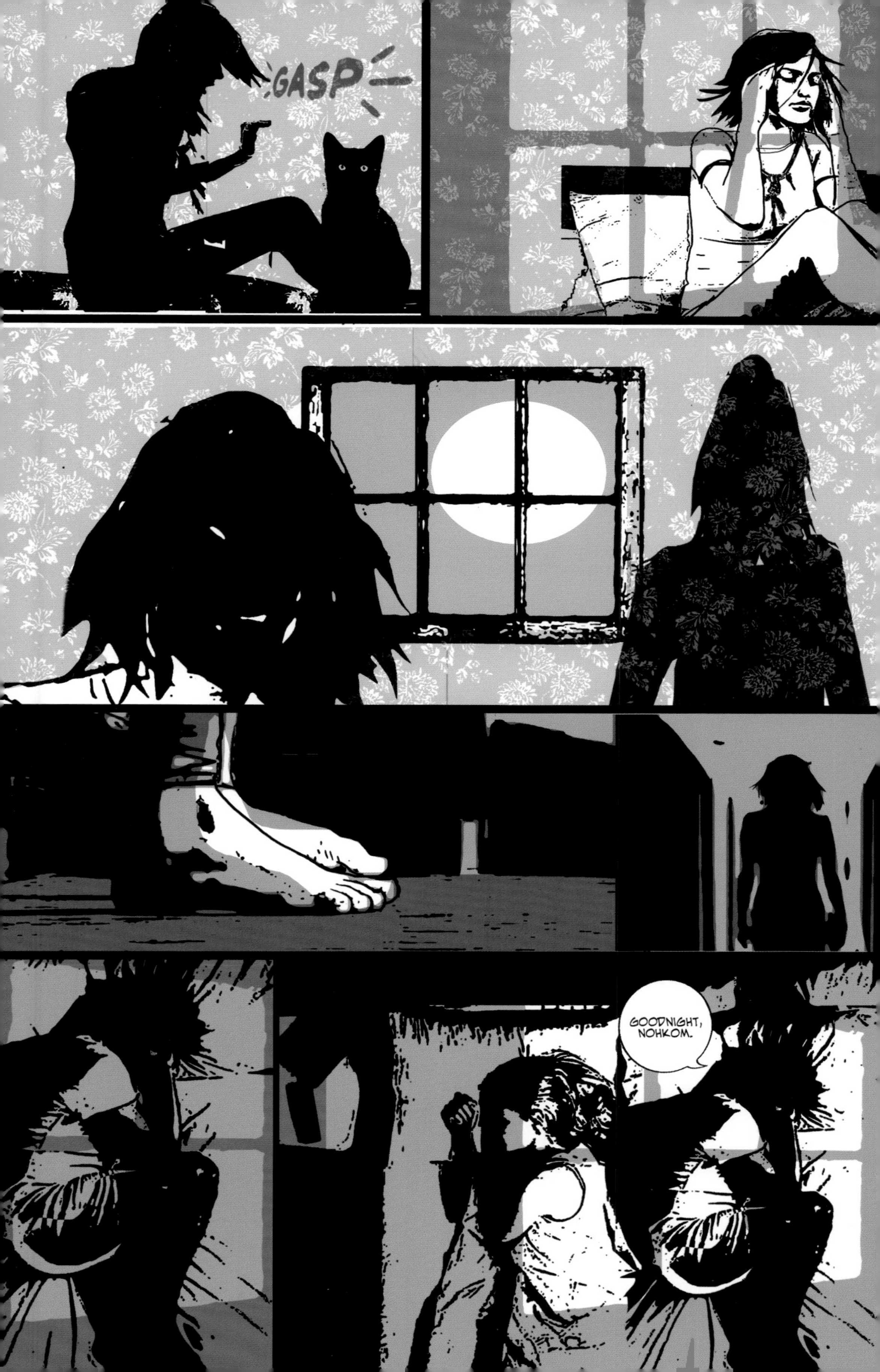
GASP
GOODNIGHT, NOHKOM.

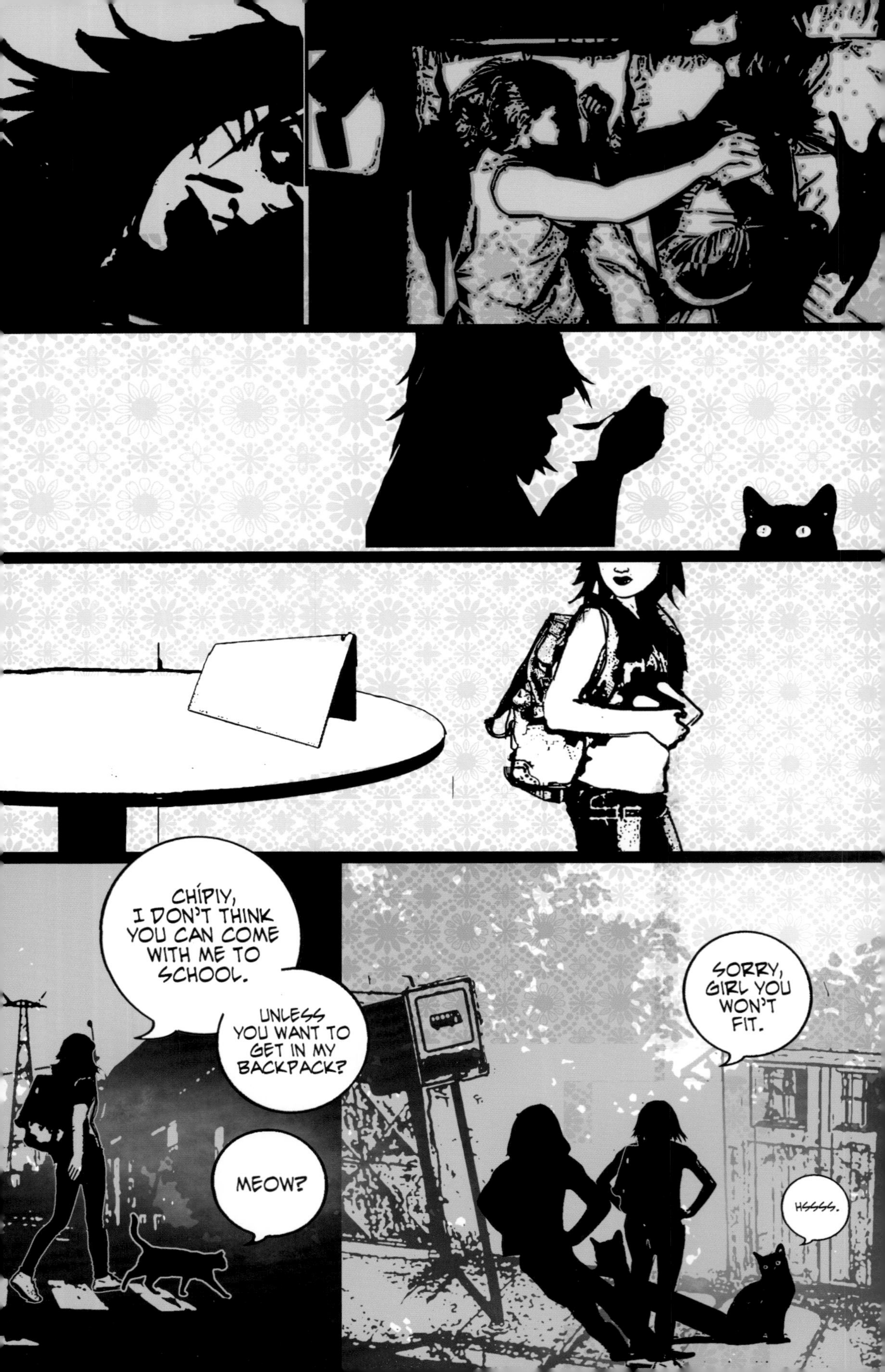
CHÍPIY, I DON'T THINK YOU CAN COME WITH ME TO SCHOOL.
UNLESS YOU WANT TO GET IN MY BACKPACK?
MEOW?
SORRY, GIRL YOU WON'T FIT.
HSSSS.

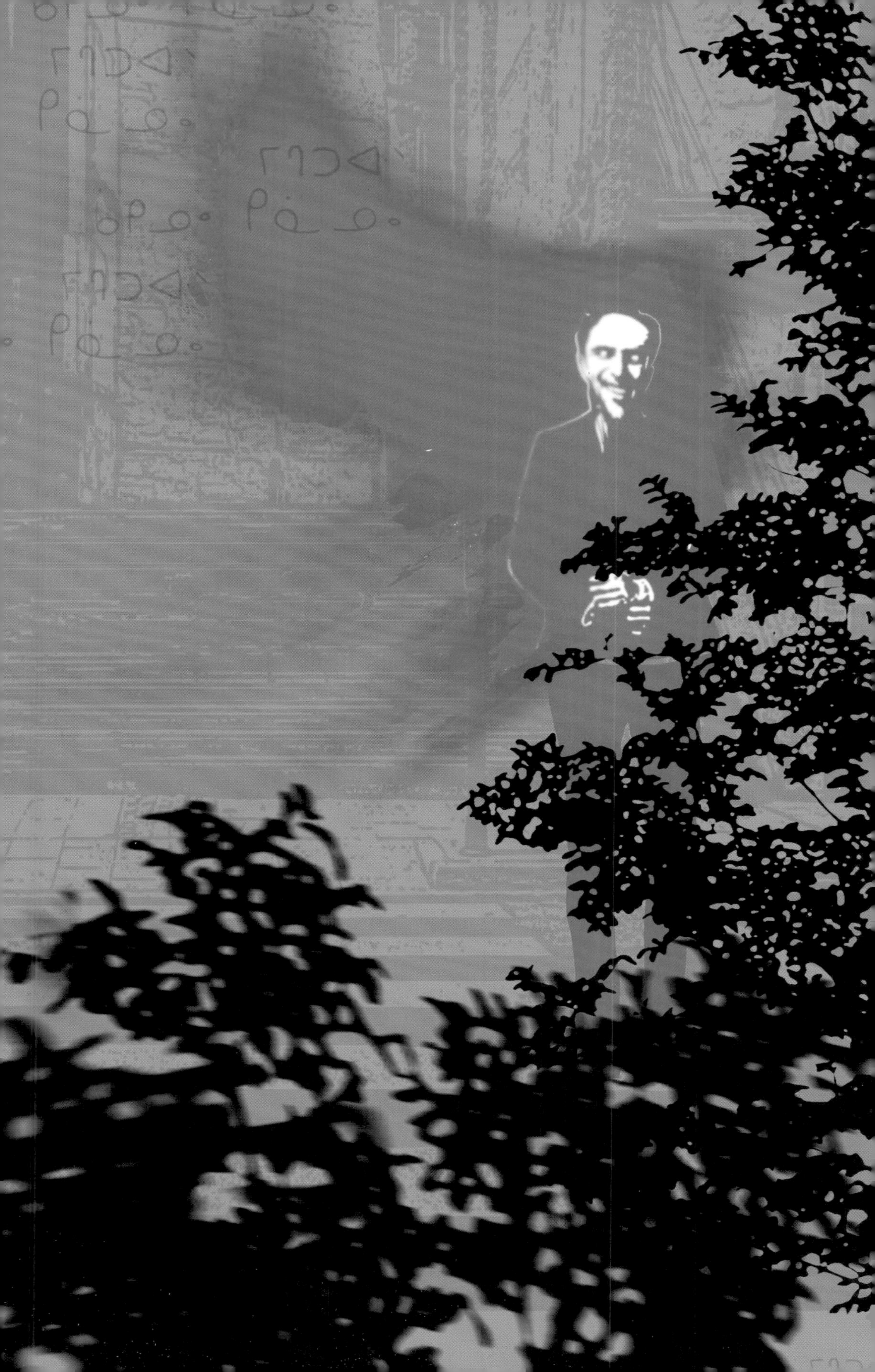

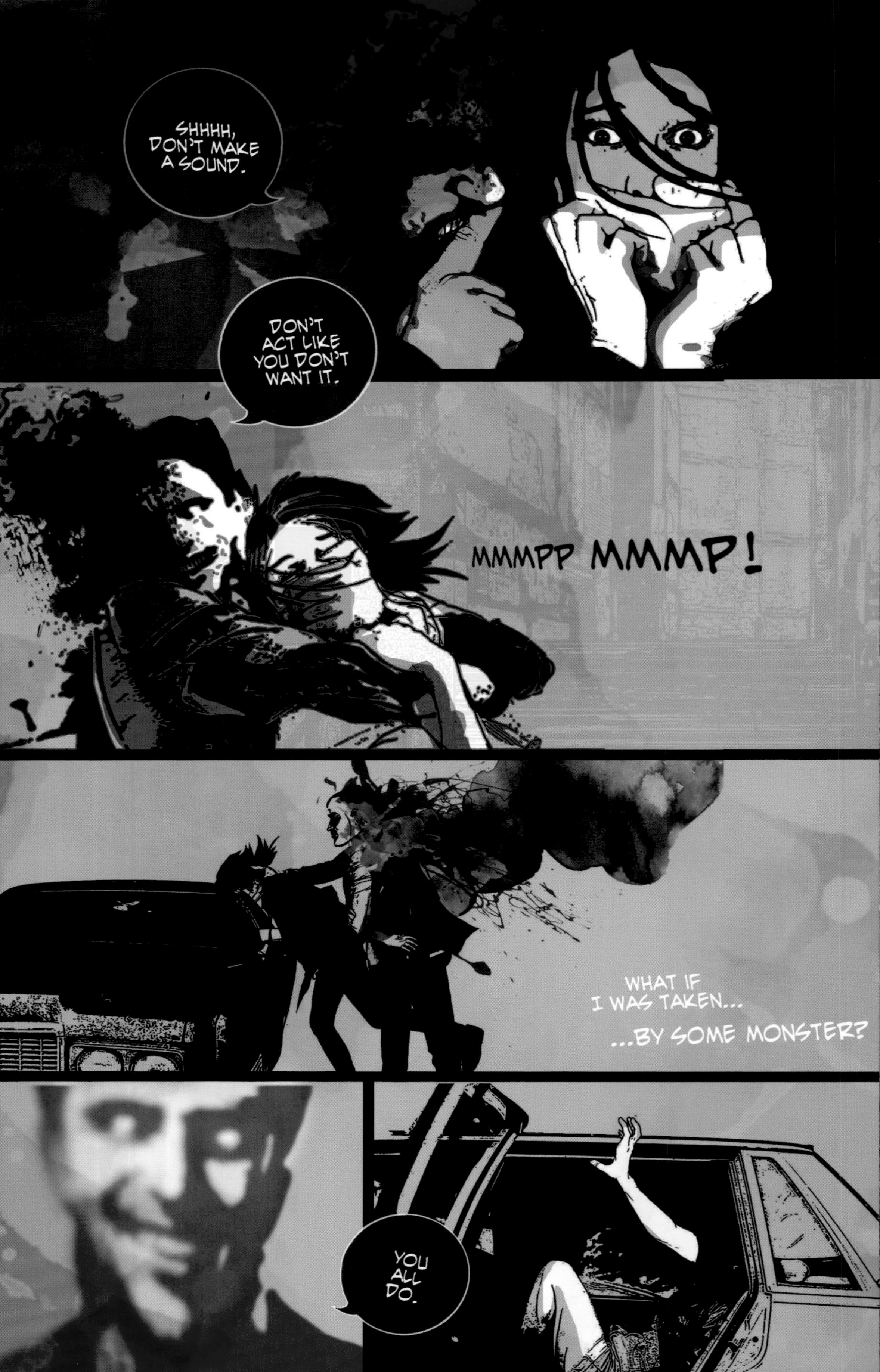
SHHHH, DON'T MAKE A SOUND.
DON'T ACT LIKE YOU DON'T WANT IT.
MMMPP MMMP!
WHAT IF I WAS TAKEN...
...BY SOME MONSTER?
YOU ALL DO.

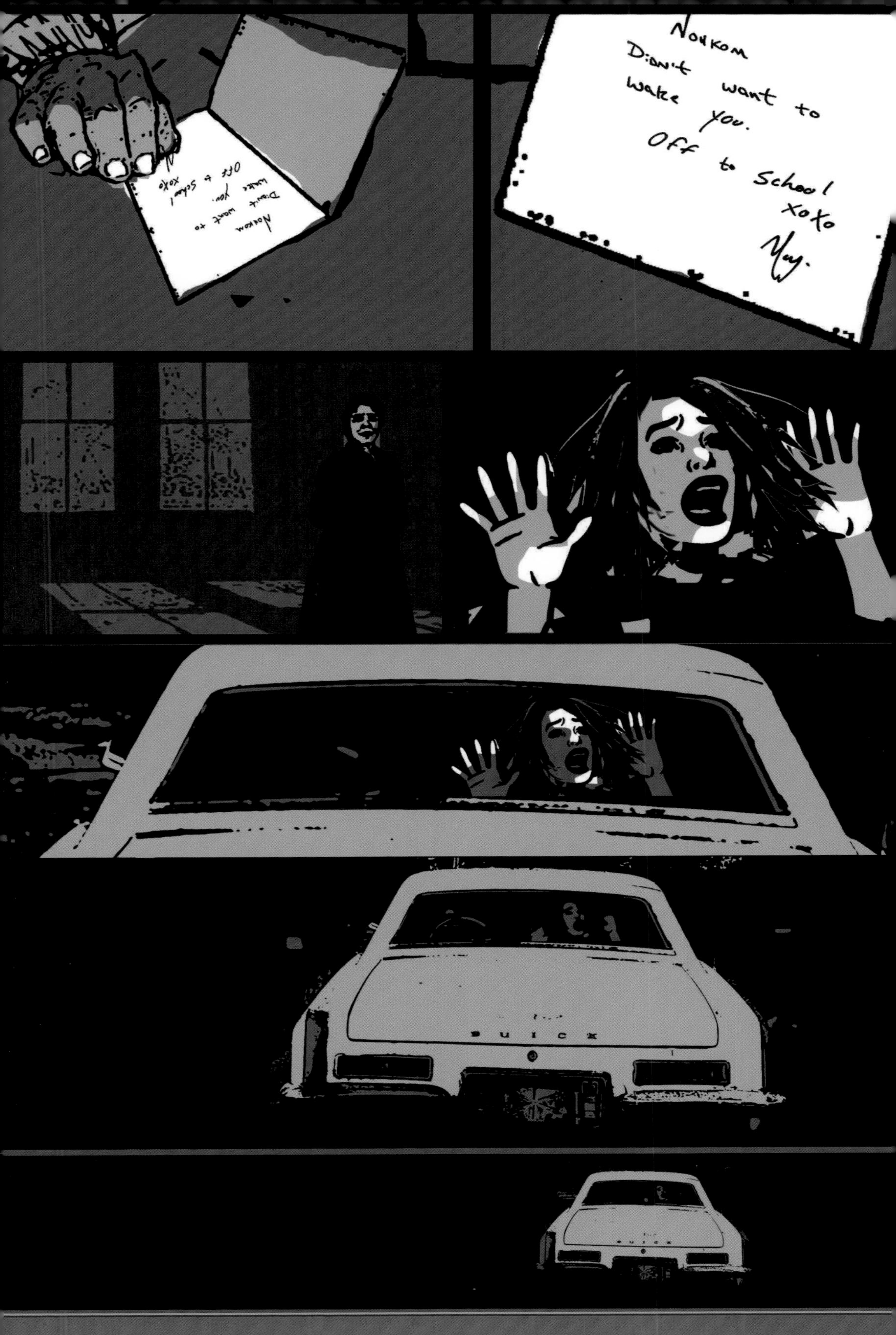
Nohkom
Didn't want to
wake you.
Off to School
xoxo

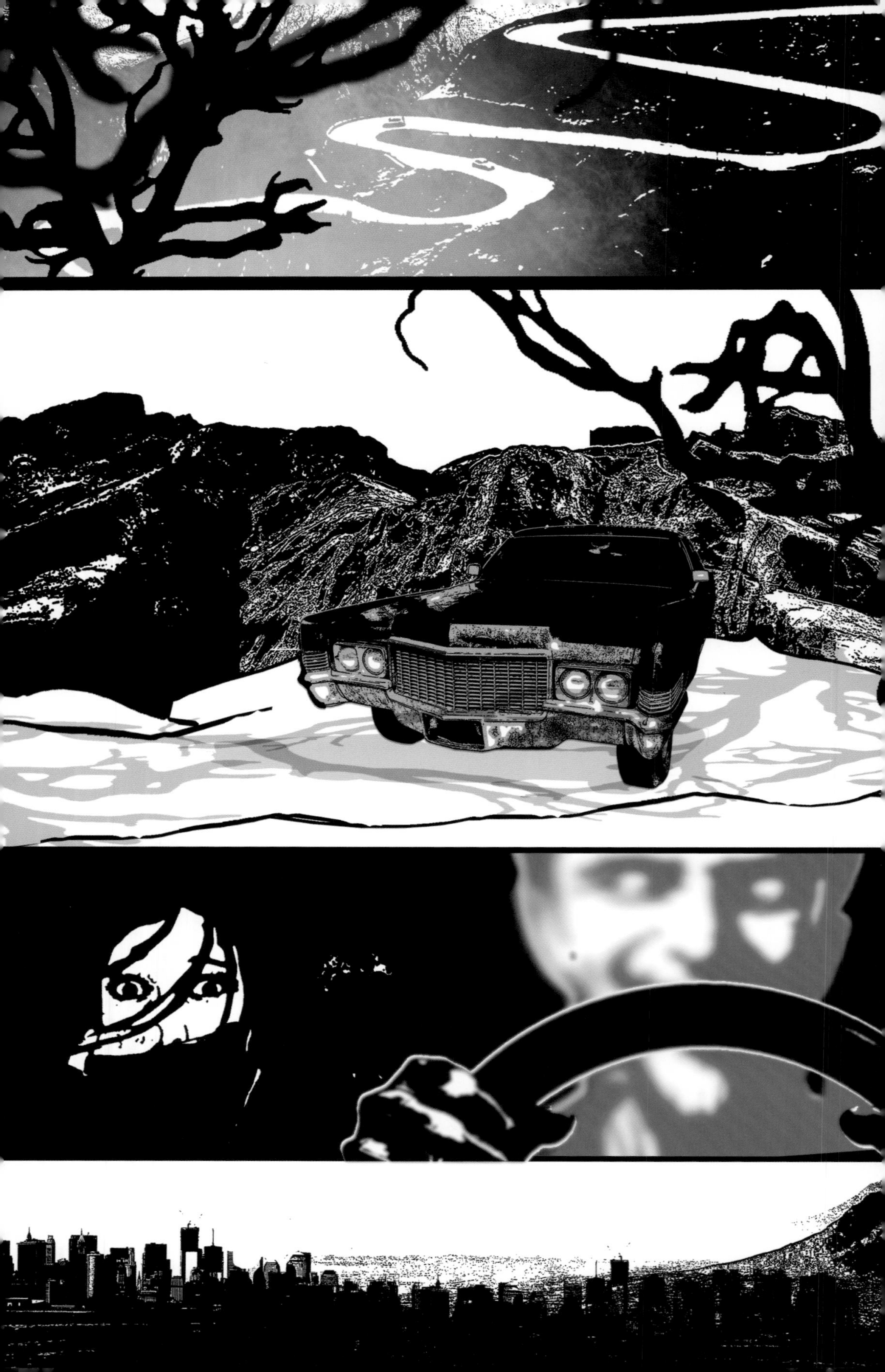

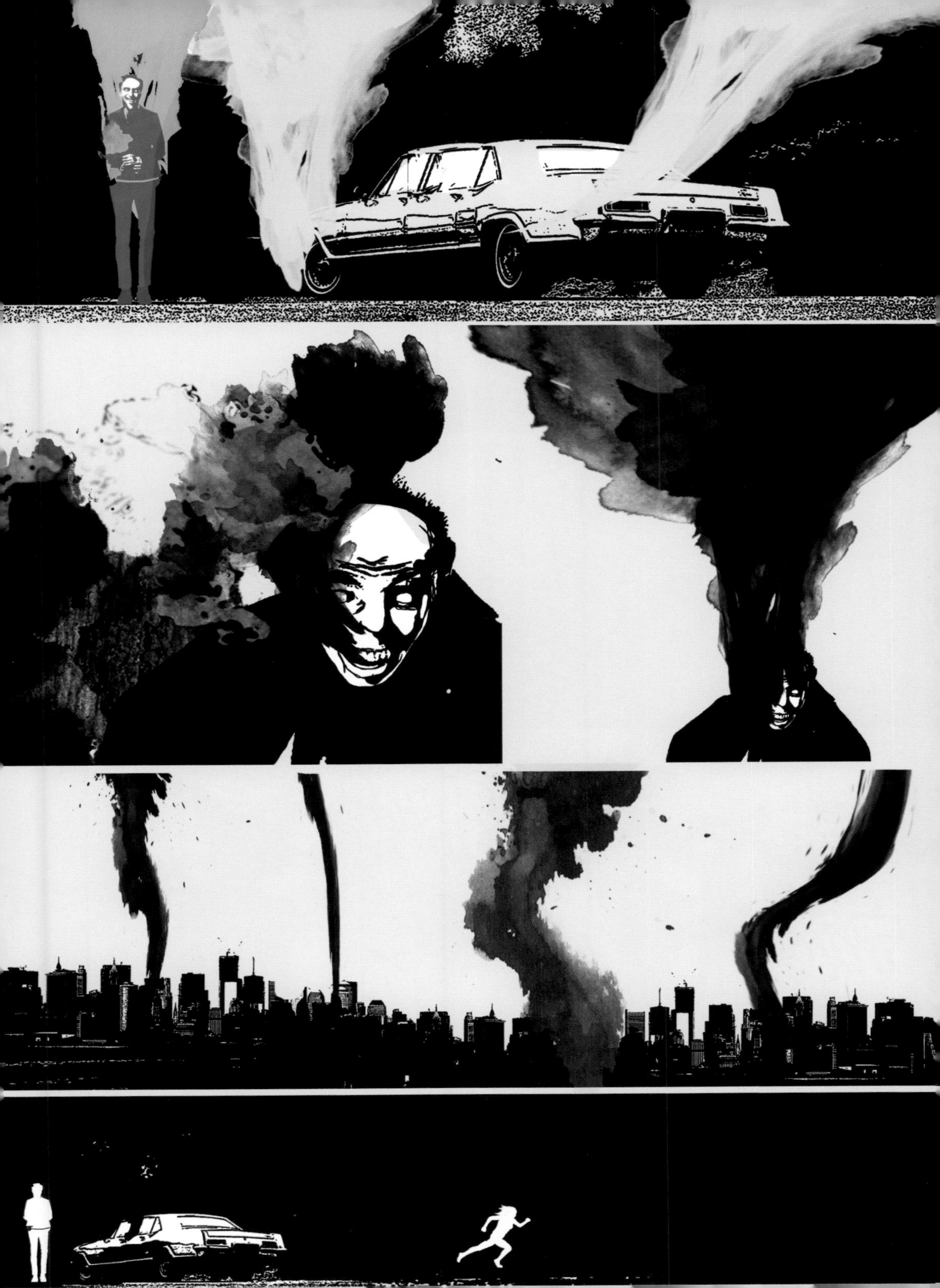

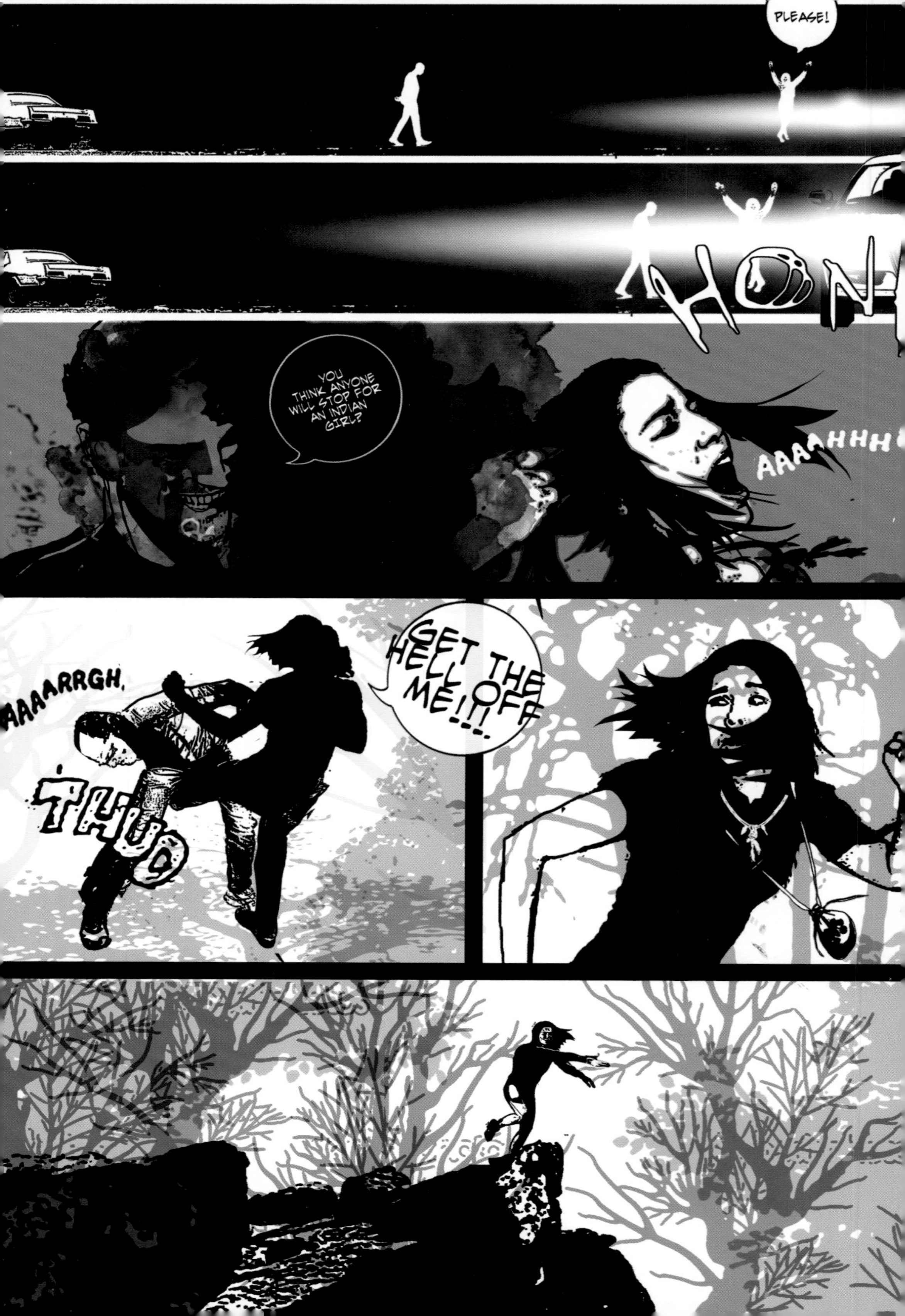
PLEASE!
HON
YOU THINK ANYONE WILL STOP FOR AN INDIAN GIRL?
AAAAHHH
AAAARRGH,
THUD
GET THE HELL OFF ME!!!

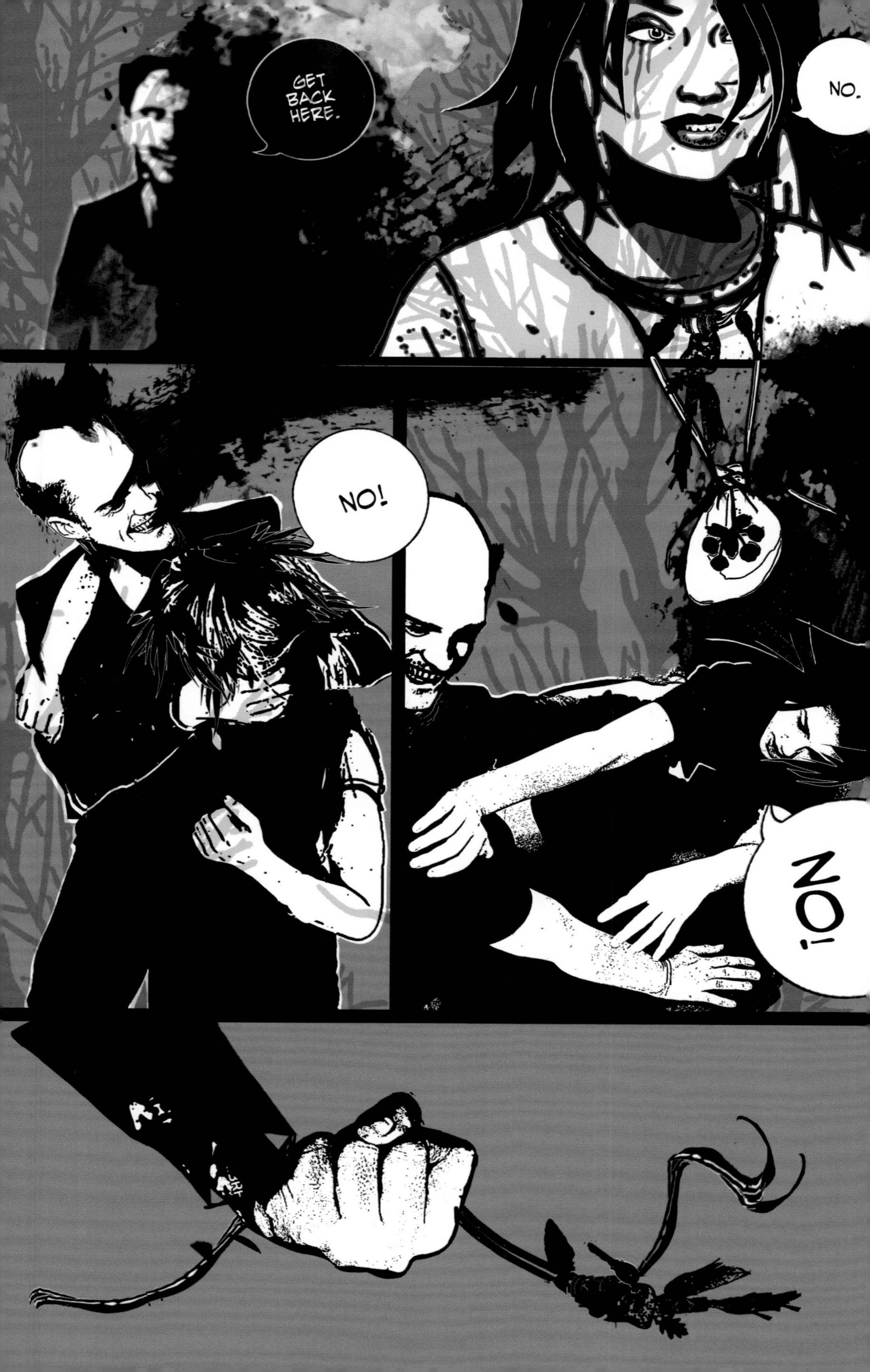

GET BACK HERE.
NO.
NO!
NO!

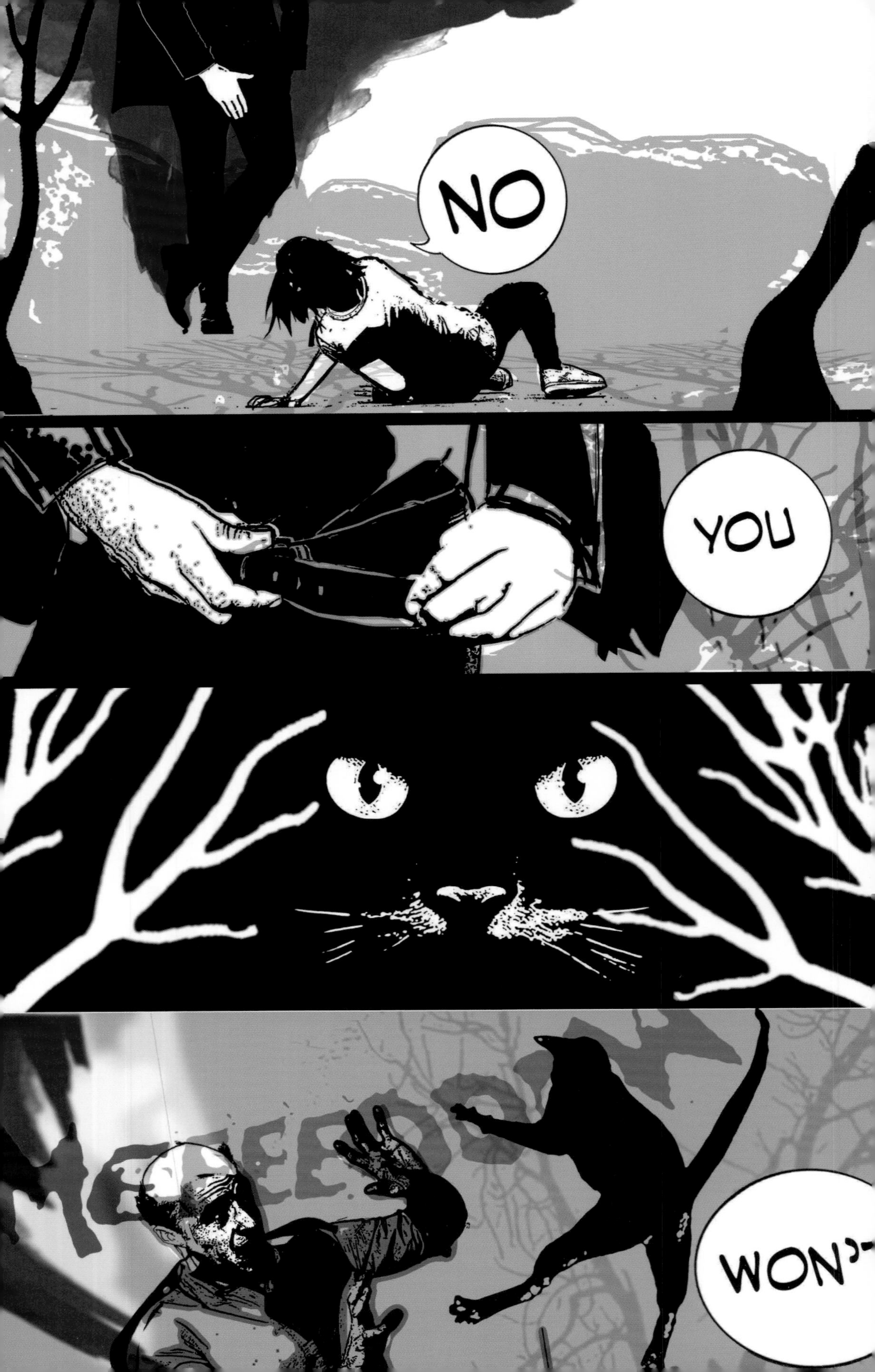
NO
YOU
WON'-

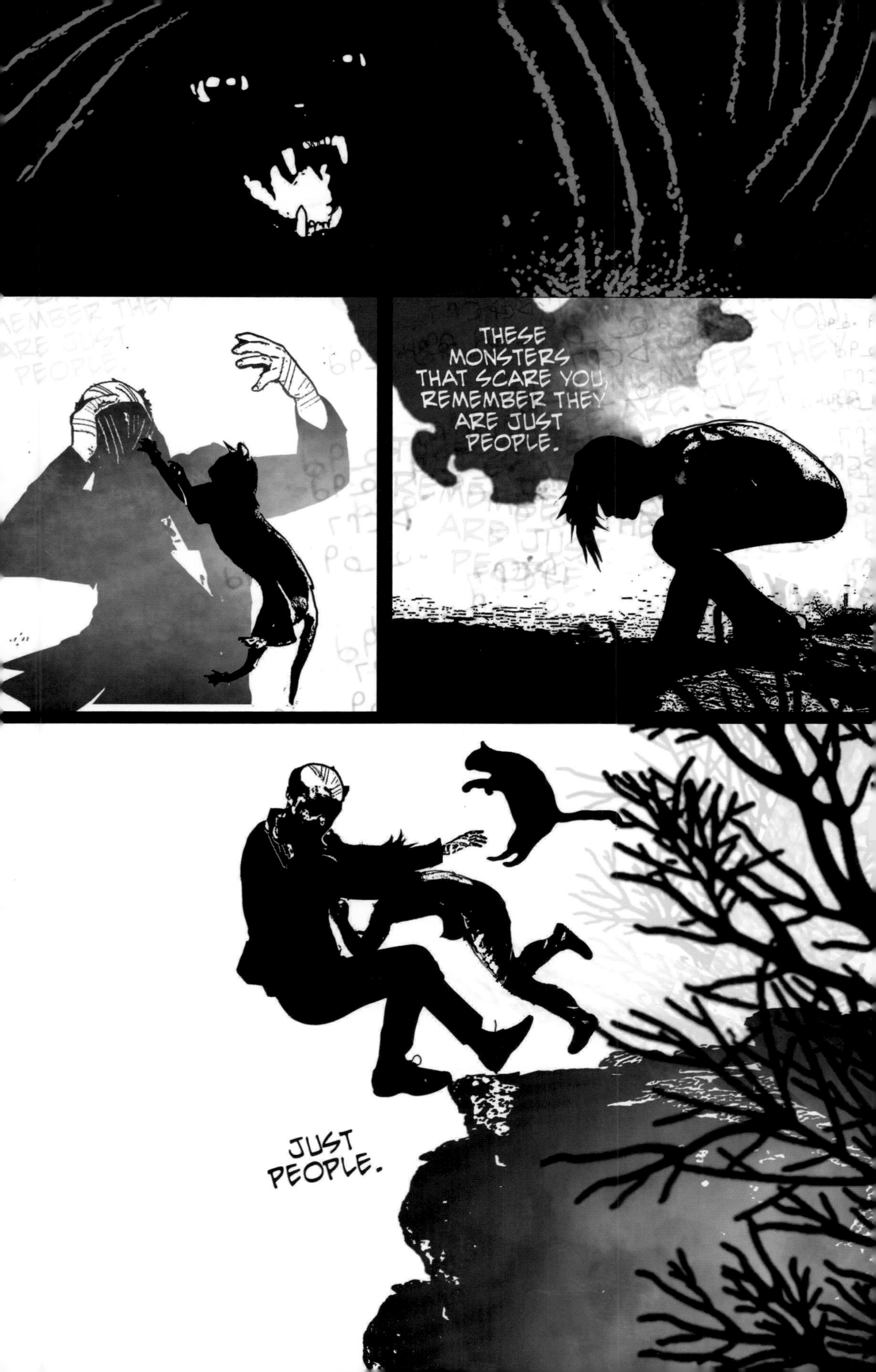
THESE MONSTERS THAT SCARE YOU, REMEMBER THEY ARE JUST PEOPLE.
JUST PEOPLE.

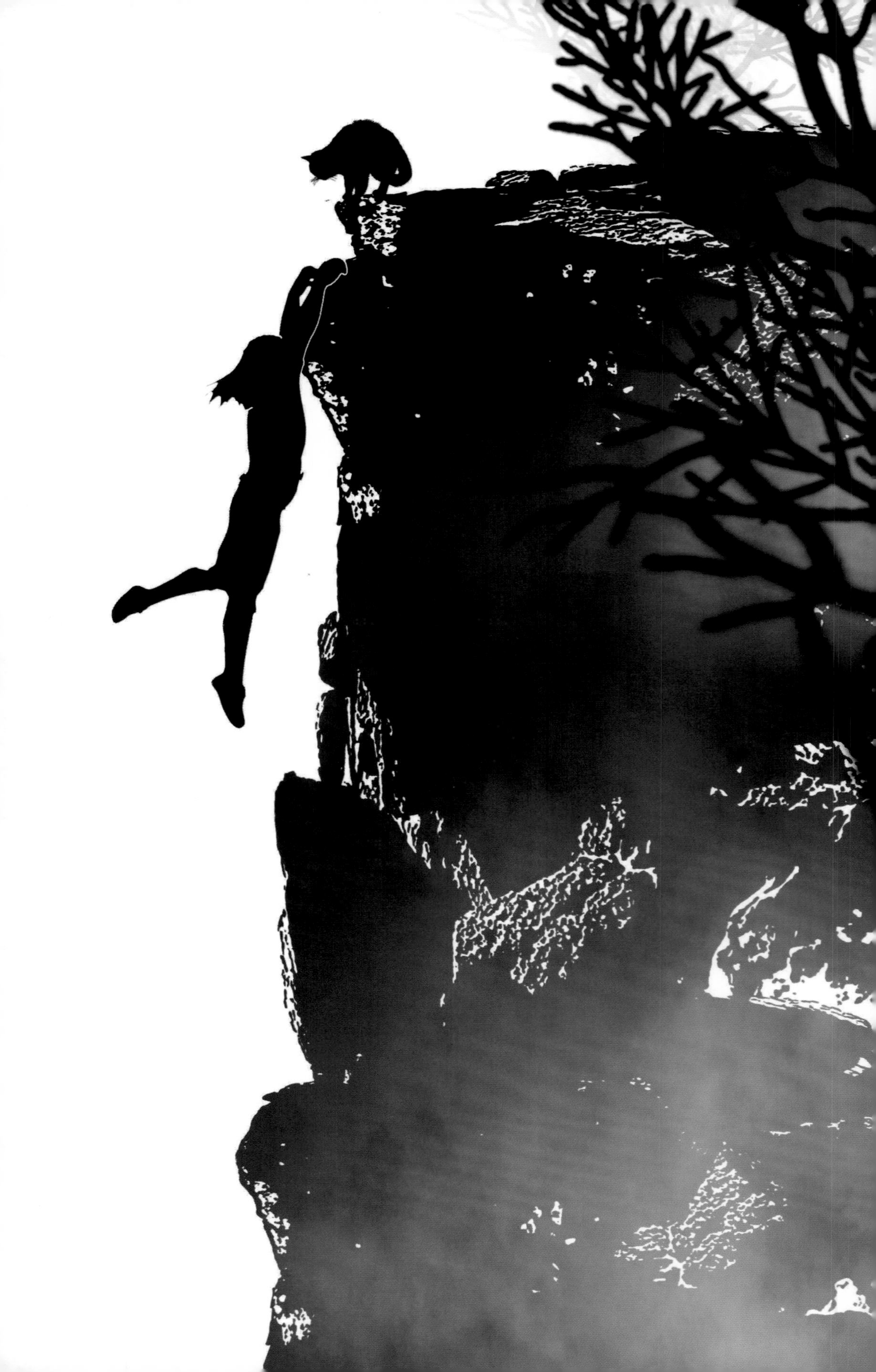

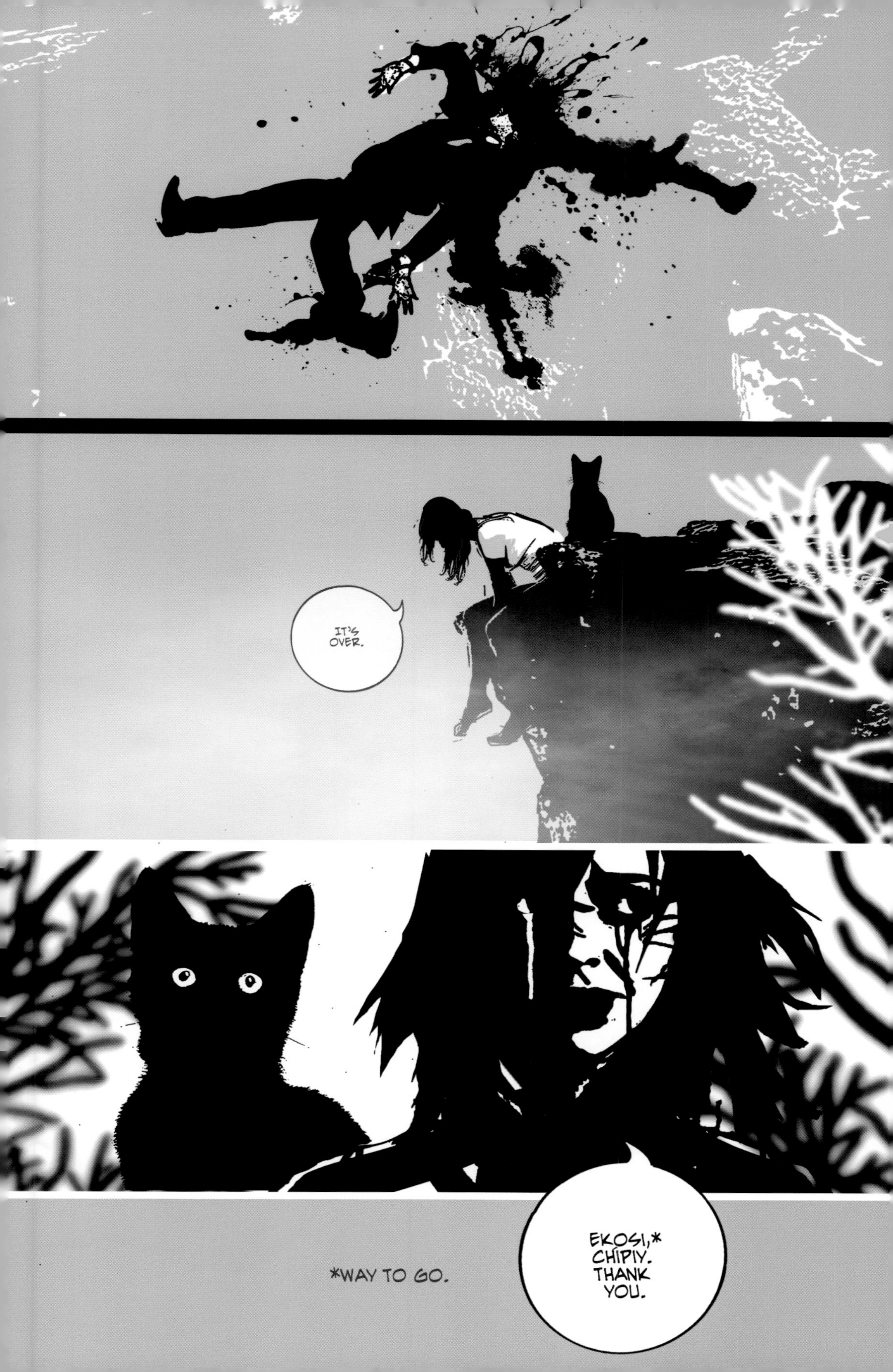
IT'S OVER.
EKOSI,* CHÍPIY. THANK YOU.
*WAY TO GO.

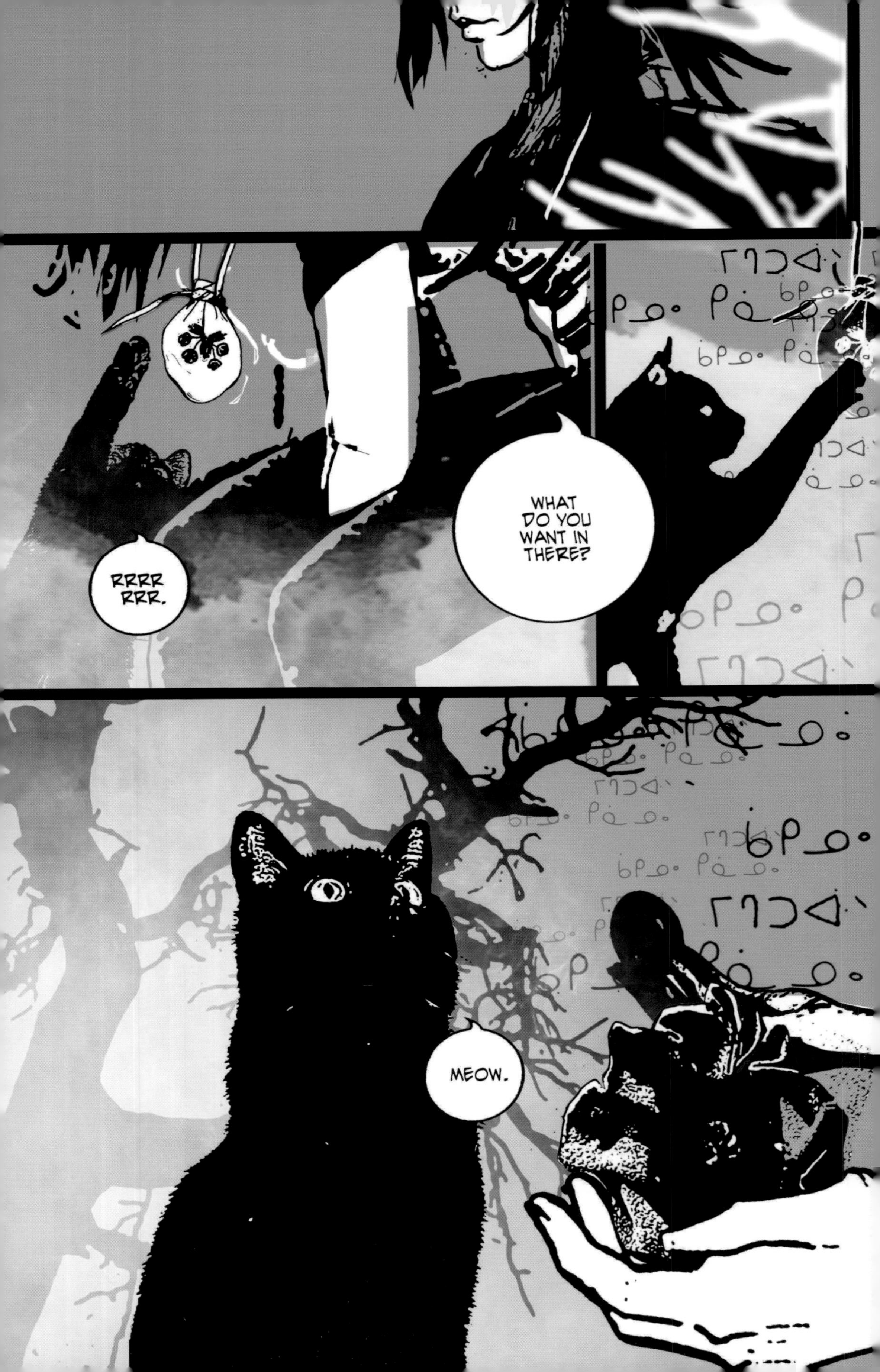
WHAT DO YOU WANT IN THERE?
RRRR RRR.
MEOW.

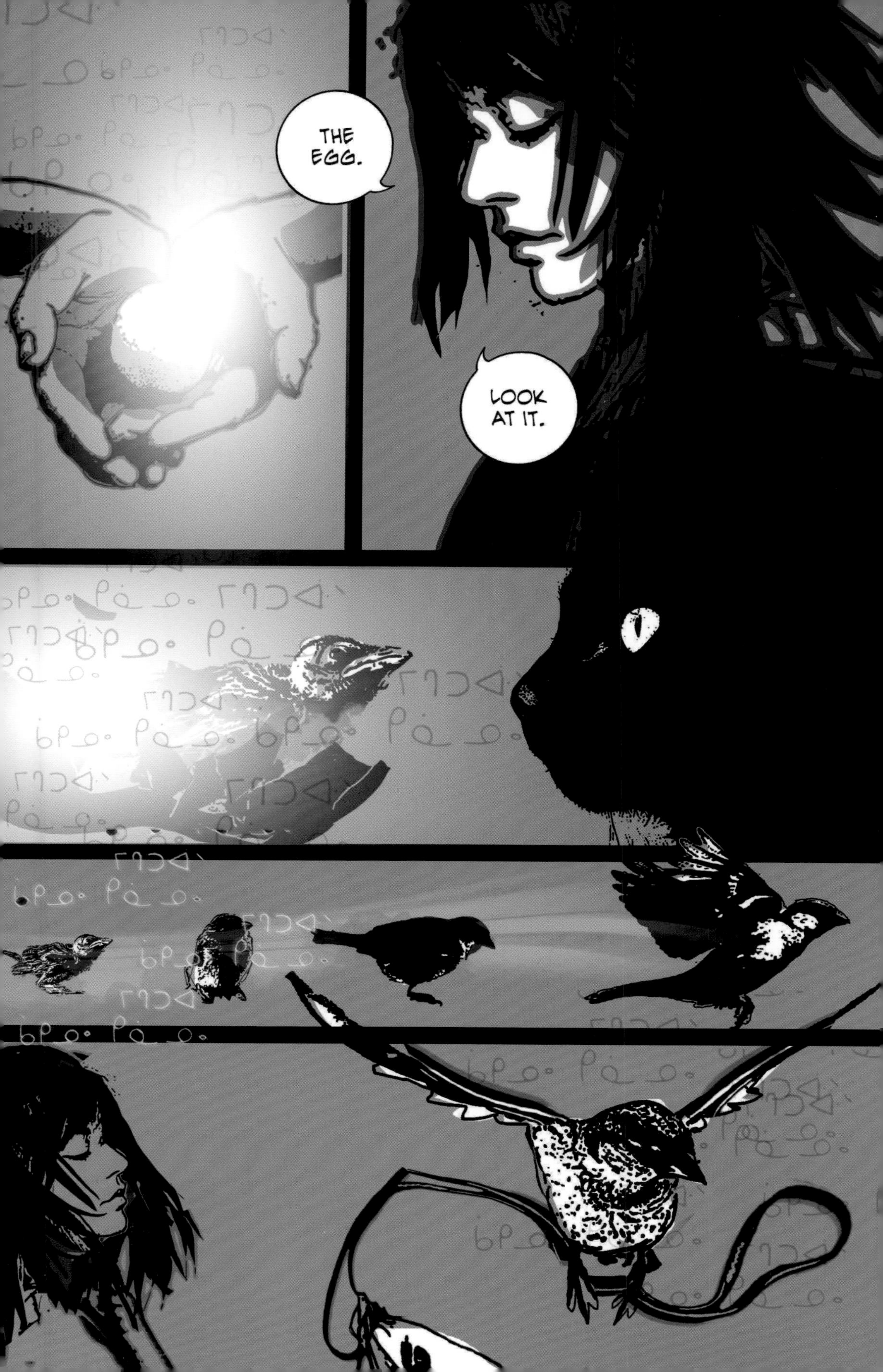
THE EGG.
LOOK AT IT.

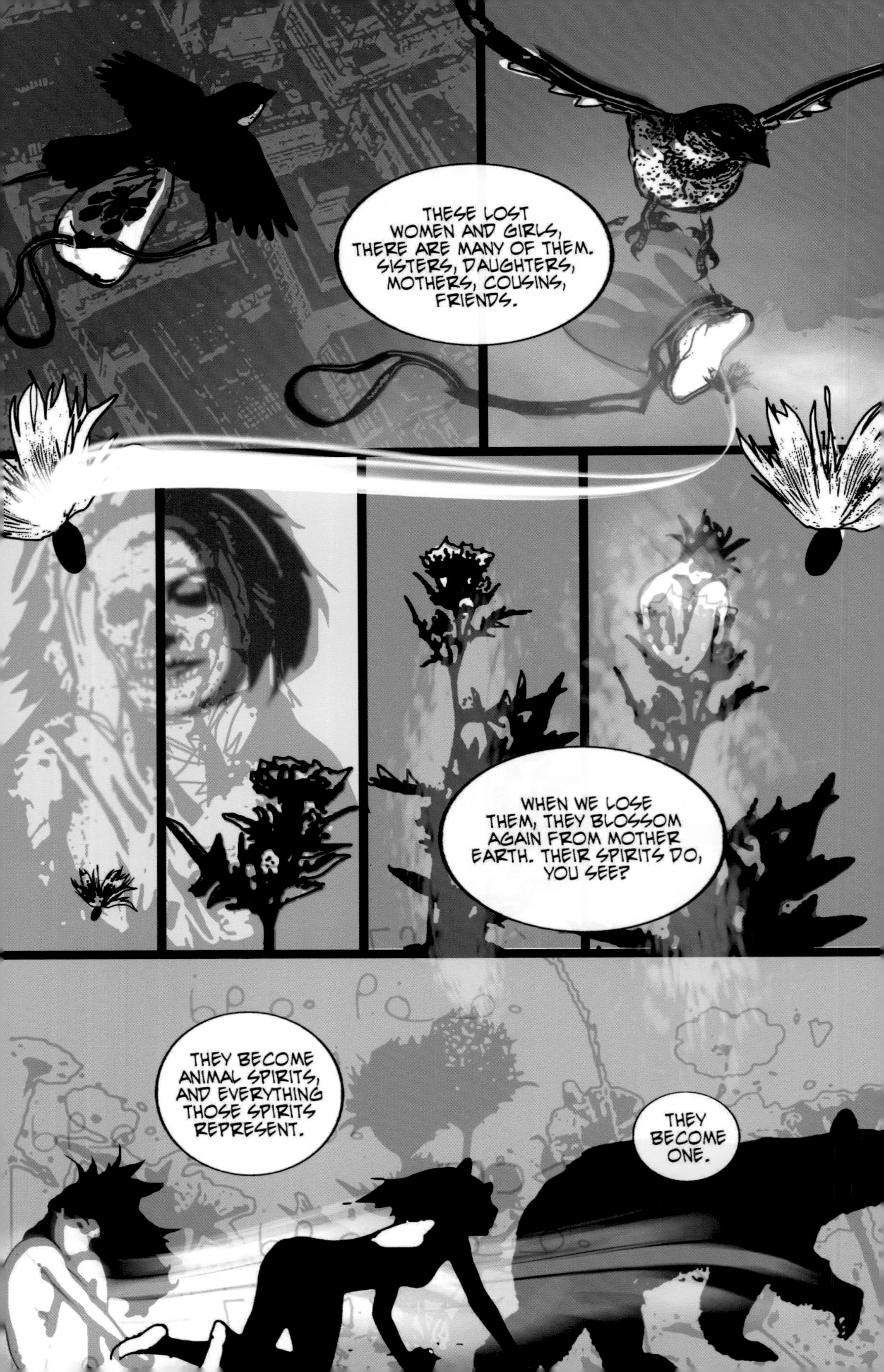
THESE LOST WOMEN AND GIRLS, THERE ARE MANY OF THEM. SISTERS, DAUGHTERS, MOTHERS, COUSINS, FRIENDS.
WHEN WE LOSE THEM, THEY BLOSSOM AGAIN FROM MOTHER EARTH. THEIR SPIRITS DO, YOU SEE?
THEY BECOME ANIMAL SPIRITS, AND EVERYTHING THOSE SPIRITS REPRESENT.
THEY BECOME ONE.

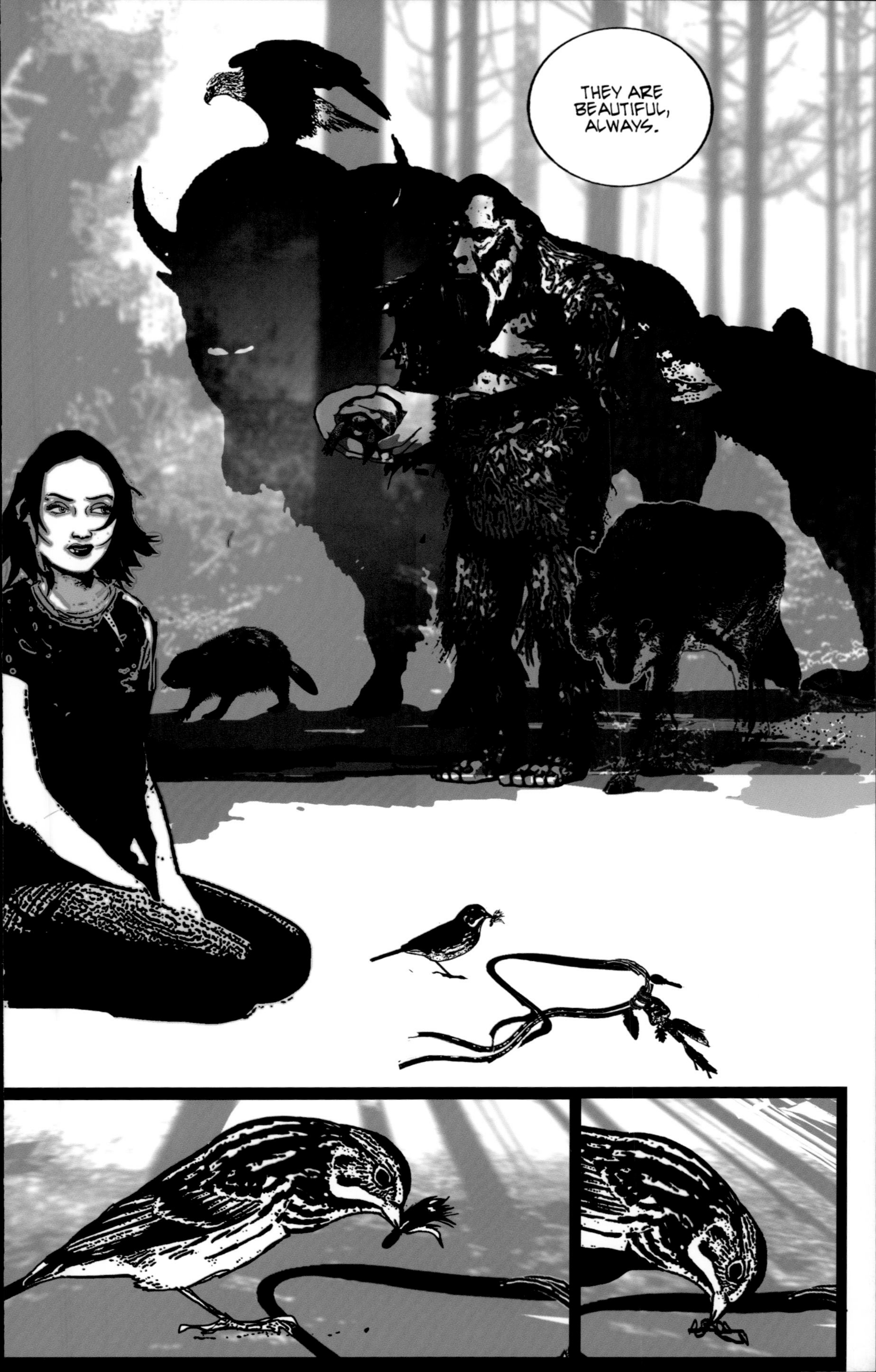
THEY ARE BEAUTIFUL, ALWAYS.

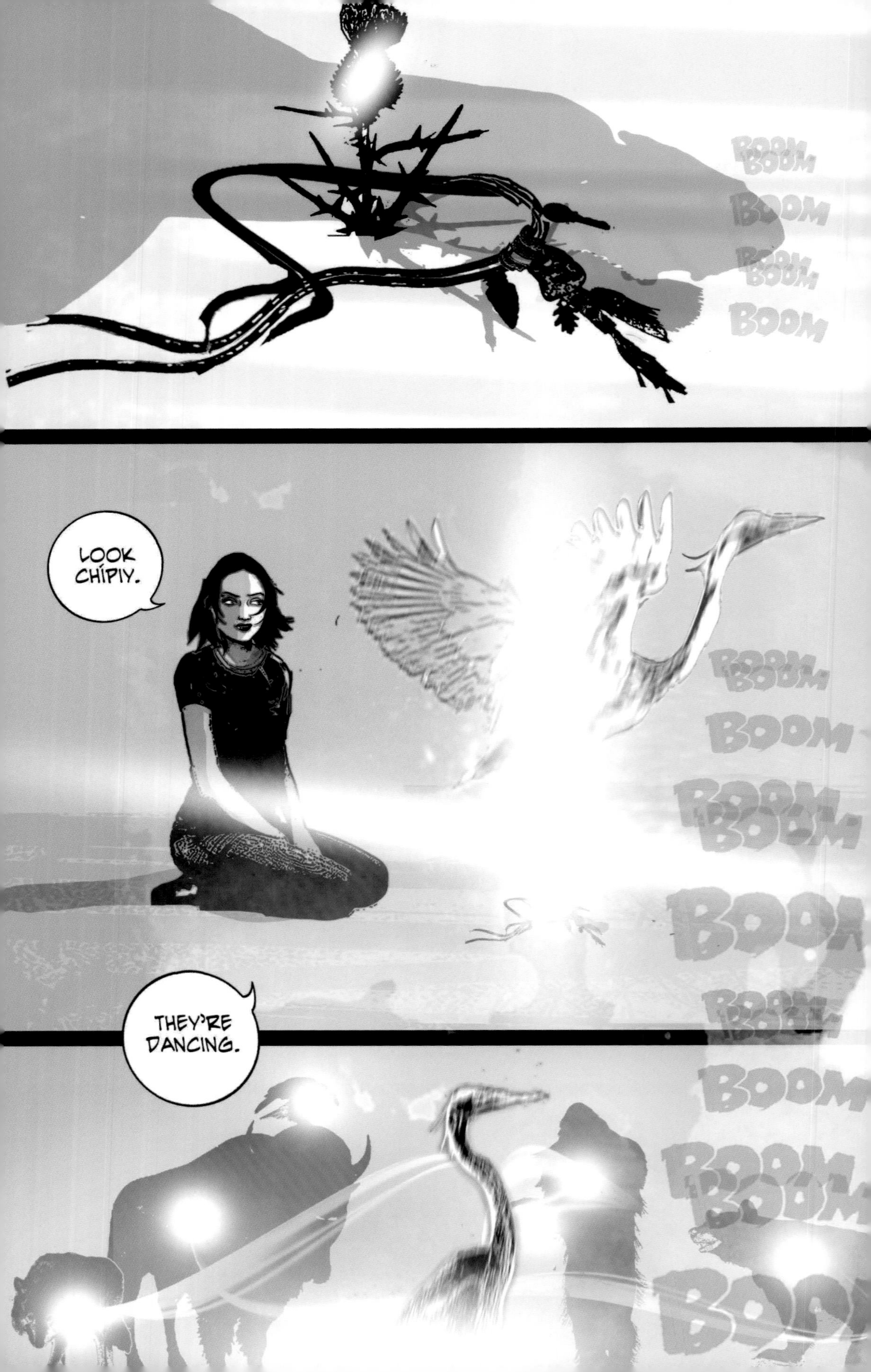
BOOM BOOM
BOOM
BOOM BOOM
BOOM
LOOK CHÍPIY.
BOOM BOOM
BOOM
BOOM BOOM
THEY'RE DANCING.
BOOM
BOOM BOOM

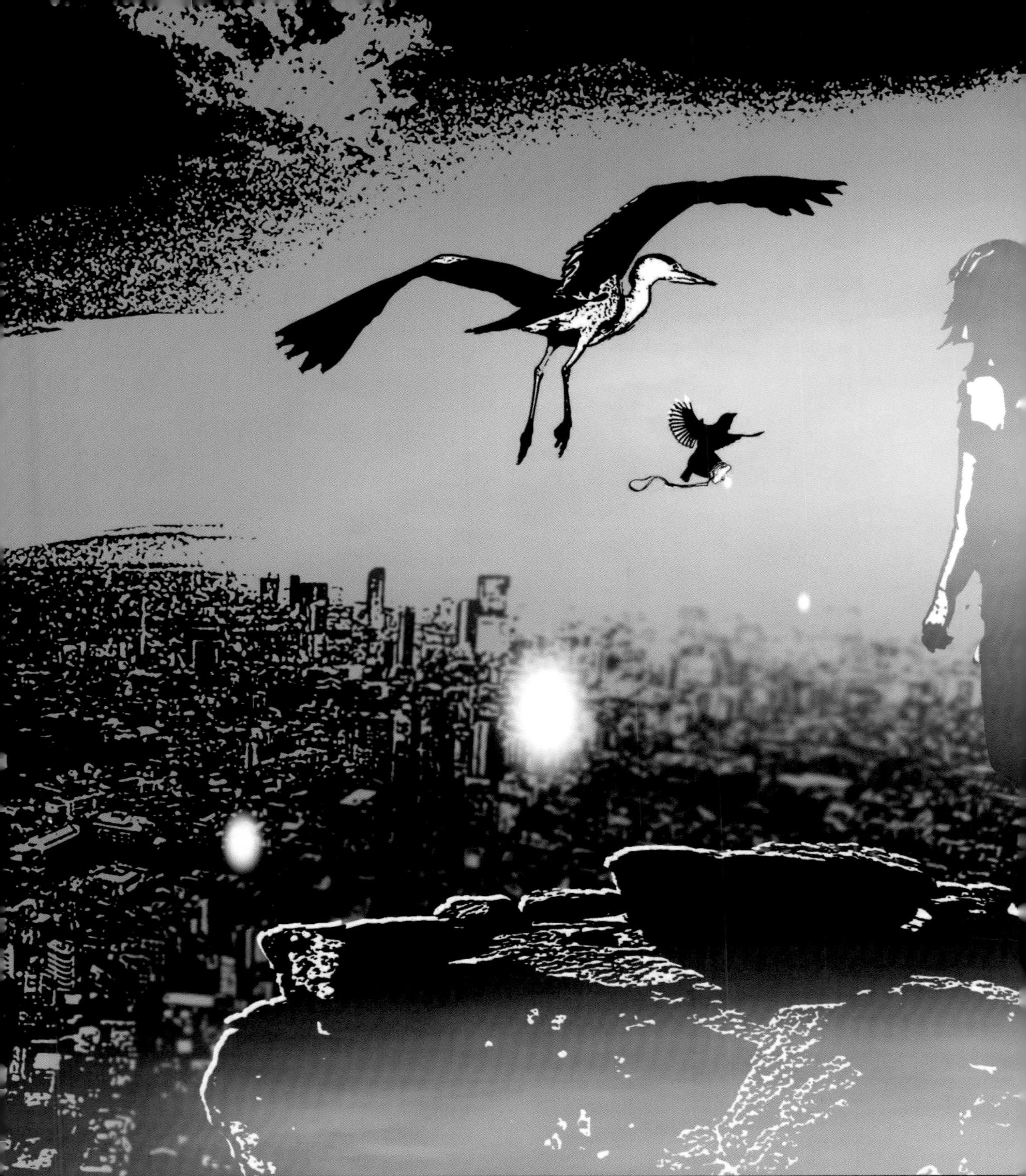
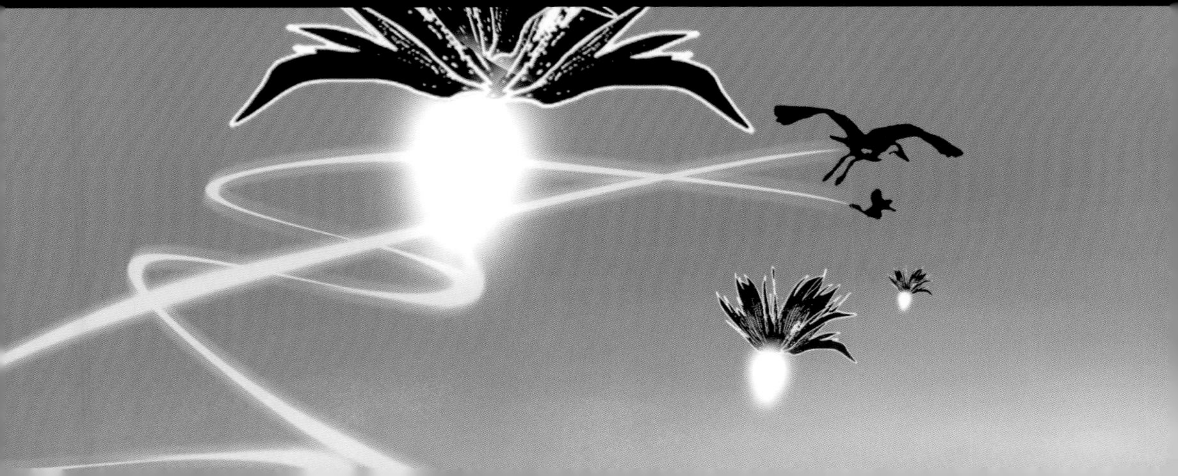

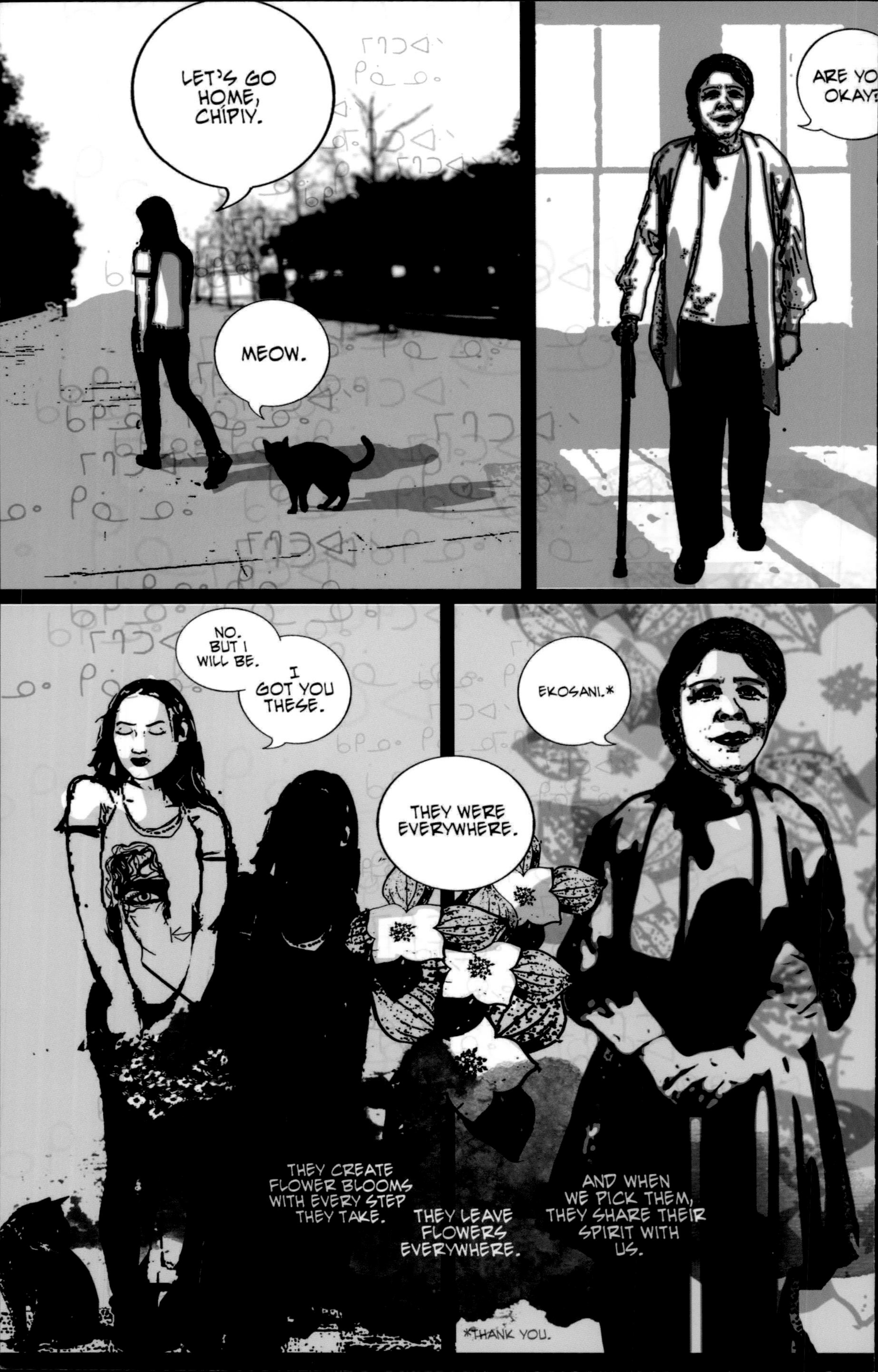
LET'S GO HOME, CHÍPIY.
MEOW.
ARE YO OKAY?
NO. BUT I WILL BE.
I GOT YOU THESE.
EKOSANI.*
THEY WERE EVERYWHERE.
THEY CREATE FLOWER BLOOMS WITH EVERY STEP THEY TAKE.
THEY LEAVE FLOWERS EVERYWHERE.
AND WHEN WE PICK THEM, THEY SHARE THEIR SPIRIT WITH US.
*THANK YOU.

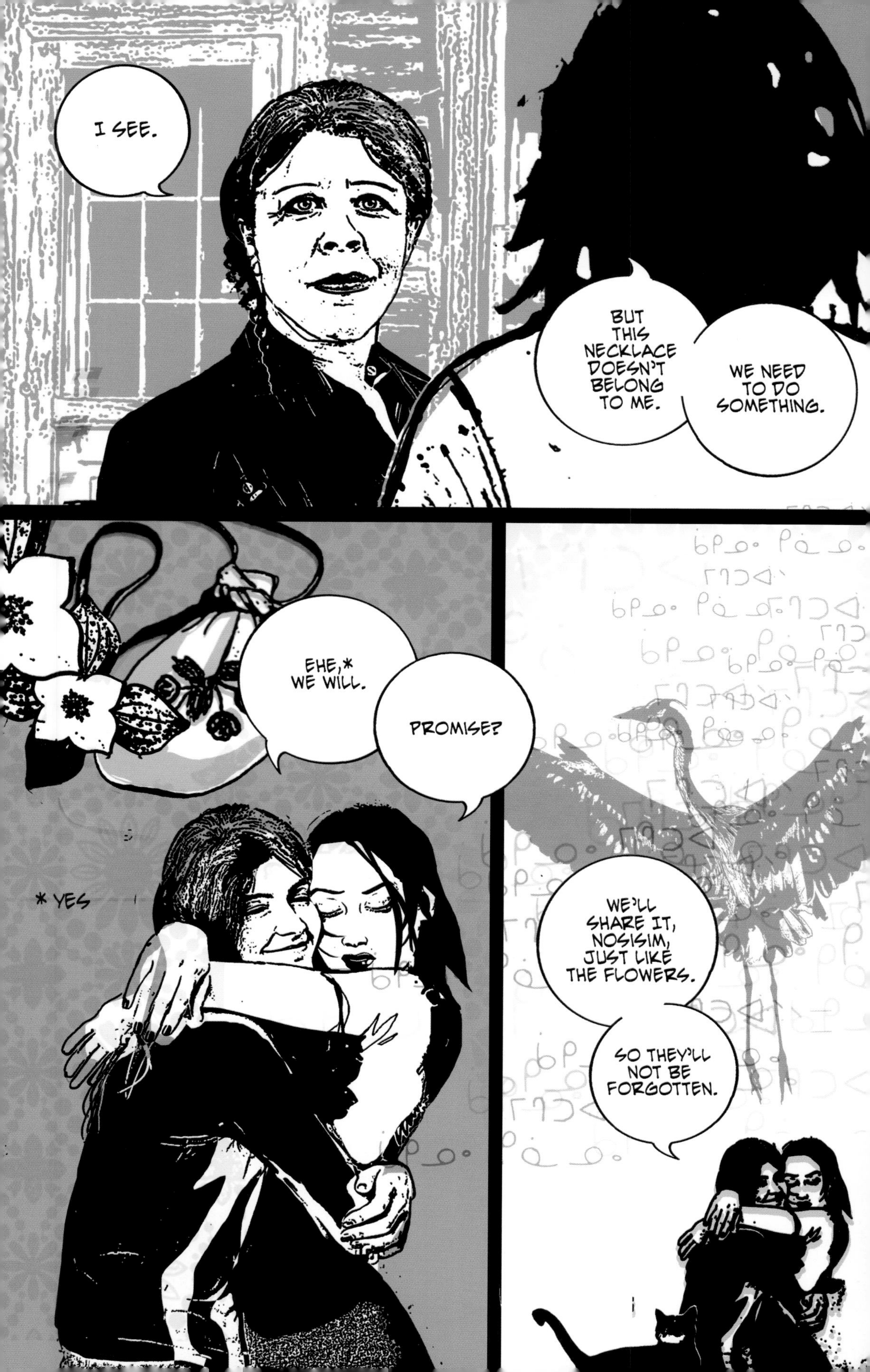
I SEE.
BUT THIS NECKLACE DOESN'T BELONG TO ME.
WE NEED TO DO SOMETHING.
EHE,* WE WILL.
PROMISE?
* YES
WE'LL SHARE IT, NOSISIM, JUST LIKE THE FLOWERS.
SO THEY'LL NOT BE FORGOTTEN.

The spirit animals in this story represent the Seven Sacred Teachings—natural virtues that form a foundation to achieve Mino-Pimatisiwin, the good life. Each animal embodies a teaching to illustrate our connection to the natural world. In receiving these teachings, we are told to respect the earth and all living things inhabited within. Indigenous Peoples lived for thousands of years with these connections to the earth through the animal world. We came from the earth, and the earth is mother to us all.

Medicine Bag: a pouch, often referred to as a bundle, which contains an individual's sacred items. This pouch hangs from the neck in order to keep these items close to our hearts.

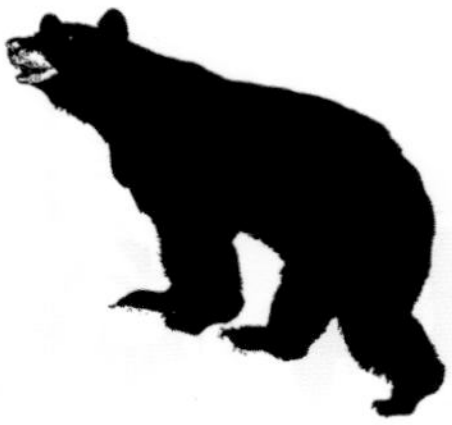

BEAR

Courage: the mental, moral, and spiritual strength to overcome fears that keep us from living the way we are meant to live.

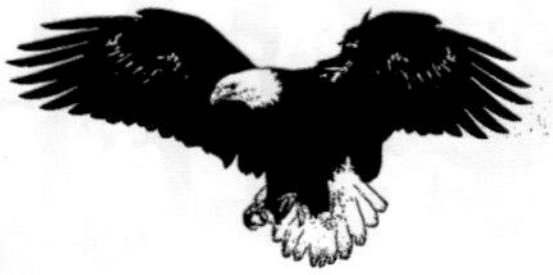

EAGLE

Love: loving oneself as the Creator loves each one of us, and extending that love to others.

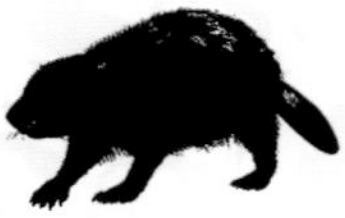

BEAVER

Wisdom: using the talents you have been gifted with for the benefit of others and to contribute to creating a healthier community.

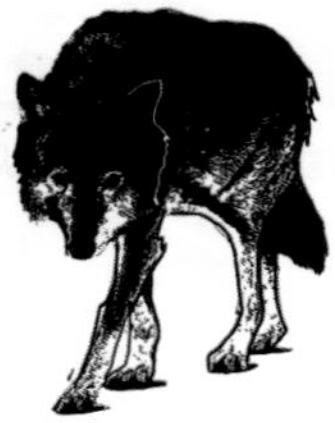

WOLF

Humility: knowing there is a higher power, and through this knowledge, understanding we are all equal to each other.

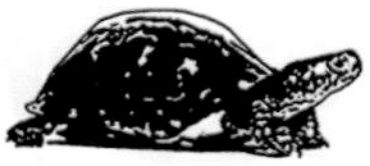

TURTLE

Truth: understanding the original laws given to us by the Creator, and remaining faithful to them.

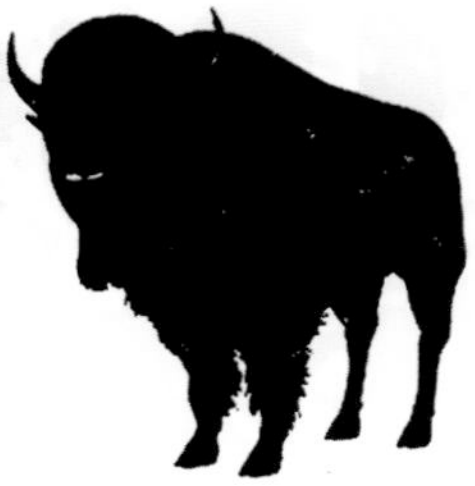

BUFFALO

Respect: showing deep respect for mother earth and all living things, including the differences that make us unique.

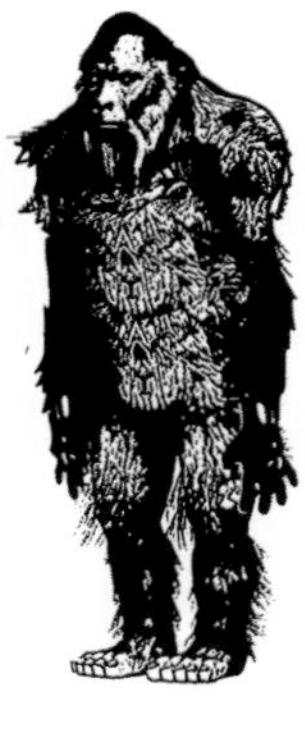

SABE or MISTAPIW

Honesty: being honest to yourself in how the Creator made you and accepting the person you are meant to be.

Nobody Knows

Lay me down now
Lay me to the ground
Lay me down now
Lay me down in the shade

I won't be afraid
No I won't
I won't be afraid
No I won't
I won't be afraid
Lay me down in the shade

And nobody knows, nobody knows
Where we've been, or where we go
Nobody knows, nobody knows
Where we've been or where we go
Nobody knows

I won't let you look away anymore

— Lyrics from the song by Iskwé

STAR WARS
EMPIRE

VOLUME FOUR: THE HEART OF THE REBELLIO

DARK HORSE BOOKS™

THESE STORIES TAKE PLACE FROM
SHORTLY BEFORE THE EVENTS
IN STAR WARS: A NEW HOPE,
TO JUST BEFORE THE EVENTS IN
THE EMPIRE STRIKES BACK.

STAR WARS: EMPIRE VOLUME 4

STAR WARS © 2005 LUCASFILM LTD. & ™. ALL RIGHTS
RESERVED. USED UNDER AUTHORIZATION. TEXT AND
ILLUSTRATIONS FOR STAR WARS ARE © 2003, 2004
AND 2005 LUCASFILM LTD. DARK HORSE BOOKS™ IS
A TRADEMARK OF DARK HORSE COMICS, INC. DARK
HORSE COMICS® IS A TRADEMARK OF DARK HORSE
COMICS, INC., REGISTERED IN VARIOUS CATEGORIES AND
COUNTRIES. ALL RIGHTS RESERVED. NO PORTION OF THIS
PUBLICATION MAY BE REPRODUCED OR TRANSMITTED, IN
ANY FORM OR BY ANY MEANS, WITHOUT THE EXPRESS
WRITTEN PERMISSION OF DARK HORSE COMICS, INC.
NAMES, CHARACTERS, PLACES, AND INCIDENTS FEATURED
IN THIS PUBLICATION EITHER ARE THE PRODUCT OF THE
AUTHOR'S IMAGINATION OR ARE USED FICTITIOUSLY. ANY
RESEMBLANCE TO ACTUAL PERSONS (LIVING OR DEAD),
EVENTS, INSTITUTIONS, OR LOCALES, WITHOUT SATIRIC
INTENT, IS COINCIDENTAL.

THIS VOLUME COLLECTS ISSUES #5-6 AND
#20-22 OF THE COMIC-BOOK SERIES STAR WARS:
EMPIRE AND STAR WARS: A VALENTINE STORY.

PUBLISHED BY
DARK HORSE BOOKS
A DIVISION OF DARK HORSE COMICS, INC.
10956 SE MAIN STREET
MILWAUKIE, OR 97222

DARKHORSE.COM
STARWARS.COM

TO FIND A COMICS SHOP IN YOUR
AREA, CALL THE COMIC SHOP
LOCATOR SERVICE TOLL-FREE
AT 1-888-266-4226

FIRST EDITION: MARCH 2005
ISBN: 1-59307-308-9

1 3 5 7 9 10 8 6 4 2

PRINTED IN CHINA

VOLUME FOUR:
THE HEART OF THE REBELLION

WRITERS WELLES HARTLEY
RON MARZ
RANDY STRADLEY
JUDD WINICK
WITH ADDITIONAL DIALOGUE BY
BRIAN DALEY

ARTISTS PAUL CHADWICK
DAVIDÉ FABBRI
& CHRISTIAN DALLA VECCHIA
TOMÁS GIORELLO
ADRIANA MELO

COLORISTS MICHAEL ATIYEH
DIGITAL CHAMELEON
KEN STEACY

LETTERERS DIGITAL CHAMELEON
JASON HVAM
SNO CONE STUDIOS
MICHAEL DAVID THOMAS

COVER ART BY DAVID MICHAEL BECK

PUBLISHER
MIKE RICHARDSON

COLLECTION DESIGNER
LANI SCHREIBSTEIN

ART DIRECTOR
LIA RIBACCHI

ASSOCIATE EDITOR
JEREMY BARLOW

EDITOR
RANDY STRADLEY

SPECIAL THANKS TO
SUE ROSTONI AND AMY GARY
AT LUCAS LICENSING

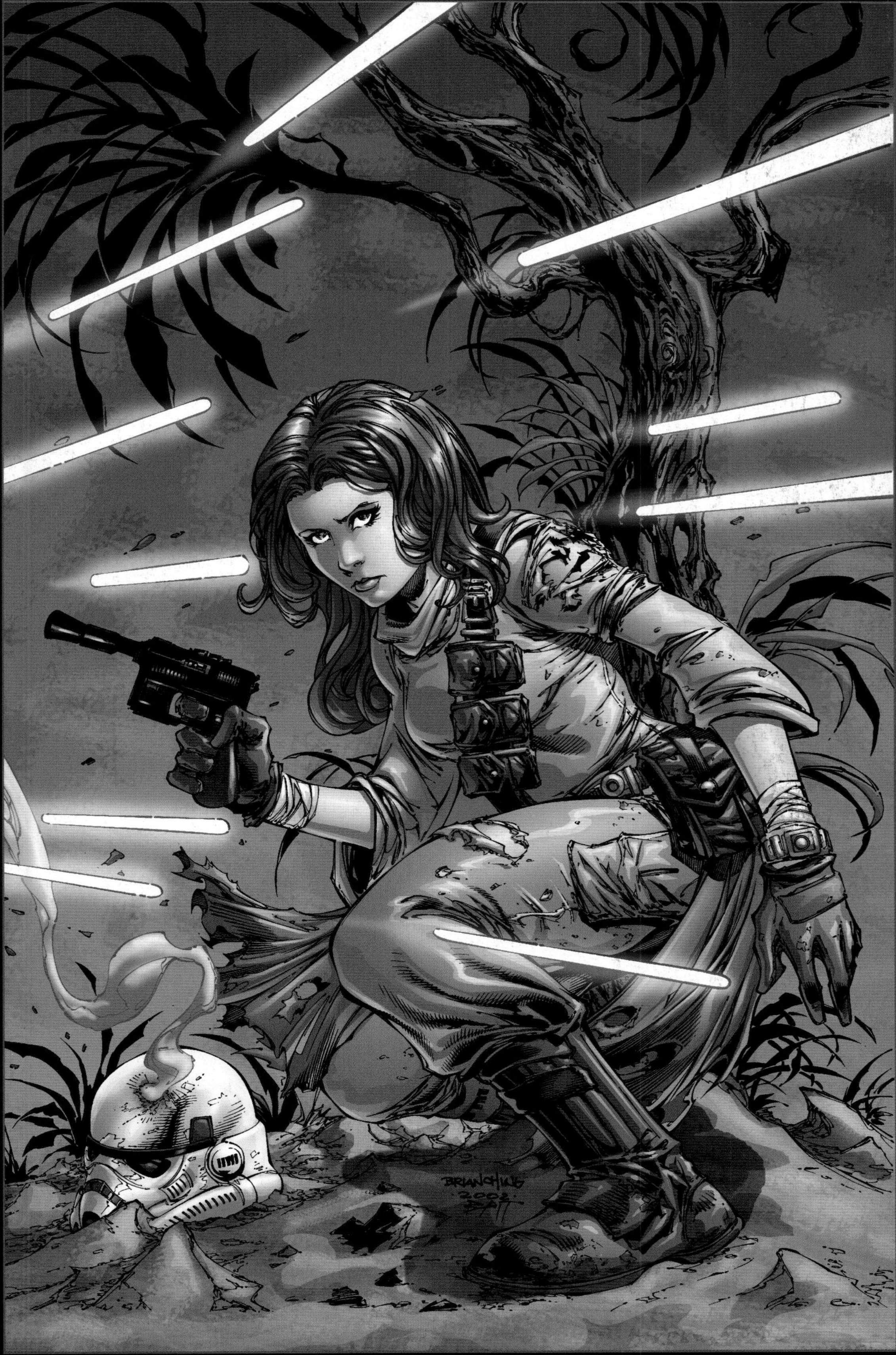

BRIAN CHING AND BATT

PRINCESS ... WARRIOR

SCRIPT RANDY STRADLEY
WITH ADDITIONAL DIALOGUE BY
BRIAN DALEY
FROM THE STAR WARS RADIO DRAMA
PENCILS DAVIDÉ FABBRI
INKS CHRISTIAN DALLA VECCHIA
COLORS DIGITAL CHAMELEON

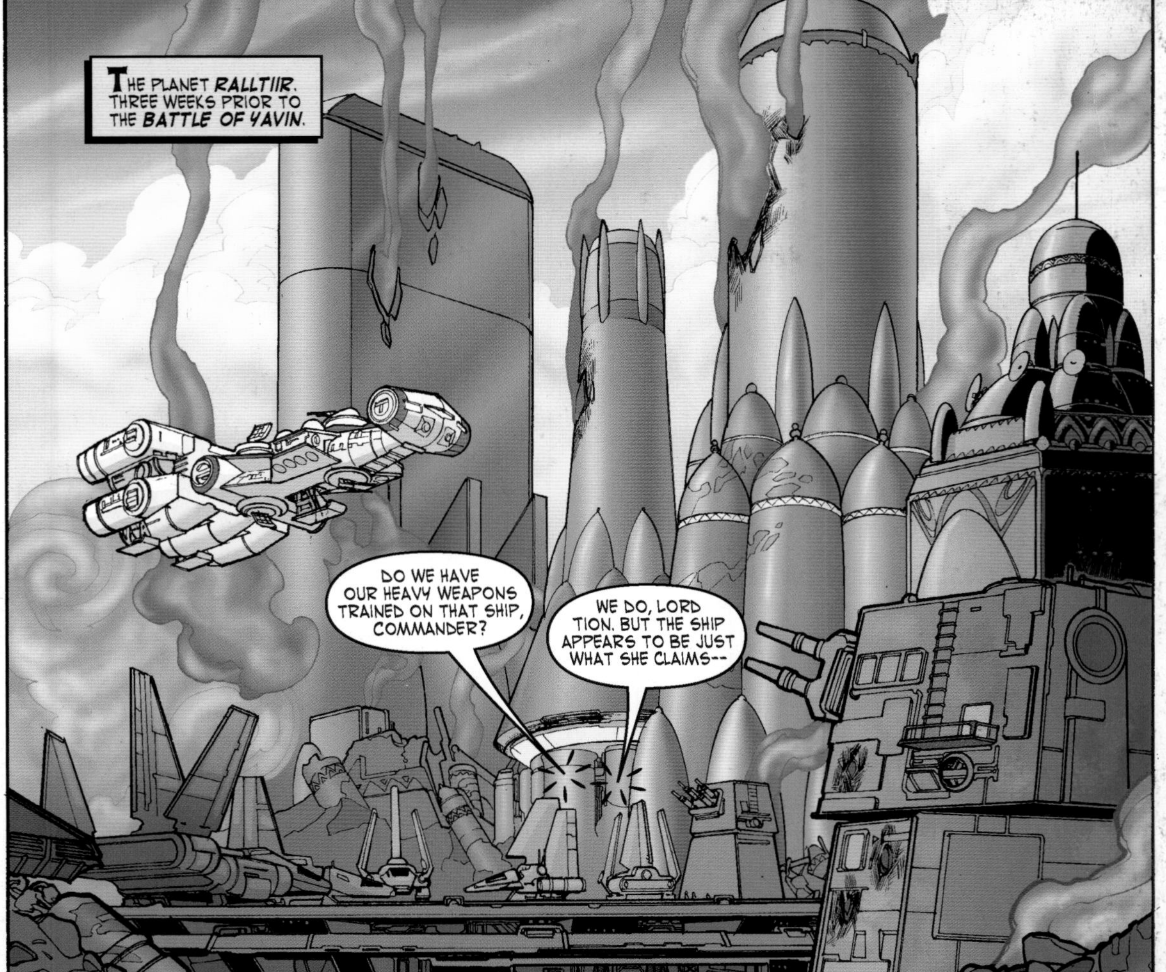
THE PLANET RALLTIIR. THREE WEEKS PRIOR TO THE BATTLE OF YAVIN.
DO WE HAVE OUR HEAVY WEAPONS TRAINED ON THAT SHIP, COMMANDER?
WE DO, LORD TION. BUT THE SHIP APPEARS TO BE JUST WHAT SHE CLAIMS--

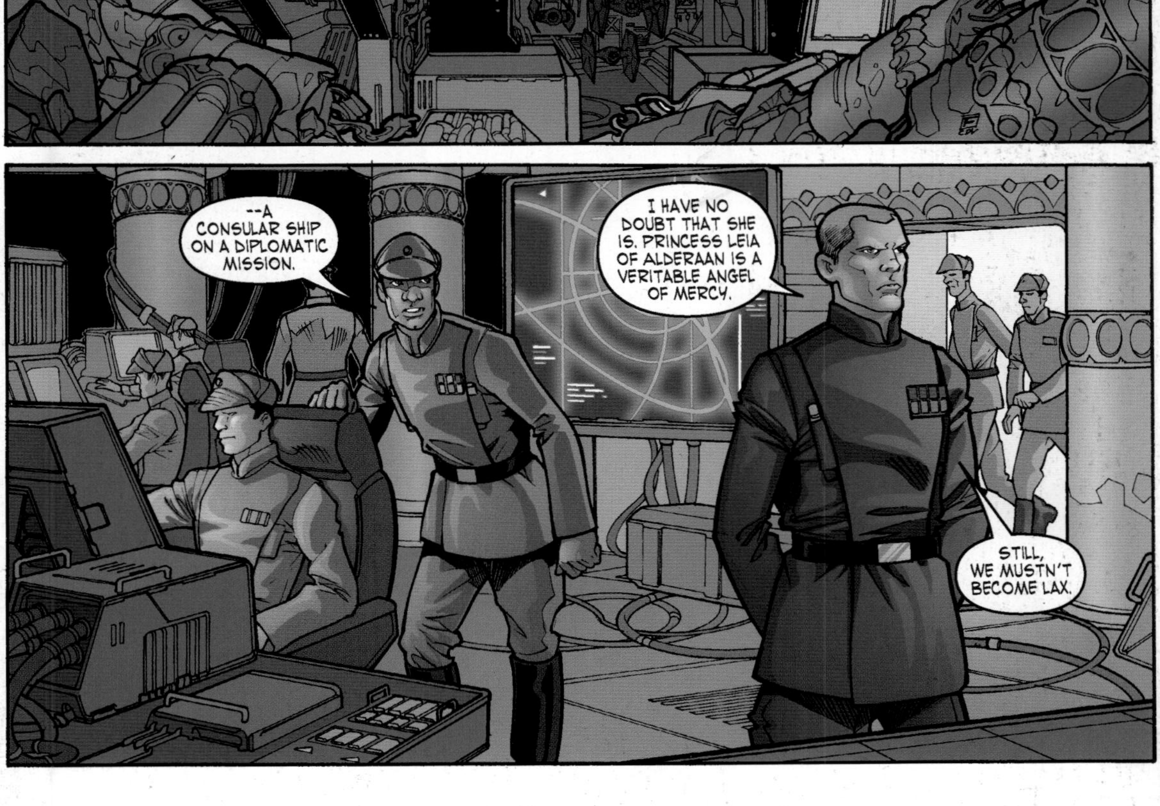
--A CONSULAR SHIP ON A DIPLOMATIC MISSION.
I HAVE NO DOUBT THAT SHE IS. PRINCESS LEIA OF ALDERAAN IS A VERITABLE ANGEL OF MERCY.
STILL, WE MUSTN'T BECOME LAX.

THEY'VE POSTED A *GUARD* AT OUR BOARDING LOCK, PRINCESS!

WHAT?! PATCH ME THROUGH TO WHOEVER'S IN CHARGE!

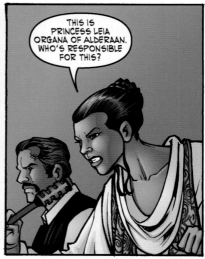

THIS IS PRINCESS LEIA ORGANA OF ALDERAAN. WHO'S RESPONSIBLE FOR THIS?

A *DELIGHT* TO HEAR YOUR VOICE AGAIN, YOUR HIGHNESS. *LORD TION,* HERE.

TION! I DON'T HAVE TIME TO FEND OFF HIS ADVANCES...

I WOULD BE HONORED TO EXPLAIN. I'LL SEND MY PERSONAL LANDSPEEDER FOR YOU.

MY OWN IS BEING LOWERED NOW, THANK YOU.

THEN I AWAIT YOU WITH GREAT ANTICIPATION.

THERE SHE GOES, *BASSO.* ARE YOU SURE YOU WANT TO GO THROUGH WITH THIS?

WE HAVE A CHOICE? OUR PEOPLE ARE BEING HERDED INTO CAMPS-- *SLAUGHTERED.*

IS THE DIVERSION TEAM READY, *JIIR?*

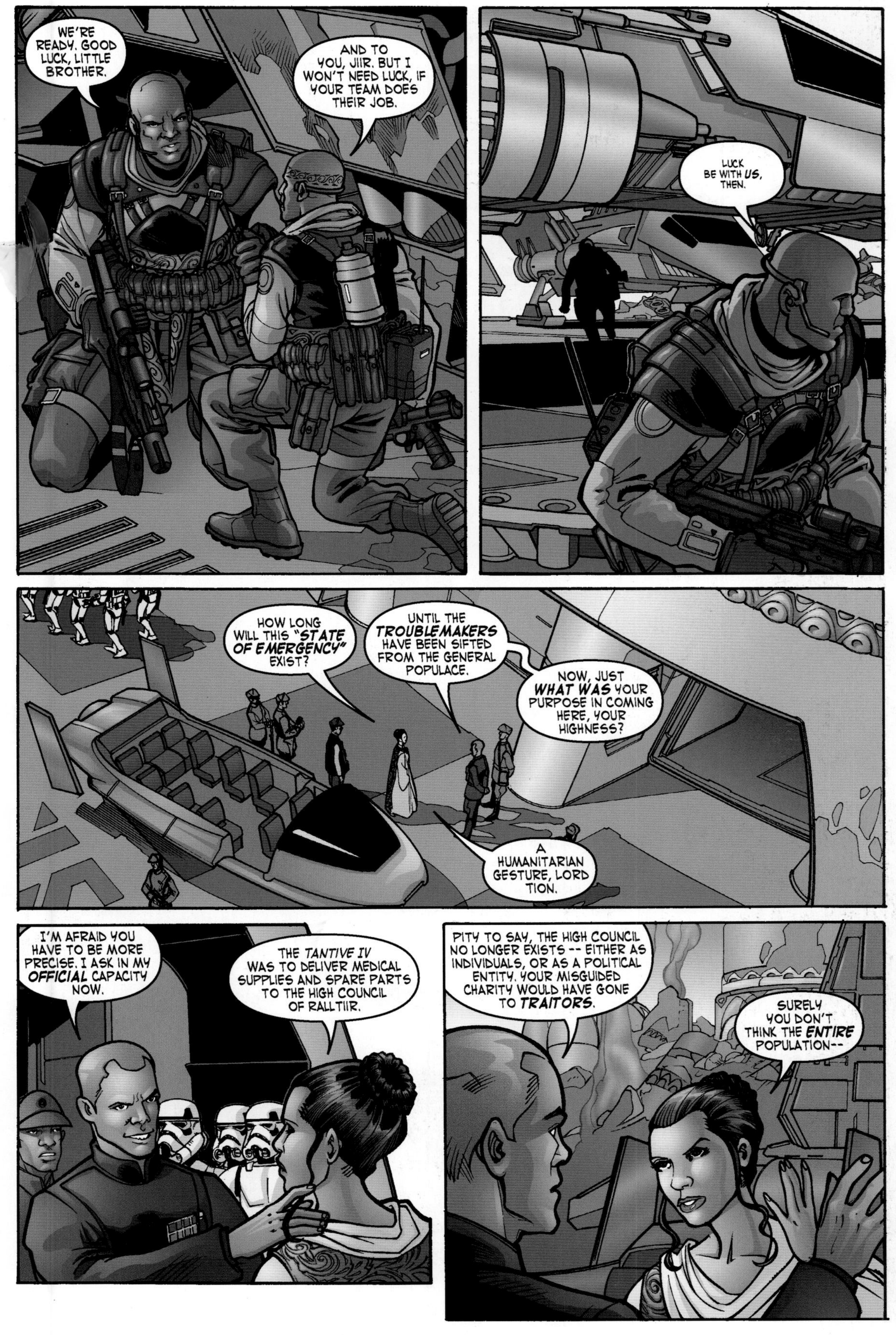
WE'RE READY. GOOD LUCK, LITTLE BROTHER.
AND TO YOU, JIIR. BUT I WON'T NEED LUCK, IF YOUR TEAM DOES THEIR JOB.
LUCK BE WITH *US*, THEN.
HOW LONG WILL THIS "*STATE OF EMERGENCY*" EXIST?
UNTIL THE *TROUBLEMAKERS* HAVE BEEN SIFTED FROM THE GENERAL POPULACE.
NOW, JUST *WHAT WAS* YOUR PURPOSE IN COMING HERE, YOUR HIGHNESS?
A HUMANITARIAN GESTURE, LORD TION.
I'M AFRAID YOU HAVE TO BE MORE PRECISE. I ASK IN MY *OFFICIAL* CAPACITY NOW.
THE *TANTIVE IV* WAS TO DELIVER MEDICAL SUPPLIES AND SPARE PARTS TO THE HIGH COUNCIL OF RALLTIIR.
PITY TO SAY, THE HIGH COUNCIL NO LONGER EXISTS -- EITHER AS INDIVIDUALS, OR AS A POLITICAL ENTITY. YOUR MISGUIDED CHARITY WOULD HAVE GONE TO *TRAITORS*.
SURELY YOU DON'T THINK THE *ENTIRE* POPULATION--

ENOUGH OF THEM WERE SYMPATHETIC TO THE *REBEL ALLIANCE* TO REQUIRE A *PURIFICATION* HERE.

THE EMPIRE WILL EXERT CLOSE GUIDANCE OVER THEM FOR THEIR OWN SAFETY.

"WITH A STARFLEET *BLOCKADE?* WITH IMPRESSMENT GANGS AND *INTERROGATION CENTERS?*"

"I RECOMMEND GREAT CARE IN CHOOSING YOUR WORDS, PRINCESS. I HAVE A HIGH REGARD FOR YOUR FAMILY AND -- IF I MAY SAY SO -- FOR *YOU* YOURSELF. BUT THERE ARE CERTAIN THINGS WHICH EVEN AN *ORGANA* MAY NOT SAY WITH IMPUNITY."

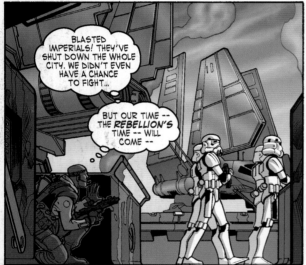

BLASTED *IMPERIALS!* THEY'VE SHUT DOWN THE WHOLE CITY. WE DIDN'T EVEN HAVE A CHANCE TO FIGHT...

BUT OUR TIME -- THE *REBELLION'S* TIME -- WILL COME --

--AND SOONER THAN THEY THINK.

THERE'S THE DIVERSION!

BDOW

BDOW

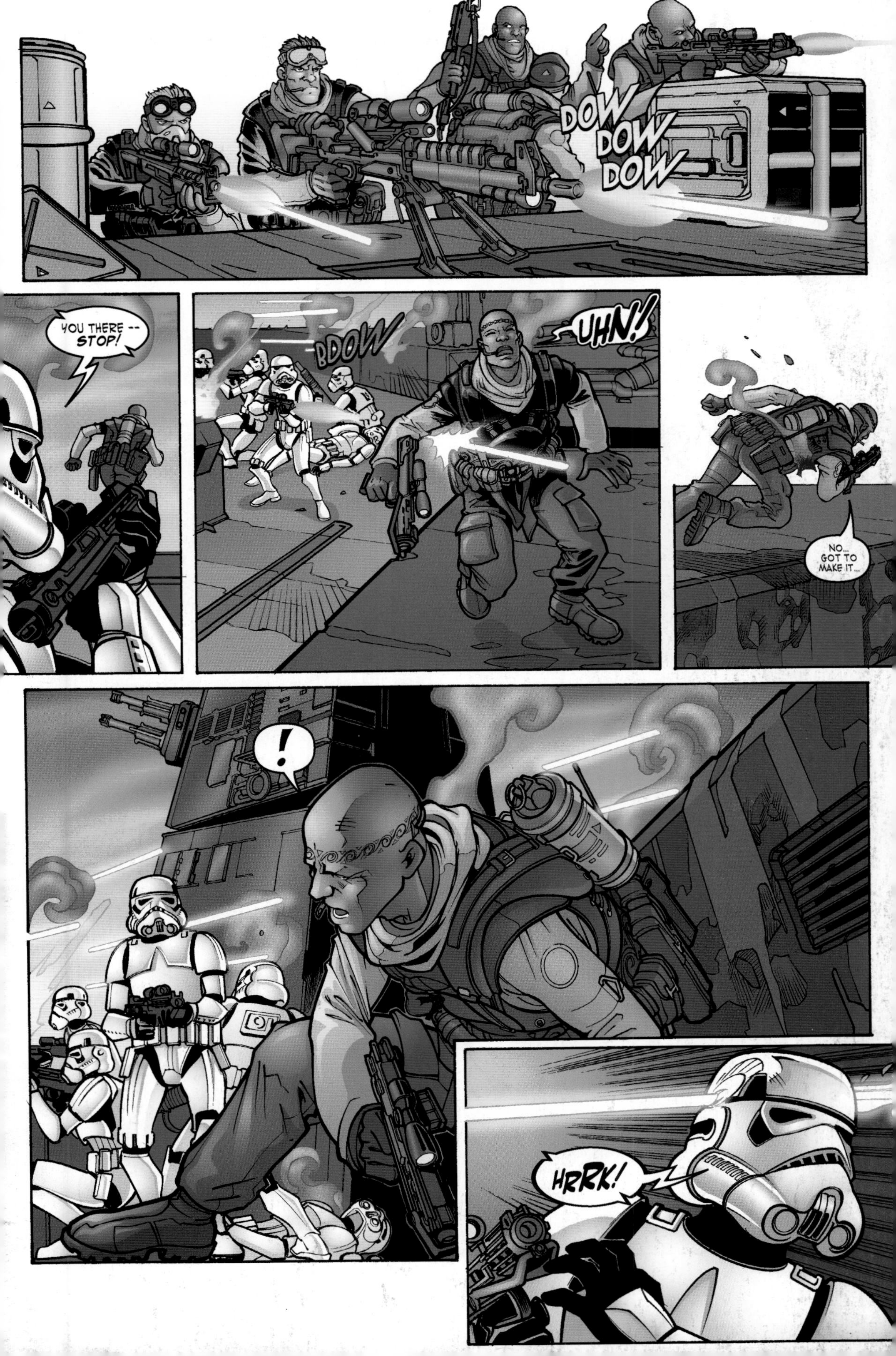
DOW
DOW
DOW
YOU THERE -- STOP!
BDOW
UHN!
NO... GOT TO MAKE IT...
!
HRRK!

...FOUR STORMTROOPERS KILLED OR WOUNDED! THE FIREFIGHT'S STILL IN PROGRESS, SIR!

COMMANDER, SEND IN ONE OF OUR RESERVE COMPANIES! I WANT PRISONERS! AND HAVE LORD VADER MEET US THERE!

YES, LORD TION!

PRINCESS LEIA, YOU'LL HAVE TO RETURN TO YOUR SHIP, FOR SAFETY'S SAKE. A FOOLISH REBEL GESTURE-- DOOMED TO FAILURE, OF COURSE. WE'VE GOT THE ENTIRE CITY WELL UNDER CONTROL. I'LL LEAVE AN ESCORT HERE FOR YOU.

I HAVE MY OWN, THANK YOU.

VERY WELL, COMMANDER! THE SOUTHERN PERIMETER, QUICKLY!

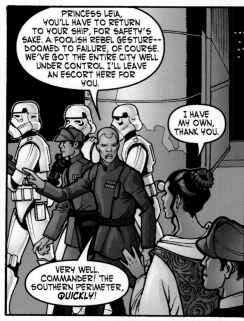

WE HAVE LITTLE CHOICE BUT TO GO BACK TO THE TANTIVE IV.

AND IF LORD TION SEARCHES HER CARGO?

MEDICAL SUPPLIES AND TECHNICAL EQUIPMENT ARE ALL HE'LL FIND.

COMBAT-TYPE MEDI-PACKS AND THREE SURGICAL FIELD STATIONS? SPARE PARTS AND POWER UNITS SUITABLE FOR MILITARY EQUIPMENT?

Y-YOUR HIGHNESS...

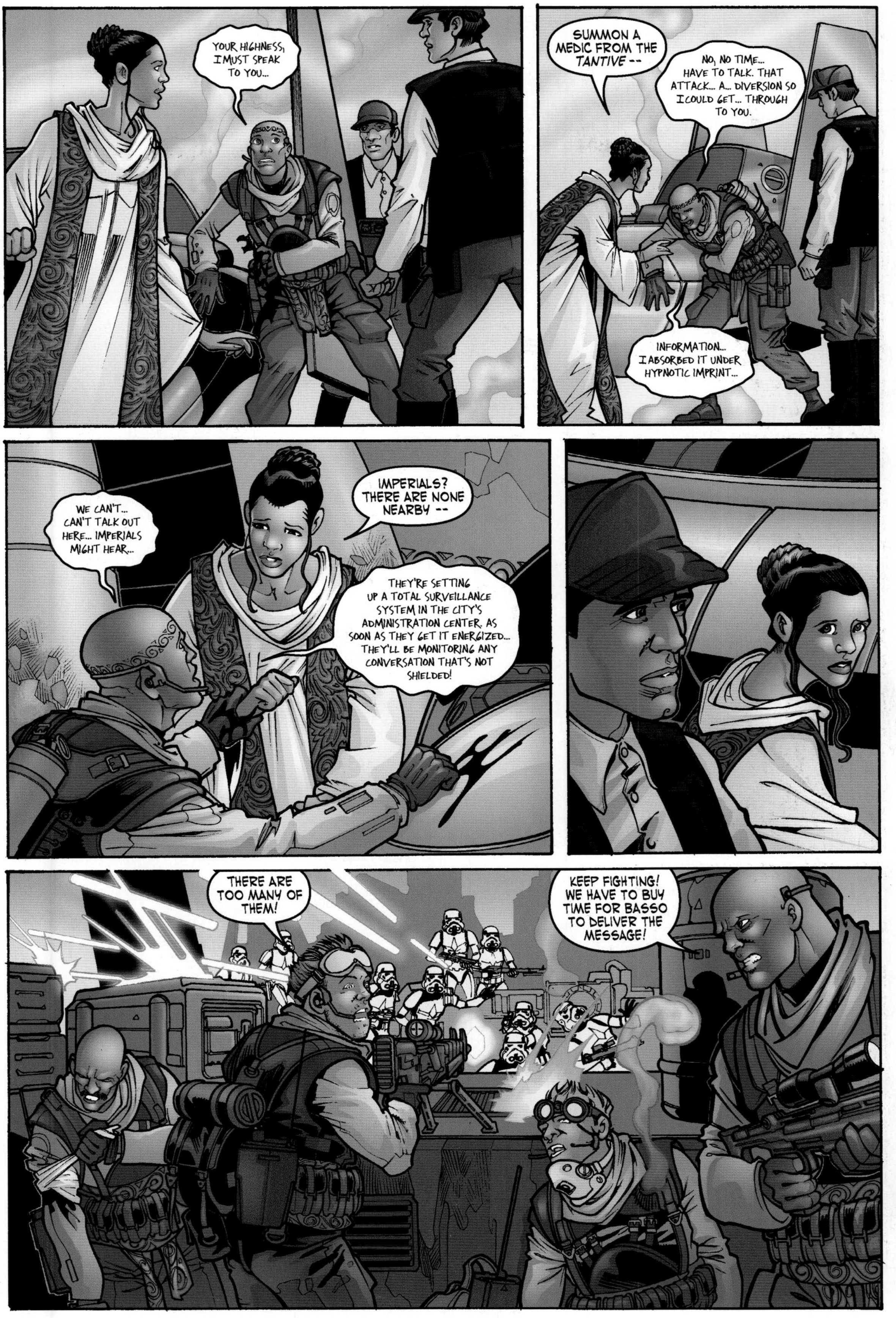
YOUR HIGHNESS, I MUST SPEAK TO YOU...
SUMMON A MEDIC FROM THE *TANTIVE* --
NO, NO TIME... HAVE TO TALK. THAT ATTACK... A... DIVERSION SO I COULD GET... THROUGH TO YOU.
INFORMATION... I ABSORBED IT UNDER HYPNOTIC IMPRINT...
WE CAN'T... CAN'T TALK OUT HERE... IMPERIALS MIGHT HEAR...
IMPERIALS? THERE ARE NONE NEARBY --
THEY'RE SETTING UP A TOTAL SURVEILLANCE SYSTEM IN THE CITY'S ADMINISTRATION CENTER. AS SOON AS THEY GET IT ENERGIZED... THEY'LL BE MONITORING ANY CONVERSATION THAT'S NOT SHIELDED!
THERE ARE TOO MANY OF THEM!
KEEP FIGHTING! WE HAVE TO BUY TIME FOR BASSO TO DELIVER THE MESSAGE!

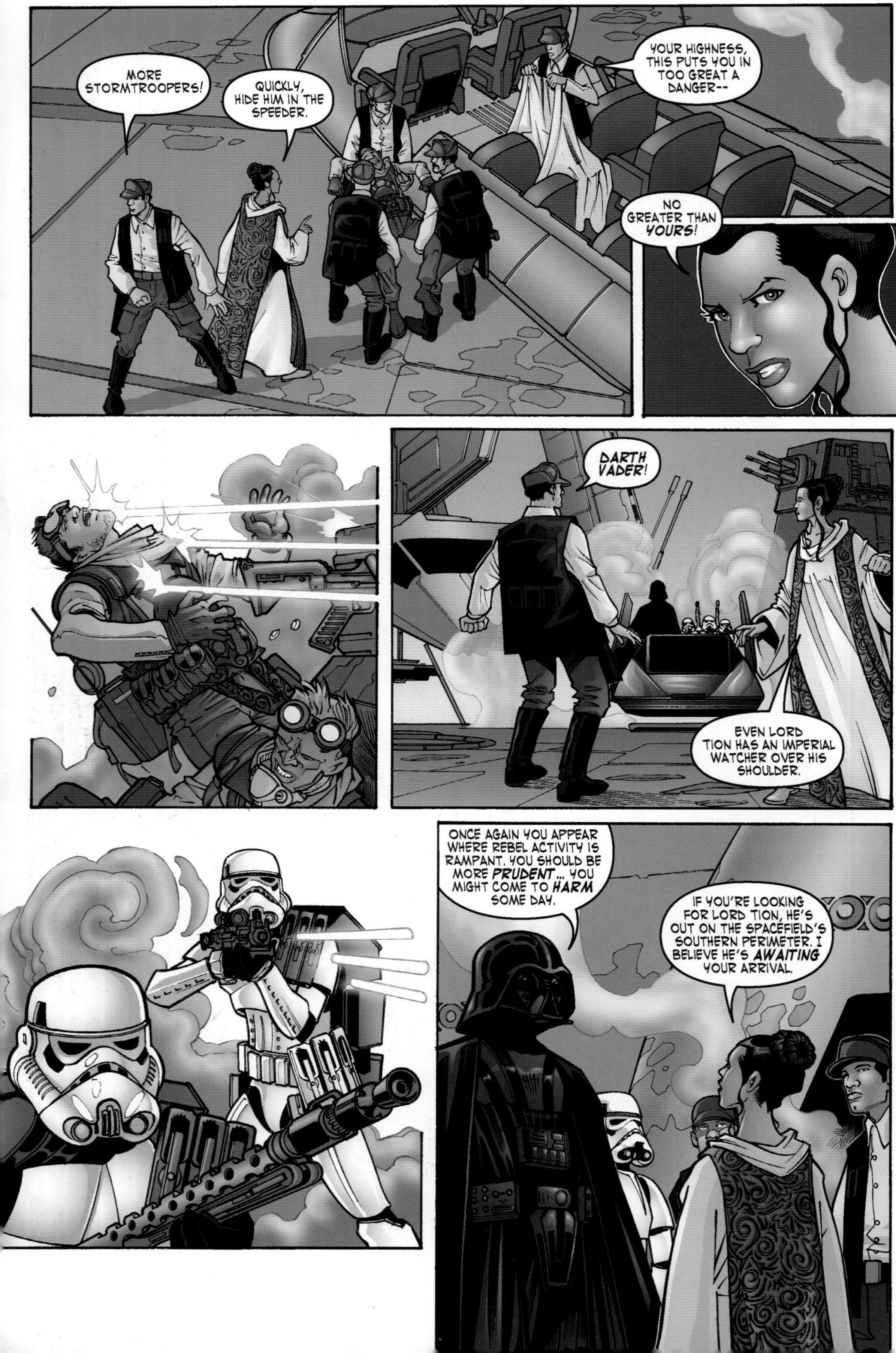
MORE STORMTROOPERS!
QUICKLY, HIDE HIM IN THE SPEEDER.
YOUR HIGHNESS, THIS PUTS YOU IN TOO GREAT A DANGER--
NO GREATER THAN YOURS!
DARTH VADER!
EVEN LORD TION HAS AN IMPERIAL WATCHER OVER HIS SHOULDER.
ONCE AGAIN YOU APPEAR WHERE REBEL ACTIVITY IS RAMPANT. YOU SHOULD BE MORE PRUDENT... YOU MIGHT COME TO HARM SOME DAY.
IF YOU'RE LOOKING FOR LORD TION, HE'S OUT ON THE SPACEFIELD'S SOUTHERN PERIMETER. I BELIEVE HE'S AWAITING YOUR ARRIVAL.

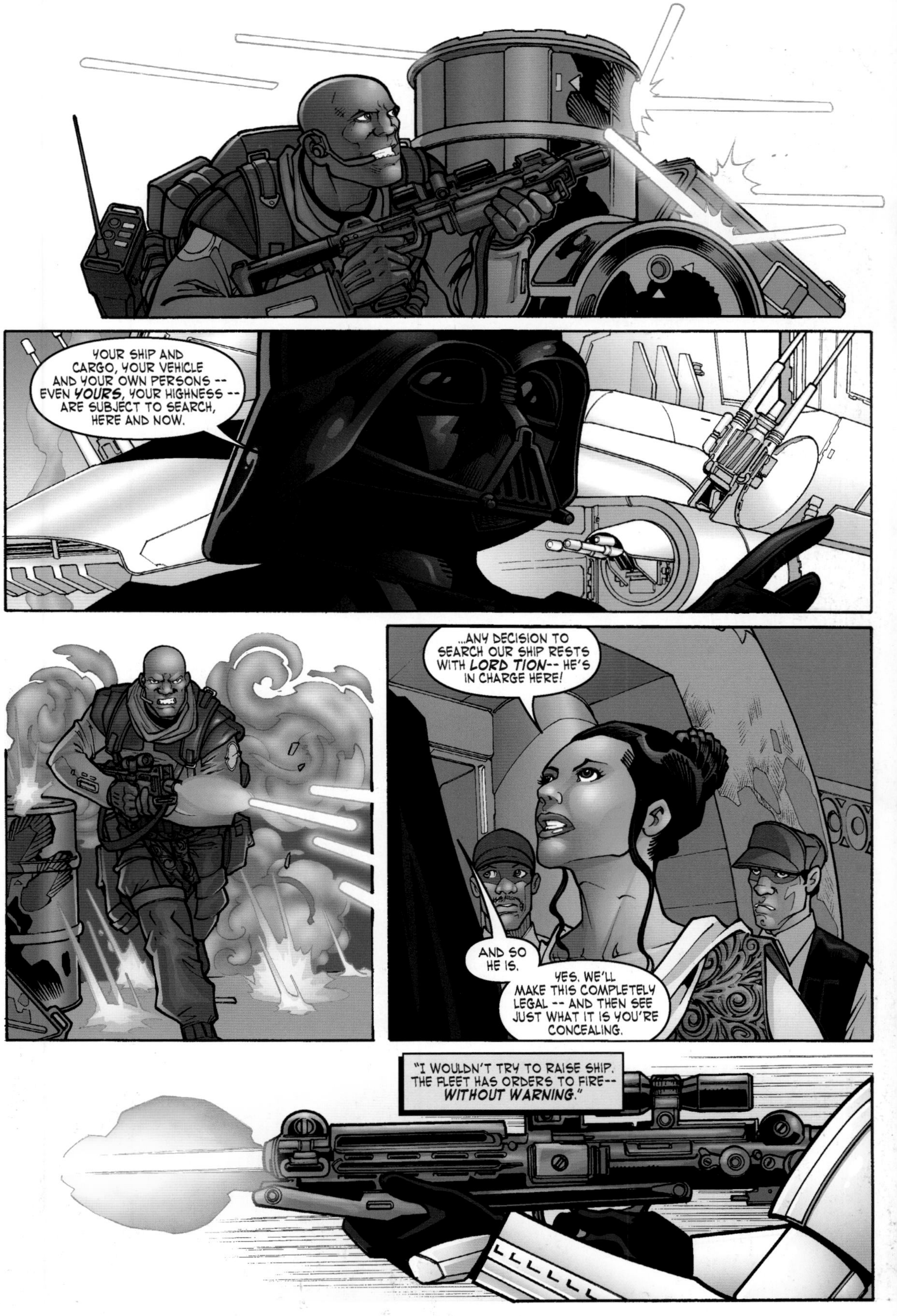
YOUR SHIP AND CARGO, YOUR VEHICLE AND YOUR OWN PERSONS -- EVEN YOURS, YOUR HIGHNESS -- ARE SUBJECT TO SEARCH, HERE AND NOW.
...ANY DECISION TO SEARCH OUR SHIP RESTS WITH LORD TION-- HE'S IN CHARGE HERE!
AND SO HE IS.
YES. WE'LL MAKE THIS COMPLETELY LEGAL -- AND THEN SEE JUST WHAT IT IS YOU'RE CONCEALING.
"I WOULDN'T TRY TO RAISE SHIP. THE FLEET HAS ORDERS TO FIRE-- WITHOUT WARNING."

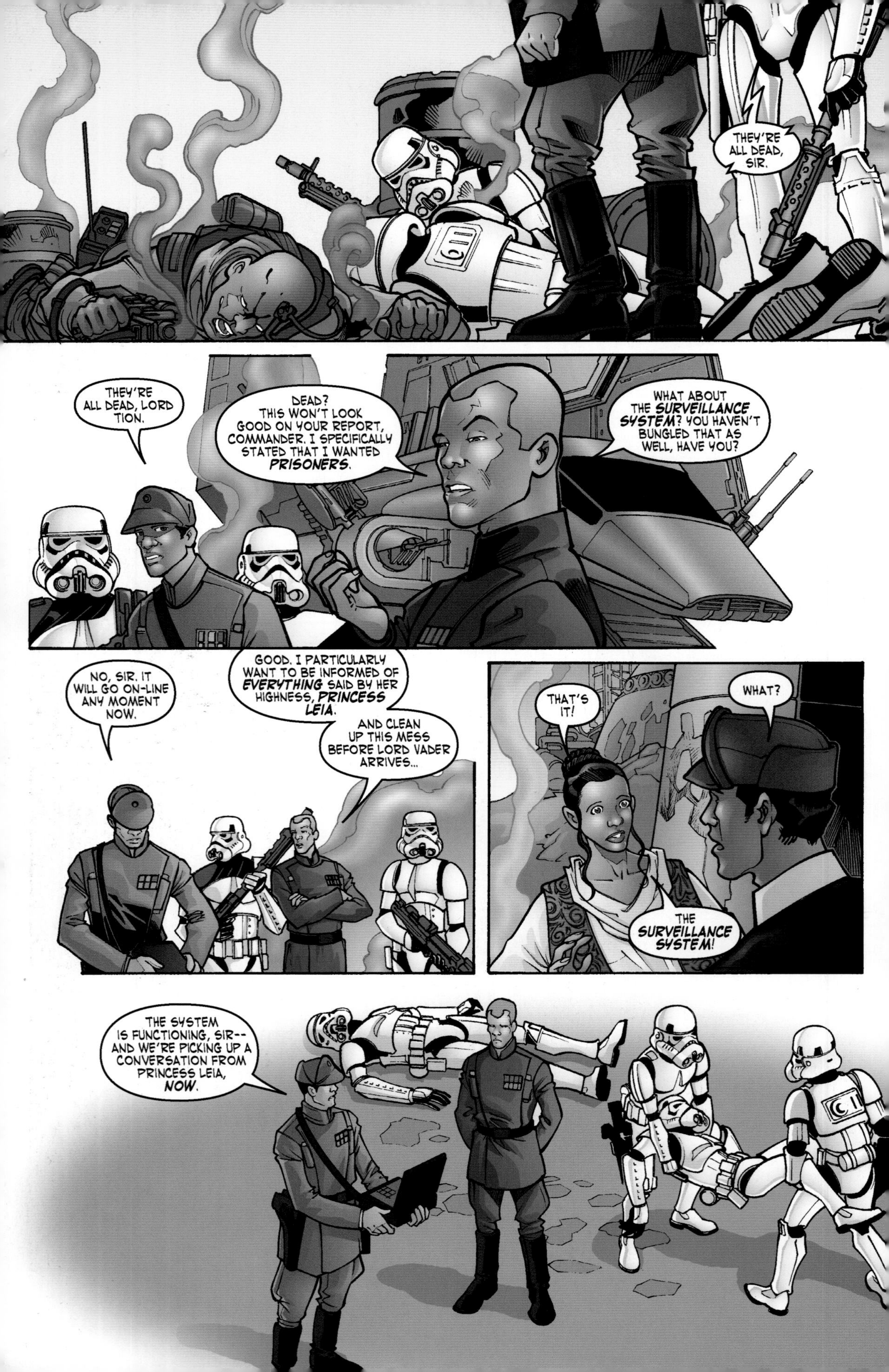
THEY'RE ALL DEAD, SIR.
THEY'RE ALL DEAD, LORD TION.
DEAD? THIS WON'T LOOK GOOD ON YOUR REPORT, COMMANDER. I SPECIFICALLY STATED THAT I WANTED PRISONERS.
WHAT ABOUT THE SURVEILLANCE SYSTEM? YOU HAVEN'T BUNGLED THAT AS WELL, HAVE YOU?
NO, SIR. IT WILL GO ON-LINE ANY MOMENT NOW.
GOOD. I PARTICULARLY WANT TO BE INFORMED OF EVERYTHING SAID BY HER HIGHNESS, PRINCESS LEIA.
AND CLEAN UP THIS MESS BEFORE LORD VADER ARRIVES...
THAT'S IT!
WHAT?
THE SURVEILLANCE SYSTEM!
THE SYSTEM IS FUNCTIONING, SIR-- AND WE'RE PICKING UP A CONVERSATION FROM PRINCESS LEIA, NOW.

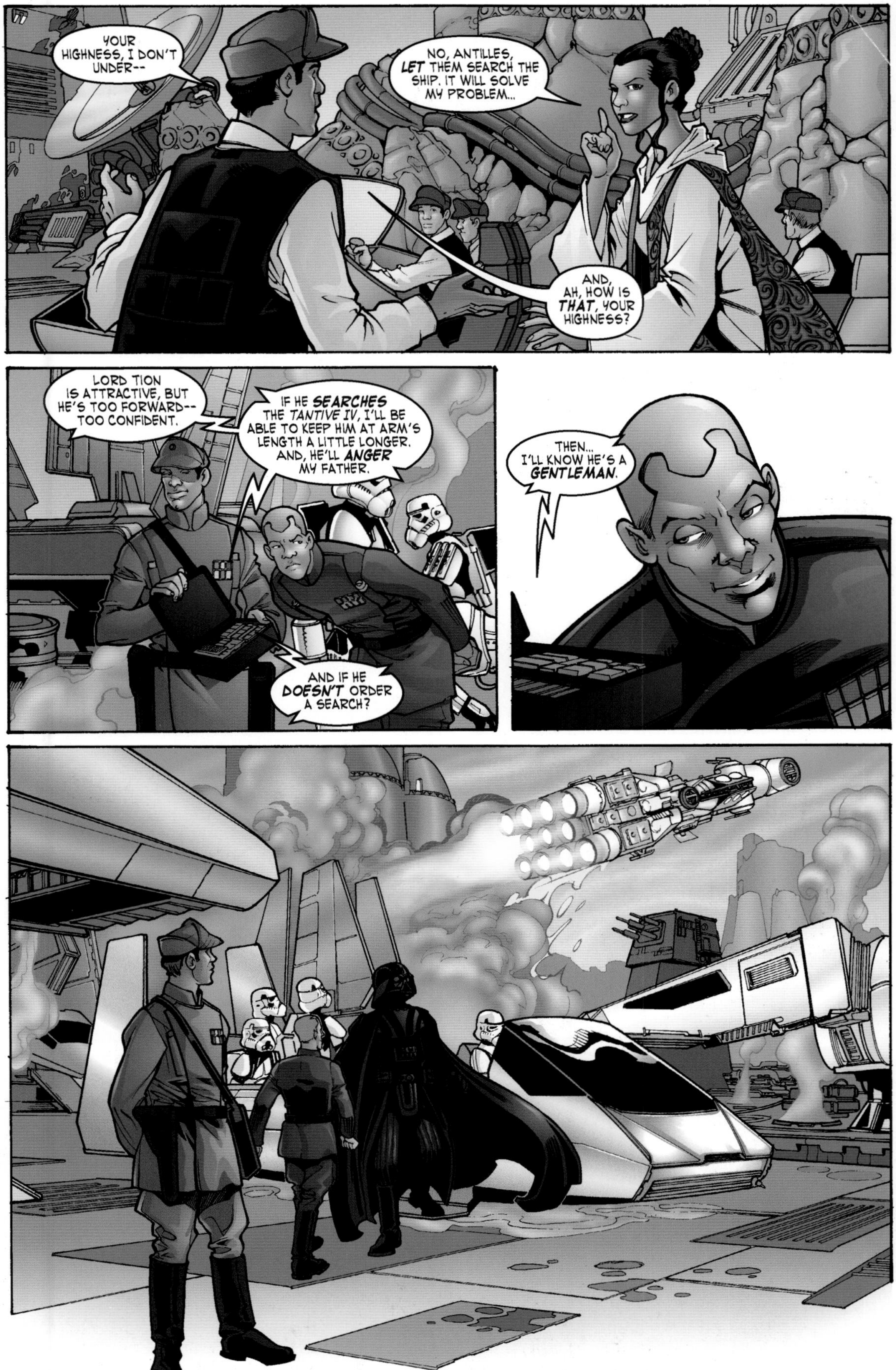
YOUR HIGHNESS, I DON'T UNDER--
NO, ANTILLES, LET THEM SEARCH THE SHIP. IT WILL SOLVE MY PROBLEM...
AND, AH, HOW IS THAT, YOUR HIGHNESS?
LORD TION IS ATTRACTIVE, BUT HE'S TOO FORWARD-- TOO CONFIDENT.
IF HE SEARCHES THE TANTIVE IV, I'LL BE ABLE TO KEEP HIM AT ARM'S LENGTH A LITTLE LONGER. AND, HE'LL ANGER MY FATHER.
AND IF HE DOESN'T ORDER A SEARCH?
THEN... I'LL KNOW HE'S A GENTLEMAN.

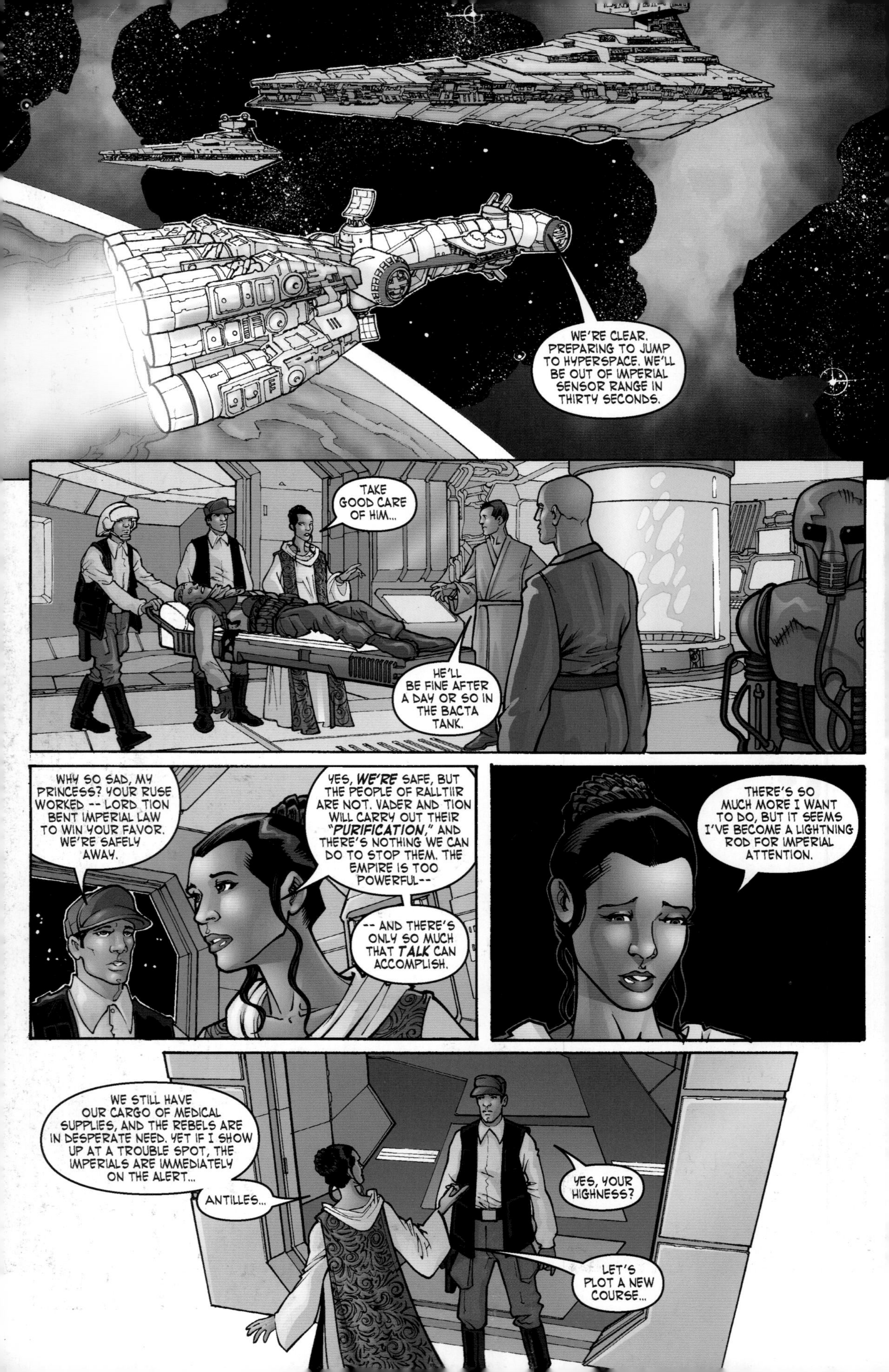
WE'RE CLEAR. PREPARING TO JUMP TO HYPERSPACE. WE'LL BE OUT OF IMPERIAL SENSOR RANGE IN THIRTY SECONDS.
TAKE GOOD CARE OF HIM...
HE'LL BE FINE AFTER A DAY OR SO IN THE BACTA TANK.
WHY SO SAD, MY PRINCESS? YOUR RUSE WORKED -- LORD TION BENT IMPERIAL LAW TO WIN YOUR FAVOR. WE'RE SAFELY AWAY.
YES, *WE'RE* SAFE, BUT THE PEOPLE OF RALLTIIR ARE NOT. VADER AND TION WILL CARRY OUT THEIR "*PURIFICATION*," AND THERE'S NOTHING WE CAN DO TO STOP THEM. THE EMPIRE IS TOO POWERFUL--
-- AND THERE'S ONLY SO MUCH THAT *TALK* CAN ACCOMPLISH.
THERE'S SO MUCH MORE I WANT TO DO, BUT IT SEEMS I'VE BECOME A LIGHTNING ROD FOR IMPERIAL ATTENTION.
WE STILL HAVE OUR CARGO OF MEDICAL SUPPLIES, AND THE REBELS ARE IN DESPERATE NEED. YET IF I SHOW UP AT A TROUBLE SPOT, THE IMPERIALS ARE IMMEDIATELY ON THE ALERT...
ANTILLES...
YES, YOUR HIGHNESS?
LET'S PLOT A NEW COURSE...

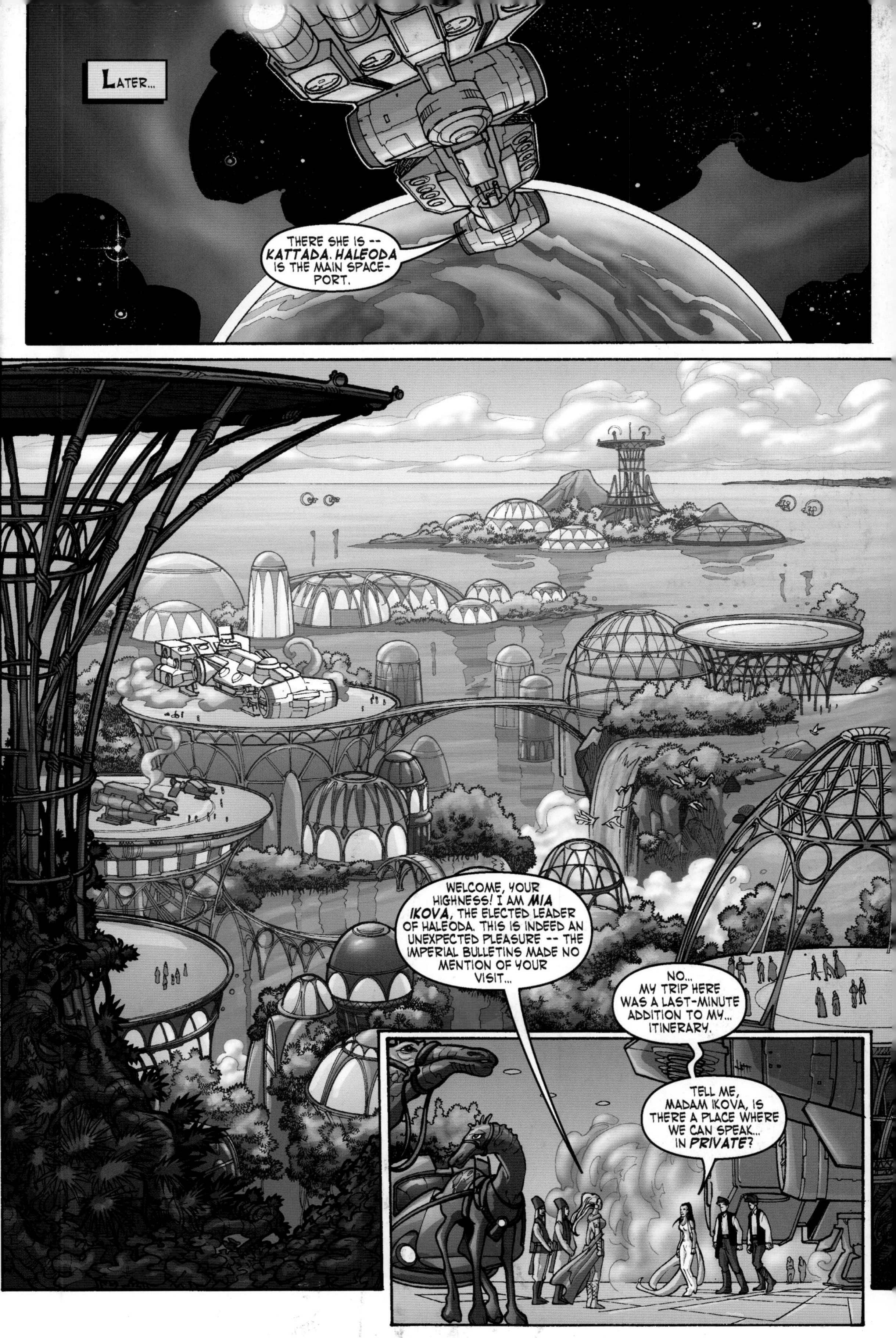
LATER...
THERE SHE IS -- KATTADA. HALEODA IS THE MAIN SPACE-PORT.
WELCOME, YOUR HIGHNESS! I AM MIA IKOVA, THE ELECTED LEADER OF HALEODA. THIS IS INDEED AN UNEXPECTED PLEASURE -- THE IMPERIAL BULLETINS MADE NO MENTION OF YOUR VISIT...
NO... MY TRIP HERE WAS A LAST-MINUTE ADDITION TO MY... ITINERARY.
TELL ME, MADAM IKOVA, IS THERE A PLACE WHERE WE CAN SPEAK... IN PRIVATE?

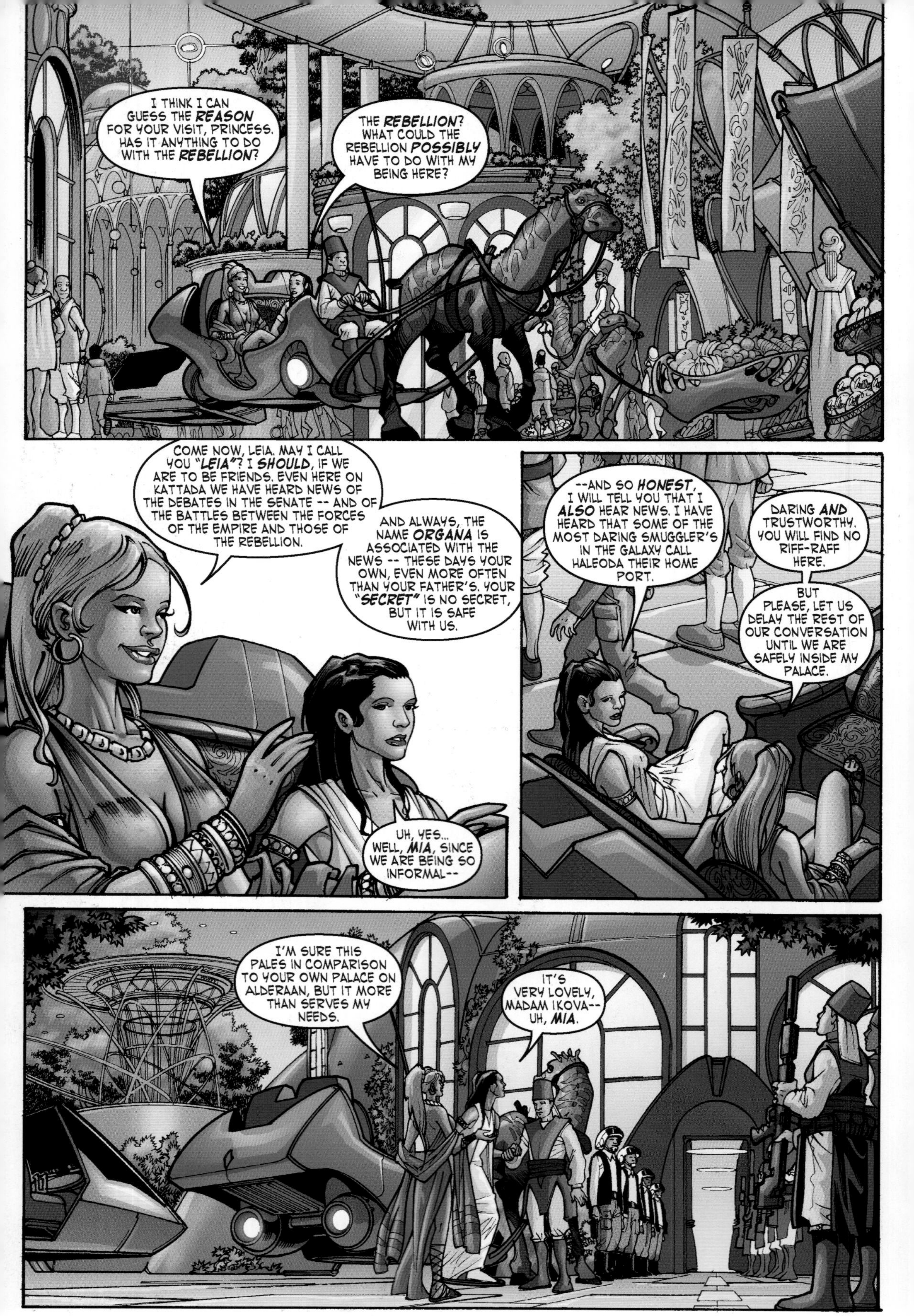
I THINK I CAN GUESS THE REASON FOR YOUR VISIT, PRINCESS. HAS IT ANYTHING TO DO WITH THE REBELLION?
THE REBELLION? WHAT COULD THE REBELLION POSSIBLY HAVE TO DO WITH MY BEING HERE?
COME NOW, LEIA. MAY I CALL YOU "LEIA"? I SHOULD, IF WE ARE TO BE FRIENDS. EVEN HERE ON KATTADA WE HAVE HEARD NEWS OF THE DEBATES IN THE SENATE -- AND OF THE BATTLES BETWEEN THE FORCES OF THE EMPIRE AND THOSE OF THE REBELLION.
AND ALWAYS, THE NAME ORGANA IS ASSOCIATED WITH THE NEWS -- THESE DAYS YOUR OWN, EVEN MORE OFTEN THAN YOUR FATHER'S. YOUR "SECRET" IS NO SECRET, BUT IT IS SAFE WITH US.
UH, YES... WELL, MIA, SINCE WE ARE BEING SO INFORMAL--
--AND SO HONEST, I WILL TELL YOU THAT I ALSO HEAR NEWS. I HAVE HEARD THAT SOME OF THE MOST DARING SMUGGLER'S IN THE GALAXY CALL HALEODA THEIR HOME PORT.
DARING AND TRUSTWORTHY. YOU WILL FIND NO RIFF-RAFF HERE.
BUT PLEASE, LET US DELAY THE REST OF OUR CONVERSATION UNTIL WE ARE SAFELY INSIDE MY PALACE.
I'M SURE THIS PALES IN COMPARISON TO YOUR OWN PALACE ON ALDERAAN, BUT IT MORE THAN SERVES MY NEEDS.
IT'S VERY LOVELY, MADAM IKOVA-- UH, MIA.

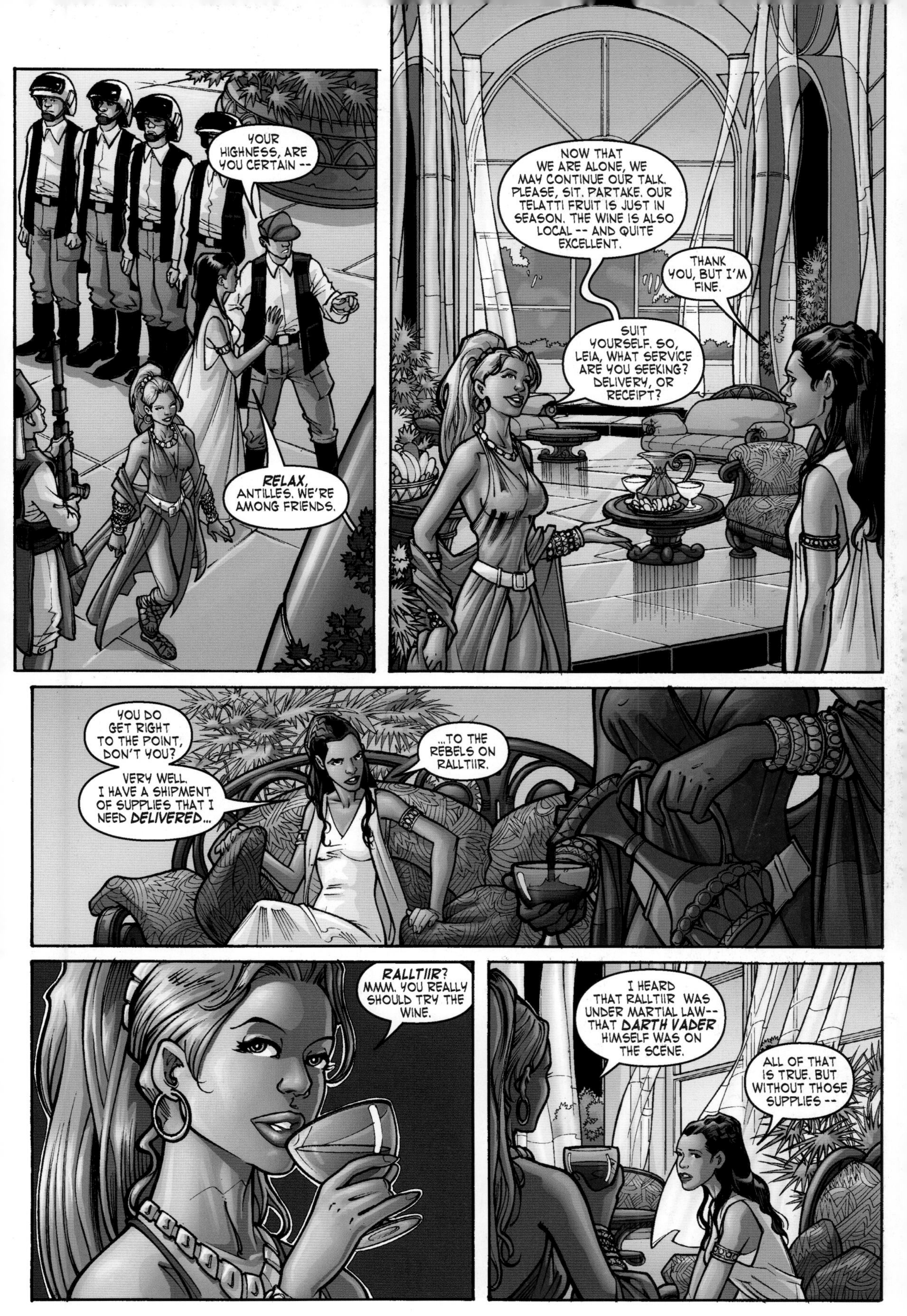
YOUR HIGHNESS, ARE YOU CERTAIN --
RELAX, ANTILLES. WE'RE AMONG FRIENDS.
NOW THAT WE ARE ALONE, WE MAY CONTINUE OUR TALK. PLEASE, SIT. PARTAKE. OUR TELATTI FRUIT IS JUST IN SEASON. THE WINE IS ALSO LOCAL -- AND QUITE EXCELLENT.
THANK YOU, BUT I'M FINE.
SUIT YOURSELF. SO, LEIA, WHAT SERVICE ARE YOU SEEKING? DELIVERY, OR RECEIPT?
YOU DO GET RIGHT TO THE POINT, DON'T YOU?
VERY WELL. I HAVE A SHIPMENT OF SUPPLIES THAT I NEED DELIVERED...
...TO THE REBELS ON RALLTIIR.
RALLTIIR? MMM. YOU REALLY SHOULD TRY THE WINE.
I HEARD THAT RALLTIIR WAS UNDER MARTIAL LAW-- THAT DARTH VADER HIMSELF WAS ON THE SCENE.
ALL OF THAT IS TRUE. BUT WITHOUT THOSE SUPPLIES --

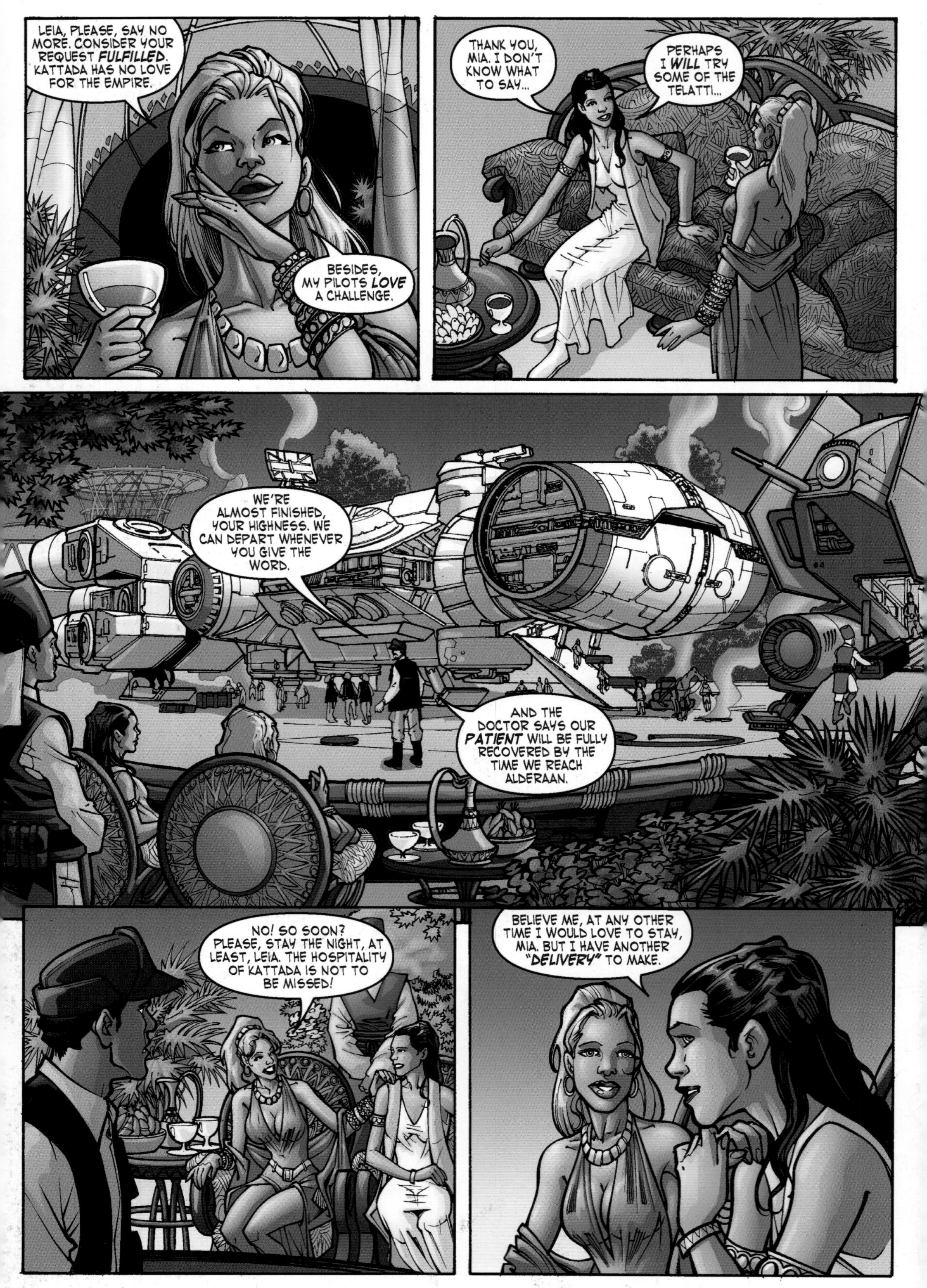
LEIA, PLEASE, SAY NO MORE. CONSIDER YOUR REQUEST FULFILLED. KATTADA HAS NO LOVE FOR THE EMPIRE.
BESIDES, MY PILOTS LOVE A CHALLENGE.
THANK YOU, MIA. I DON'T KNOW WHAT TO SAY...
PERHAPS I WILL TRY SOME OF THE TELATTI...
WE'RE ALMOST FINISHED, YOUR HIGHNESS. WE CAN DEPART WHENEVER YOU GIVE THE WORD.
AND THE DOCTOR SAYS OUR PATIENT WILL BE FULLY RECOVERED BY THE TIME WE REACH ALDERAAN.
NO! SO SOON? PLEASE, STAY THE NIGHT, AT LEAST, LEIA. THE HOSPITALITY OF KATTADA IS NOT TO BE MISSED!
BELIEVE ME, AT ANY OTHER TIME I WOULD LOVE TO STAY, MIA. BUT I HAVE ANOTHER "DELIVERY" TO MAKE.

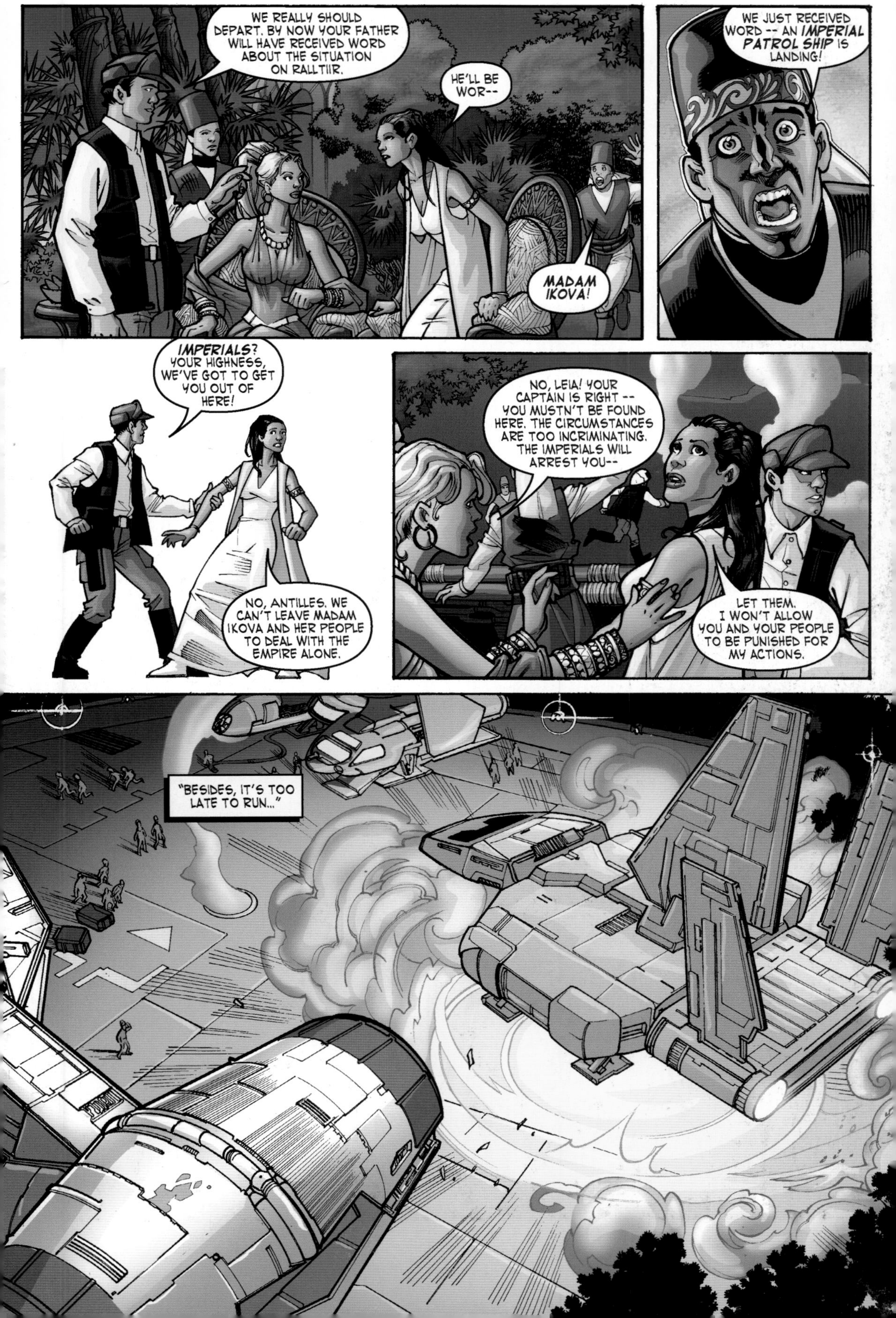
WE REALLY SHOULD DEPART. BY NOW YOUR FATHER WILL HAVE RECEIVED WORD ABOUT THE SITUATION ON RALLTIIR.
HE'LL BE WOR--
MADAM IKOVA!
WE JUST RECEIVED WORD -- AN IMPERIAL PATROL SHIP IS LANDING!
IMPERIALS? YOUR HIGHNESS, WE'VE GOT TO GET YOU OUT OF HERE!
NO, ANTILLES. WE CAN'T LEAVE MADAM IKOVA AND HER PEOPLE TO DEAL WITH THE EMPIRE ALONE.
NO, LEIA! YOUR CAPTAIN IS RIGHT -- YOU MUSTN'T BE FOUND HERE. THE CIRCUMSTANCES ARE TOO INCRIMINATING. THE IMPERIALS WILL ARREST YOU--
LET THEM. I WON'T ALLOW YOU AND YOUR PEOPLE TO BE PUNISHED FOR MY ACTIONS.
"BESIDES, IT'S TOO LATE TO RUN..."

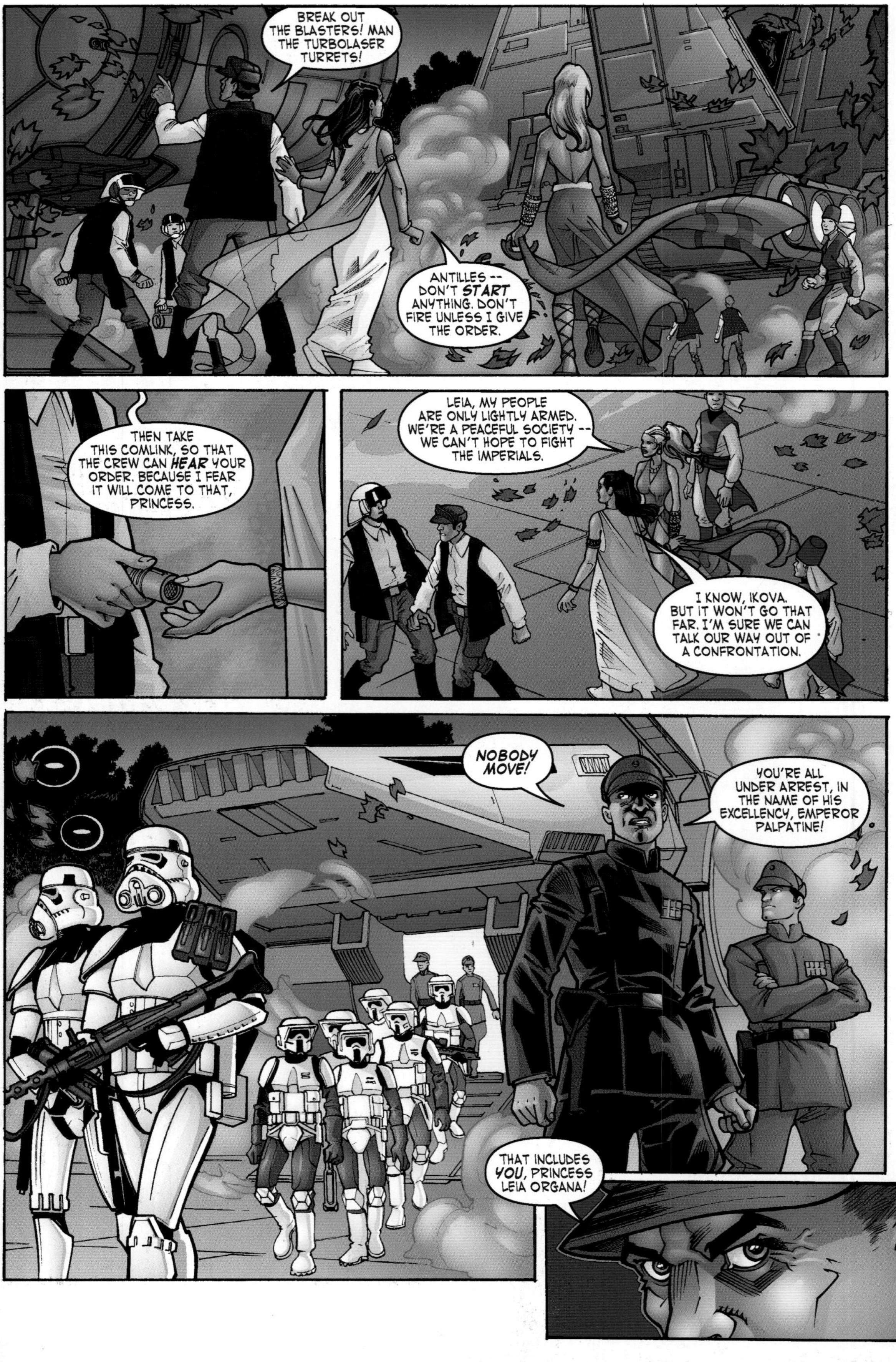
BREAK OUT THE BLASTERS! MAN THE TURBOLASER TURRETS!
ANTILLES -- DON'T START ANYTHING. DON'T FIRE UNLESS I GIVE THE ORDER.
THEN TAKE THIS COMLINK, SO THAT THE CREW CAN HEAR YOUR ORDER. BECAUSE I FEAR IT WILL COME TO THAT, PRINCESS.
LEIA, MY PEOPLE ARE ONLY LIGHTLY ARMED. WE'RE A PEACEFUL SOCIETY -- WE CAN'T HOPE TO FIGHT THE IMPERIALS.
I KNOW, IKOVA. BUT IT WON'T GO THAT FAR. I'M SURE WE CAN TALK OUR WAY OUT OF A CONFRONTATION.
NOBODY MOVE!
YOU'RE ALL UNDER ARREST, IN THE NAME OF HIS EXCELLENCY, EMPEROR PALPATINE!
THAT INCLUDES YOU, PRINCESS LEIA ORGANA!

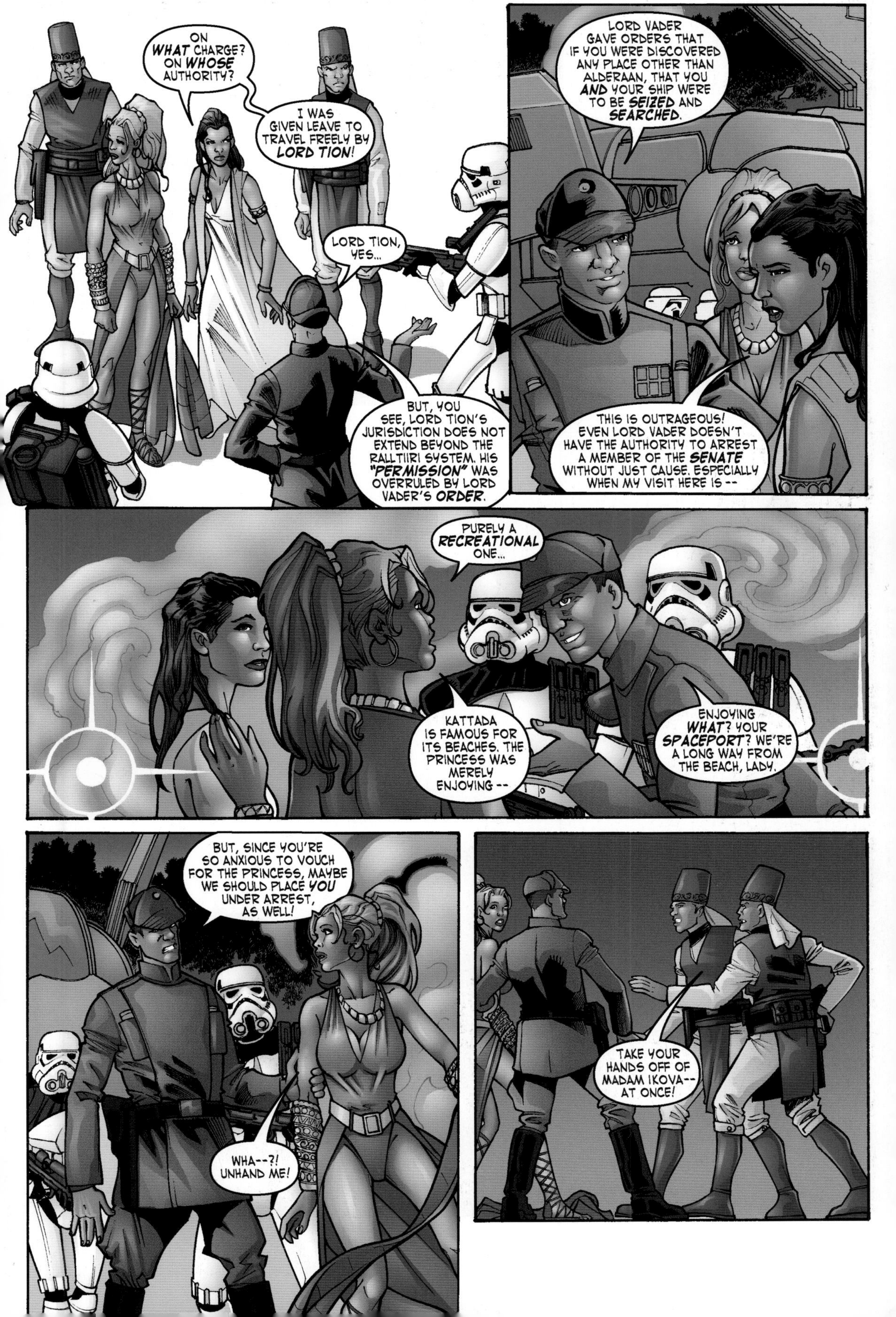
ON WHAT CHARGE? ON WHOSE AUTHORITY?
I WAS GIVEN LEAVE TO TRAVEL FREELY BY LORD TION!
LORD TION, YES...
BUT, YOU SEE, LORD TION'S JURISDICTION DOES NOT EXTEND BEYOND THE RALLTIIRI SYSTEM. HIS "PERMISSION" WAS OVERRULED BY LORD VADER'S ORDER.
LORD VADER GAVE ORDERS THAT IF YOU WERE DISCOVERED ANY PLACE OTHER THAN ALDERAAN, THAT YOU AND YOUR SHIP WERE TO BE SEIZED AND SEARCHED.
THIS IS OUTRAGEOUS! EVEN LORD VADER DOESN'T HAVE THE AUTHORITY TO ARREST A MEMBER OF THE SENATE WITHOUT JUST CAUSE. ESPECIALLY WHEN MY VISIT HERE IS --
PURELY A RECREATIONAL ONE...
KATTADA IS FAMOUS FOR ITS BEACHES. THE PRINCESS WAS MERELY ENJOYING --
ENJOYING WHAT? YOUR SPACEPORT? WE'RE A LONG WAY FROM THE BEACH, LADY.
BUT, SINCE YOU'RE SO ANXIOUS TO VOUCH FOR THE PRINCESS, MAYBE WE SHOULD PLACE YOU UNDER ARREST, AS WELL!
WHA--?! UNHAND ME!
TAKE YOUR HANDS OFF OF MADAM IKOVA-- AT ONCE!

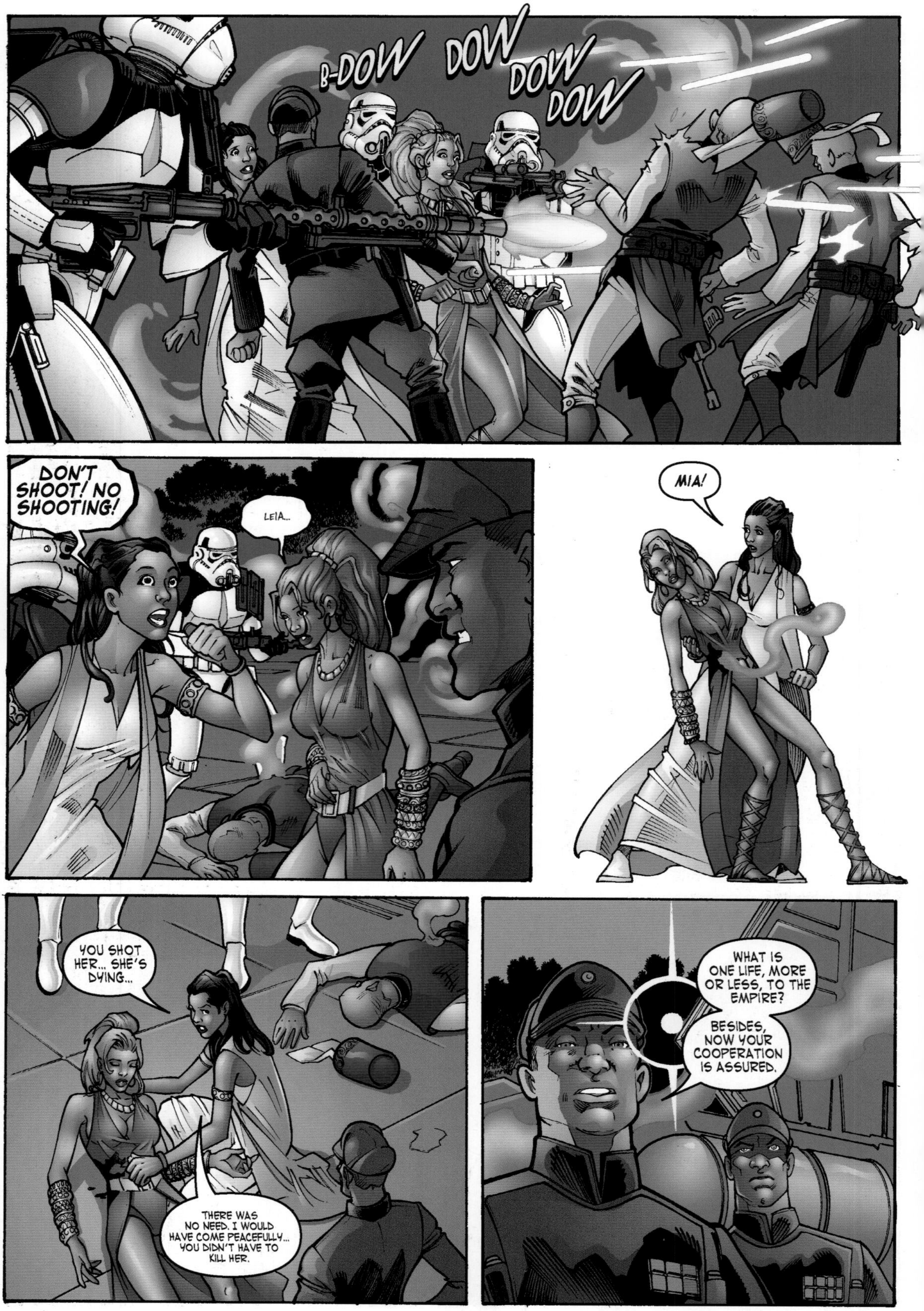
B-DOW DOW DOW DOW
DON'T SHOOT! NO SHOOTING!
LEIA...
MIA!
YOU SHOT HER... SHE'S DYING...
THERE WAS NO NEED. I WOULD HAVE COME PEACEFULLY... YOU DIDN'T HAVE TO KILL HER.
WHAT IS ONE LIFE, MORE OR LESS, TO THE EMPIRE?
BESIDES, NOW YOUR COOPERATION IS ASSURED.

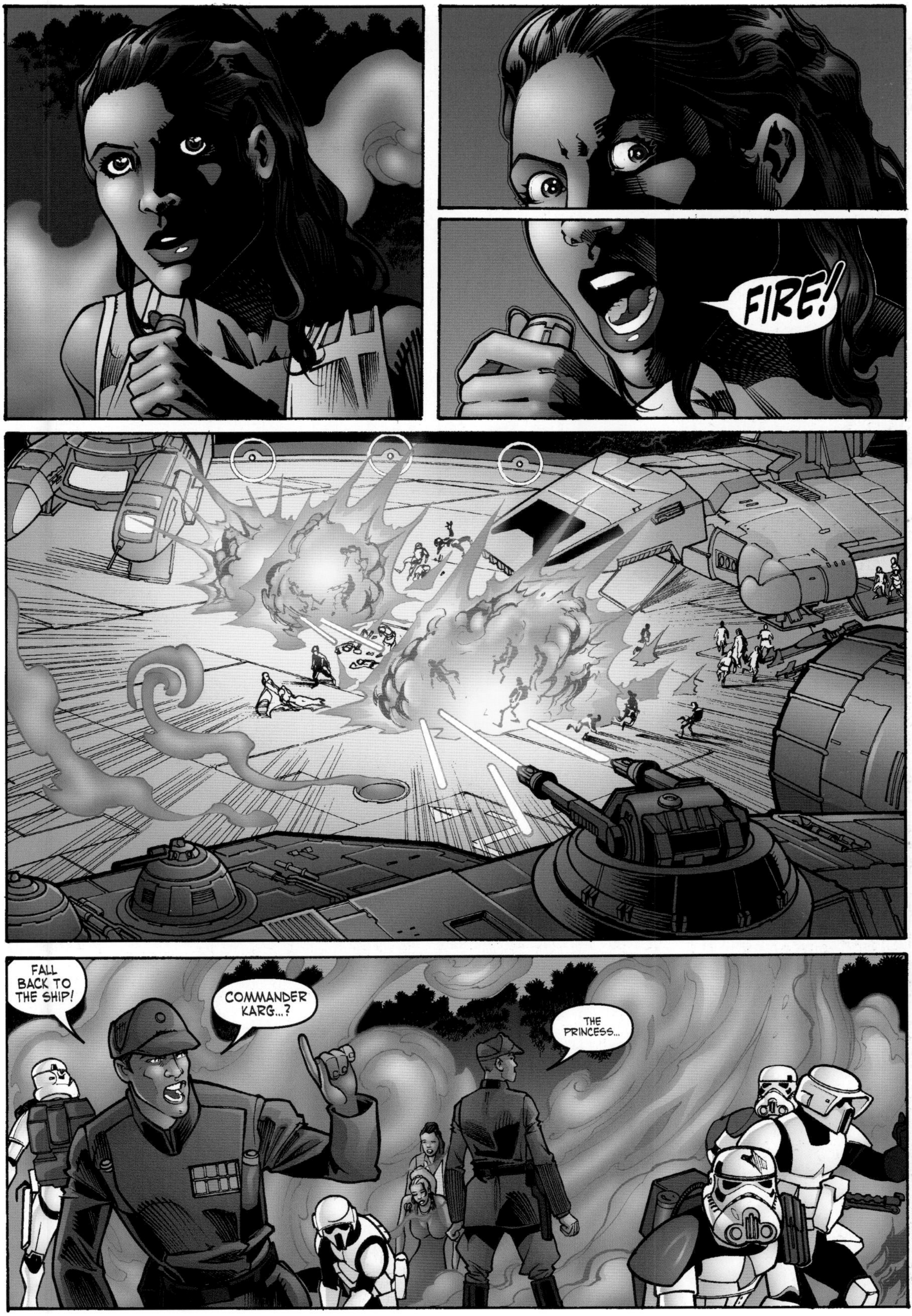
FIRE!
FALL BACK TO THE SHIP!
COMMANDER KARG...?
THE PRINCESS...

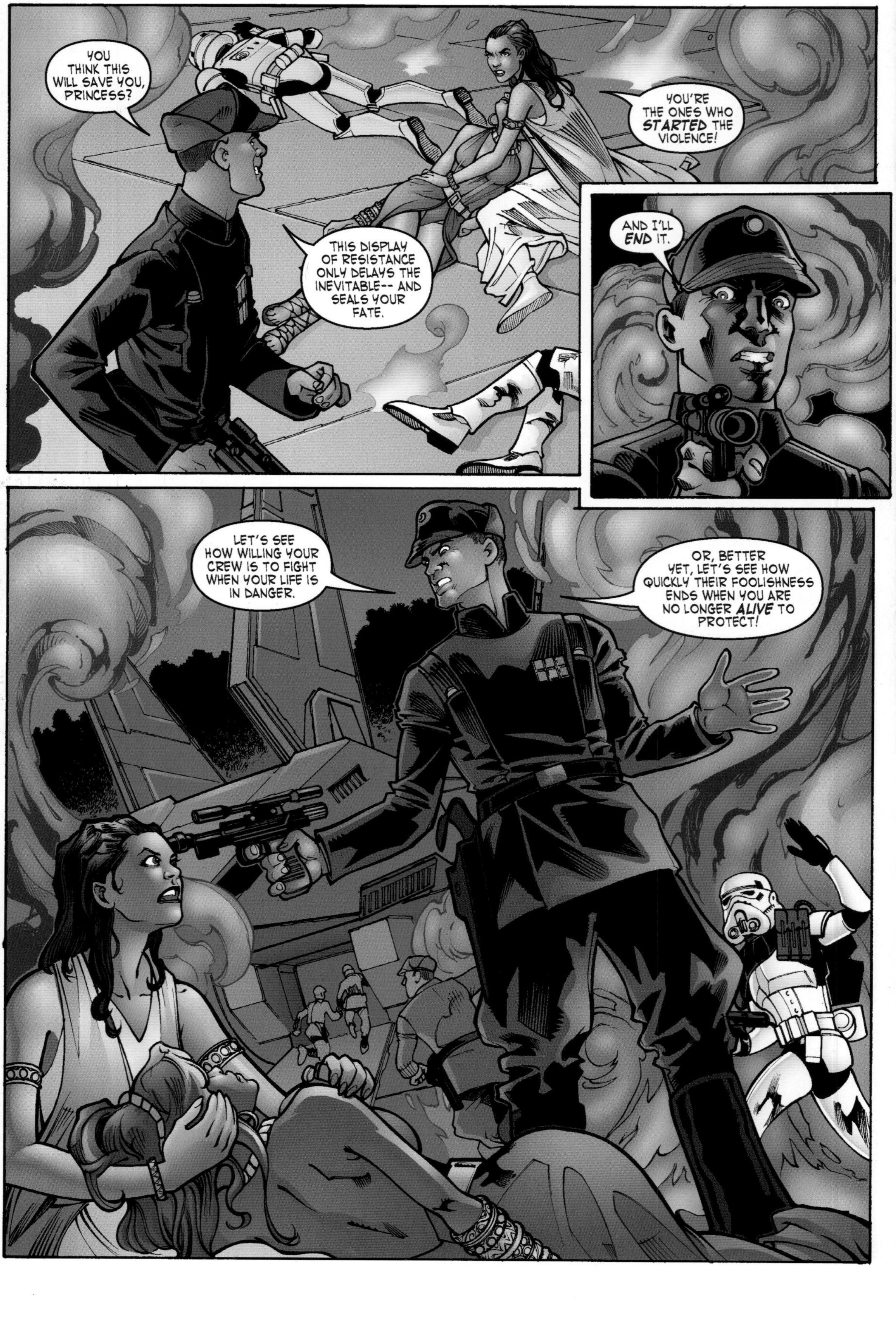
YOU THINK THIS WILL SAVE YOU, PRINCESS?
YOU'RE THE ONES WHO STARTED THE VIOLENCE!
THIS DISPLAY OF RESISTANCE ONLY DELAYS THE INEVITABLE-- AND SEALS YOUR FATE.
AND I'LL END IT.
LET'S SEE HOW WILLING YOUR CREW IS TO FIGHT WHEN YOUR LIFE IS IN DANGER.
OR, BETTER YET, LET'S SEE HOW QUICKLY THEIR FOOLISHNESS ENDS WHEN YOU ARE NO LONGER ALIVE TO PROTECT!

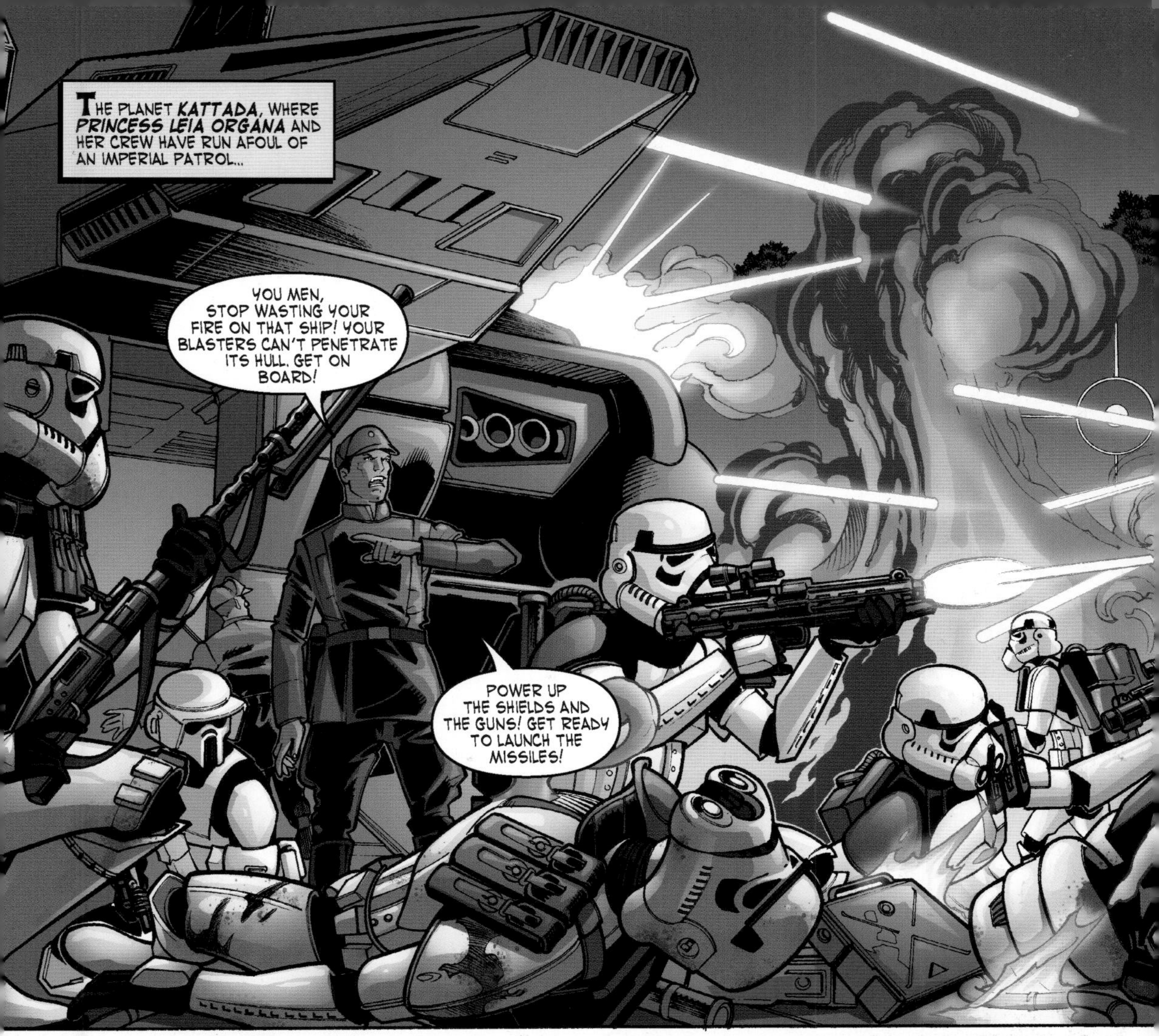
THE PLANET KATTADA, WHERE PRINCESS LEIA ORGANA AND HER CREW HAVE RUN AFOUL OF AN IMPERIAL PATROL...
YOU MEN, STOP WASTING YOUR FIRE ON THAT SHIP! YOUR BLASTERS CAN'T PENETRATE ITS HULL. GET ON BOARD!
POWER UP THE SHIELDS AND THE GUNS! GET READY TO LAUNCH THE MISSILES!

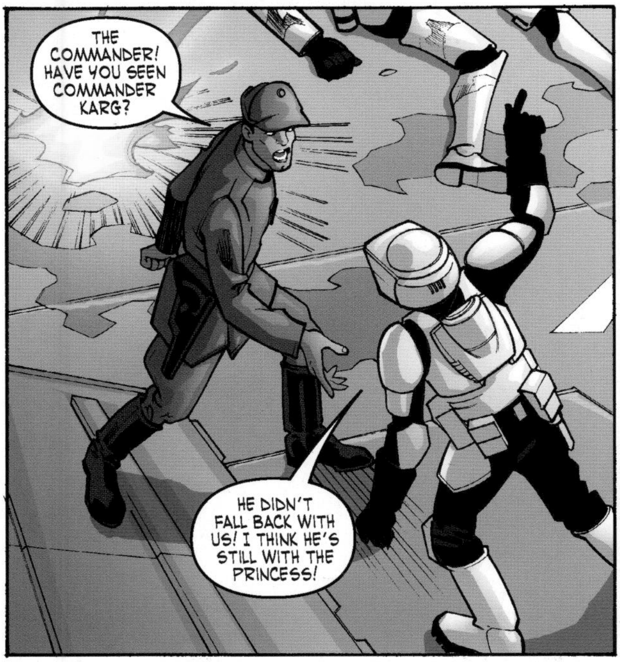
THE COMMANDER! HAVE YOU SEEN COMMANDER KARG?
HE DIDN'T FALL BACK WITH US! I THINK HE'S STILL WITH THE PRINCESS!

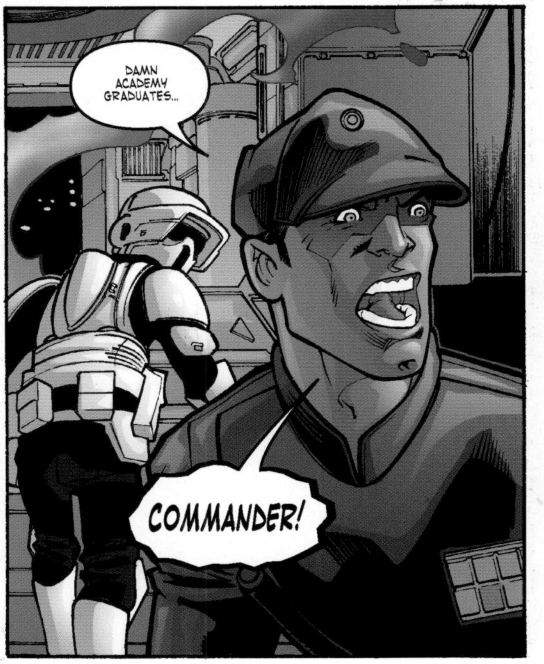
DAMN ACADEMY GRADUATES...
COMMANDER!

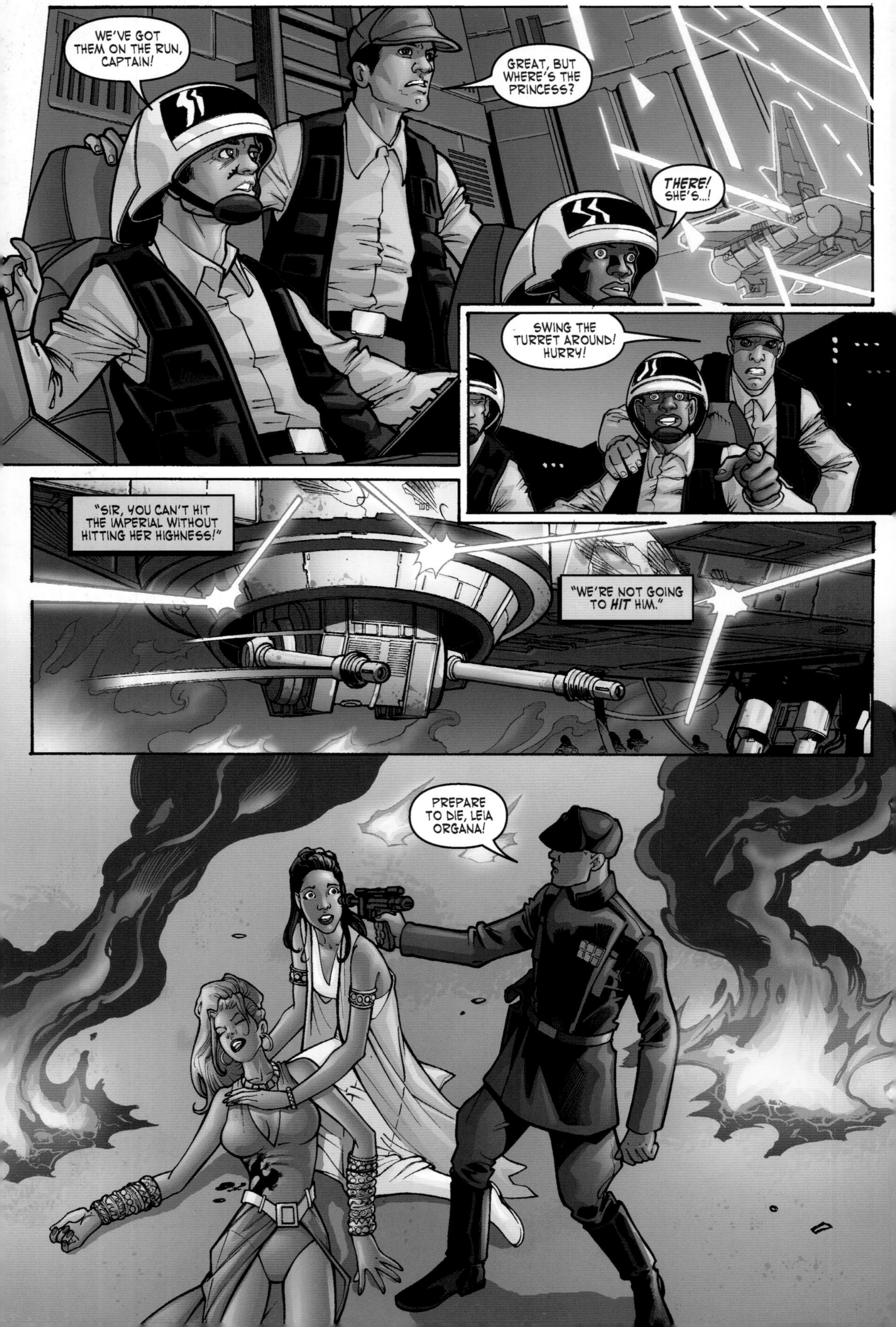
WE'VE GOT THEM ON THE RUN, CAPTAIN!
GREAT, BUT WHERE'S THE PRINCESS?
THERE! SHE'S...!
SWING THE TURRET AROUND! HURRY!
"SIR, YOU CAN'T HIT THE IMPERIAL WITHOUT HITTING HER HIGHNESS!"
"WE'RE NOT GOING TO HIT HIM."
PREPARE TO DIE, LEIA ORGANA!

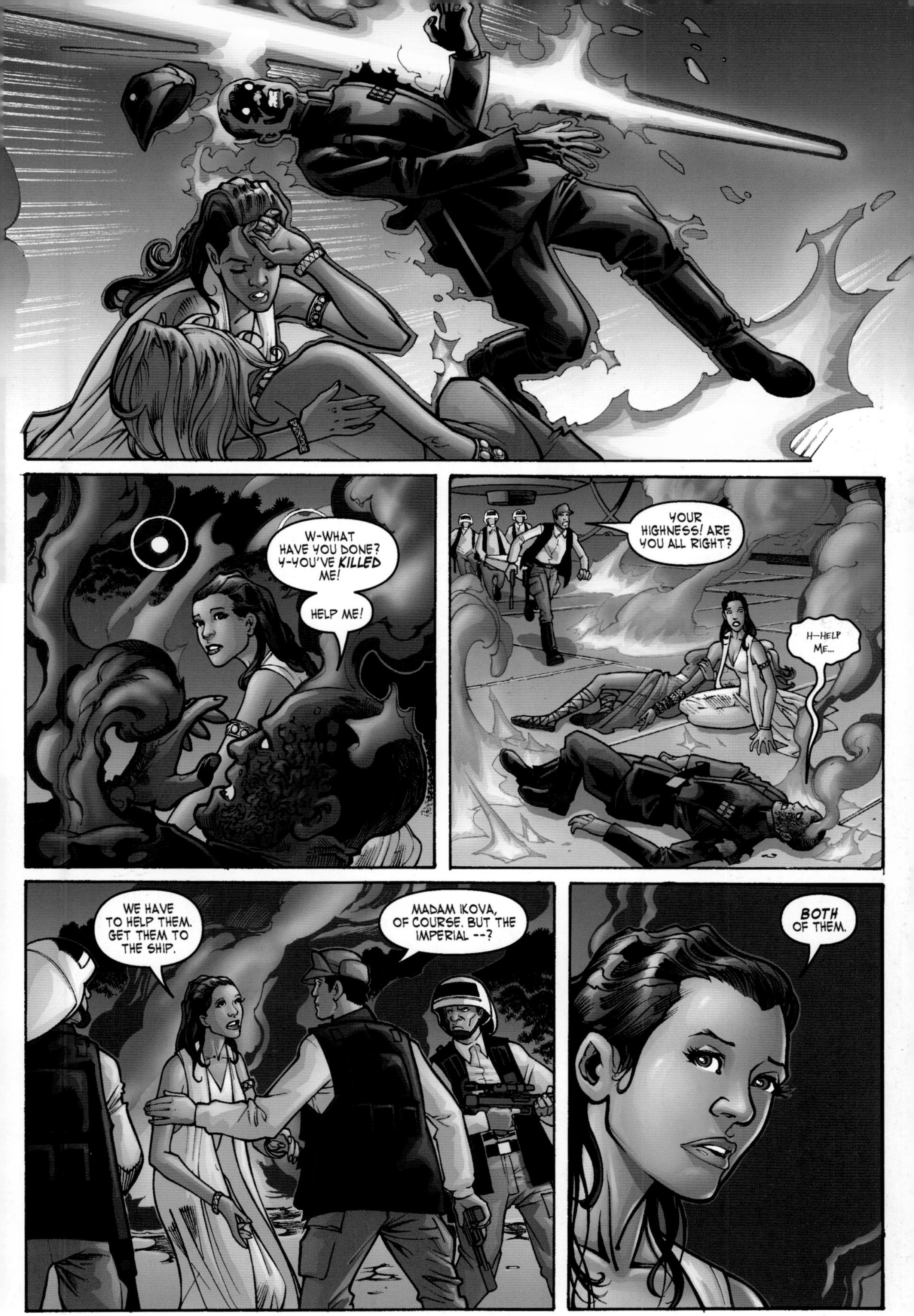
W-WHAT HAVE YOU DONE? Y-YOU'VE KILLED ME!
HELP ME!
YOUR HIGHNESS! ARE YOU ALL RIGHT?
H--HELP ME...
WE HAVE TO HELP THEM. GET THEM TO THE SHIP.
MADAM IKOVA, OF COURSE. BUT THE IMPERIAL --?
BOTH OF THEM.

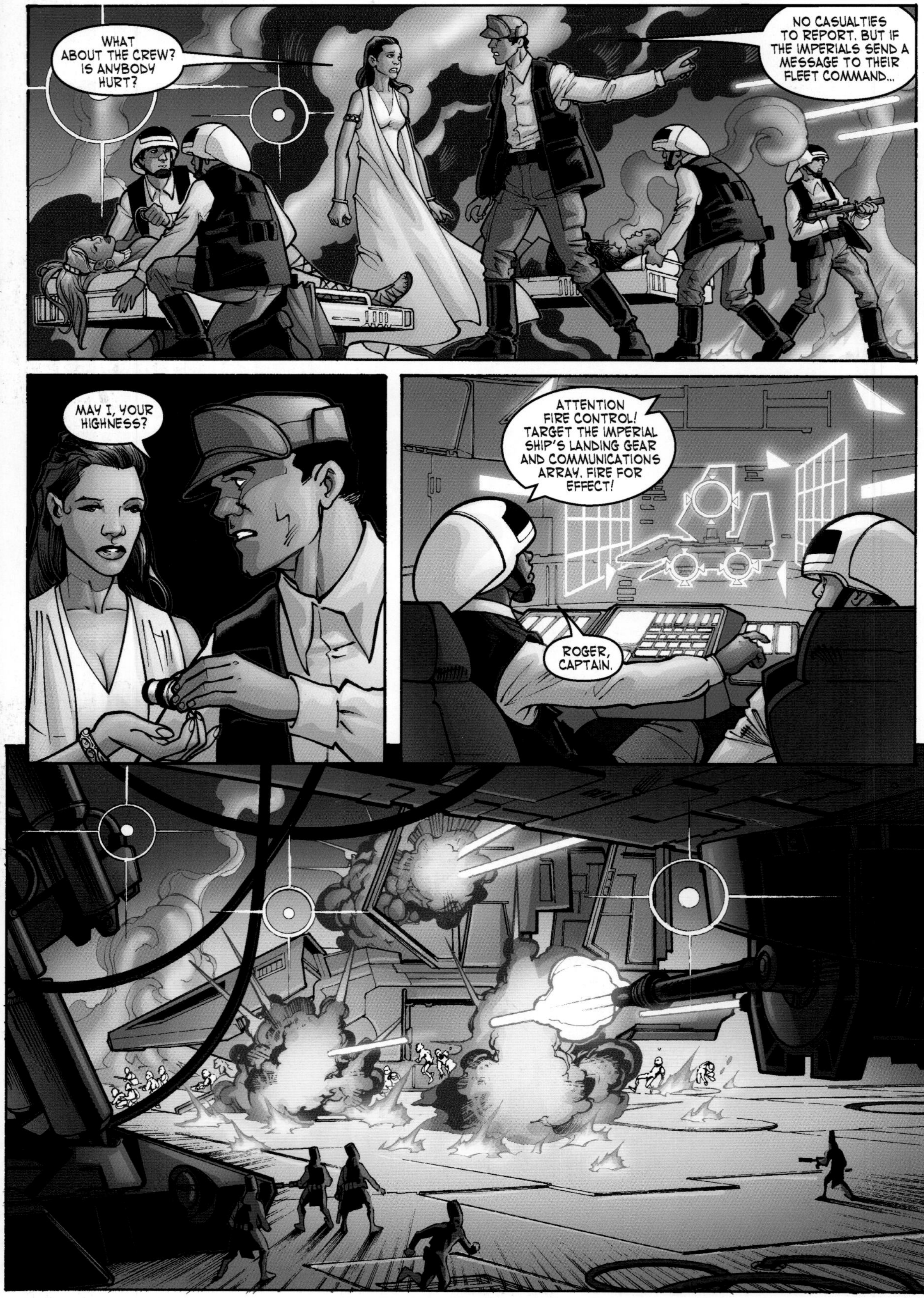
WHAT ABOUT THE CREW? IS ANYBODY HURT?
NO CASUALTIES TO REPORT. BUT IF THE IMPERIALS SEND A MESSAGE TO THEIR FLEET COMMAND...
MAY I, YOUR HIGHNESS?
ATTENTION FIRE CONTROL! TARGET THE IMPERIAL SHIP'S LANDING GEAR AND COMMUNICATIONS ARRAY. FIRE FOR EFFECT!
ROGER, CAPTAIN.

THAT WILL GIVE THEM SOMETHING TO THINK ABOUT -- BUT WE STILL HAVE A *FIGHT* AHEAD OF US! WE SHOULD FINISH THEM NOW WHILE --

THERE WILL BE *NO MORE* FIGHTING!

BUT, YOUR HIGHNESS...

OUR ONLY CONCERN NOW IS TO SEE TO MADAM IKOVA'S WOUNDS -- AND TO MOVE THE *TANTIVE IV* OUT OF HARM'S WAY!

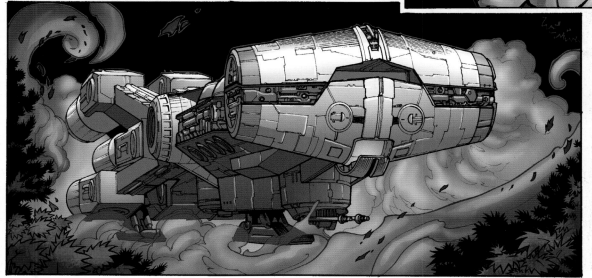

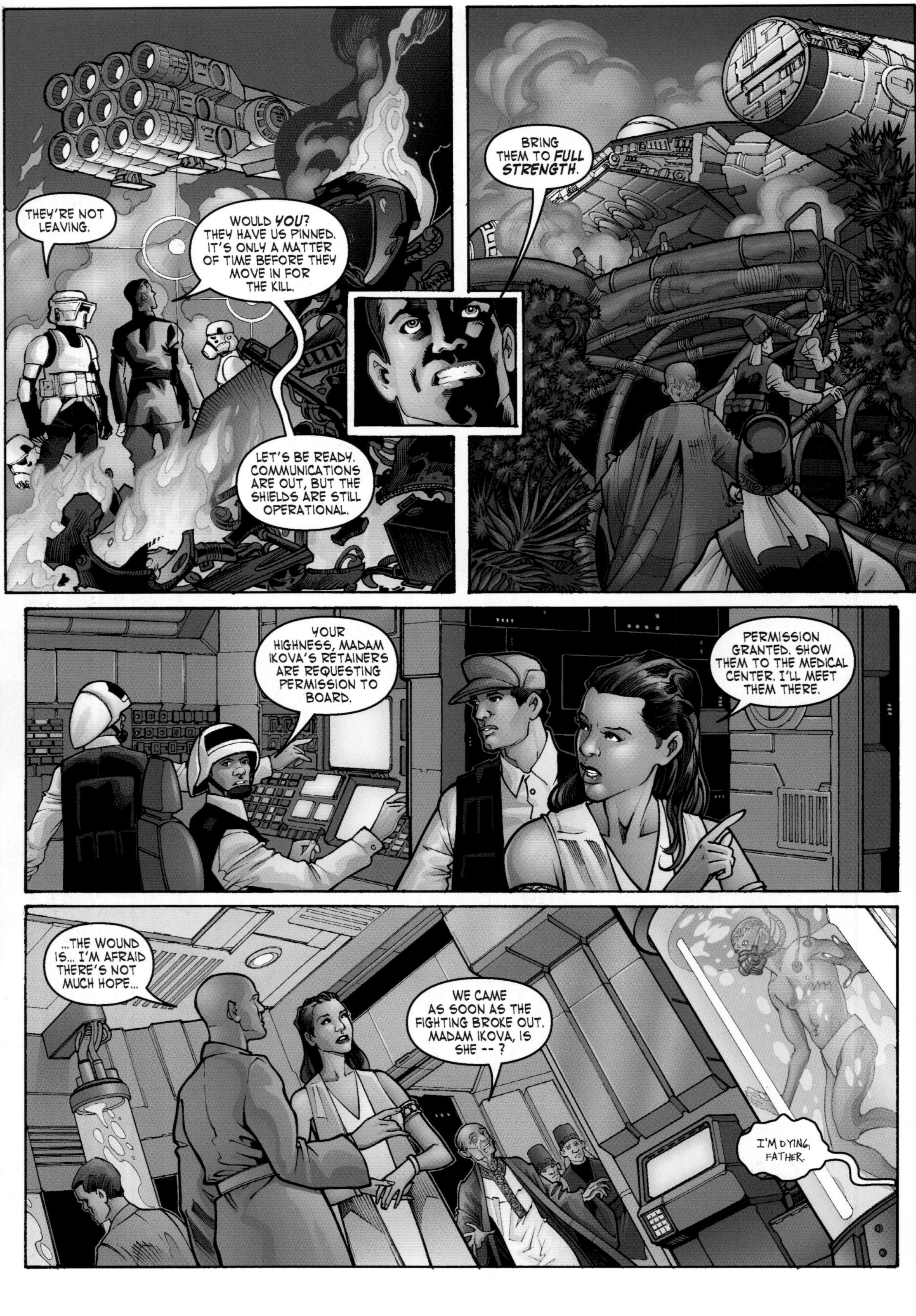
THEY'RE NOT LEAVING.
WOULD YOU? THEY HAVE US PINNED. IT'S ONLY A MATTER OF TIME BEFORE THEY MOVE IN FOR THE KILL.
LET'S BE READY. COMMUNICATIONS ARE OUT, BUT THE SHIELDS ARE STILL OPERATIONAL.
BRING THEM TO FULL STRENGTH.
YOUR HIGHNESS, MADAM IKOVA'S RETAINERS ARE REQUESTING PERMISSION TO BOARD.
PERMISSION GRANTED. SHOW THEM TO THE MEDICAL CENTER. I'LL MEET THEM THERE.
...THE WOUND IS... I'M AFRAID THERE'S NOT MUCH HOPE...
WE CAME AS SOON AS THE FIGHTING BROKE OUT. MADAM IKOVA, IS SHE -- ?
I'M DYING, FATHER.

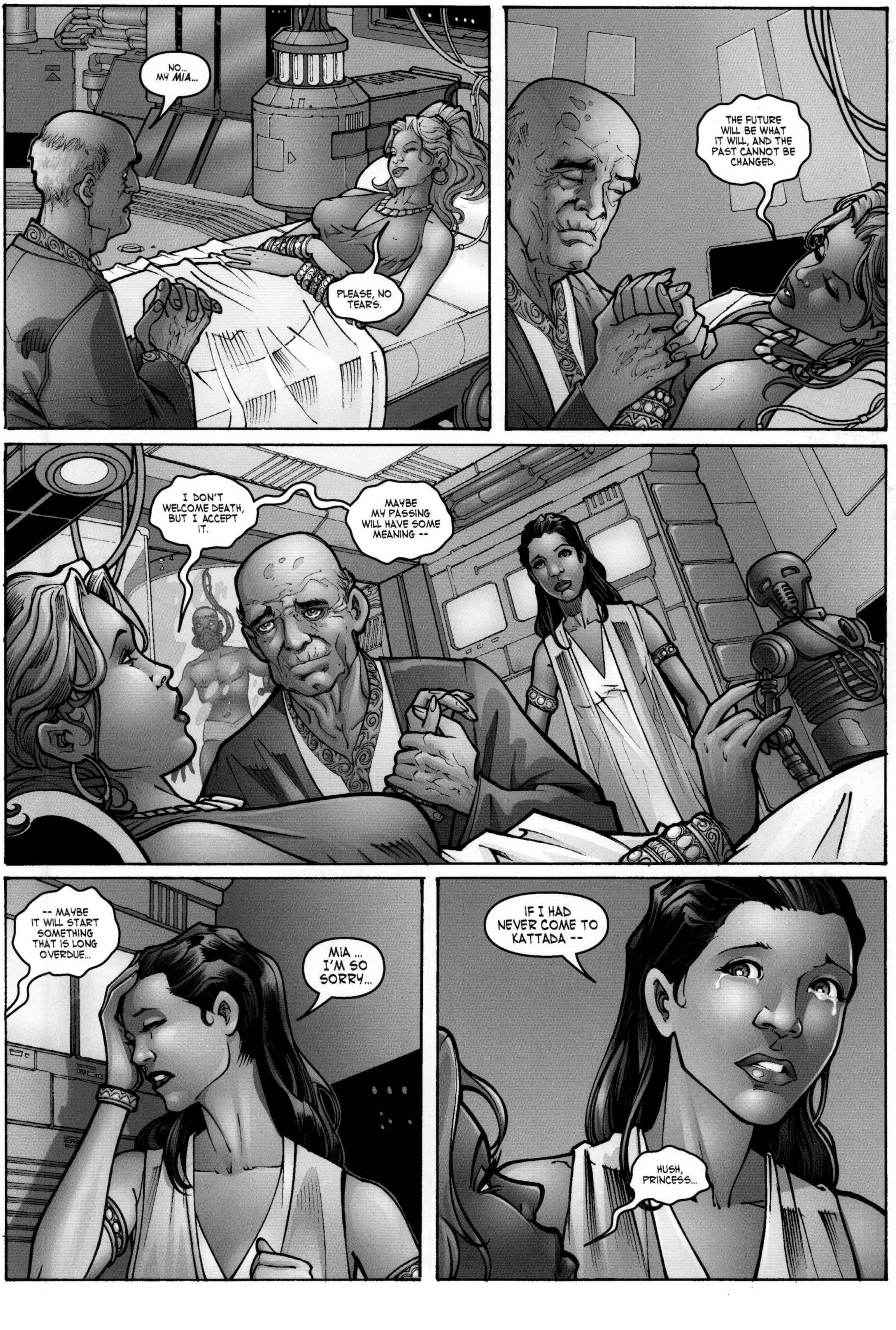
NO... MY MÍA...
PLEASE, NO TEARS.
THE FUTURE WILL BE WHAT IT WILL, AND THE PAST CANNOT BE CHANGED.
I DON'T WELCOME DEATH, BUT I ACCEPT IT.
MAYBE MY PASSING WILL HAVE SOME MEANING --
-- MAYBE IT WILL START SOMETHING THAT IS LONG OVERDUE...
MÍA ... I'M SO SORRY...
IF I HAD NEVER COME TO KATTADA --
HUSH, PRINCESS...

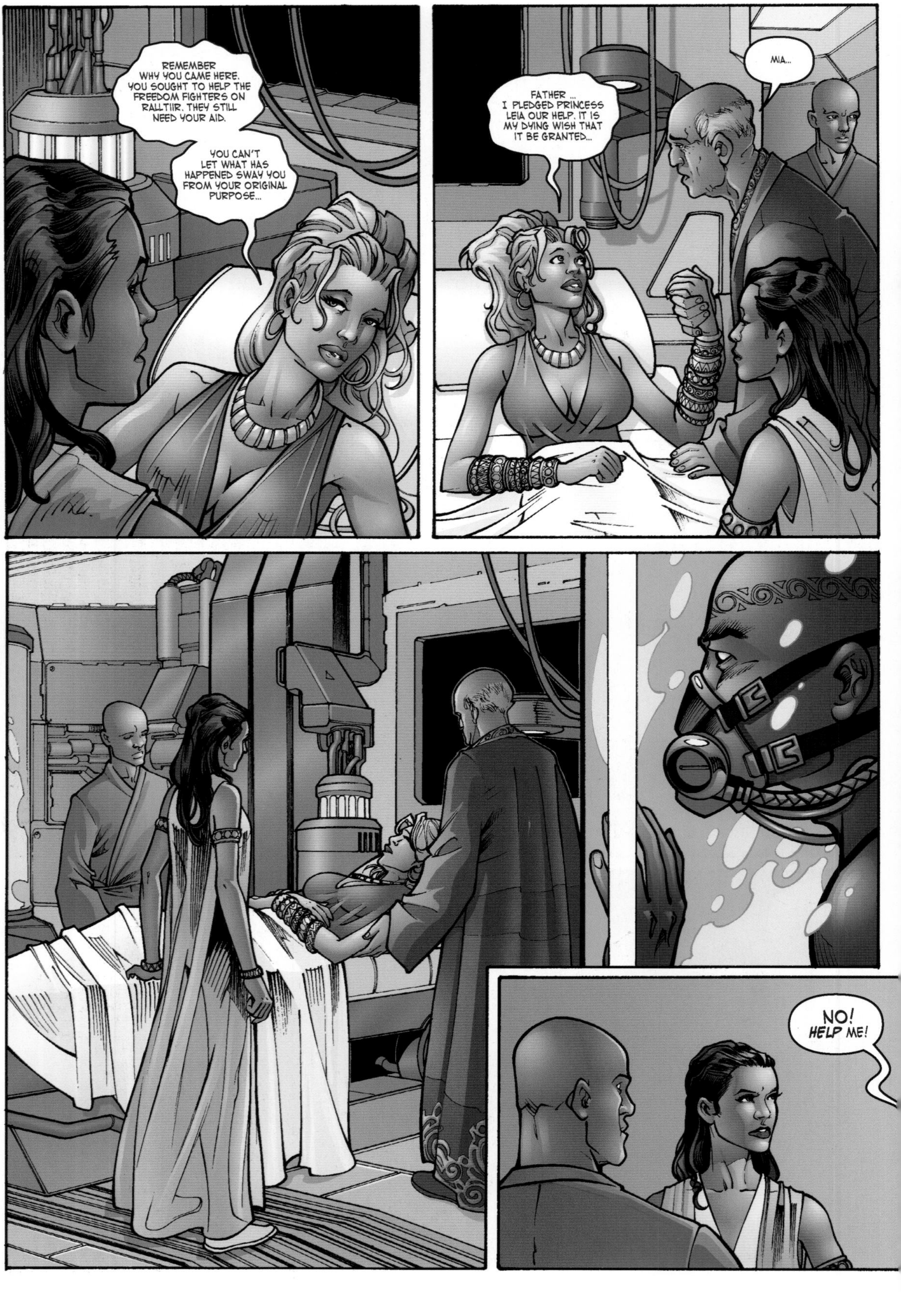
REMEMBER WHY YOU CAME HERE. YOU SOUGHT TO HELP THE FREEDOM FIGHTERS ON RALLTIIR. THEY STILL NEED YOUR AID.
YOU CAN'T LET WHAT HAS HAPPENED SWAY YOU FROM YOUR ORIGINAL PURPOSE...
FATHER ... I PLEDGED PRINCESS LEIA OUR HELP. IT IS MY DYING WISH THAT IT BE GRANTED...
MIA...
NO! HELP ME!

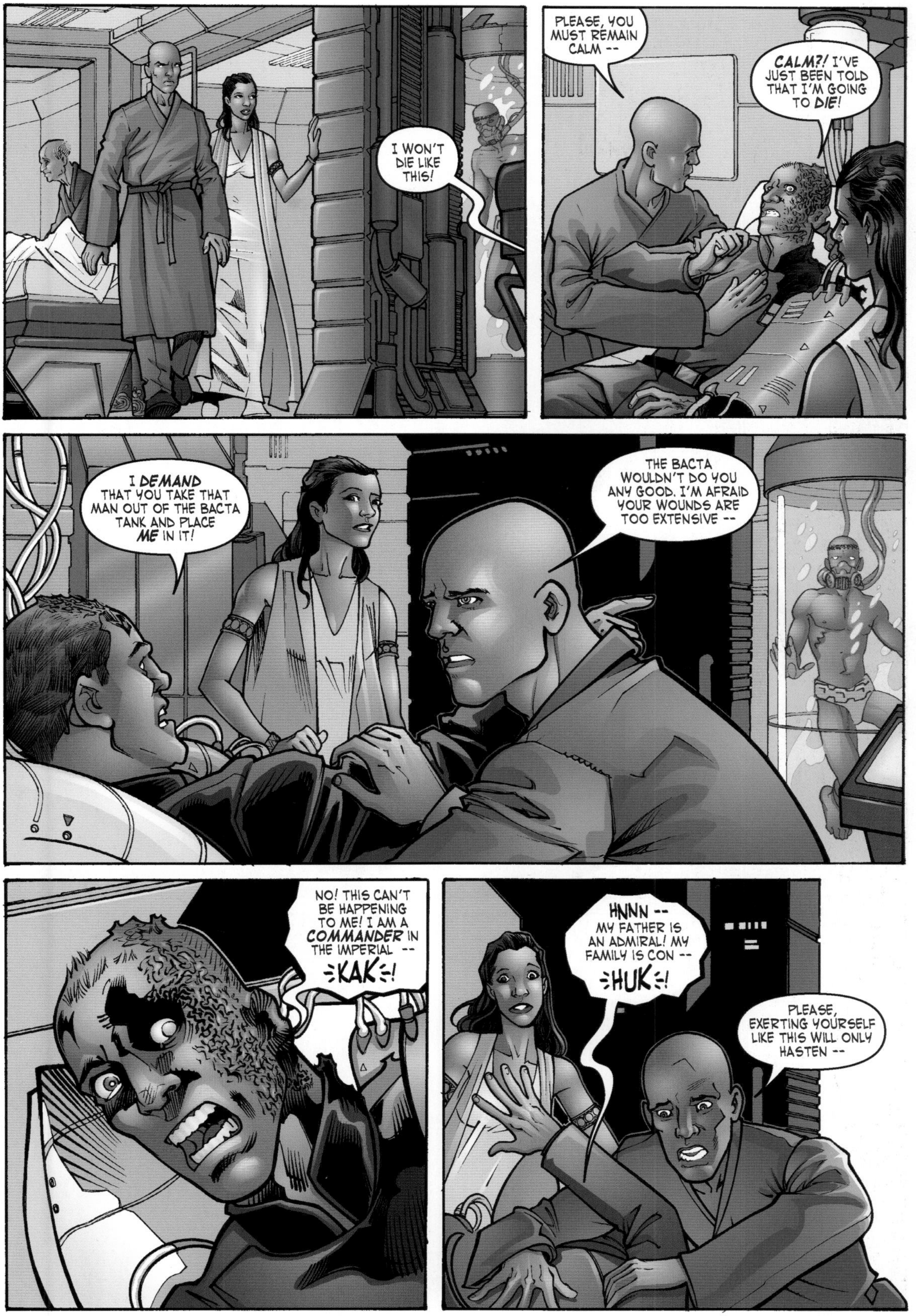

I WON'T DIE LIKE THIS!
PLEASE, YOU MUST REMAIN CALM --
CALM?! I'VE JUST BEEN TOLD THAT I'M GOING TO DIE!
I DEMAND THAT YOU TAKE THAT MAN OUT OF THE BACTA TANK AND PLACE ME IN IT!
THE BACTA WOULDN'T DO YOU ANY GOOD. I'M AFRAID YOUR WOUNDS ARE TOO EXTENSIVE --
NO! THIS CAN'T BE HAPPENING TO ME! I AM A COMMANDER IN THE IMPERIAL --
KAK!
HNNN -- MY FATHER IS AN ADMIRAL! MY FAMILY IS CON --
HUK!
PLEASE, EXERTING YOURSELF LIKE THIS WILL ONLY HASTEN --

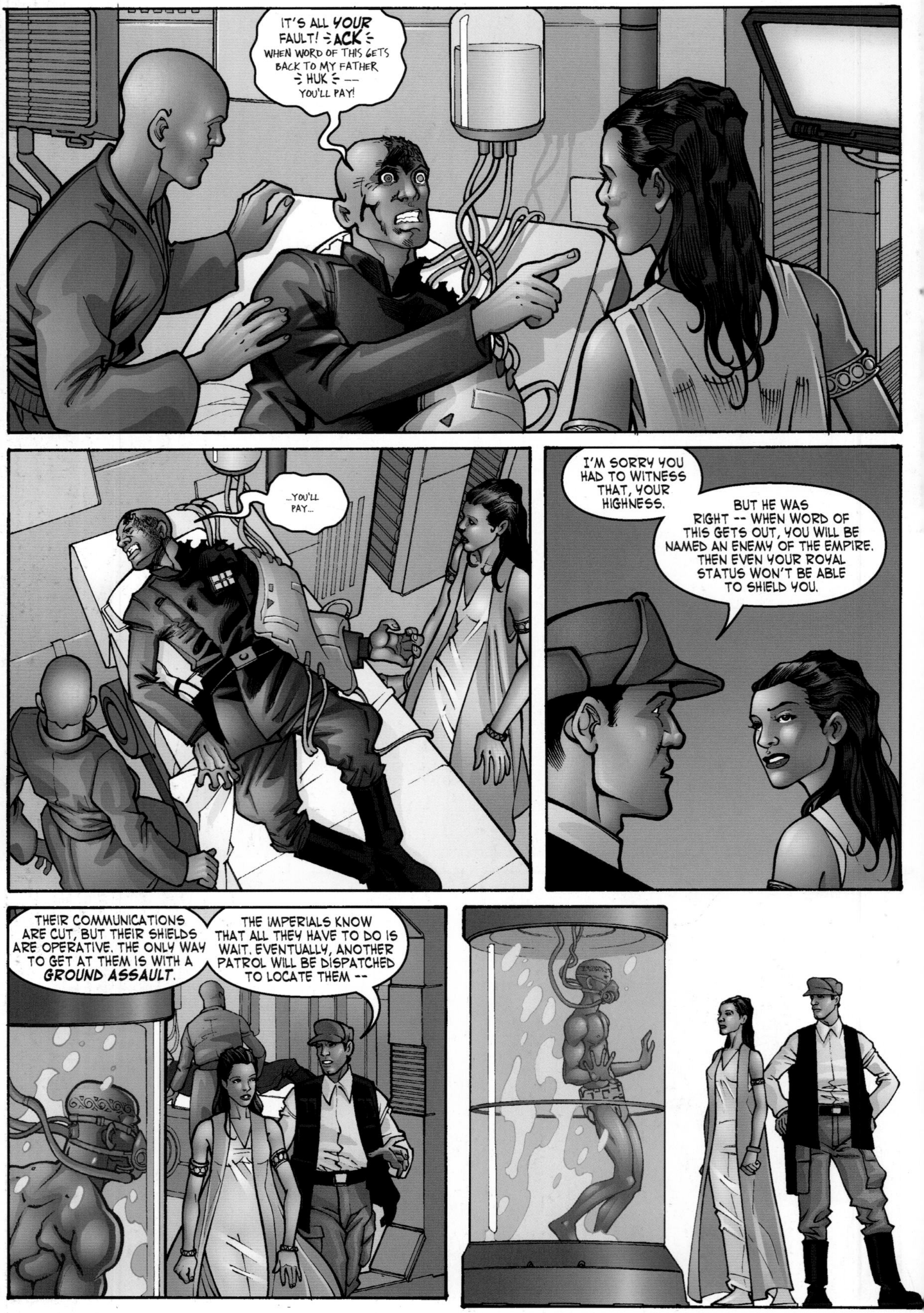
IT'S ALL YOUR FAULT! ACK WHEN WORD OF THIS GETS BACK TO MY FATHER HUK -- YOU'LL PAY!
...YOU'LL PAY...
I'M SORRY YOU HAD TO WITNESS THAT, YOUR HIGHNESS.
BUT HE WAS RIGHT -- WHEN WORD OF THIS GETS OUT, YOU WILL BE NAMED AN ENEMY OF THE EMPIRE. THEN EVEN YOUR ROYAL STATUS WON'T BE ABLE TO SHIELD YOU.
THEIR COMMUNICATIONS ARE CUT, BUT THEIR SHIELDS ARE OPERATIVE. THE ONLY WAY TO GET AT THEM IS WITH A GROUND ASSAULT.
THE IMPERIALS KNOW THAT ALL THEY HAVE TO DO IS WAIT. EVENTUALLY, ANOTHER PATROL WILL BE DISPATCHED TO LOCATE THEM --

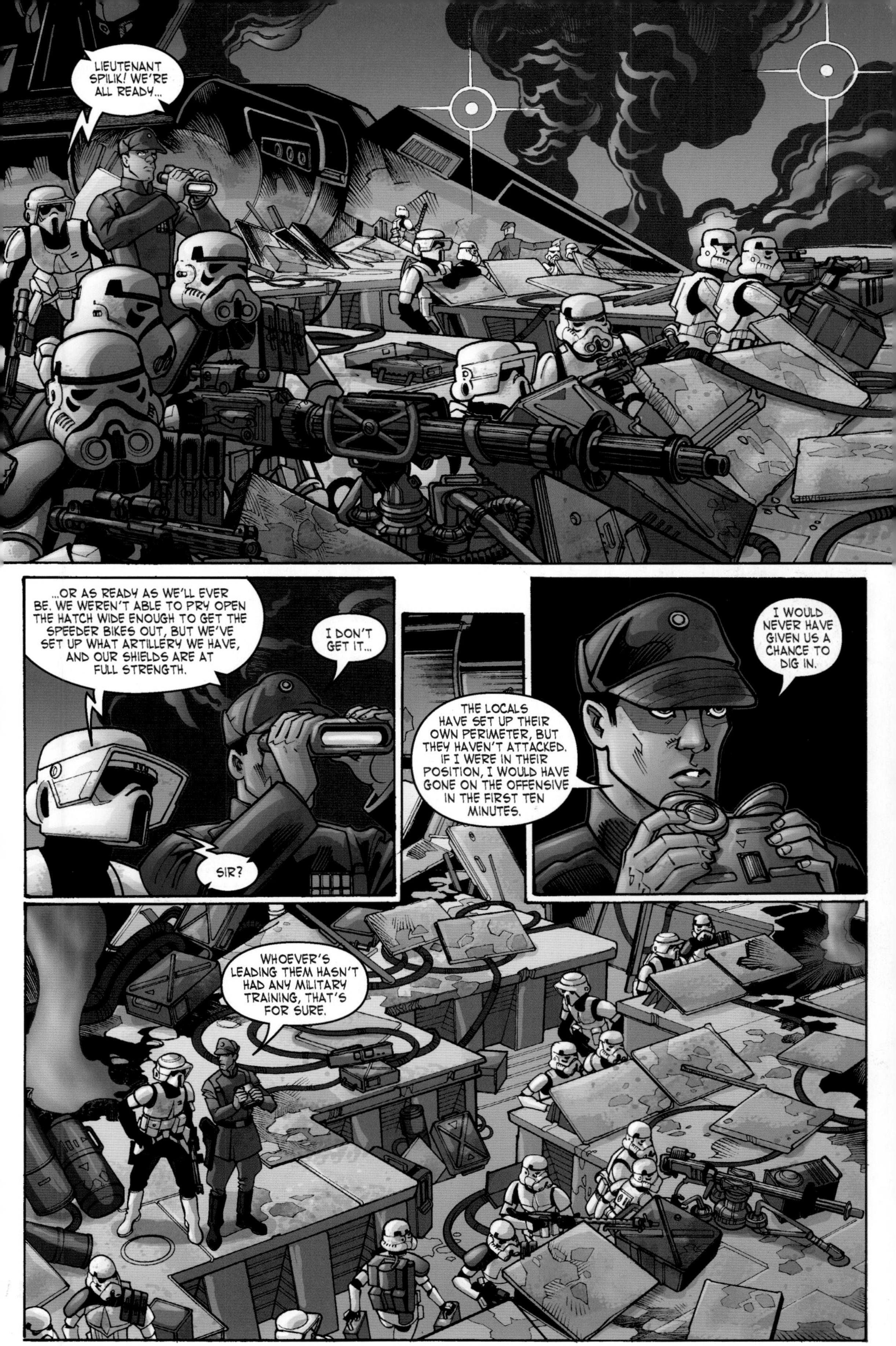
LIEUTENANT SPILIK! WE'RE ALL READY...
...OR AS READY AS WE'LL EVER BE. WE WEREN'T ABLE TO PRY OPEN THE HATCH WIDE ENOUGH TO GET THE SPEEDER BIKES OUT, BUT WE'VE SET UP WHAT ARTILLERY WE HAVE, AND OUR SHIELDS ARE AT FULL STRENGTH.
I DON'T GET IT...
SIR?
THE LOCALS HAVE SET UP THEIR OWN PERIMETER, BUT THEY HAVEN'T ATTACKED. IF I WERE IN THEIR POSITION, I WOULD HAVE GONE ON THE OFFENSIVE IN THE FIRST TEN MINUTES.
I WOULD NEVER HAVE GIVEN US A CHANCE TO DIG IN.
WHOEVER'S LEADING THEM HASN'T HAD ANY MILITARY TRAINING, THAT'S FOR SURE.

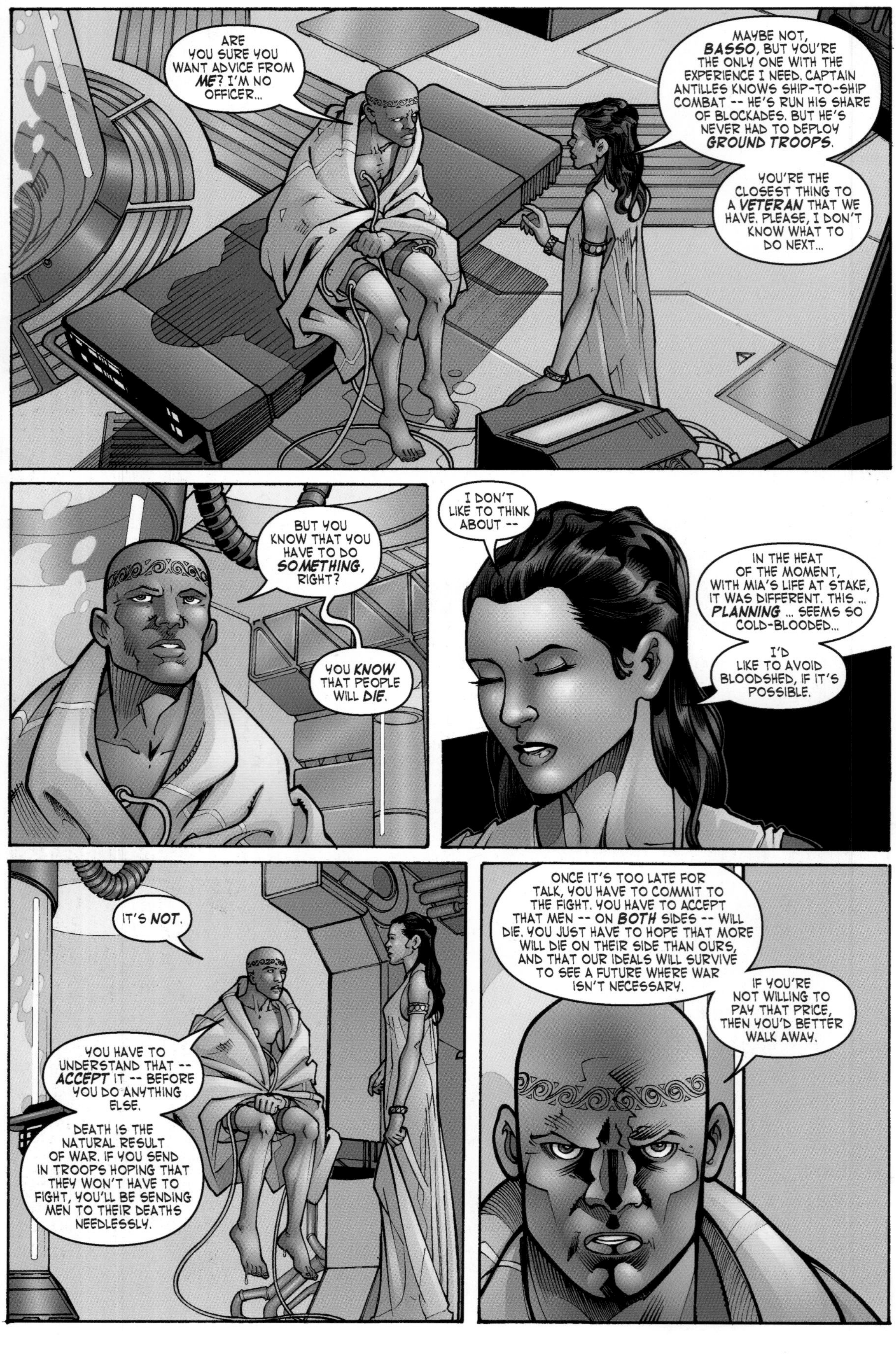
ARE YOU SURE YOU WANT ADVICE FROM ME? I'M NO OFFICER...
MAYBE NOT, BASSO, BUT YOU'RE THE ONLY ONE WITH THE EXPERIENCE I NEED. CAPTAIN ANTILLES KNOWS SHIP-TO-SHIP COMBAT -- HE'S RUN HIS SHARE OF BLOCKADES. BUT HE'S NEVER HAD TO DEPLOY GROUND TROOPS.
YOU'RE THE CLOSEST THING TO A VETERAN THAT WE HAVE. PLEASE, I DON'T KNOW WHAT TO DO NEXT...
BUT YOU KNOW THAT YOU HAVE TO DO SOMETHING, RIGHT?
YOU KNOW THAT PEOPLE WILL DIE.
I DON'T LIKE TO THINK ABOUT --
IN THE HEAT OF THE MOMENT, WITH MIA'S LIFE AT STAKE, IT WAS DIFFERENT. THIS ... PLANNING ... SEEMS SO COLD-BLOODED...
I'D LIKE TO AVOID BLOODSHED, IF IT'S POSSIBLE.
IT'S NOT.
YOU HAVE TO UNDERSTAND THAT -- ACCEPT IT -- BEFORE YOU DO ANYTHING ELSE.
DEATH IS THE NATURAL RESULT OF WAR. IF YOU SEND IN TROOPS HOPING THAT THEY WON'T HAVE TO FIGHT, YOU'LL BE SENDING MEN TO THEIR DEATHS NEEDLESSLY.
ONCE IT'S TOO LATE FOR TALK, YOU HAVE TO COMMIT TO THE FIGHT. YOU HAVE TO ACCEPT THAT MEN -- ON BOTH SIDES -- WILL DIE. YOU JUST HAVE TO HOPE THAT MORE WILL DIE ON THEIR SIDE THAN OURS, AND THAT OUR IDEALS WILL SURVIVE TO SEE A FUTURE WHERE WAR ISN'T NECESSARY.
IF YOU'RE NOT WILLING TO PAY THAT PRICE, THEN YOU'D BETTER WALK AWAY.

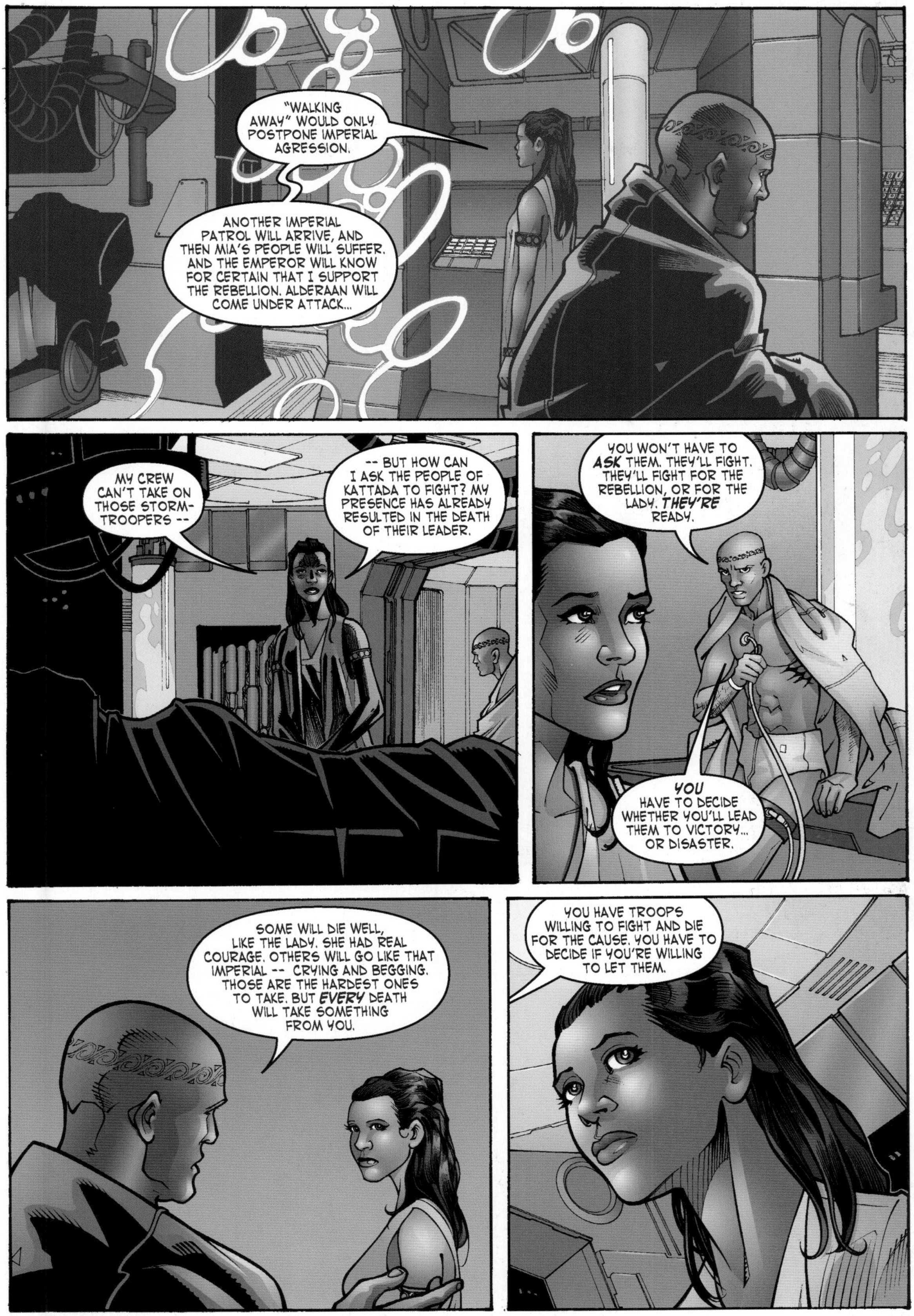
"WALKING AWAY" WOULD ONLY POSTPONE IMPERIAL AGRESSION.
ANOTHER IMPERIAL PATROL WILL ARRIVE, AND THEN MIA'S PEOPLE WILL SUFFER. AND THE EMPEROR WILL KNOW FOR CERTAIN THAT I SUPPORT THE REBELLION. ALDERAAN WILL COME UNDER ATTACK...
MY CREW CAN'T TAKE ON THOSE STORM-TROOPERS --
-- BUT HOW CAN I ASK THE PEOPLE OF KATTADA TO FIGHT? MY PRESENCE HAS ALREADY RESULTED IN THE DEATH OF THEIR LEADER.
YOU WON'T HAVE TO ASK THEM. THEY'LL FIGHT. THEY'LL FIGHT FOR THE REBELLION, OR FOR THE LADY. THEY'RE READY.
YOU HAVE TO DECIDE WHETHER YOU'LL LEAD THEM TO VICTORY... OR DISASTER.
SOME WILL DIE WELL, LIKE THE LADY. SHE HAD REAL COURAGE. OTHERS WILL GO LIKE THAT IMPERIAL -- CRYING AND BEGGING. THOSE ARE THE HARDEST ONES TO TAKE. BUT EVERY DEATH WILL TAKE SOMETHING FROM YOU.
YOU HAVE TROOPS WILLING TO FIGHT AND DIE FOR THE CAUSE. YOU HAVE TO DECIDE IF YOU'RE WILLING TO LET THEM.

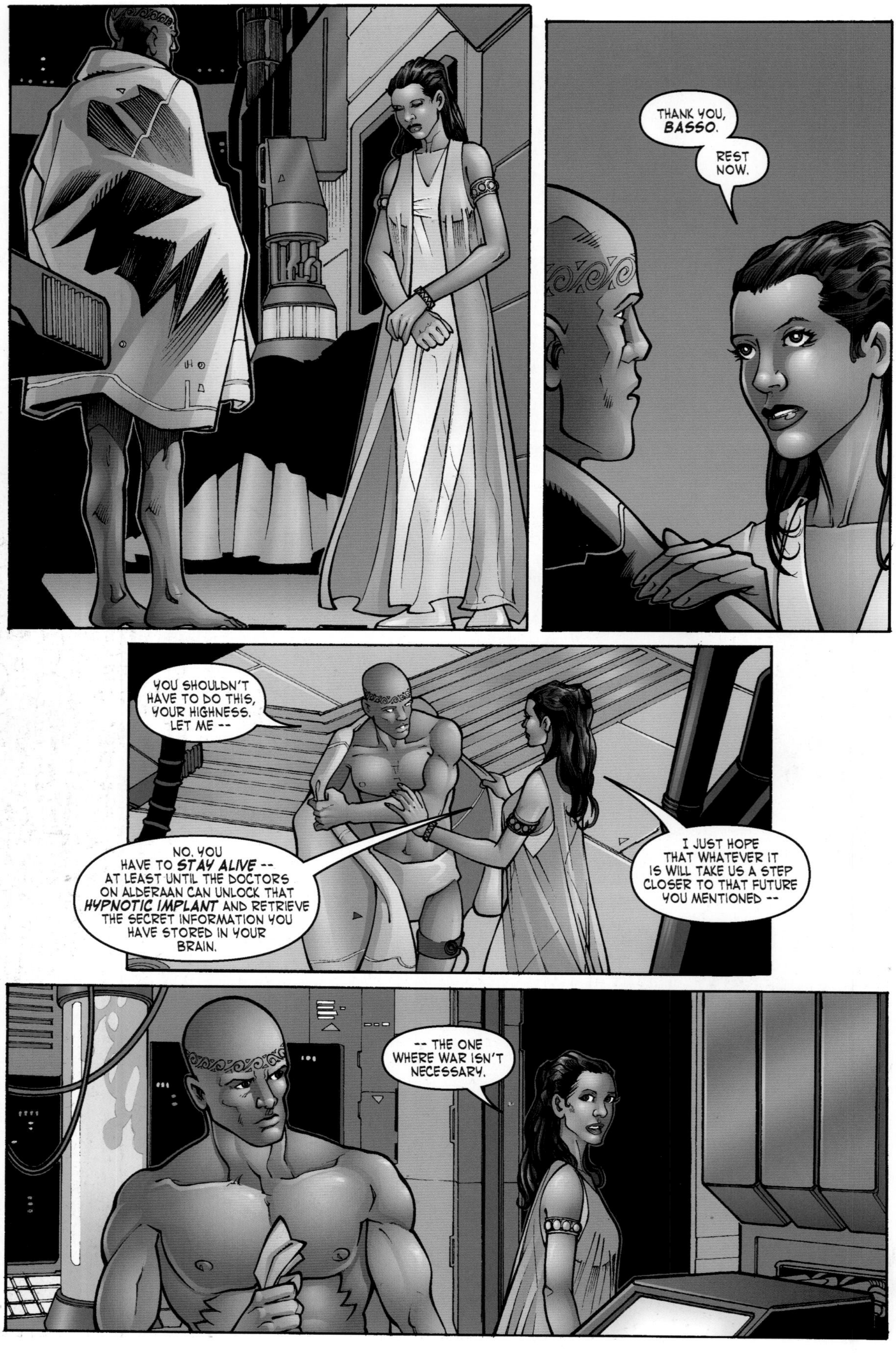
THANK YOU, BASSO.
REST NOW.
YOU SHOULDN'T HAVE TO DO THIS, YOUR HIGHNESS. LET ME --
NO. YOU HAVE TO STAY ALIVE -- AT LEAST UNTIL THE DOCTORS ON ALDERAAN CAN UNLOCK THAT HYPNOTIC IMPLANT AND RETRIEVE THE SECRET INFORMATION YOU HAVE STORED IN YOUR BRAIN.
I JUST HOPE THAT WHATEVER IT IS WILL TAKE US A STEP CLOSER TO THAT FUTURE YOU MENTIONED --
-- THE ONE WHERE WAR ISN'T NECESSARY.

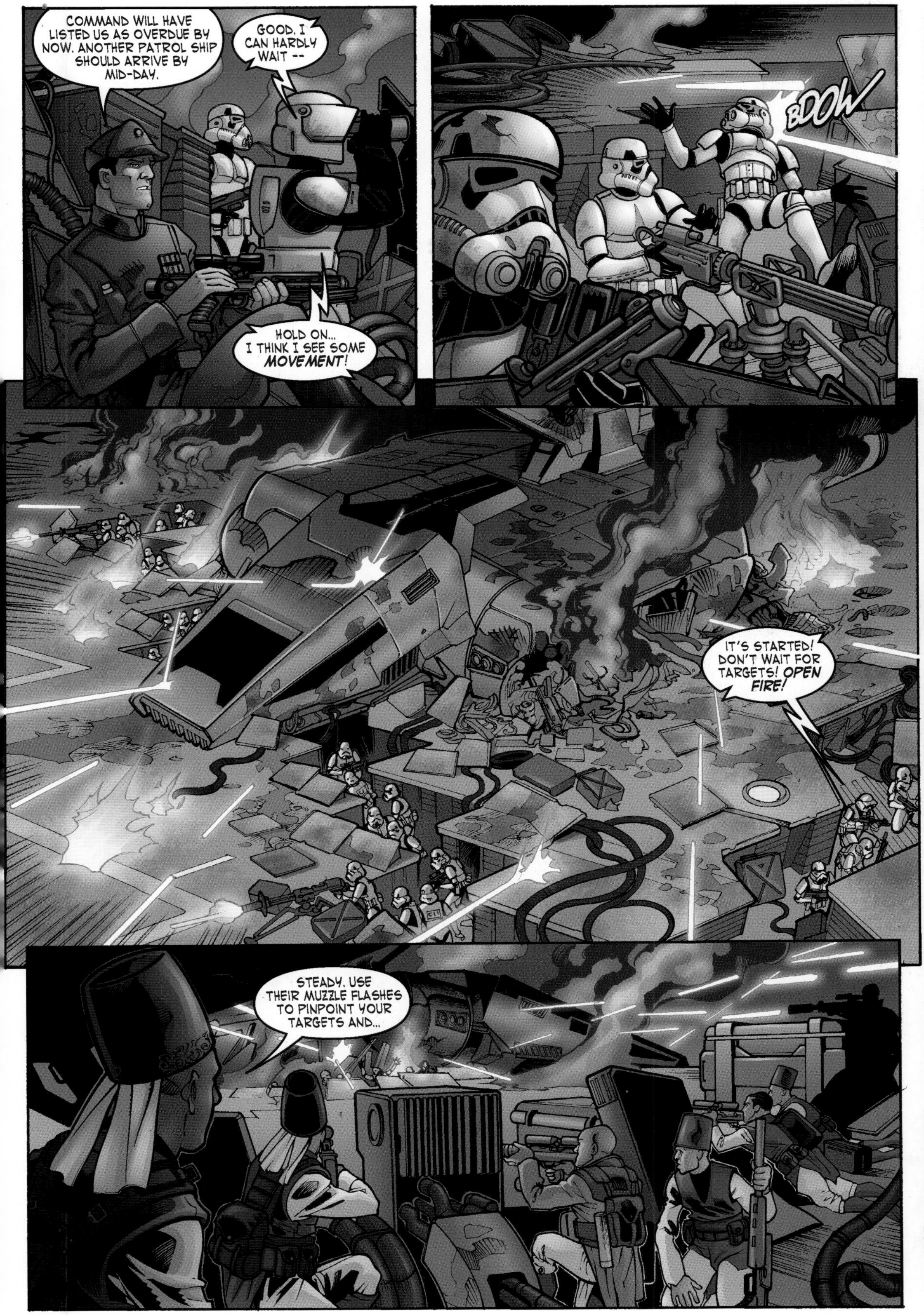
COMMAND WILL HAVE LISTED US AS OVERDUE BY NOW. ANOTHER PATROL SHIP SHOULD ARRIVE BY MID-DAY.
GOOD. I CAN HARDLY WAIT --
HOLD ON... I THINK I SEE SOME MOVEMENT!
BDOW
IT'S STARTED! DON'T WAIT FOR TARGETS! OPEN FIRE!
STEADY. USE THEIR MUZZLE FLASHES TO PINPOINT YOUR TARGETS AND...

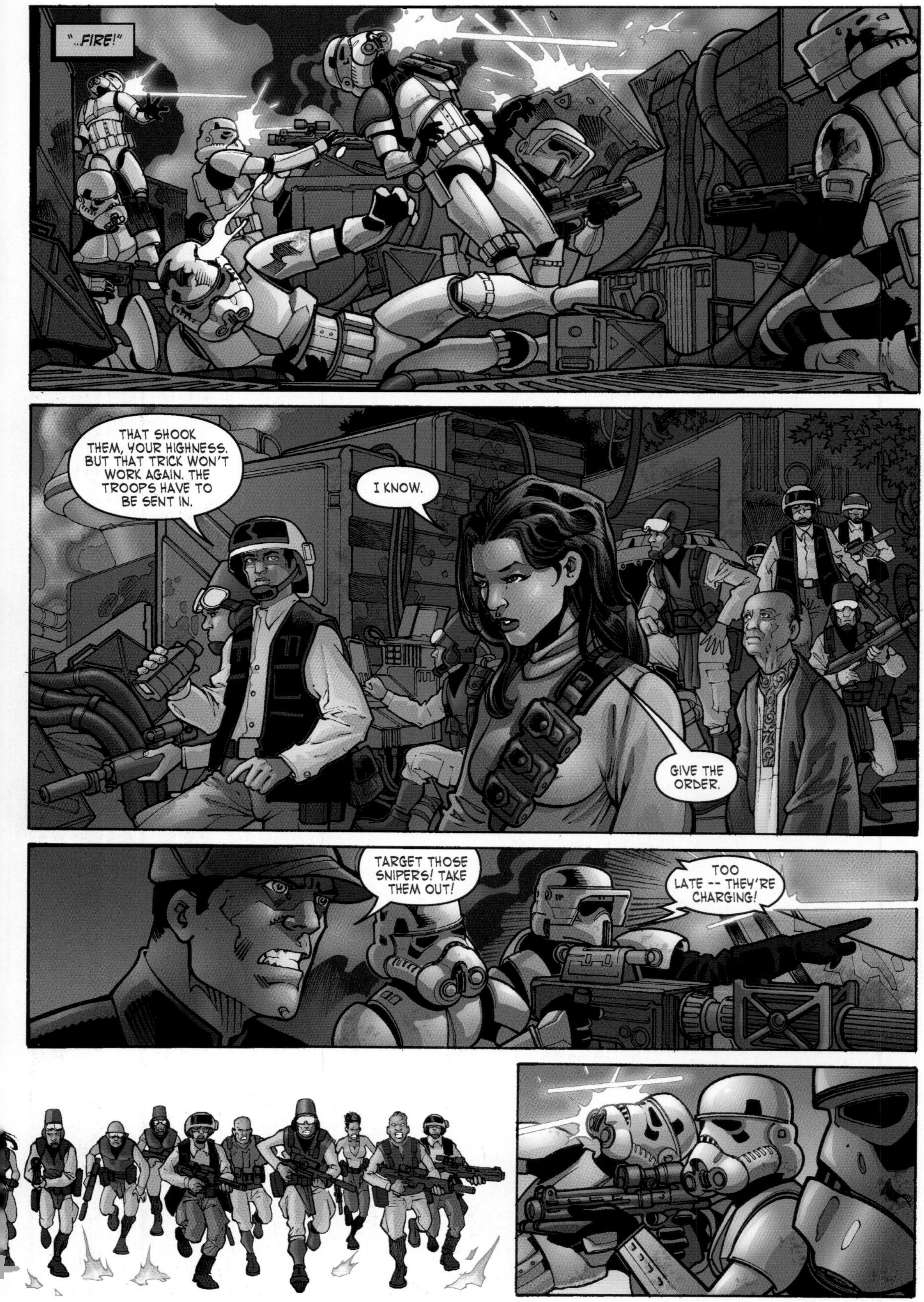
"..FIRE!"
THAT SHOOK THEM, YOUR HIGHNESS. BUT THAT TRICK WON'T WORK AGAIN. THE TROOPS HAVE TO BE SENT IN.
I KNOW.
GIVE THE ORDER.
TARGET THOSE SNIPERS! TAKE THEM OUT!
TOO LATE -- THEY'RE CHARGING!

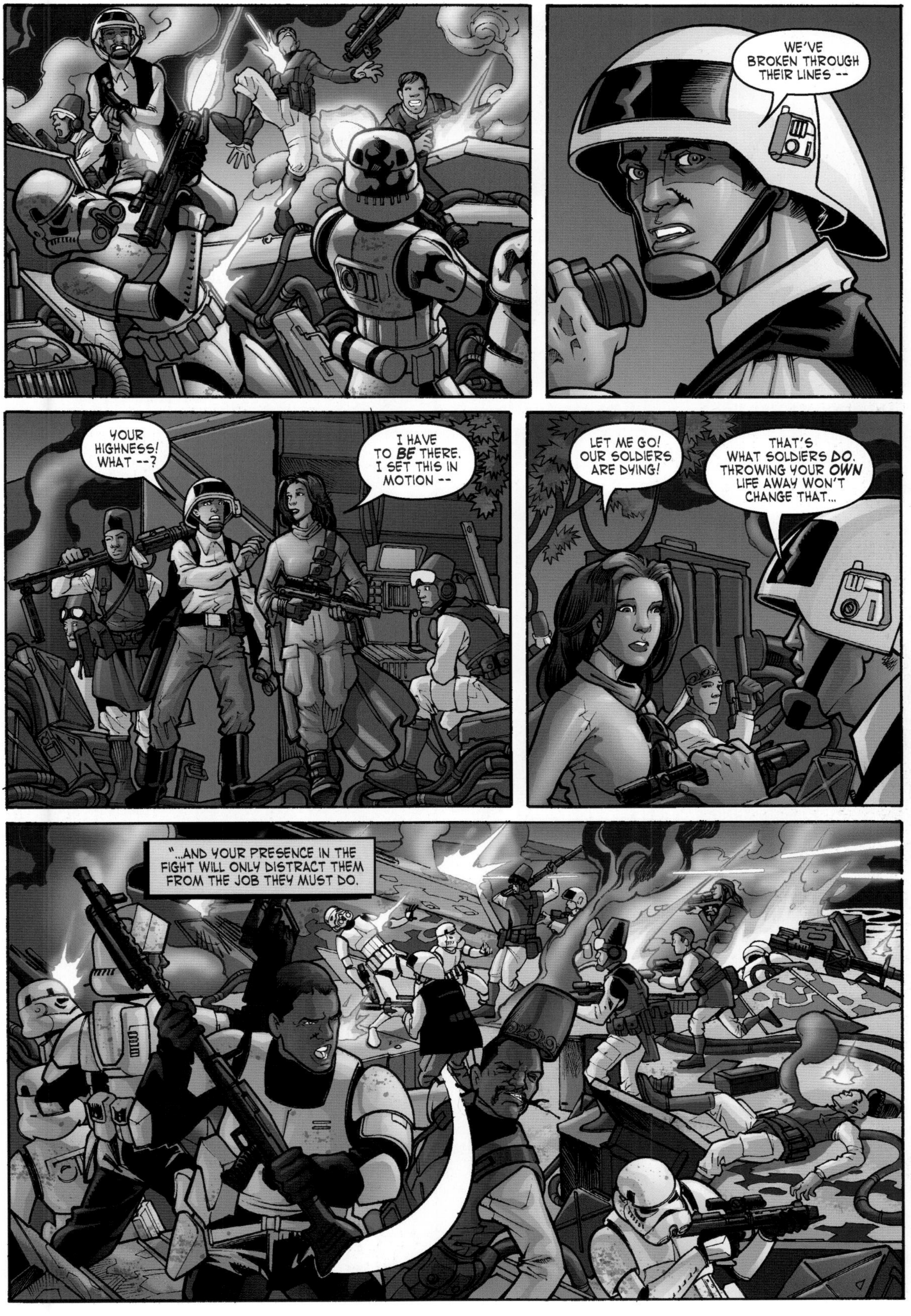
WE'VE BROKEN THROUGH THEIR LINES --
YOUR HIGHNESS! WHAT --?
I HAVE TO BE THERE. I SET THIS IN MOTION --
LET ME GO! OUR SOLDIERS ARE DYING!
THAT'S WHAT SOLDIERS DO. THROWING YOUR OWN LIFE AWAY WON'T CHANGE THAT...
"...AND YOUR PRESENCE IN THE FIGHT WILL ONLY DISTRACT THEM FROM THE JOB THEY MUST DO.

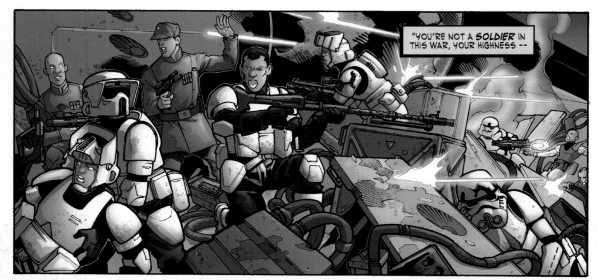

"YOU'RE NOT A *SOLDIER* IN THIS WAR, YOUR HIGHNESS --

"-- YOU'RE A *LEADER*, A *SYMBOL*.

"IN THE LONG RUN, YOUR DEATH MIGHT MAKE YOU A MARTYR...

"...BUT ITS IMMEDIATE EFFECT WOULD BE TO DEMORALIZE YOUR TROOPS AND KNOCK THE FIGHT OUT OF THEM."

WE JUST RECEIVED WORD FROM THE FRONT. THE BATTLE IS OVER.

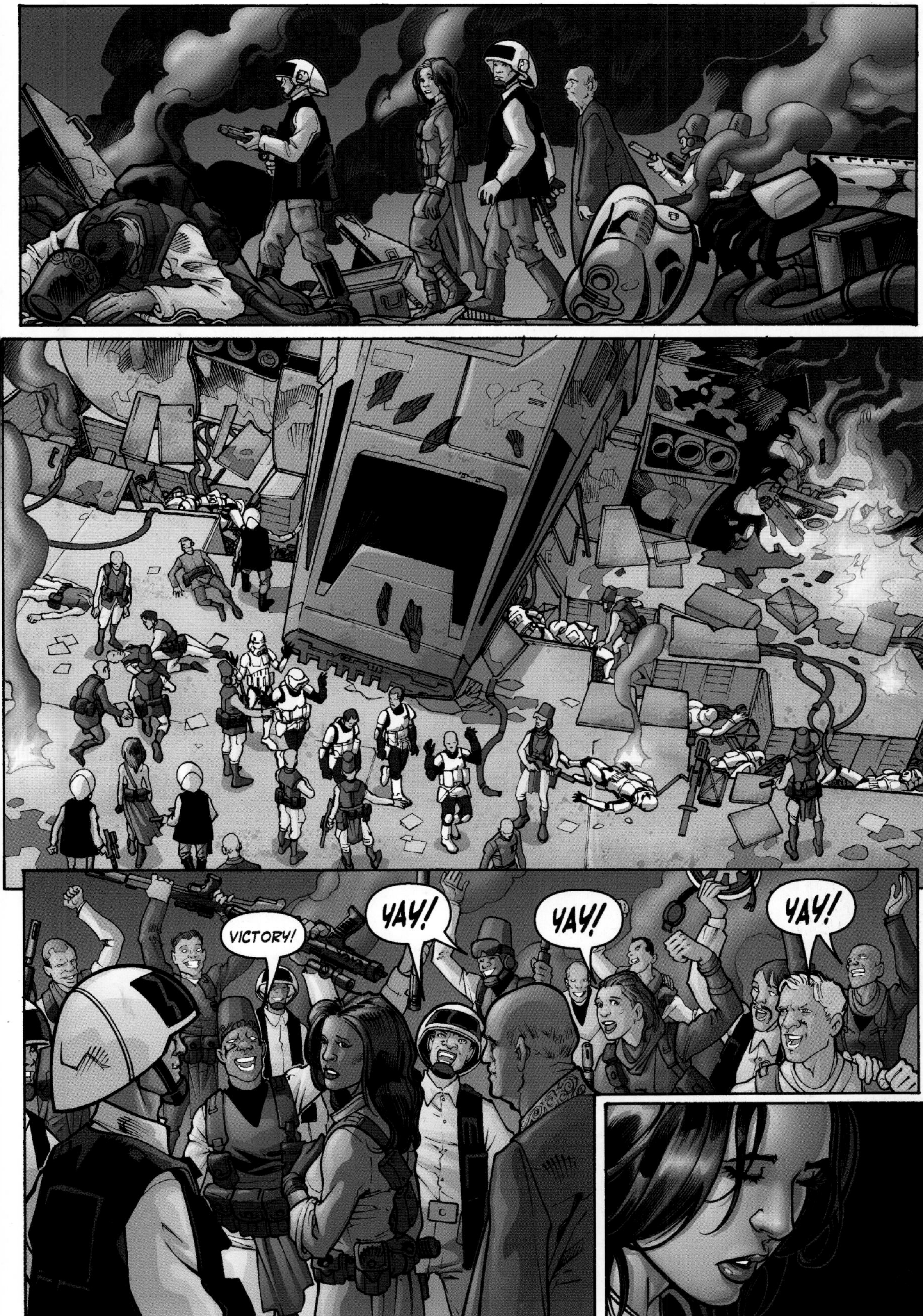
VICTORY!
YAY!
YAY!
YAY!

OUR PEOPLE WILL HAVE THE IMPERIAL SHIP DISMANTLED, AND ALL TRACES OF THE BATTLE HIDDEN BEFORE ANOTHER PATROL ARRIVES. NOT A WORD OF WHAT TRANSPIRED HERE WILL PASS ANYONE'S LIPS.

BUT YOU MUST BE AWAY -- SOON.

YES...

I'M SO SORRY FOR YOUR LOSS, SIR. I FEEL RESPONSIBLE FOR YOUR DAUGHTER'S DEATH --

PLEASE, YOUR HIGHNESS, PUT AWAY YOUR SORROW.

MIA DIED FOR A CAUSE SHE BELIEVED IN, AND THE VICTORY TO WHICH YOU LED US WOULD HAVE MADE HER PROUD.

PROUD...

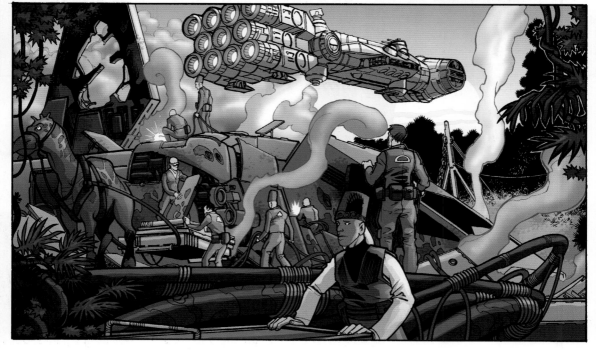

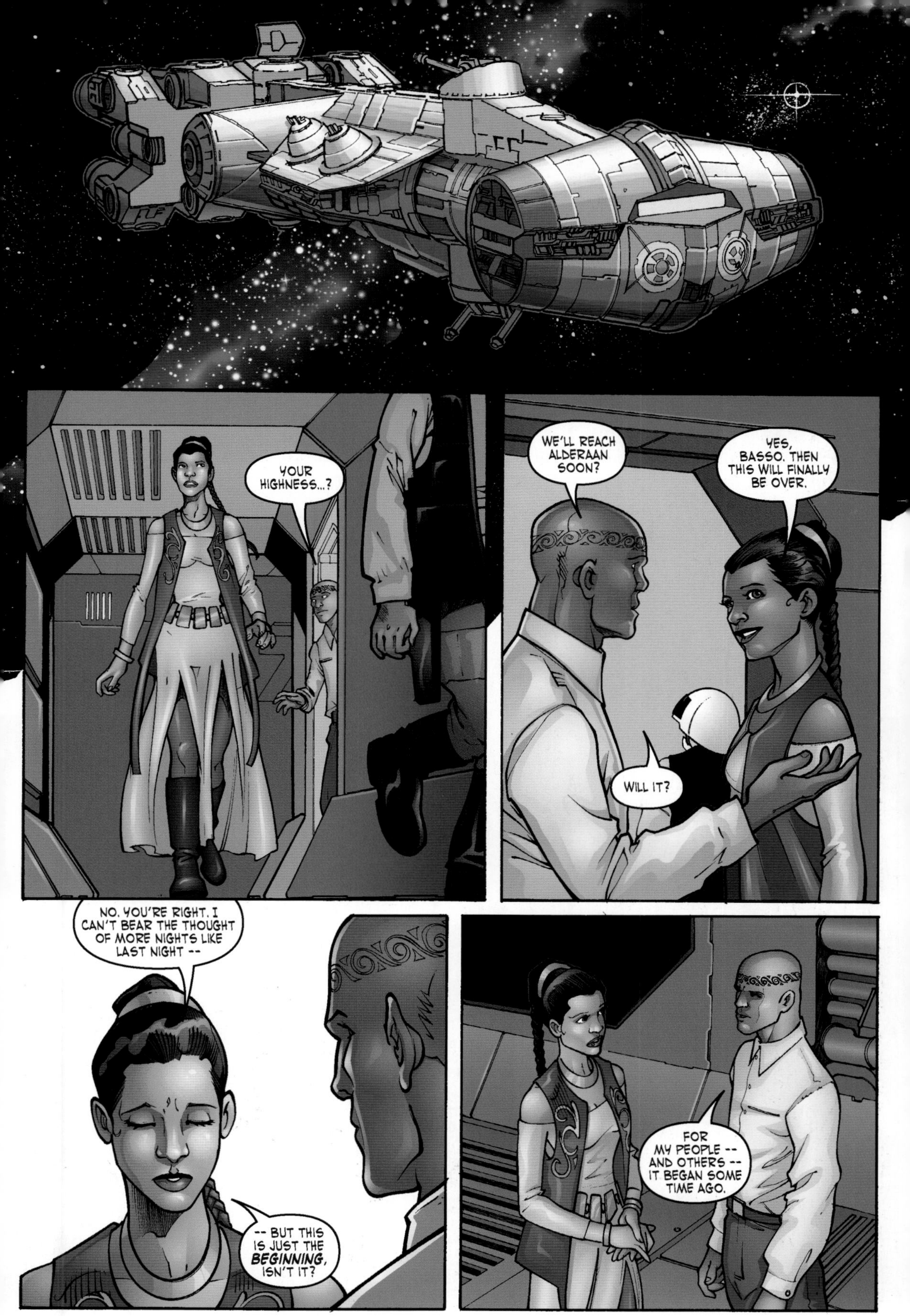
YOUR HIGHNESS...?
WE'LL REACH ALDERAAN SOON?
YES, BASSO. THEN THIS WILL FINALLY BE OVER.
WILL IT?
NO. YOU'RE RIGHT. I CAN'T BEAR THE THOUGHT OF MORE NIGHTS LIKE LAST NIGHT --
-- BUT THIS IS JUST THE *BEGINNING*, ISN'T IT?
FOR MY PEOPLE -- AND OTHERS -- IT BEGAN SOME TIME AGO.

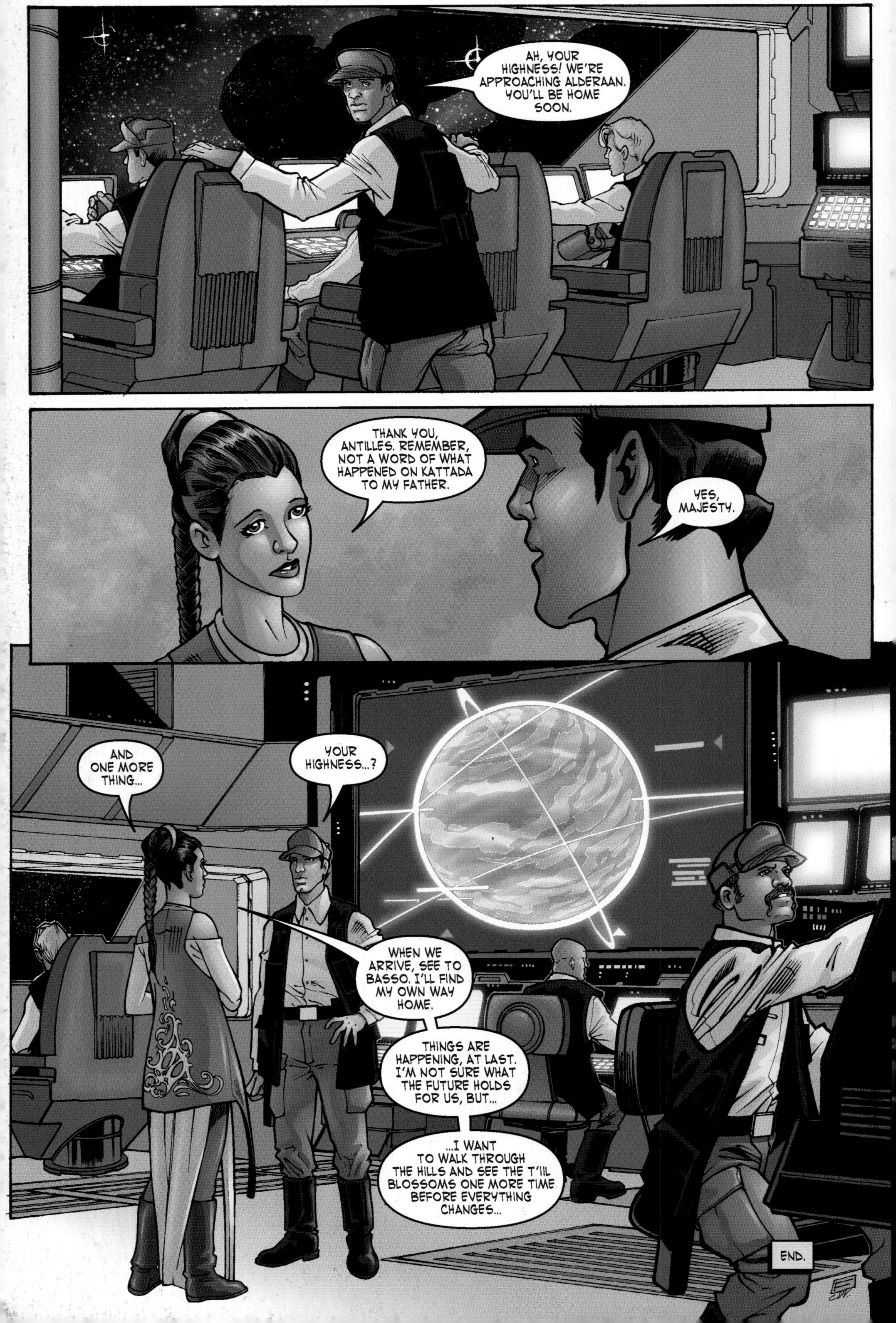
AH, YOUR HIGHNESS! WE'RE APPROACHING ALDERAAN. YOU'LL BE HOME SOON.
THANK YOU, ANTILLES. REMEMBER, NOT A WORD OF WHAT HAPPENED ON KATTADA TO MY FATHER.
YES, MAJESTY.
AND ONE MORE THING...
YOUR HIGHNESS...?
WHEN WE ARRIVE, SEE TO BASSO. I'LL FIND MY OWN WAY HOME.
THINGS ARE HAPPENING, AT LAST. I'M NOT SURE WHAT THE FUTURE HOLDS FOR US, BUT...
...I WANT TO WALK THROUGH THE HILLS AND SEE THE T'IIL BLOSSOMS ONE MORE TIME BEFORE EVERYTHING CHANGES...
END.

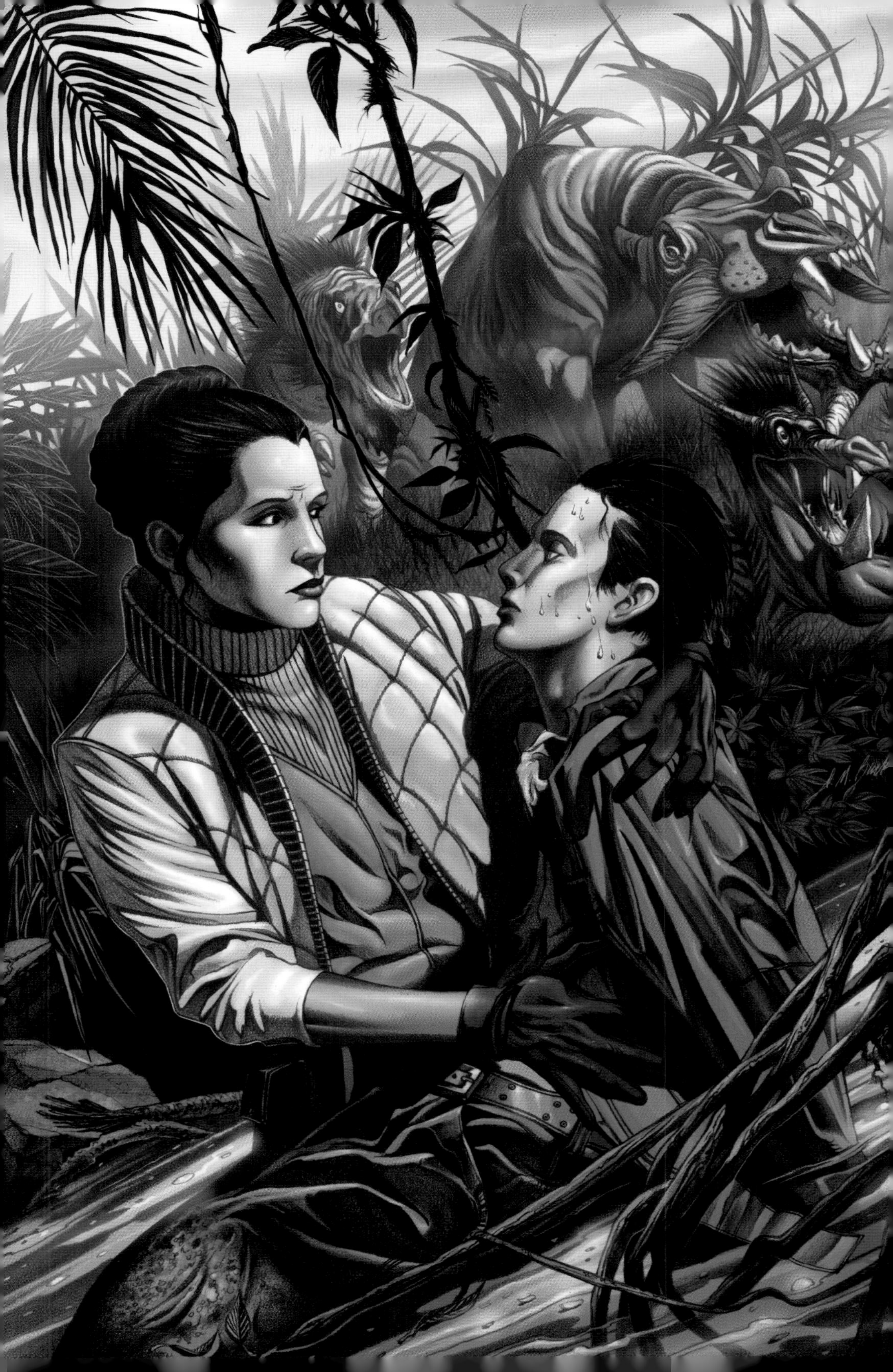

A LITTLE PIECE OF HOME

Script RON MARZ
Art TOMÁS GIORELLO
Colors MICHAEL ATIYEH

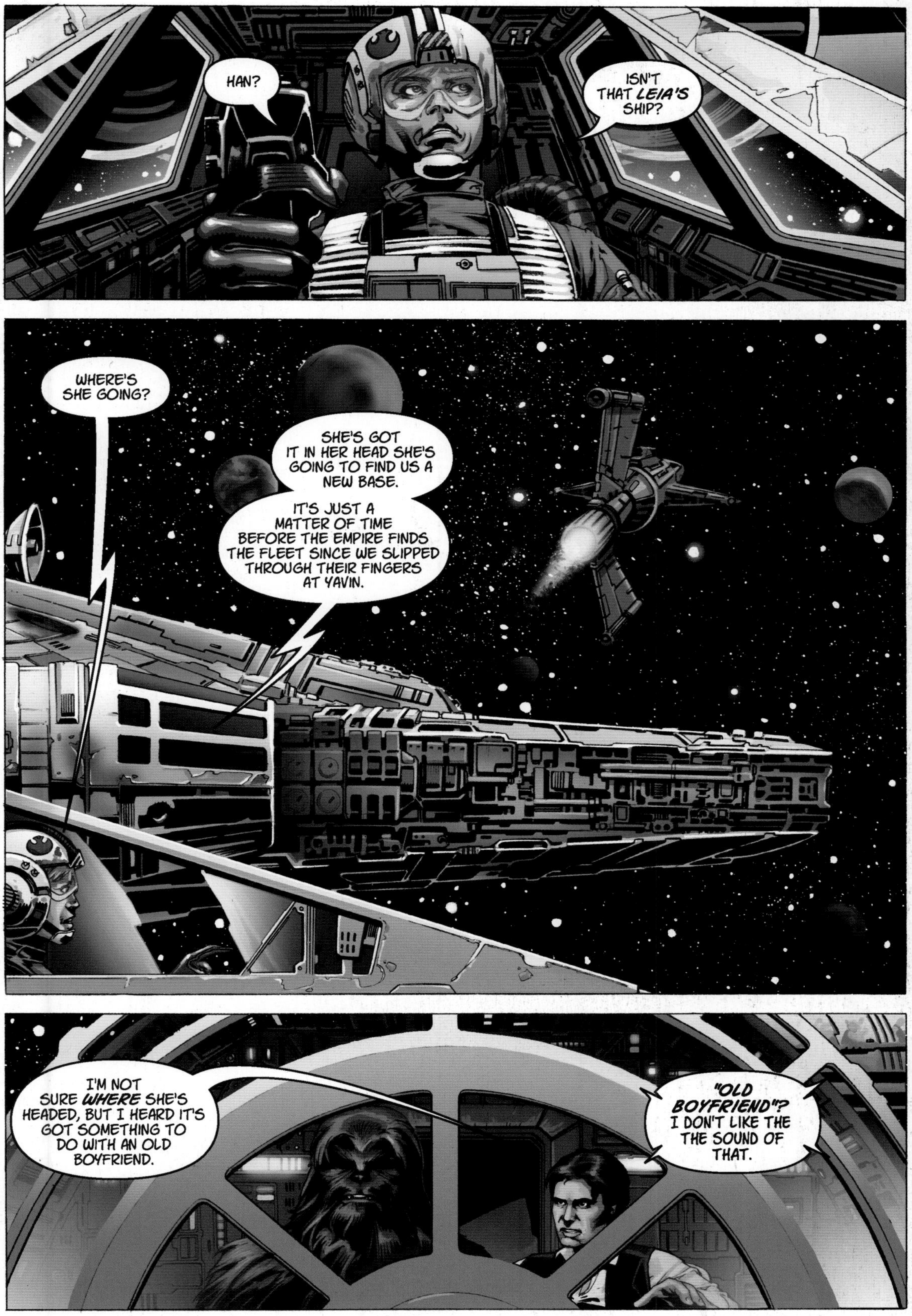
HAN?
ISN'T THAT LEIA'S SHIP?
WHERE'S SHE GOING?
SHE'S GOT IT IN HER HEAD SHE'S GOING TO FIND US A NEW BASE.
IT'S JUST A MATTER OF TIME BEFORE THE EMPIRE FINDS THE FLEET SINCE WE SLIPPED THROUGH THEIR FINGERS AT YAVIN.
I'M NOT SURE WHERE SHE'S HEADED, BUT I HEARD IT'S GOT SOMETHING TO DO WITH AN OLD BOYFRIEND.
"OLD BOYFRIEND"? I DON'T LIKE THE THE SOUND OF THAT.

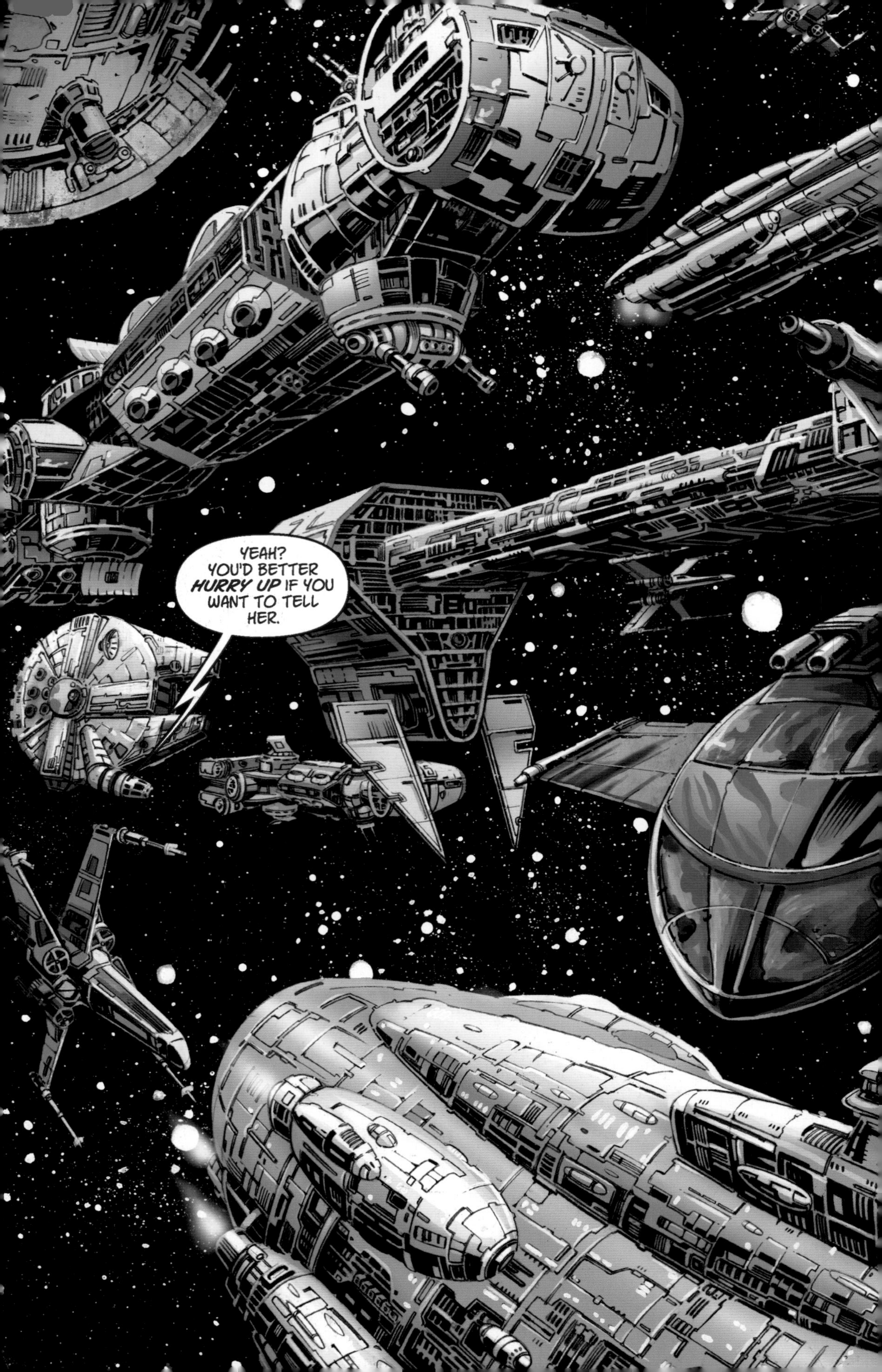
YEAH? YOU'D BETTER HURRY UP IF YOU WANT TO TELL HER.

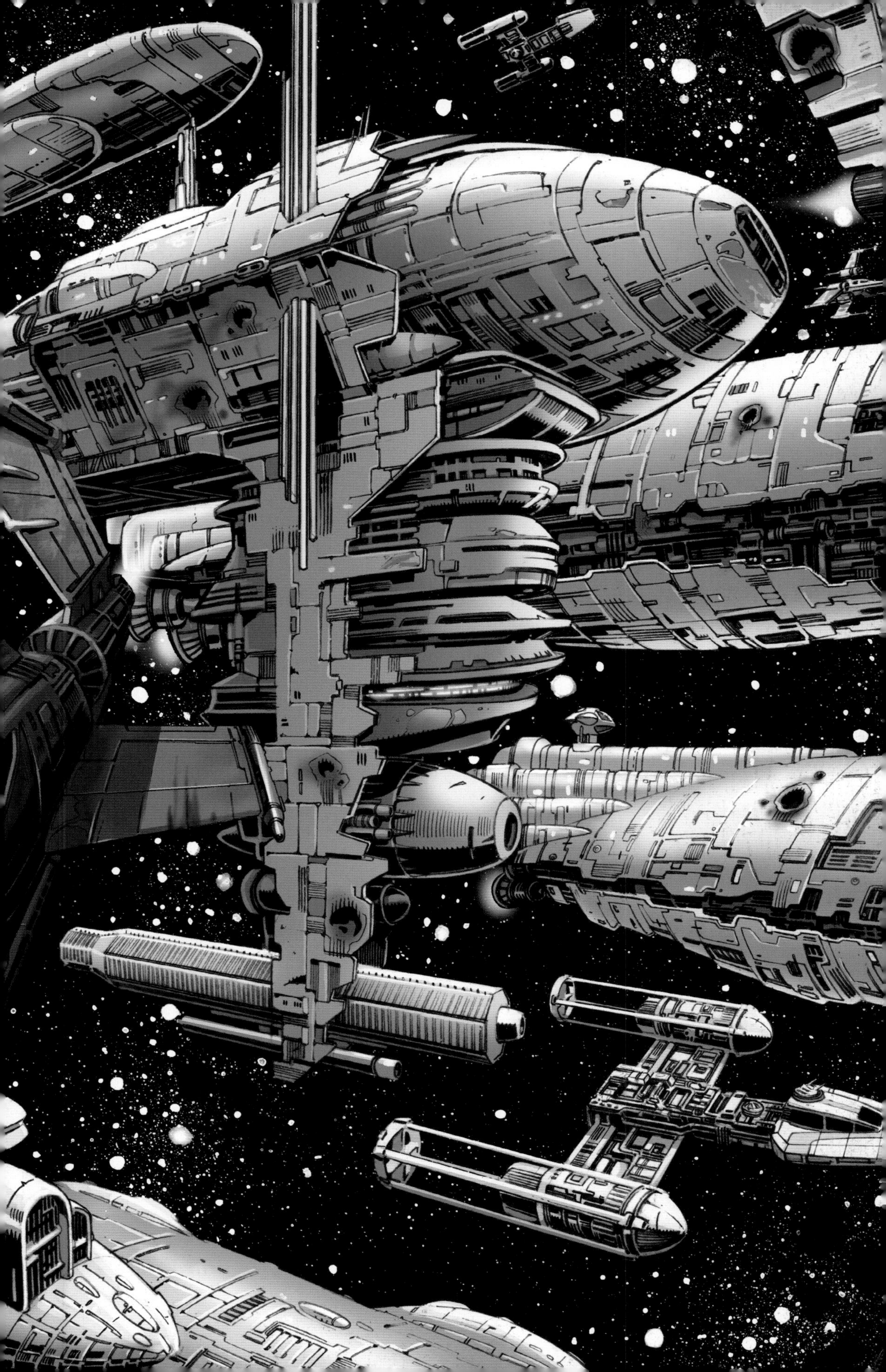

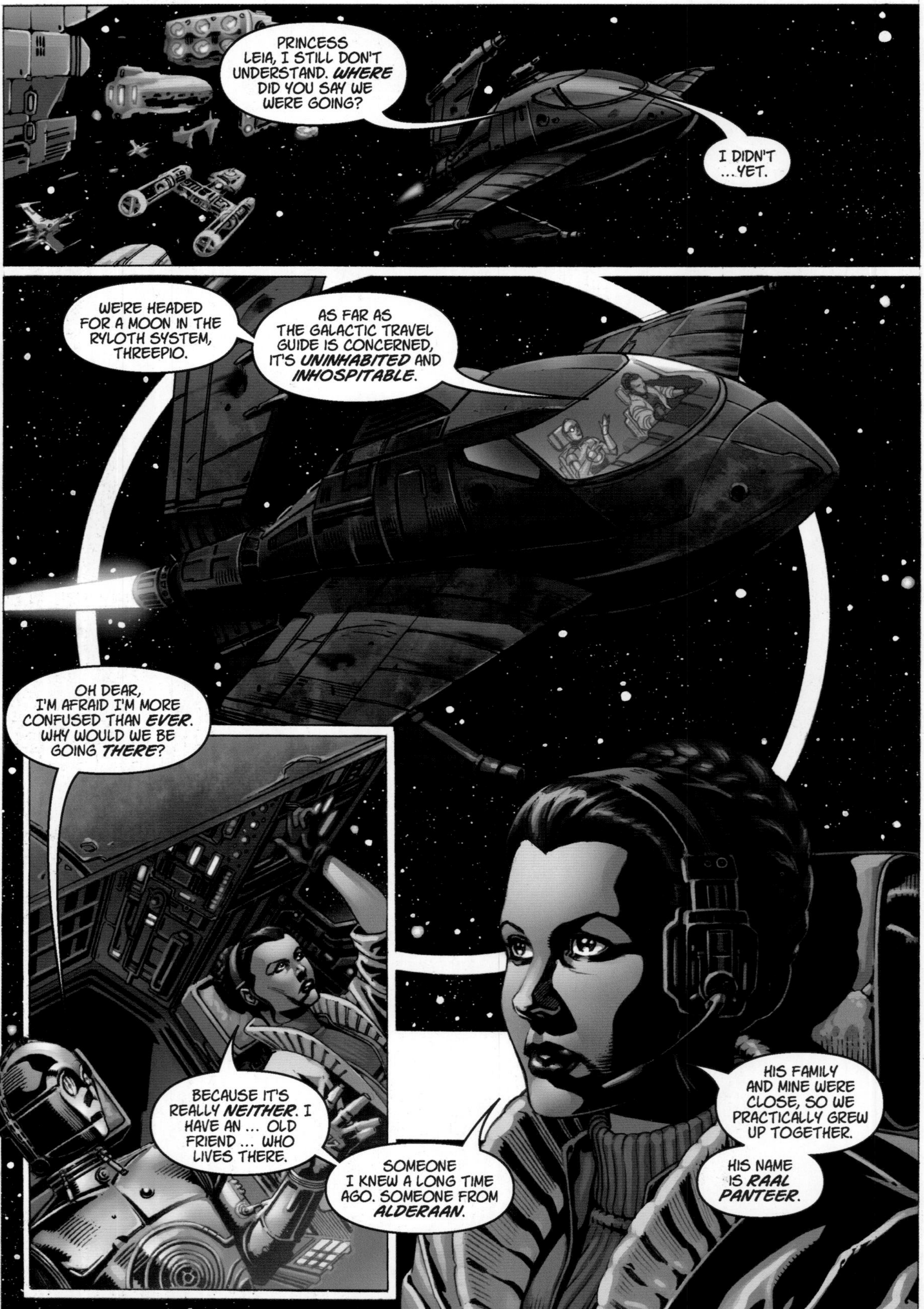
PRINCESS LEIA, I STILL DON'T UNDERSTAND. WHERE DID YOU SAY WE WERE GOING?
I DIDN'T ... YET.
WE'RE HEADED FOR A MOON IN THE RYLOTH SYSTEM, THREEPIO.
AS FAR AS THE GALACTIC TRAVEL GUIDE IS CONCERNED, IT'S UNINHABITED AND INHOSPITABLE.
OH DEAR, I'M AFRAID I'M MORE CONFUSED THAN EVER. WHY WOULD WE BE GOING THERE?
BECAUSE IT'S REALLY NEITHER. I HAVE AN ... OLD FRIEND ... WHO LIVES THERE.
SOMEONE I KNEW A LONG TIME AGO. SOMEONE FROM ALDERAAN.
HIS FAMILY AND MINE WERE CLOSE, SO WE PRACTICALLY GREW UP TOGETHER.
HIS NAME IS RAAL PANTEER.

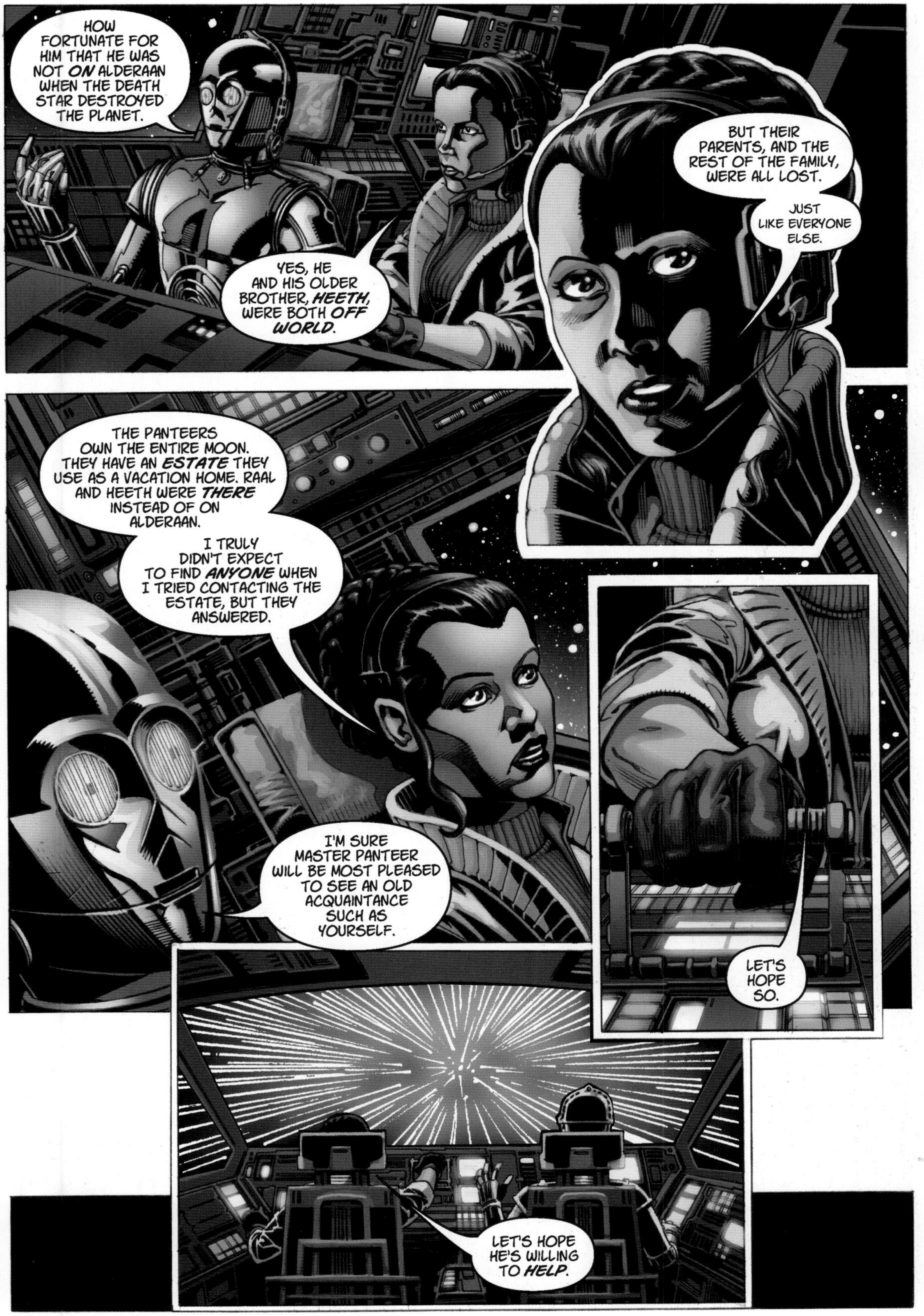
HOW FORTUNATE FOR HIM THAT HE WAS NOT *ON* ALDERAAN WHEN THE DEATH STAR DESTROYED THE PLANET.
YES, HE AND HIS OLDER BROTHER, *HEETH*, WERE BOTH *OFF WORLD*.
BUT THEIR PARENTS, AND THE REST OF THE FAMILY, WERE ALL LOST.
JUST LIKE EVERYONE ELSE.
THE PANTEERS OWN THE ENTIRE MOON. THEY HAVE AN *ESTATE* THEY USE AS A VACATION HOME. RAAL AND HEETH WERE *THERE* INSTEAD OF ON ALDERAAN.
I TRULY DIDN'T EXPECT TO FIND *ANYONE* WHEN I TRIED CONTACTING THE ESTATE, BUT THEY ANSWERED.
I'M SURE MASTER PANTEER WILL BE MOST PLEASED TO SEE AN OLD ACQUAINTANCE SUCH AS YOURSELF.
LET'S HOPE SO.
LET'S HOPE HE'S WILLING TO *HELP*.

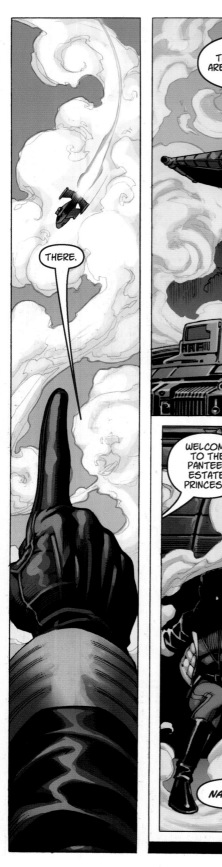

THERE.

HOW IS IT THAT YOUR EYES ARE *STILL* SHARPER THAN MINE?

DO YOU THINK SHE'S *CHANGED* MUCH?

IN MY EXPERIENCE ... *EVERYONE* DOES, TO ONE DEGREE OR ANOTHER.

WELCOME TO THE PANTEER ESTATE, PRINCESS.

YES. I WAS HERE SERVING MASTERS RAAL AND HEETH WHEN THE TRAGEDY OCCURRED. IF YOU'LL FORGIVE MY FAMILIARITY, I SHOULD LIKE TO SAY IT'S MOST PLEASING TO SEE YOU AGAIN. WE ARE *ALL* BETTER FOR YOUR PRESENCE HERE.

I'M PLEASED TO SEE *YOU* AS WELL. I DON'T KNOW WHY, BUT I NEVER THOUGHT THAT YOU'D BE HERE TOO.

NALLEN?

LEIA!

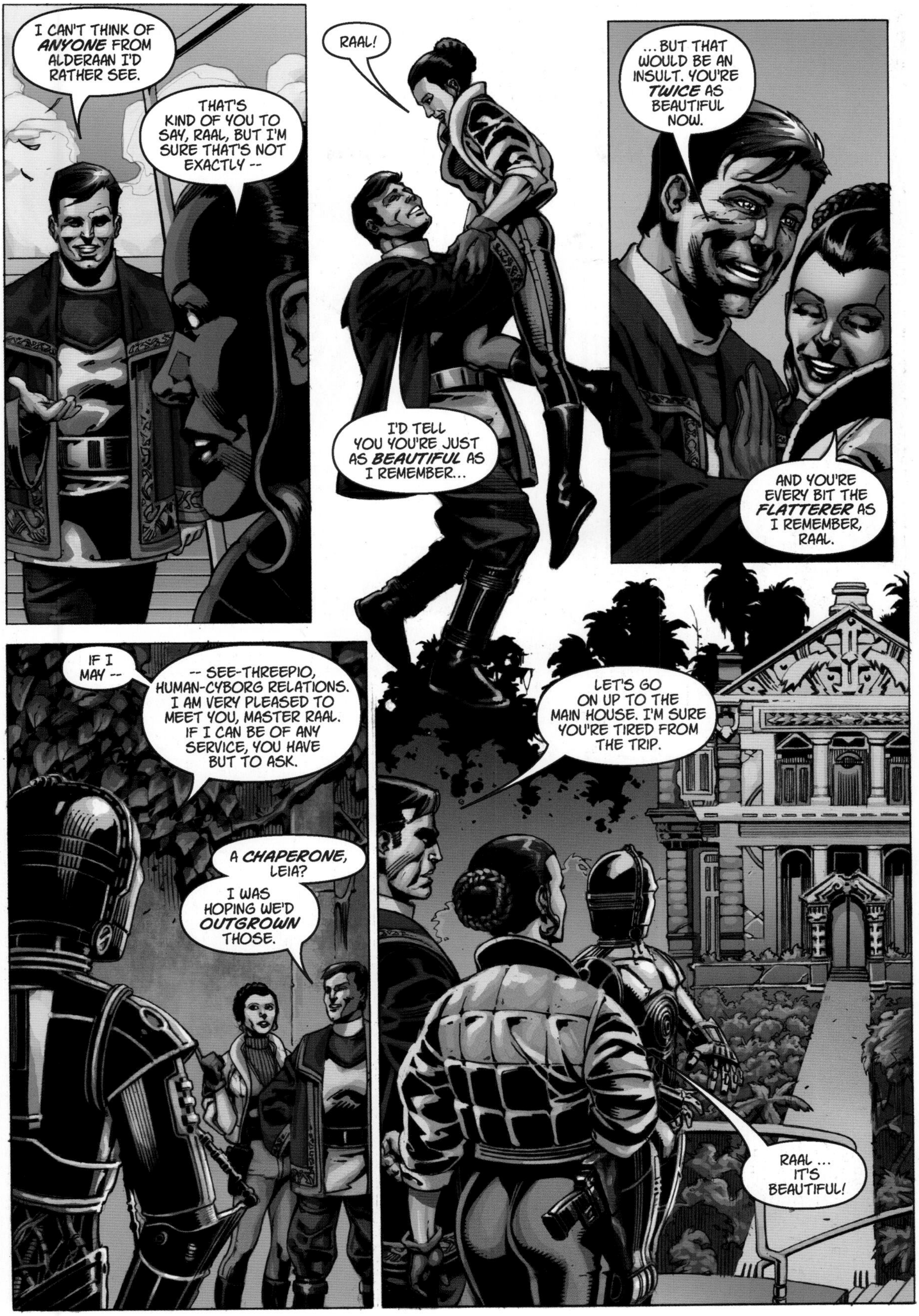
I CAN'T THINK OF ANYONE FROM ALDERAAN I'D RATHER SEE.
THAT'S KIND OF YOU TO SAY, RAAL, BUT I'M SURE THAT'S NOT EXACTLY --
RAAL!
I'D TELL YOU YOU'RE JUST AS BEAUTIFUL AS I REMEMBER...
... BUT THAT WOULD BE AN INSULT. YOU'RE TWICE AS BEAUTIFUL NOW.
AND YOU'RE EVERY BIT THE FLATTERER AS I REMEMBER, RAAL.
IF I MAY --
-- SEE-THREEPIO, HUMAN-CYBORG RELATIONS. I AM VERY PLEASED TO MEET YOU, MASTER RAAL. IF I CAN BE OF ANY SERVICE, YOU HAVE BUT TO ASK.
A CHAPERONE, LEIA?
I WAS HOPING WE'D OUTGROWN THOSE.
LET'S GO ON UP TO THE MAIN HOUSE. I'M SURE YOU'RE TIRED FROM THE TRIP.
RAAL ... IT'S BEAUTIFUL!

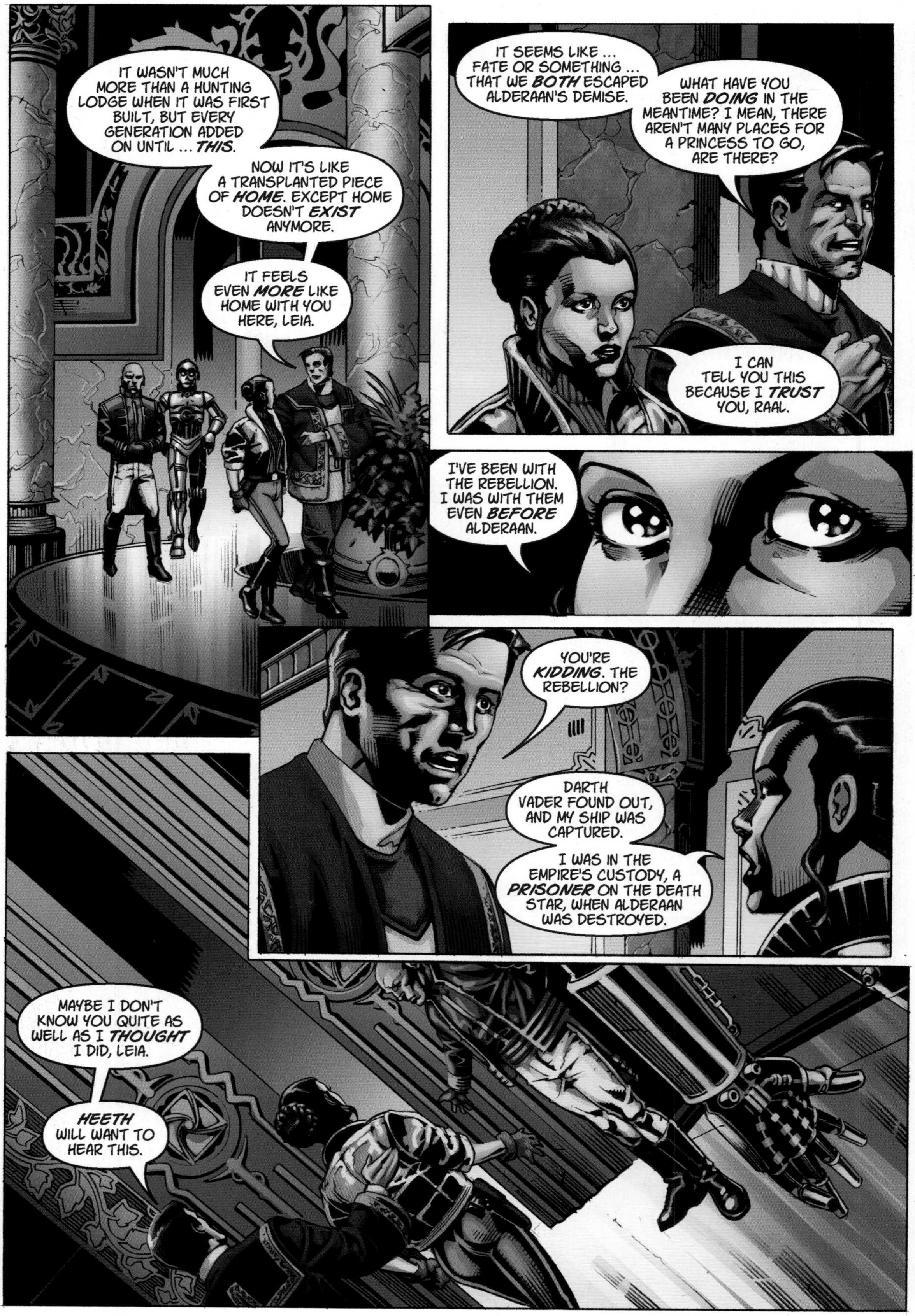
IT WASN'T MUCH MORE THAN A HUNTING LODGE WHEN IT WAS FIRST BUILT, BUT EVERY GENERATION ADDED ON UNTIL ... THIS.
NOW IT'S LIKE A TRANSPLANTED PIECE OF HOME. EXCEPT HOME DOESN'T EXIST ANYMORE.
IT FEELS EVEN MORE LIKE HOME WITH YOU HERE, LEIA.
IT SEEMS LIKE ... FATE OR SOMETHING ... THAT WE BOTH ESCAPED ALDERAAN'S DEMISE.
WHAT HAVE YOU BEEN DOING IN THE MEANTIME? I MEAN, THERE AREN'T MANY PLACES FOR A PRINCESS TO GO, ARE THERE?
I CAN TELL YOU THIS BECAUSE I TRUST YOU, RAAL.
I'VE BEEN WITH THE REBELLION. I WAS WITH THEM EVEN BEFORE ALDERAAN.
YOU'RE KIDDING. THE REBELLION?
DARTH VADER FOUND OUT, AND MY SHIP WAS CAPTURED.
I WAS IN THE EMPIRE'S CUSTODY, A PRISONER ON THE DEATH STAR, WHEN ALDERAAN WAS DESTROYED.
MAYBE I DON'T KNOW YOU QUITE AS WELL AS I THOUGHT I DID, LEIA.
HEETH WILL WANT TO HEAR THIS.

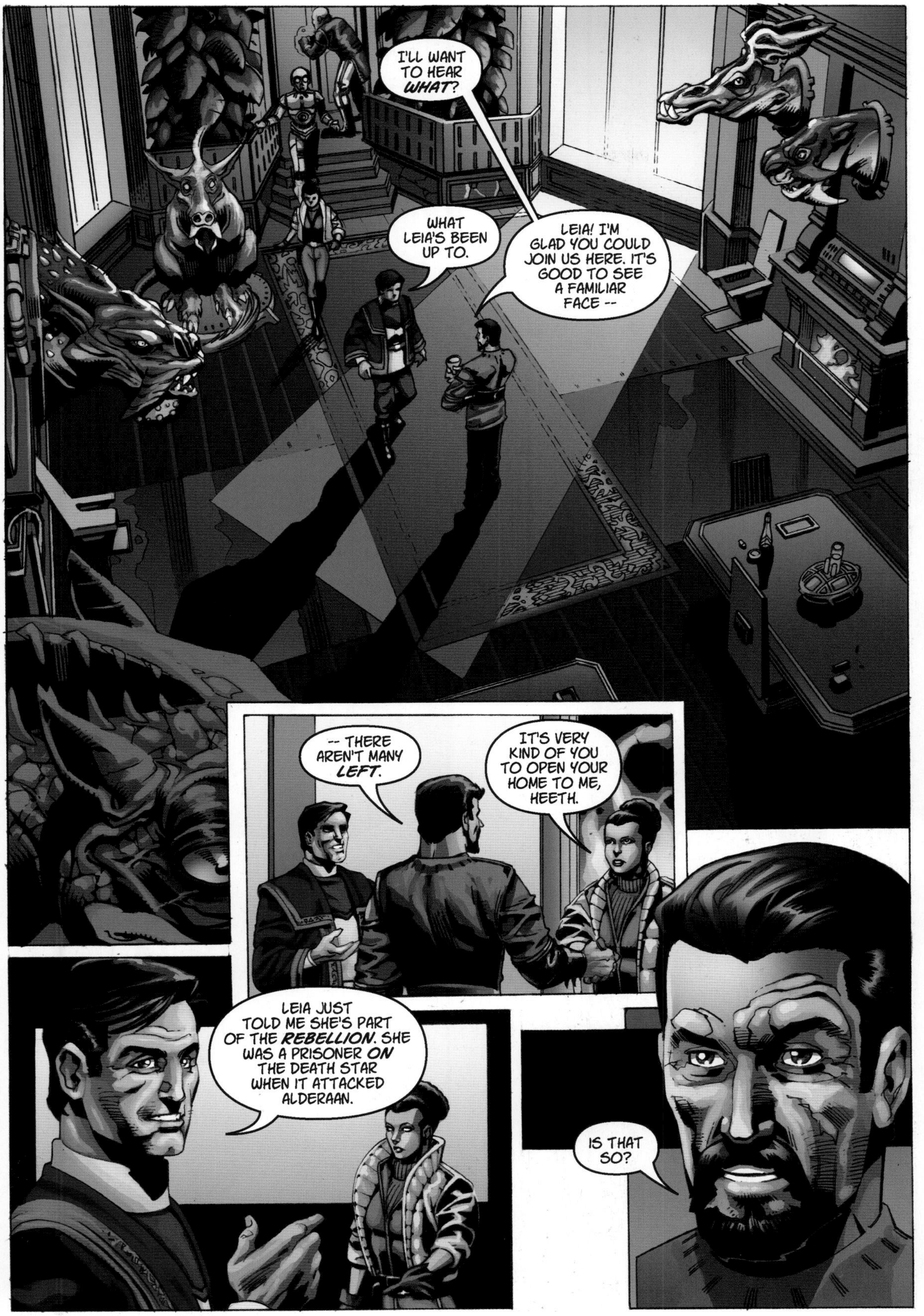
I'LL WANT TO HEAR *WHAT*?
WHAT LEIA'S BEEN UP TO.
LEIA! I'M GLAD YOU COULD JOIN US HERE. IT'S GOOD TO SEE A FAMILIAR FACE --
-- THERE AREN'T MANY *LEFT*.
IT'S VERY KIND OF YOU TO OPEN YOUR HOME TO ME, HEETH.
LEIA JUST TOLD ME SHE'S PART OF THE *REBELLION*. SHE WAS A PRISONER *ON* THE DEATH STAR WHEN IT ATTACKED ALDERAAN.
IS THAT SO?

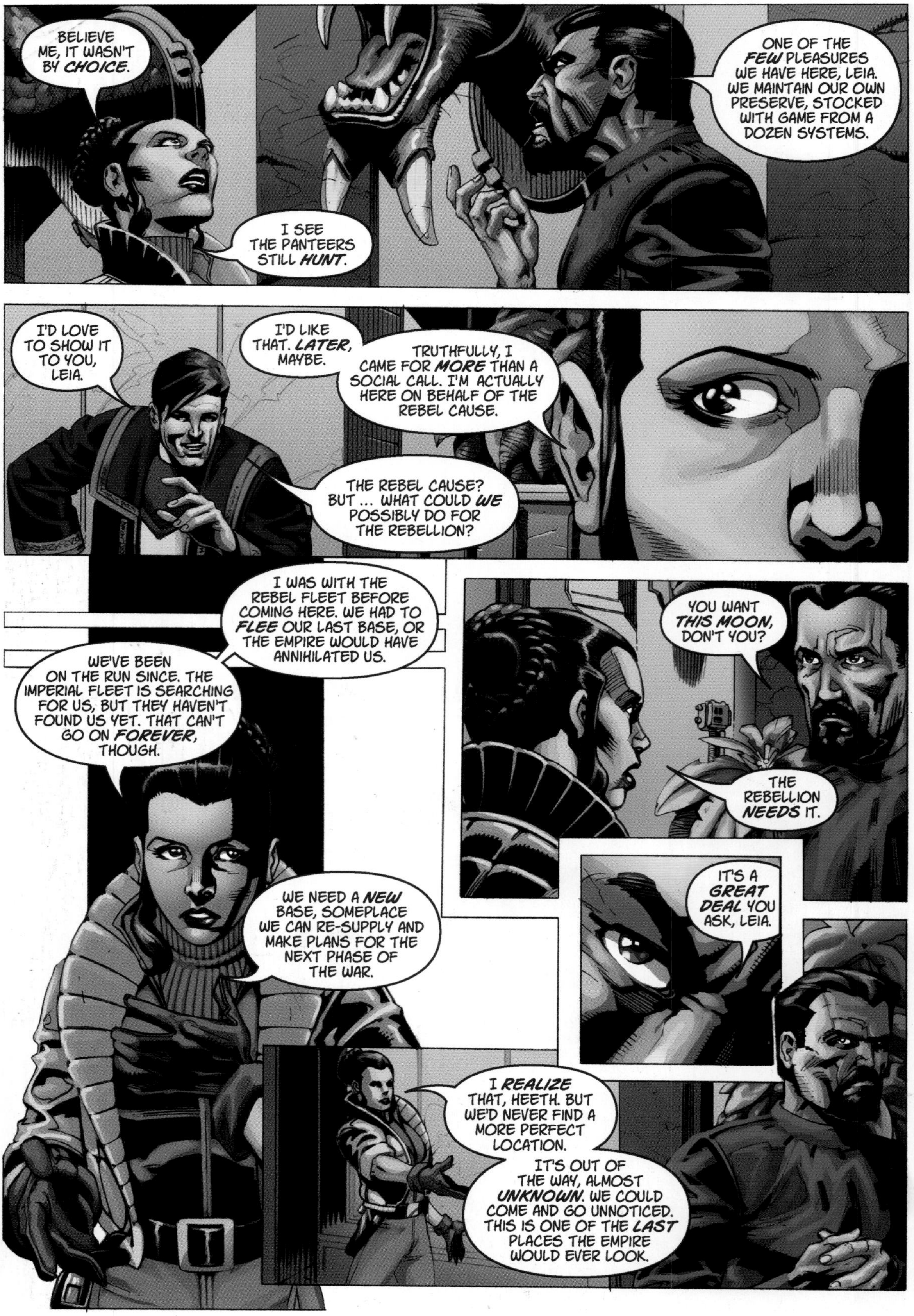

BELIEVE ME, IT WASN'T BY CHOICE.
ONE OF THE FEW PLEASURES WE HAVE HERE, LEIA. WE MAINTAIN OUR OWN PRESERVE, STOCKED WITH GAME FROM A DOZEN SYSTEMS.
I SEE THE PANTEERS STILL HUNT.
I'D LOVE TO SHOW IT TO YOU, LEIA.
I'D LIKE THAT. LATER, MAYBE.
TRUTHFULLY, I CAME FOR MORE THAN A SOCIAL CALL. I'M ACTUALLY HERE ON BEHALF OF THE REBEL CAUSE.
THE REBEL CAUSE? BUT ... WHAT COULD WE POSSIBLY DO FOR THE REBELLION?
I WAS WITH THE REBEL FLEET BEFORE COMING HERE. WE HAD TO FLEE OUR LAST BASE, OR THE EMPIRE WOULD HAVE ANNIHILATED US.
WE'VE BEEN ON THE RUN SINCE. THE IMPERIAL FLEET IS SEARCHING FOR US, BUT THEY HAVEN'T FOUND US YET. THAT CAN'T GO ON FOREVER, THOUGH.
WE NEED A NEW BASE, SOMEPLACE WE CAN RE-SUPPLY AND MAKE PLANS FOR THE NEXT PHASE OF THE WAR.
YOU WANT THIS MOON, DON'T YOU?
THE REBELLION NEEDS IT.
IT'S A GREAT DEAL YOU ASK, LEIA.
I REALIZE THAT, HEETH. BUT WE'D NEVER FIND A MORE PERFECT LOCATION.
IT'S OUT OF THE WAY, ALMOST UNKNOWN. WE COULD COME AND GO UNNOTICED. THIS IS ONE OF THE LAST PLACES THE EMPIRE WOULD EVER LOOK.

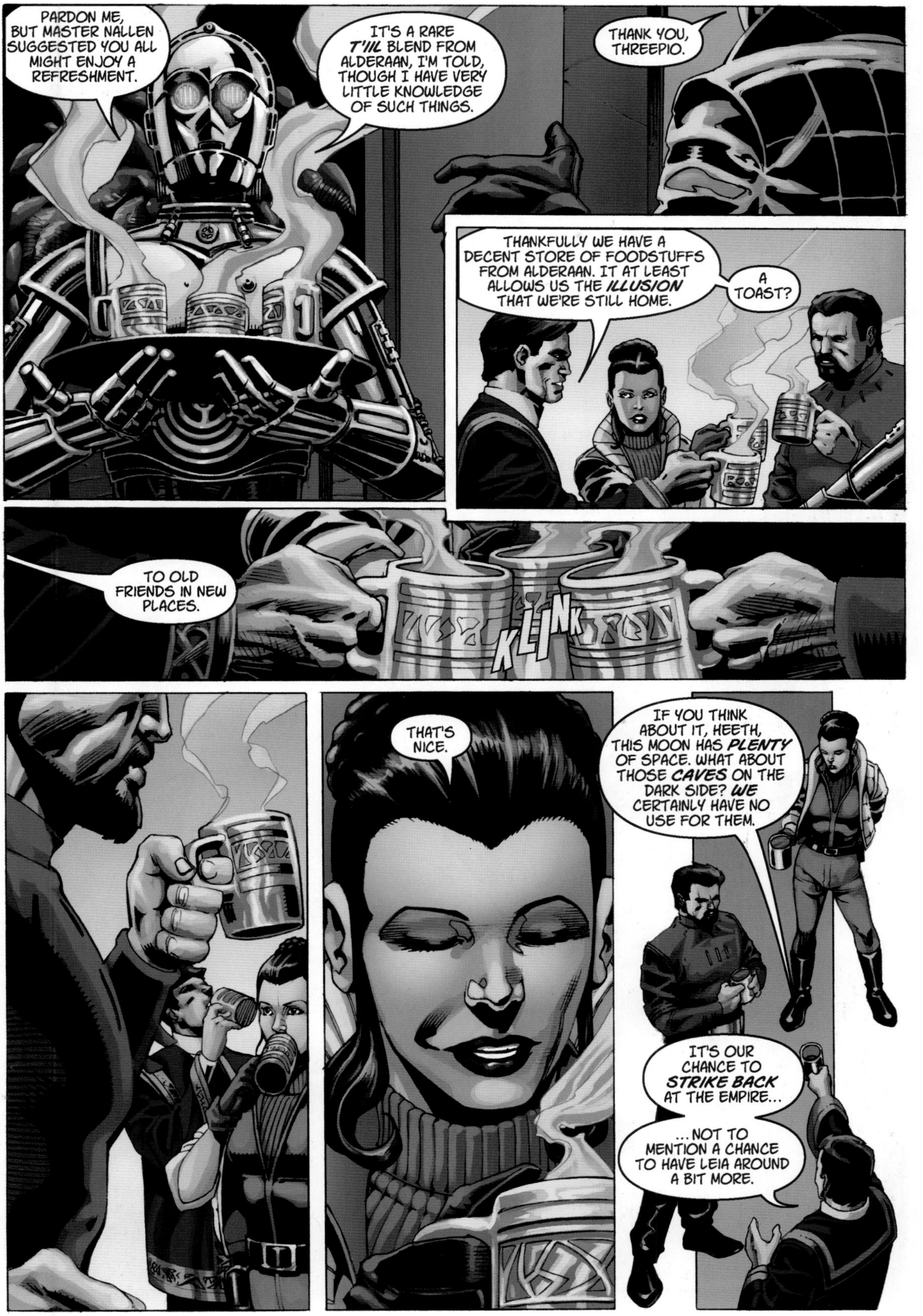
PARDON ME, BUT MASTER NALLEN SUGGESTED YOU ALL MIGHT ENJOY A REFRESHMENT.
IT'S A RARE T'IIL BLEND FROM ALDERAAN, I'M TOLD, THOUGH I HAVE VERY LITTLE KNOWLEDGE OF SUCH THINGS.
THANK YOU, THREEPIO.
THANKFULLY WE HAVE A DECENT STORE OF FOODSTUFFS FROM ALDERAAN. IT AT LEAST ALLOWS US THE ILLUSION THAT WE'RE STILL HOME.
A TOAST?
TO OLD FRIENDS IN NEW PLACES.
KLINK
THAT'S NICE.
IF YOU THINK ABOUT IT, HEETH, THIS MOON HAS PLENTY OF SPACE. WHAT ABOUT THOSE CAVES ON THE DARK SIDE? WE CERTAINLY HAVE NO USE FOR THEM.
IT'S OUR CHANCE TO STRIKE BACK AT THE EMPIRE...
...NOT TO MENTION A CHANCE TO HAVE LEIA AROUND A BIT MORE.

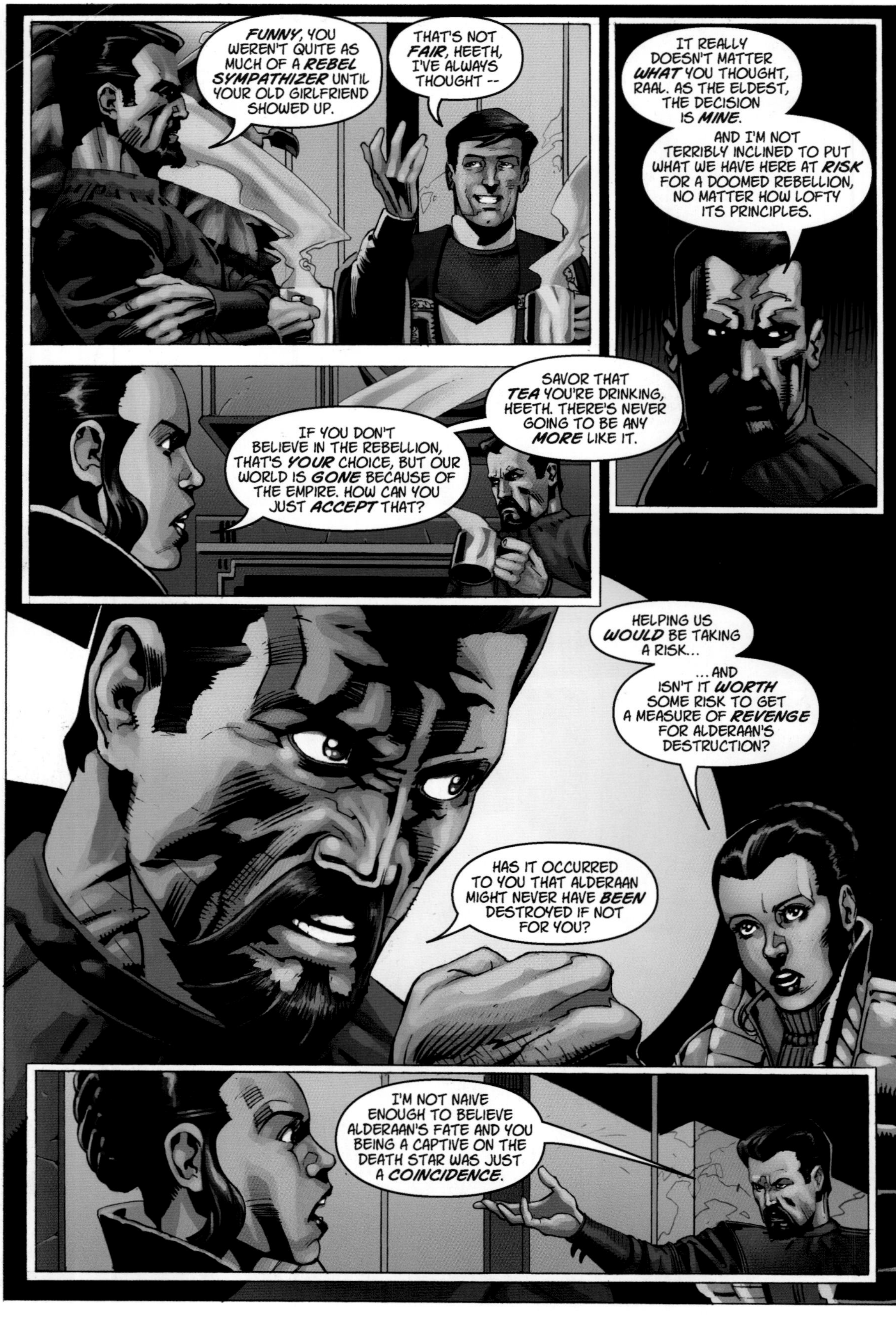
FUNNY, YOU WEREN'T QUITE AS MUCH OF A REBEL SYMPATHIZER UNTIL YOUR OLD GIRLFRIEND SHOWED UP.
THAT'S NOT FAIR, HEETH, I'VE ALWAYS THOUGHT --
IT REALLY DOESN'T MATTER WHAT YOU THOUGHT, RAAL. AS THE ELDEST, THE DECISION IS MINE.
AND I'M NOT TERRIBLY INCLINED TO PUT WHAT WE HAVE HERE AT RISK FOR A DOOMED REBELLION, NO MATTER HOW LOFTY ITS PRINCIPLES.
IF YOU DON'T BELIEVE IN THE REBELLION, THAT'S YOUR CHOICE, BUT OUR WORLD IS GONE BECAUSE OF THE EMPIRE. HOW CAN YOU JUST ACCEPT THAT?
SAVOR THAT TEA YOU'RE DRINKING, HEETH. THERE'S NEVER GOING TO BE ANY MORE LIKE IT.
HELPING US WOULD BE TAKING A RISK...
...AND ISN'T IT WORTH SOME RISK TO GET A MEASURE OF REVENGE FOR ALDERAAN'S DESTRUCTION?
HAS IT OCCURRED TO YOU THAT ALDERAAN MIGHT NEVER HAVE BEEN DESTROYED IF NOT FOR YOU?
I'M NOT NAIVE ENOUGH TO BELIEVE ALDERAAN'S FATE AND YOU BEING A CAPTIVE ON THE DEATH STAR WAS JUST A COINCIDENCE.

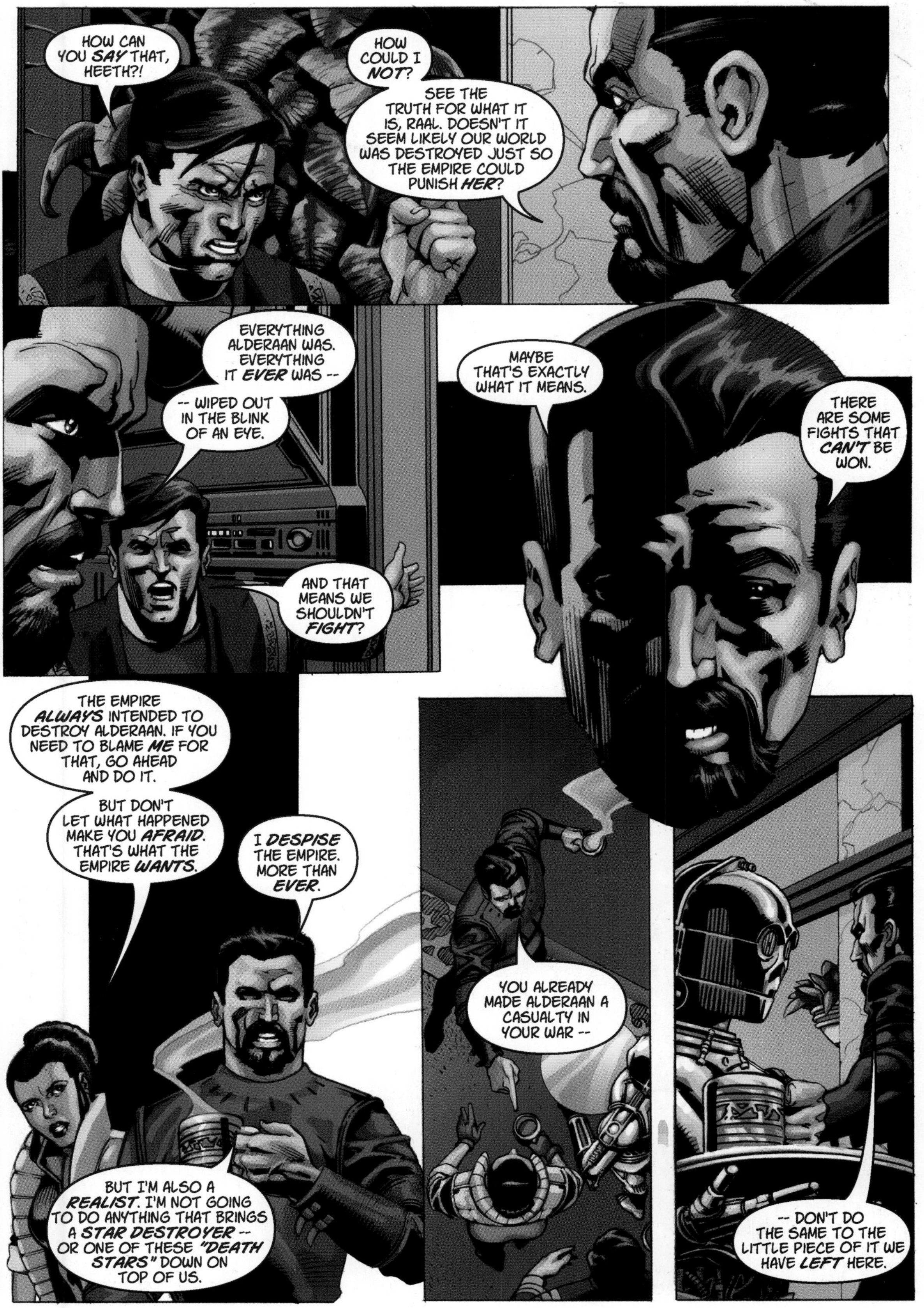
HOW CAN YOU SAY THAT, HEETH?!
HOW COULD I NOT?
SEE THE TRUTH FOR WHAT IT IS, RAAL. DOESN'T IT SEEM LIKELY OUR WORLD WAS DESTROYED JUST SO THE EMPIRE COULD PUNISH HER?
EVERYTHING ALDERAAN WAS. EVERYTHING IT EVER WAS --
-- WIPED OUT IN THE BLINK OF AN EYE.
AND THAT MEANS WE SHOULDN'T FIGHT?
MAYBE THAT'S EXACTLY WHAT IT MEANS.
THERE ARE SOME FIGHTS THAT CAN'T BE WON.
THE EMPIRE ALWAYS INTENDED TO DESTROY ALDERAAN. IF YOU NEED TO BLAME ME FOR THAT, GO AHEAD AND DO IT.
BUT DON'T LET WHAT HAPPENED MAKE YOU AFRAID. THAT'S WHAT THE EMPIRE WANTS.
I DESPISE THE EMPIRE. MORE THAN EVER.
BUT I'M ALSO A REALIST. I'M NOT GOING TO DO ANYTHING THAT BRINGS A STAR DESTROYER -- OR ONE OF THESE "DEATH STARS" DOWN ON TOP OF US.
YOU ALREADY MADE ALDERAAN A CASUALTY IN YOUR WAR --
-- DON'T DO THE SAME TO THE LITTLE PIECE OF IT WE HAVE LEFT HERE.

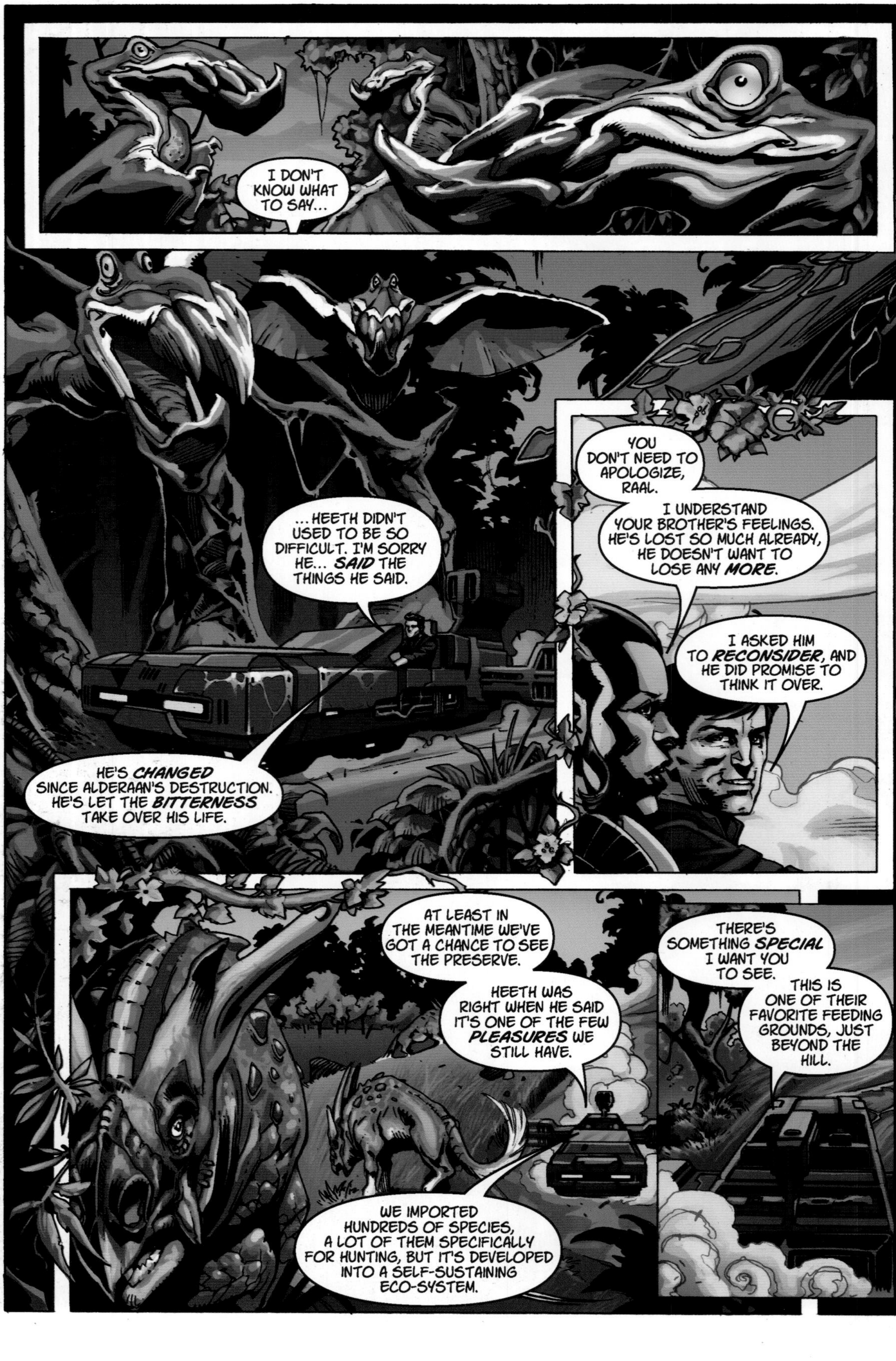
I DON'T KNOW WHAT TO SAY...
...HEETH DIDN'T USED TO BE SO DIFFICULT. I'M SORRY HE... *SAID* THE THINGS HE SAID.
HE'S *CHANGED* SINCE ALDERAAN'S DESTRUCTION. HE'S LET THE *BITTERNESS* TAKE OVER HIS LIFE.
YOU DON'T NEED TO APOLOGIZE, RAAL.
I UNDERSTAND YOUR BROTHER'S FEELINGS. HE'S LOST SO MUCH ALREADY, HE DOESN'T WANT TO LOSE ANY *MORE*.
I ASKED HIM TO *RECONSIDER*, AND HE DID PROMISE TO THINK IT OVER.
AT LEAST IN THE MEANTIME WE'VE GOT A CHANCE TO SEE THE PRESERVE.
HEETH WAS RIGHT WHEN HE SAID IT'S ONE OF THE FEW *PLEASURES* WE STILL HAVE.
WE IMPORTED HUNDREDS OF SPECIES, A LOT OF THEM SPECIFICALLY FOR HUNTING, BUT IT'S DEVELOPED INTO A SELF-SUSTAINING ECO-SYSTEM.
THERE'S SOMETHING *SPECIAL* I WANT YOU TO SEE.
THIS IS ONE OF THEIR FAVORITE FEEDING GROUNDS, JUST BEYOND THE HILL.

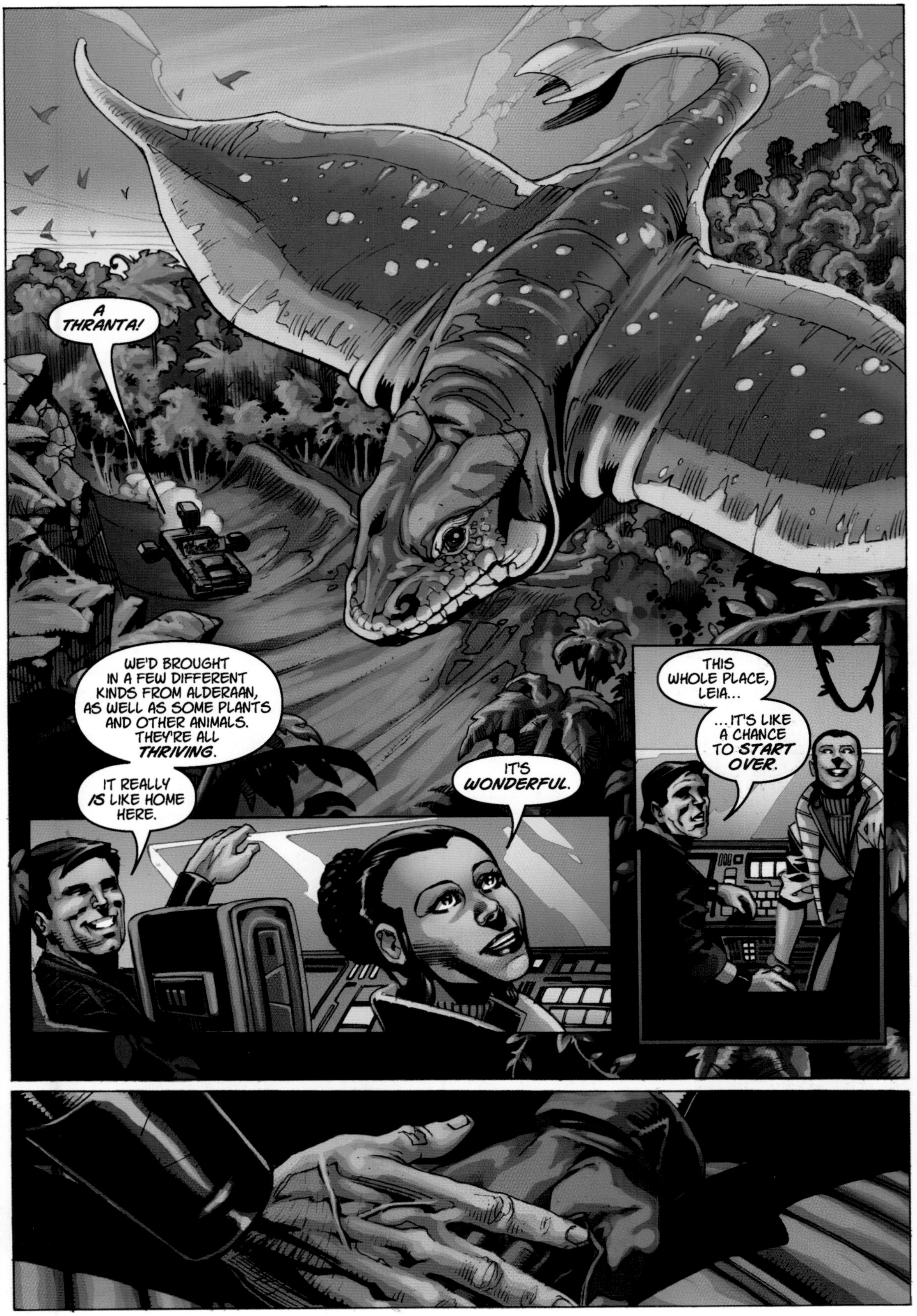
A THRANTA!
WE'D BROUGHT IN A FEW DIFFERENT KINDS FROM ALDERAAN, AS WELL AS SOME PLANTS AND OTHER ANIMALS. THEY'RE ALL THRIVING.
IT REALLY IS LIKE HOME HERE.
IT'S WONDERFUL.
THIS WHOLE PLACE, LEIA...
...IT'S LIKE A CHANCE TO START OVER.

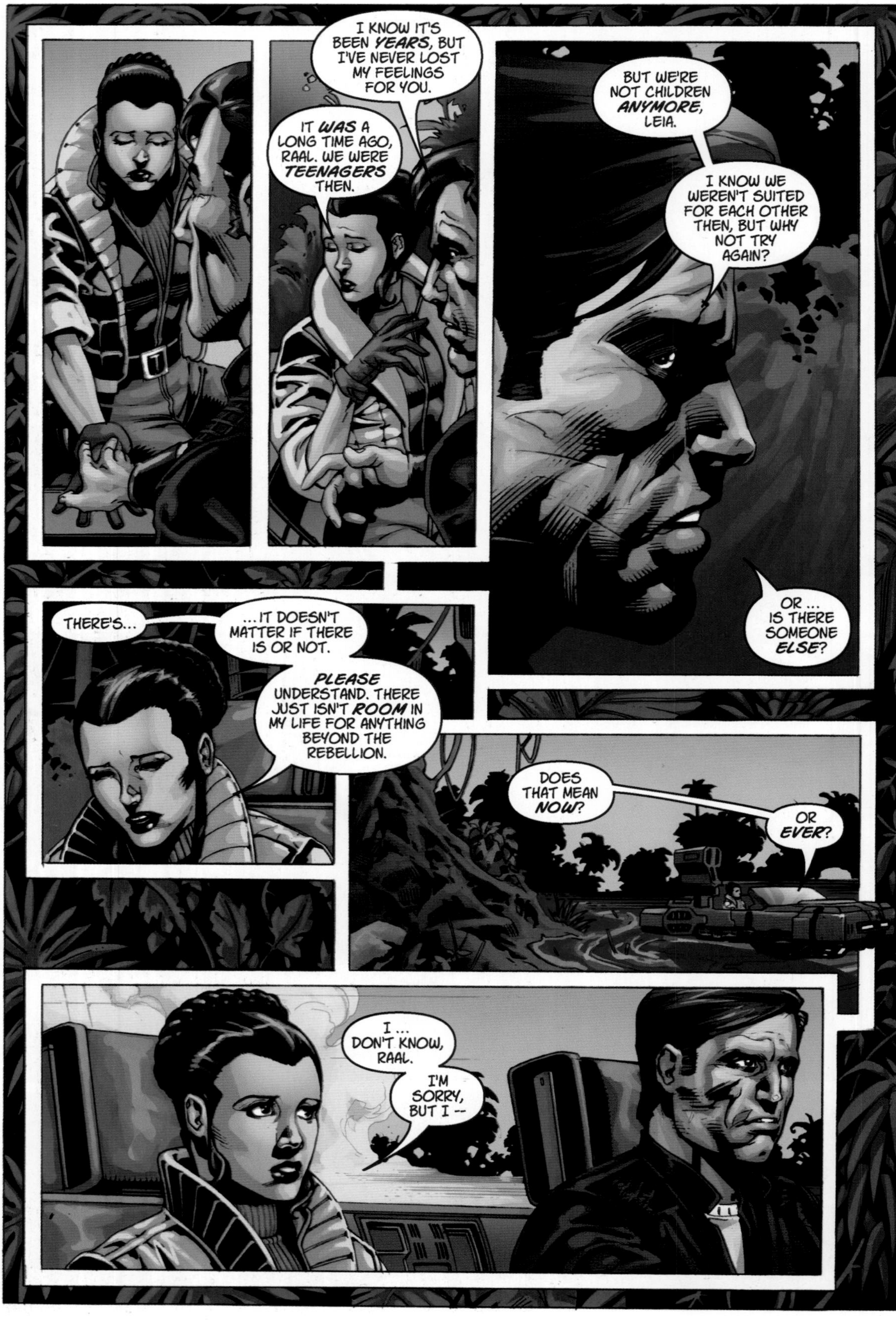
I KNOW IT'S BEEN *YEARS*, BUT I'VE NEVER LOST MY FEELINGS FOR YOU.
IT *WAS* A LONG TIME AGO, RAAL. WE WERE *TEENAGERS* THEN.
BUT WE'RE NOT CHILDREN *ANYMORE*, LEIA.
I KNOW WE WEREN'T SUITED FOR EACH OTHER THEN, BUT WHY NOT TRY AGAIN?
OR ... IS THERE SOMEONE *ELSE*?
THERE'S...
...IT DOESN'T MATTER IF THERE IS OR NOT.
PLEASE UNDERSTAND. THERE JUST ISN'T *ROOM* IN MY LIFE FOR ANYTHING BEYOND THE REBELLION.
DOES THAT MEAN *NOW*?
OR *EVER*?
I ... DON'T KNOW, RAAL.
I'M SORRY, BUT I --

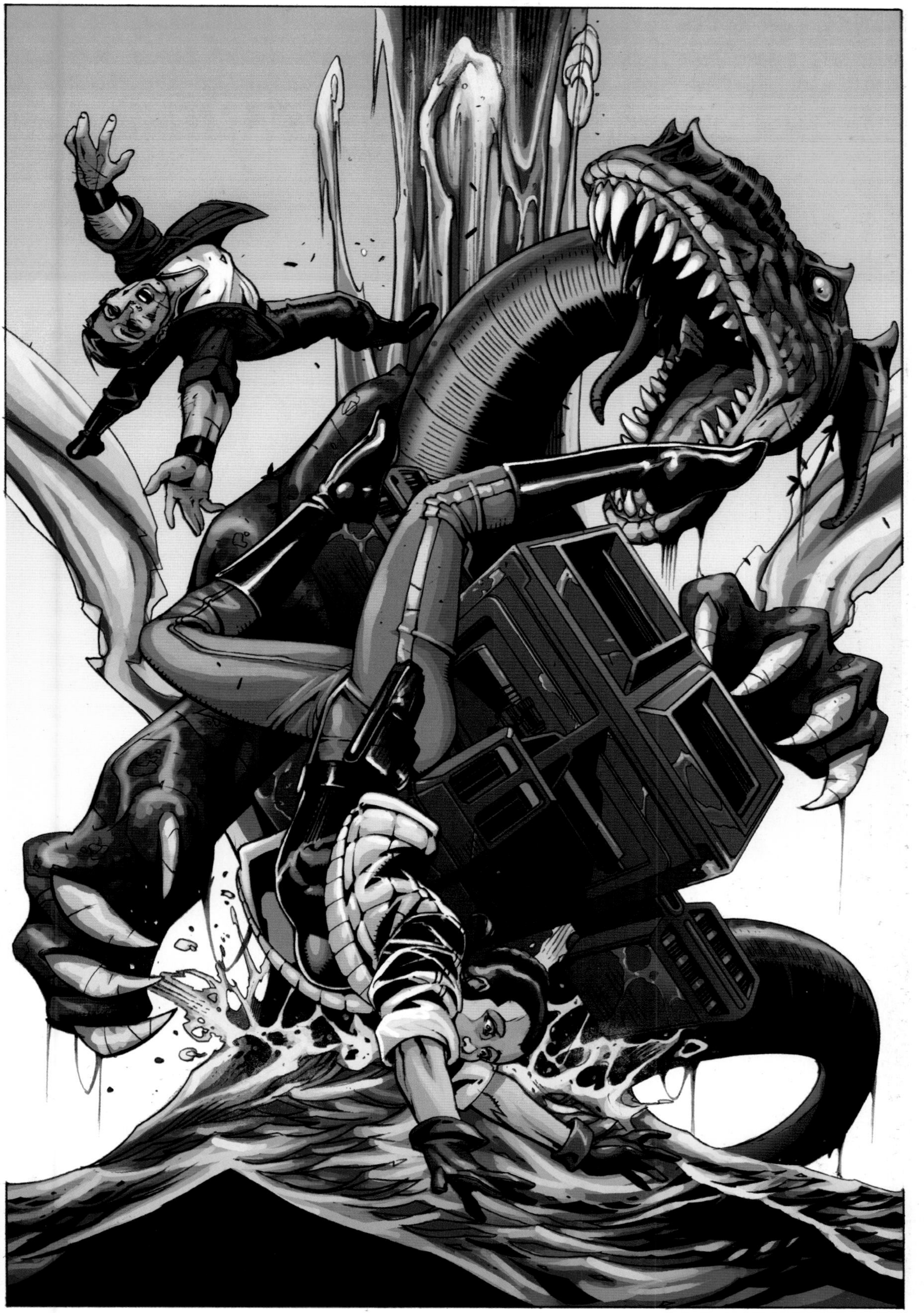

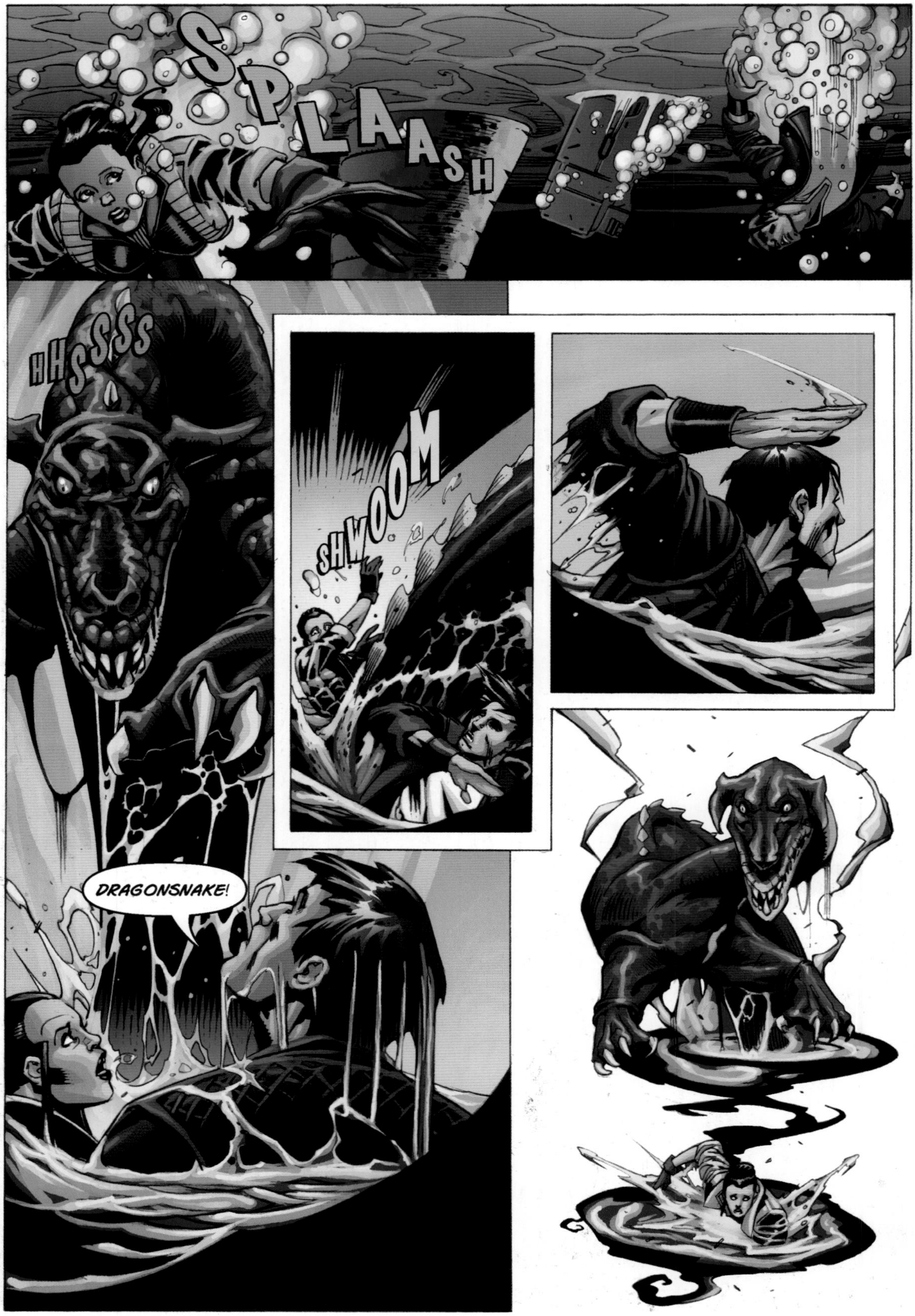
SPLAASH
HHSSSSS
SHWOOM
DRAGONSNAKE!

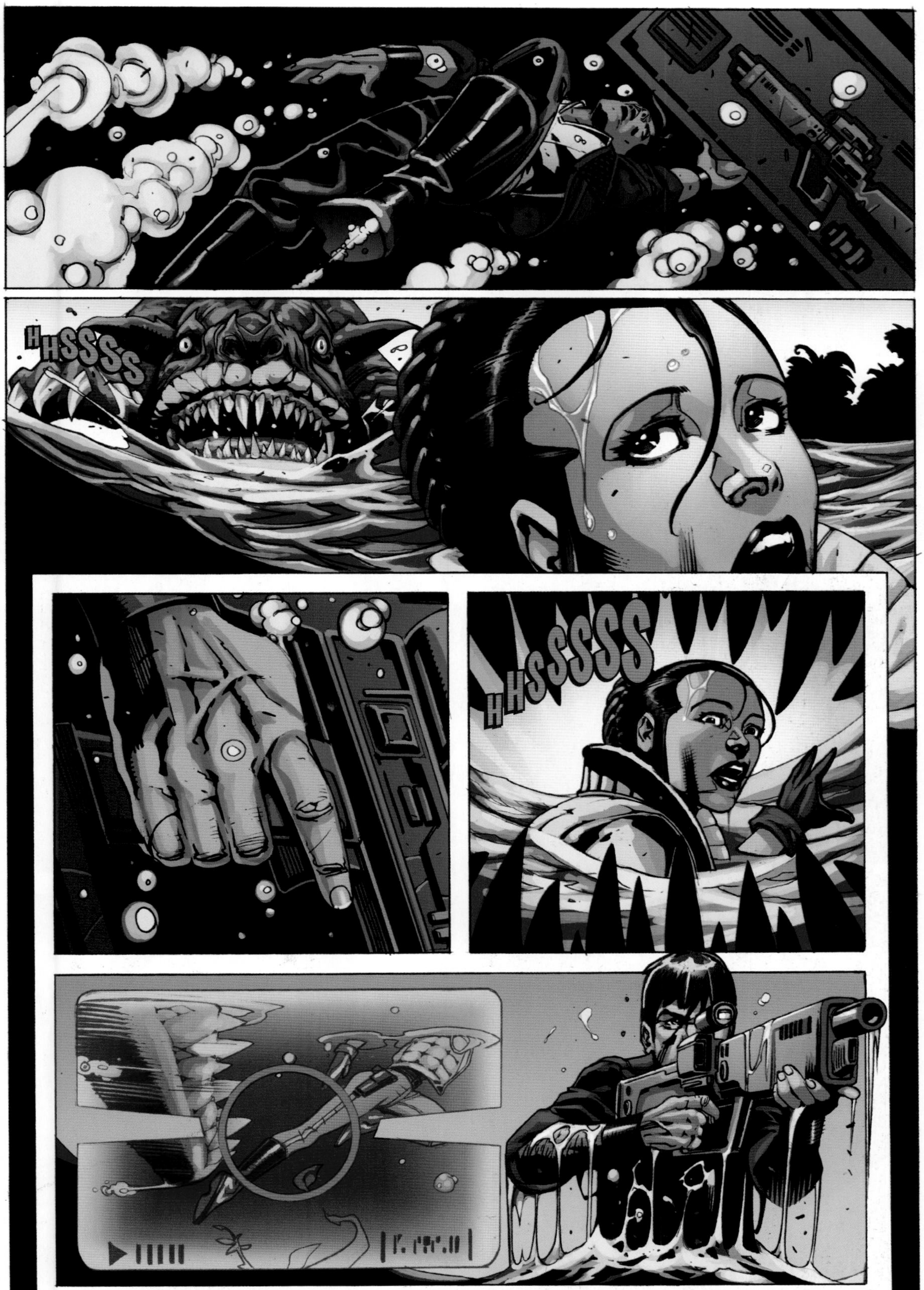
HHSSSSS
HHSSSSS

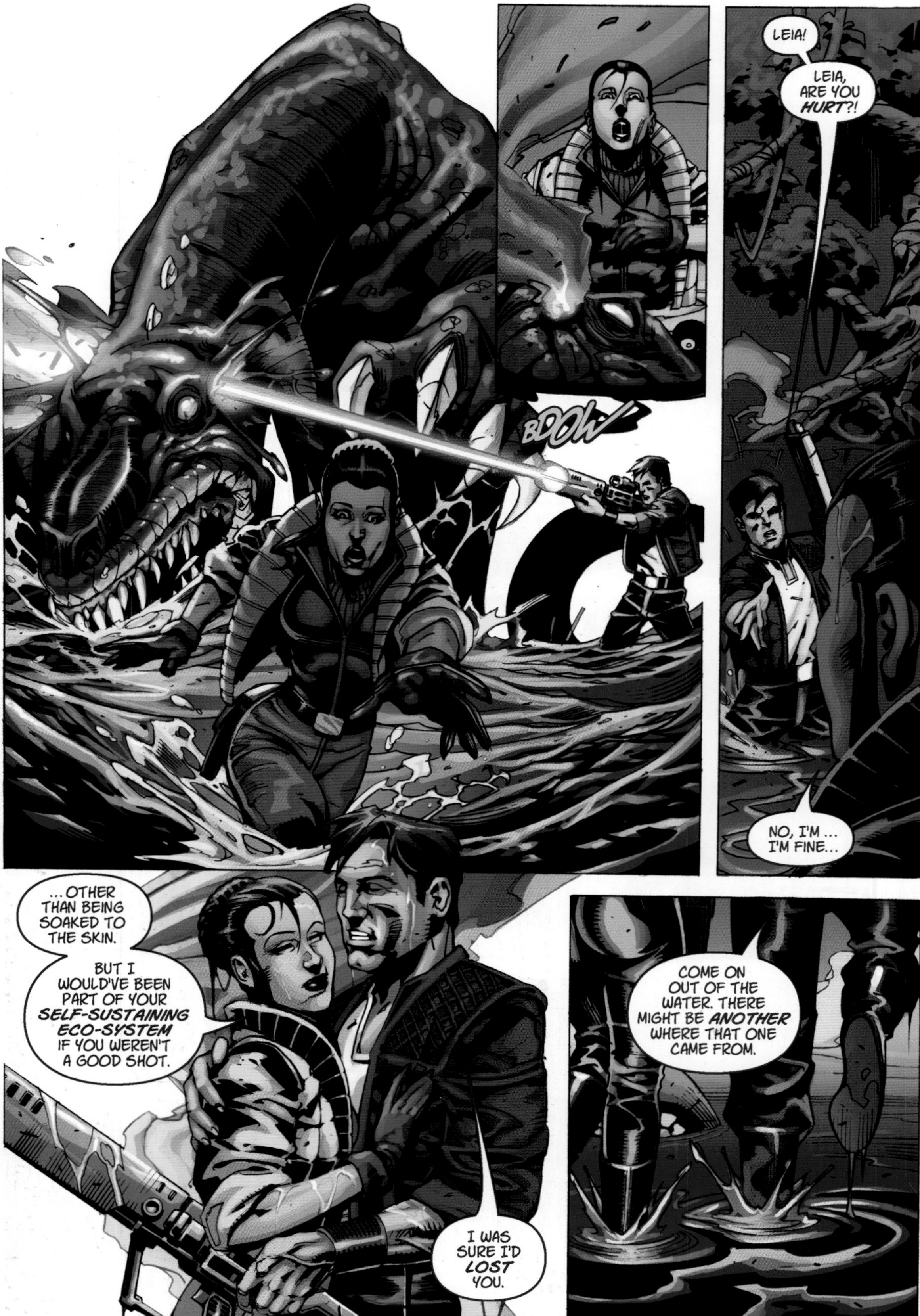

BDOW!
LEIA!
LEIA, ARE YOU HURT?!
NO, I'M ... I'M FINE...
...OTHER THAN BEING SOAKED TO THE SKIN.
BUT I WOULD'VE BEEN PART OF YOUR SELF-SUSTAINING ECO-SYSTEM IF YOU WEREN'T A GOOD SHOT.
I WAS SURE I'D LOST YOU.
COME ON OUT OF THE WATER. THERE MIGHT BE ANOTHER WHERE THAT ONE CAME FROM.

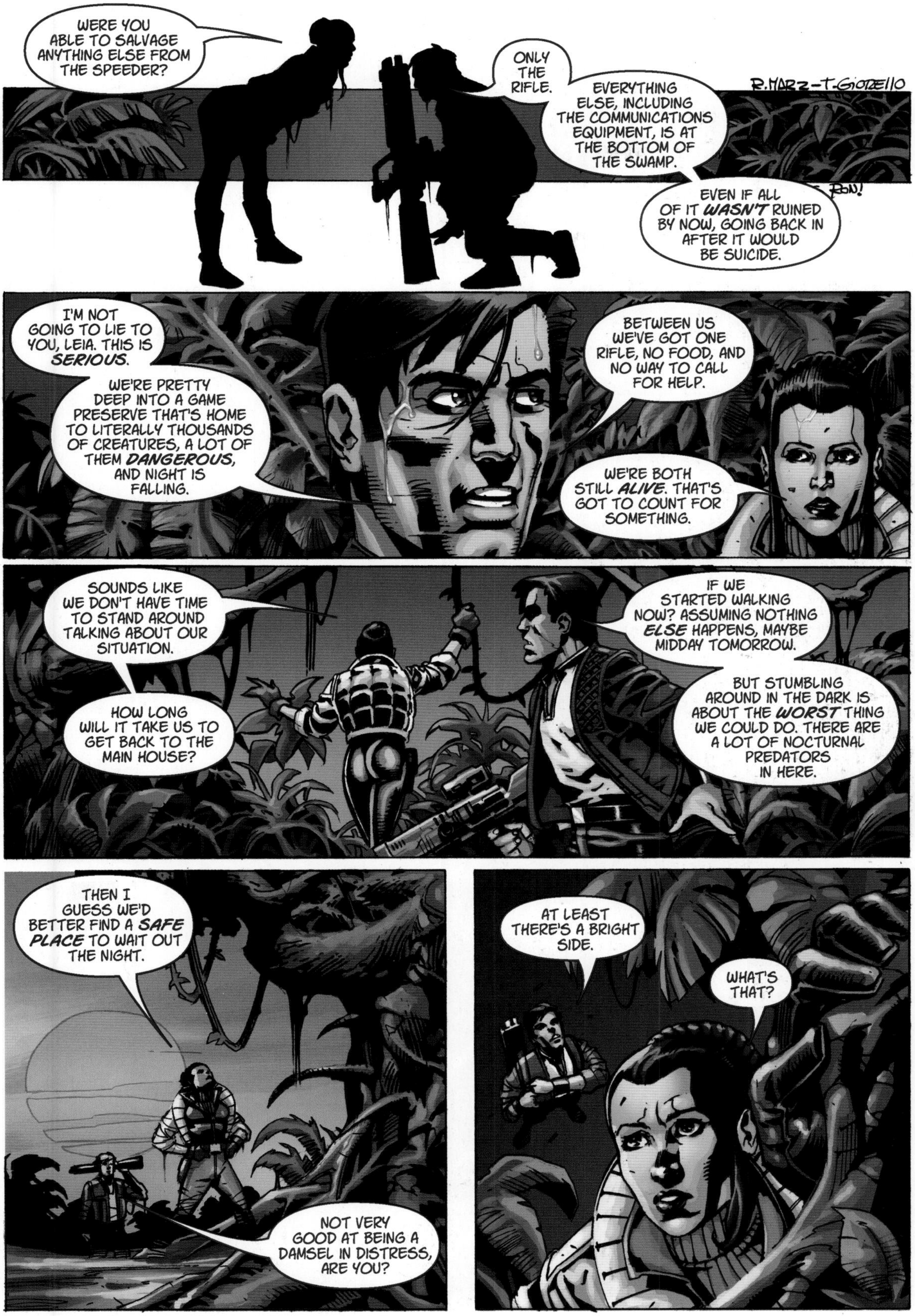
WERE YOU ABLE TO SALVAGE ANYTHING ELSE FROM THE SPEEDER?
ONLY THE RIFLE.
EVERYTHING ELSE, INCLUDING THE COMMUNICATIONS EQUIPMENT, IS AT THE BOTTOM OF THE SWAMP.
R.MARZ-T.GIORELLO
EVEN IF ALL OF IT WASN'T RUINED BY NOW, GOING BACK IN AFTER IT WOULD BE SUICIDE.
I'M NOT GOING TO LIE TO YOU, LEIA. THIS IS SERIOUS.
WE'RE PRETTY DEEP INTO A GAME PRESERVE THAT'S HOME TO LITERALLY THOUSANDS OF CREATURES, A LOT OF THEM DANGEROUS, AND NIGHT IS FALLING.
BETWEEN US WE'VE GOT ONE RIFLE, NO FOOD, AND NO WAY TO CALL FOR HELP.
WE'RE BOTH STILL ALIVE. THAT'S GOT TO COUNT FOR SOMETHING.
SOUNDS LIKE WE DON'T HAVE TIME TO STAND AROUND TALKING ABOUT OUR SITUATION.
HOW LONG WILL IT TAKE US TO GET BACK TO THE MAIN HOUSE?
IF WE STARTED WALKING NOW? ASSUMING NOTHING ELSE HAPPENS, MAYBE MIDDAY TOMORROW.
BUT STUMBLING AROUND IN THE DARK IS ABOUT THE WORST THING WE COULD DO. THERE ARE A LOT OF NOCTURNAL PREDATORS IN HERE.
THEN I GUESS WE'D BETTER FIND A SAFE PLACE TO WAIT OUT THE NIGHT.
NOT VERY GOOD AT BEING A DAMSEL IN DISTRESS, ARE YOU?
AT LEAST THERE'S A BRIGHT SIDE.
WHAT'S THAT?

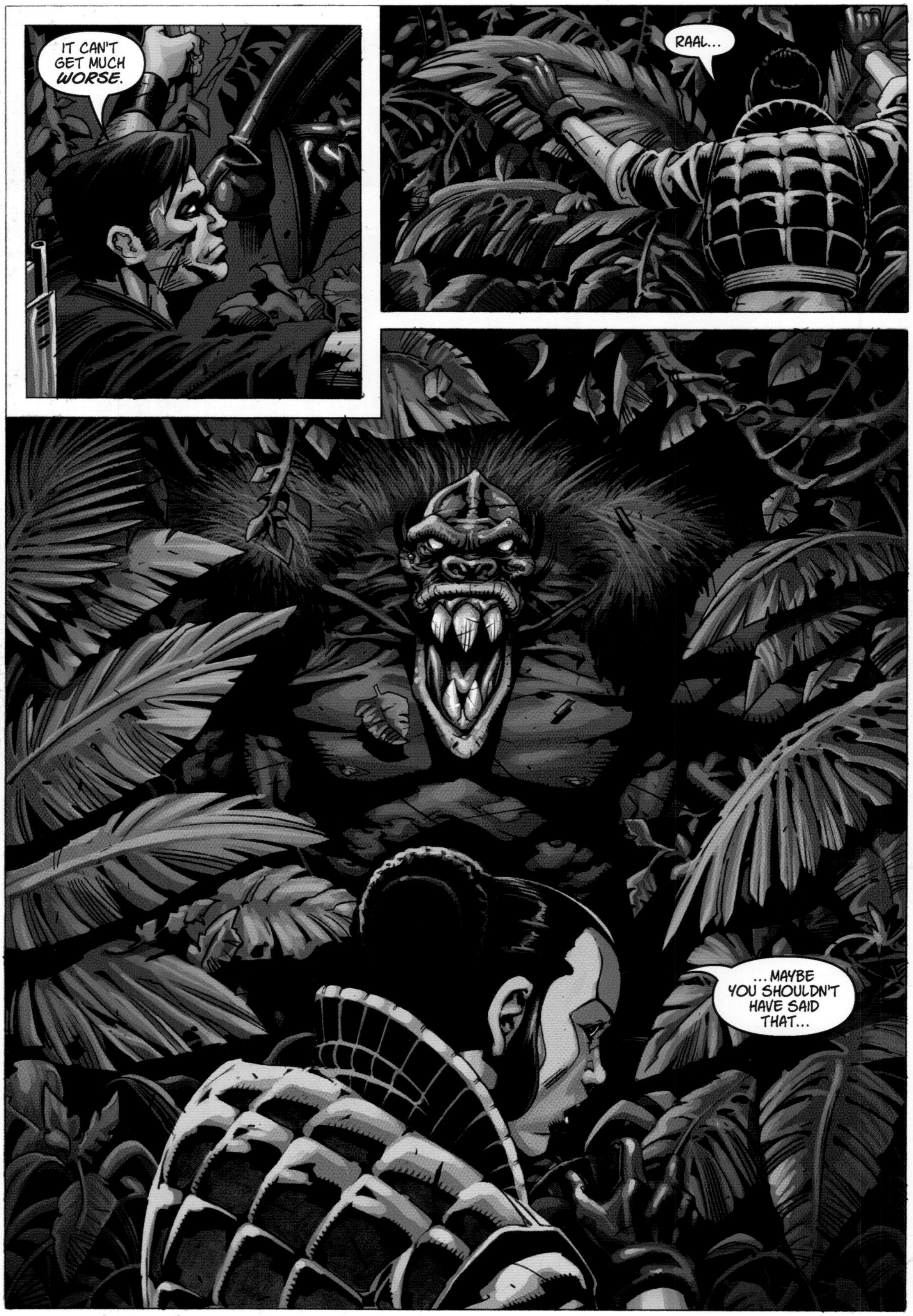
IT CAN'T GET MUCH *WORSE*.
RAAL...
...MAYBE YOU SHOULDN'T HAVE SAID THAT...

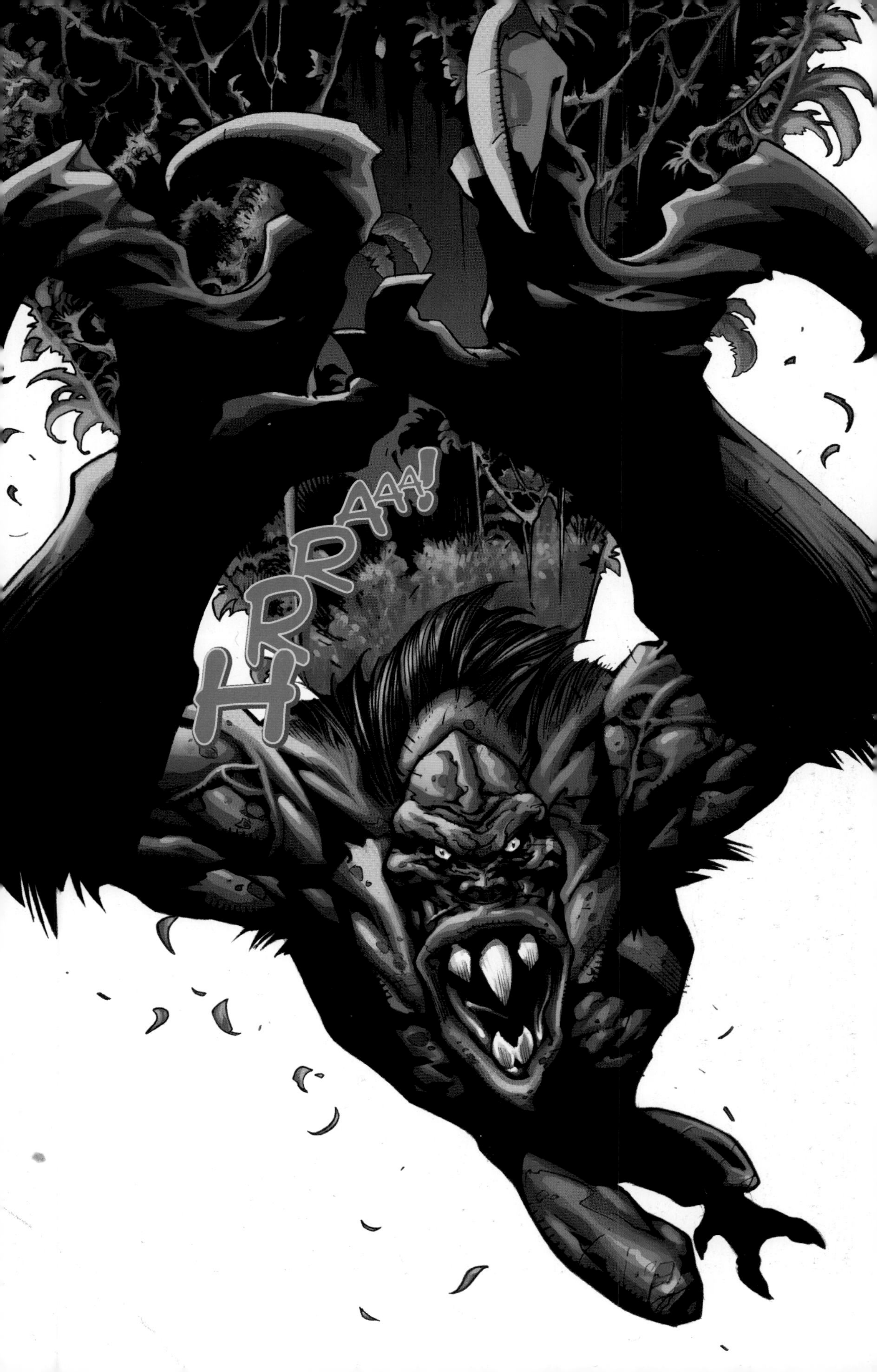
HRRAAA!

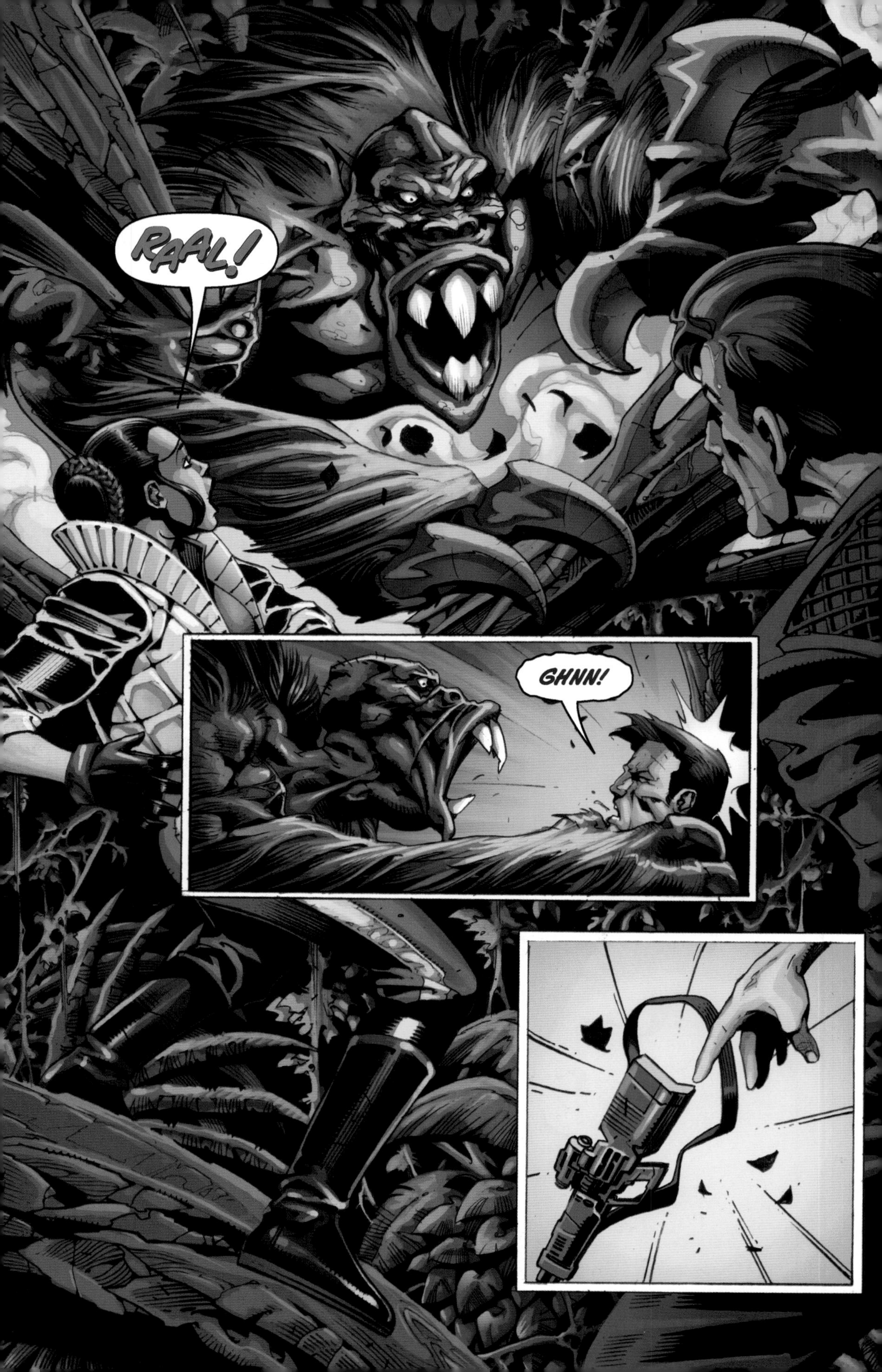
RAAL!
GHNN!

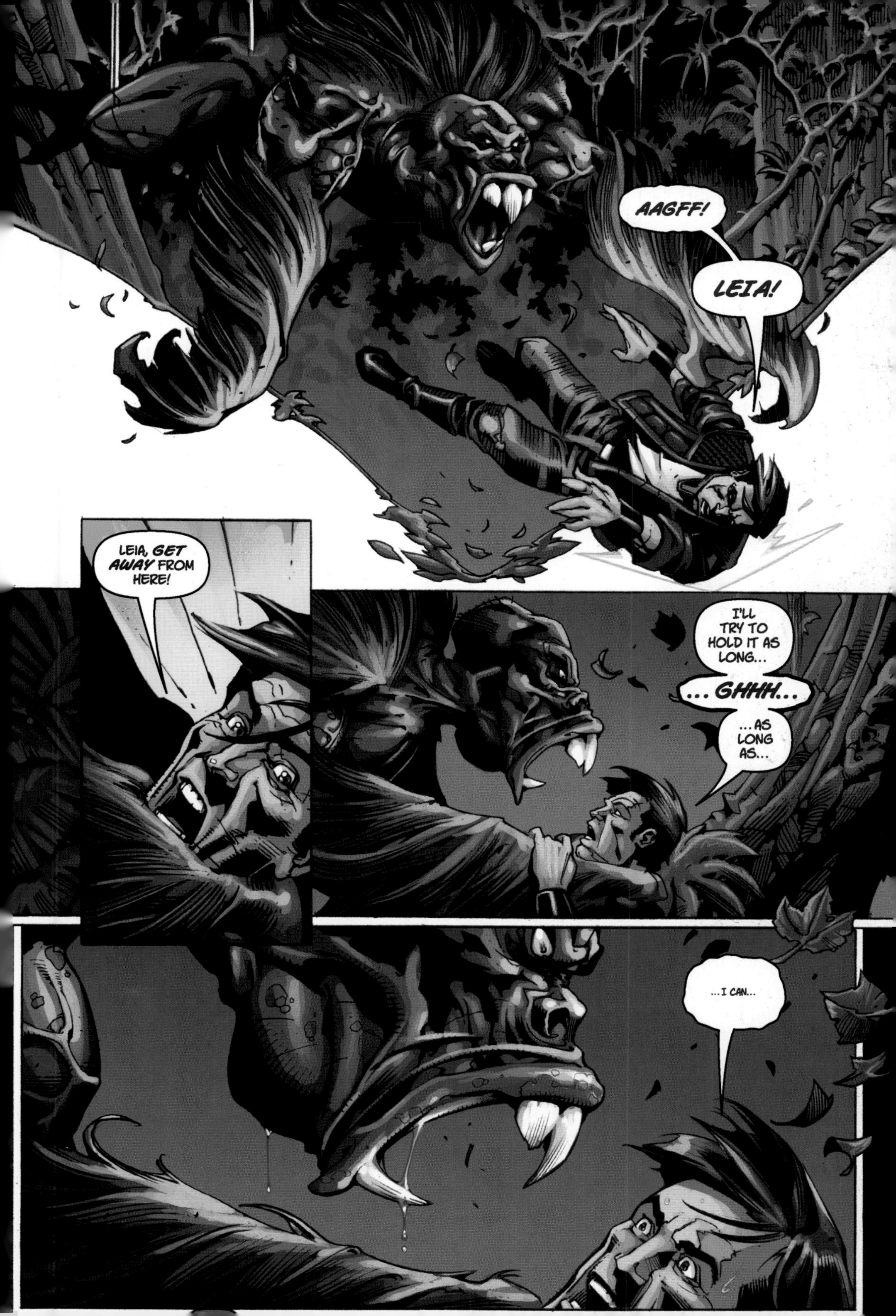
AAGFF!
LEIA!
LEIA, GET AWAY FROM HERE!
I'LL TRY TO HOLD IT AS LONG...
...GHHH...
...AS LONG AS...
...I CAN...

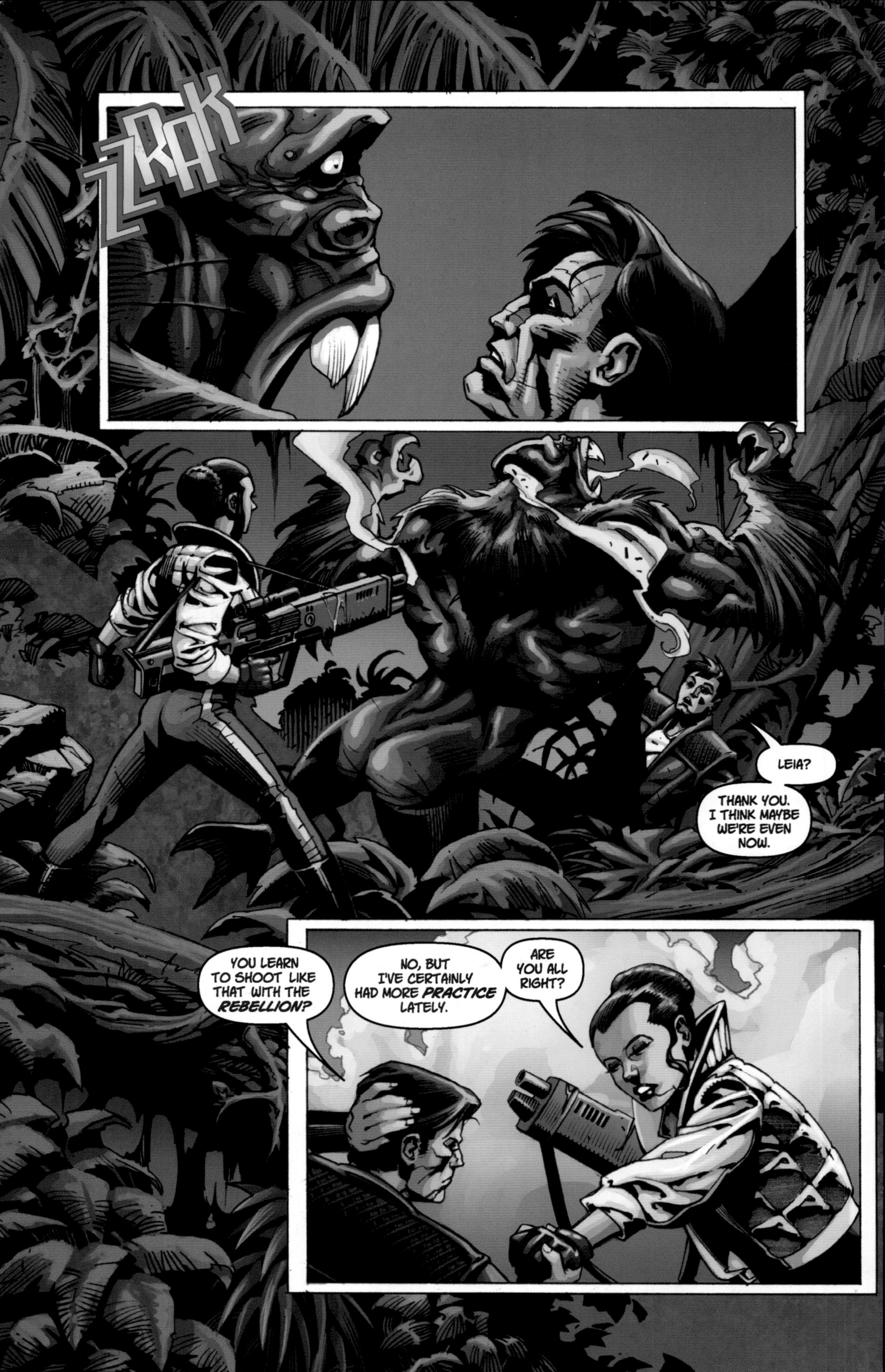
ZZRAK
LEIA?
THANK YOU. I THINK MAYBE WE'RE EVEN NOW.
YOU LEARN TO SHOOT LIKE THAT WITH THE REBELLION?
NO, BUT I'VE CERTAINLY HAD MORE PRACTICE LATELY.
ARE YOU ALL RIGHT?

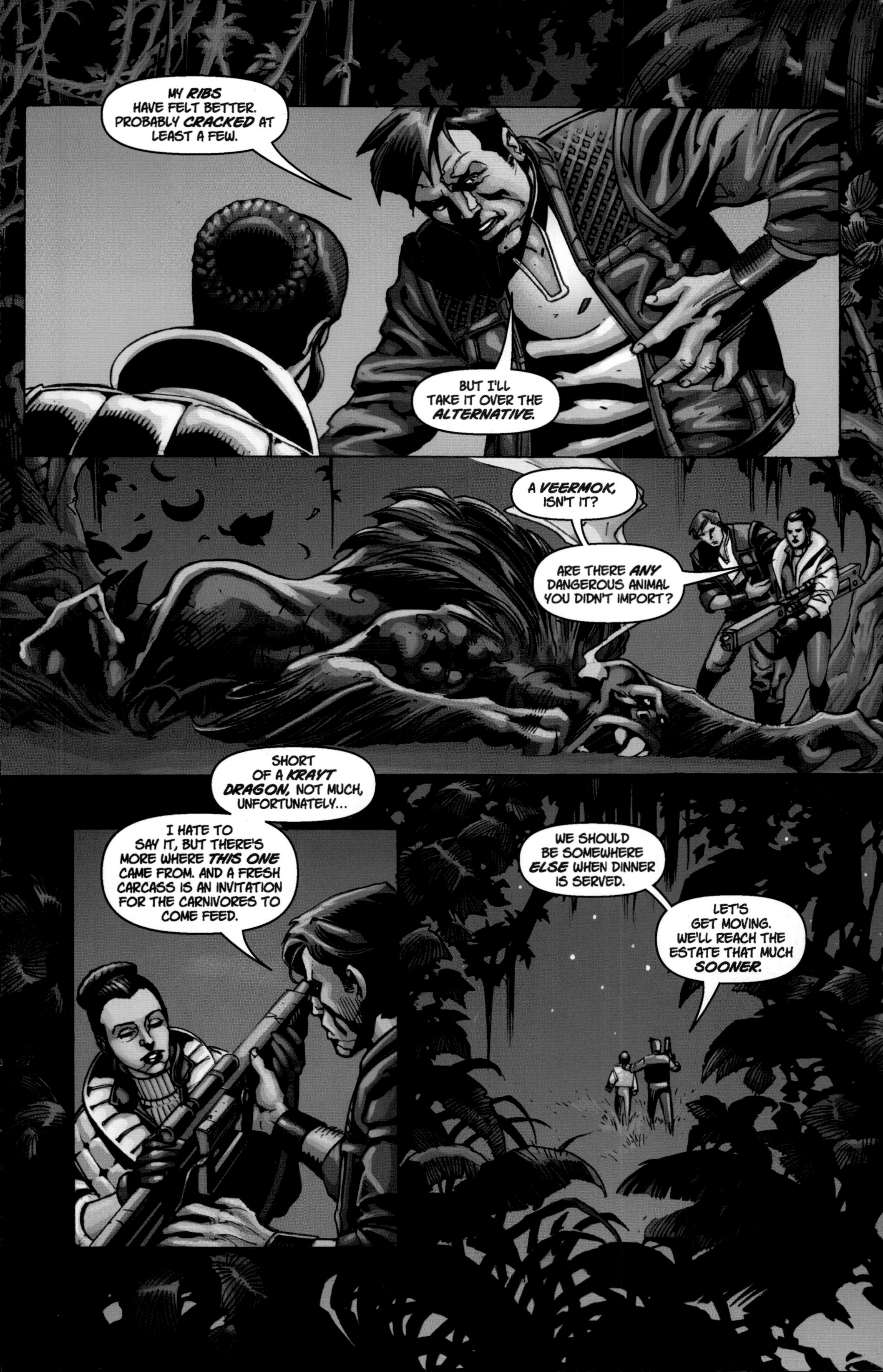
MY RIBS HAVE FELT BETTER. PROBABLY CRACKED AT LEAST A FEW.
BUT I'LL TAKE IT OVER THE ALTERNATIVE.
A VEERMOK, ISN'T IT?
ARE THERE ANY DANGEROUS ANIMAL YOU DIDN'T IMPORT?
SHORT OF A KRAYT DRAGON, NOT MUCH, UNFORTUNATELY...
I HATE TO SAY IT, BUT THERE'S MORE WHERE THIS ONE CAME FROM. AND A FRESH CARCASS IS AN INVITATION FOR THE CARNIVORES TO COME FEED.
WE SHOULD BE SOMEWHERE ELSE WHEN DINNER IS SERVED.
LET'S GET MOVING. WE'LL REACH THE ESTATE THAT MUCH SOONER.

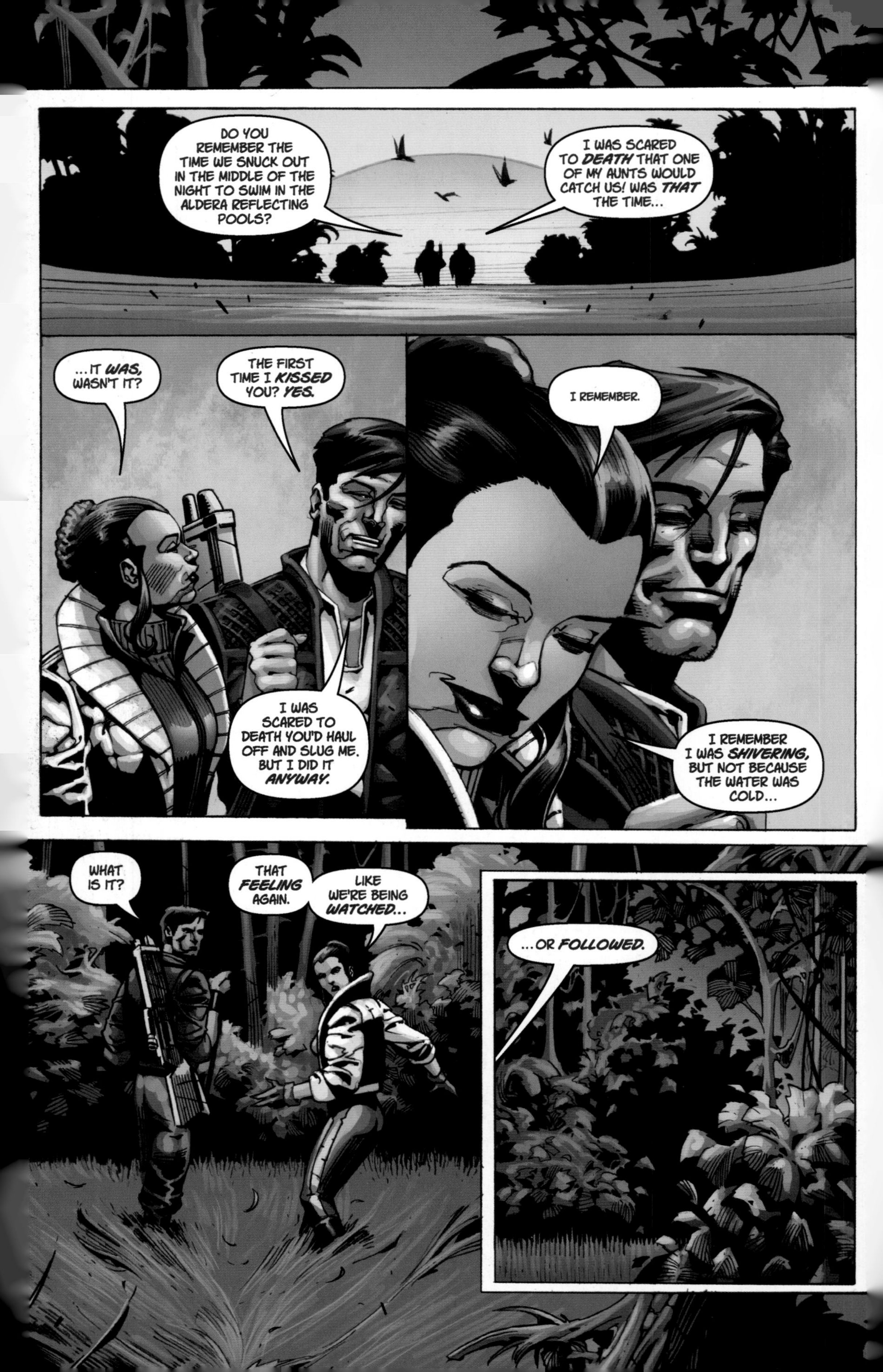
DO YOU REMEMBER THE TIME WE SNUCK OUT IN THE MIDDLE OF THE NIGHT TO SWIM IN THE ALDERA REFLECTING POOLS?
I WAS SCARED TO DEATH THAT ONE OF MY AUNTS WOULD CATCH US! WAS THAT THE TIME...
...IT WAS, WASN'T IT?
THE FIRST TIME I KISSED YOU? YES.
I WAS SCARED TO DEATH YOU'D HAUL OFF AND SLUG ME. BUT I DID IT ANYWAY.
I REMEMBER.
I REMEMBER I WAS SHIVERING, BUT NOT BECAUSE THE WATER WAS COLD...
WHAT IS IT?
THAT FEELING AGAIN.
LIKE WE'RE BEING WATCHED...
...OR FOLLOWED.

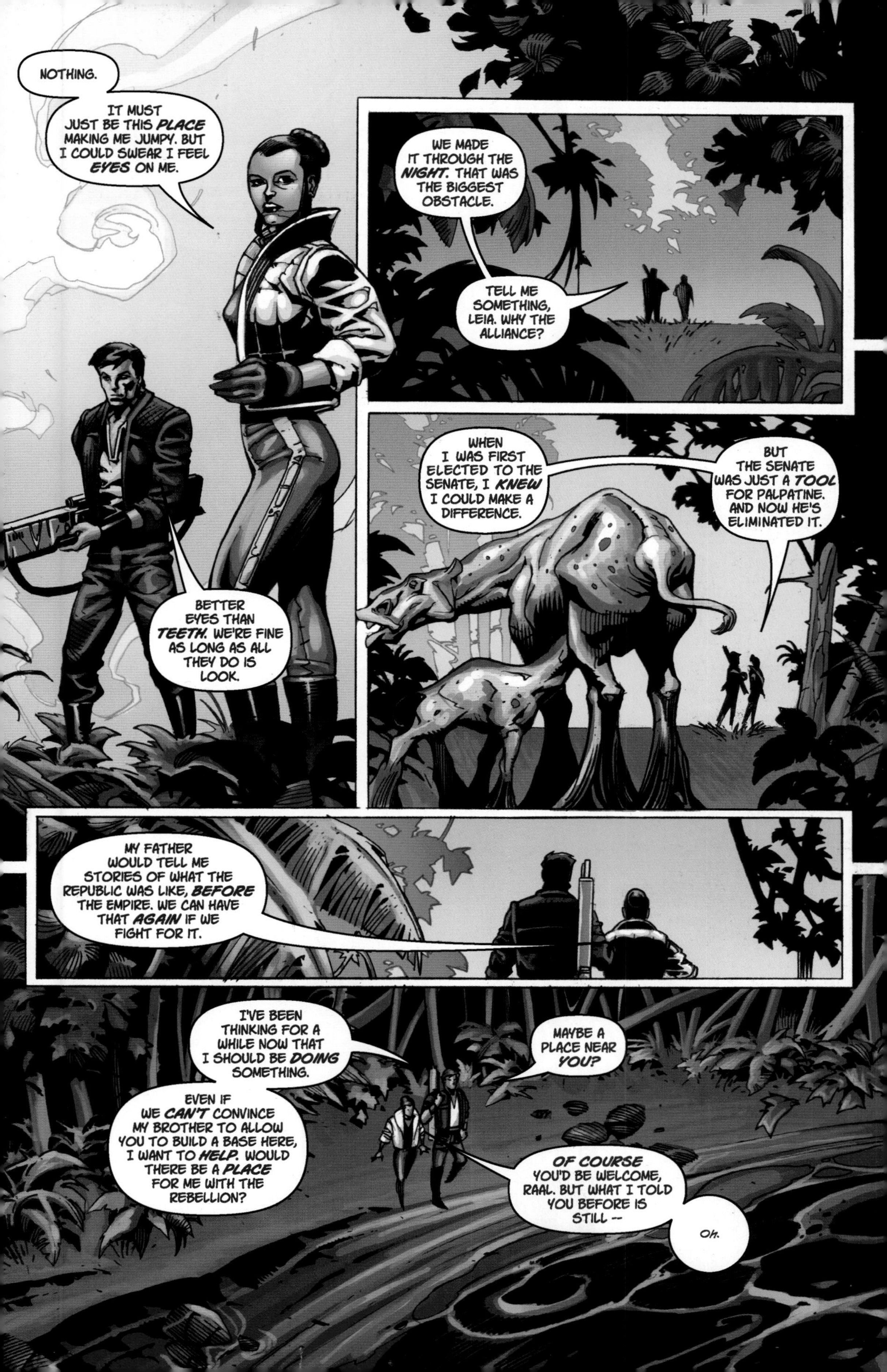
NOTHING.
IT MUST JUST BE THIS PLACE MAKING ME JUMPY. BUT I COULD SWEAR I FEEL EYES ON ME.
BETTER EYES THAN TEETH. WE'RE FINE AS LONG AS ALL THEY DO IS LOOK.
WE MADE IT THROUGH THE NIGHT. THAT WAS THE BIGGEST OBSTACLE.
TELL ME SOMETHING, LEIA. WHY THE ALLIANCE?
WHEN I WAS FIRST ELECTED TO THE SENATE, I KNEW I COULD MAKE A DIFFERENCE.
BUT THE SENATE WAS JUST A TOOL FOR PALPATINE. AND NOW HE'S ELIMINATED IT.
MY FATHER WOULD TELL ME STORIES OF WHAT THE REPUBLIC WAS LIKE, BEFORE THE EMPIRE. WE CAN HAVE THAT AGAIN IF WE FIGHT FOR IT.
I'VE BEEN THINKING FOR A WHILE NOW THAT I SHOULD BE DOING SOMETHING.
EVEN IF WE CAN'T CONVINCE MY BROTHER TO ALLOW YOU TO BUILD A BASE HERE, I WANT TO HELP. WOULD THERE BE A PLACE FOR ME WITH THE REBELLION?
MAYBE A PLACE NEAR YOU?
OF COURSE YOU'D BE WELCOME, RAAL. BUT WHAT I TOLD YOU BEFORE IS STILL --
Oh.

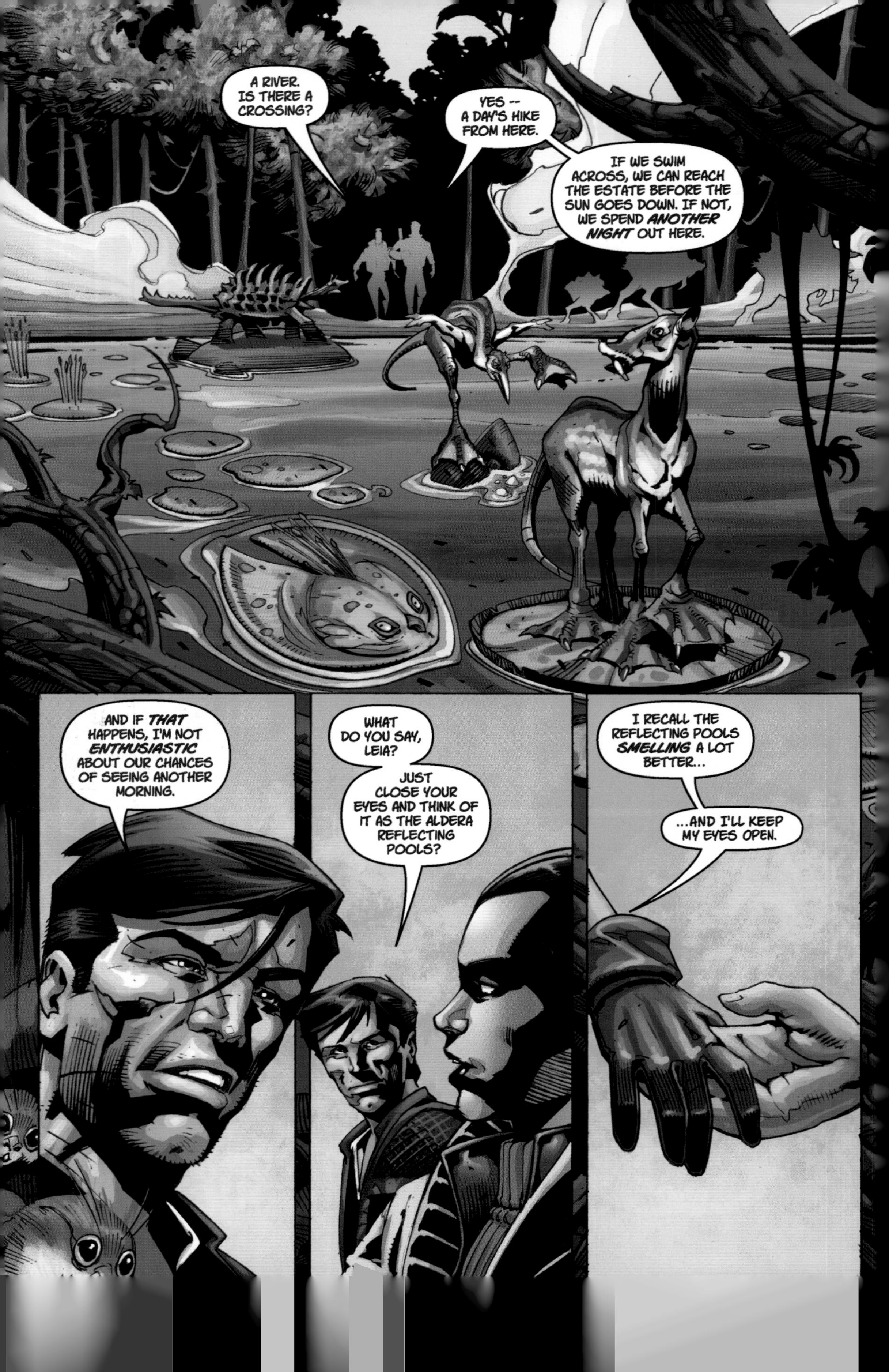
A RIVER. IS THERE A CROSSING?
YES -- A DAY'S HIKE FROM HERE.
IF WE SWIM ACROSS, WE CAN REACH THE ESTATE BEFORE THE SUN GOES DOWN. IF NOT, WE SPEND *ANOTHER NIGHT* OUT HERE.
AND IF *THAT* HAPPENS, I'M NOT *ENTHUSIASTIC* ABOUT OUR CHANCES OF SEEING ANOTHER MORNING.
WHAT DO YOU SAY, LEIA?
JUST CLOSE YOUR EYES AND THINK OF IT AS THE ALDERA REFLECTING POOLS?
I RECALL THE REFLECTING POOLS *SMELLING* A LOT BETTER...
...AND I'LL KEEP MY EYES OPEN.

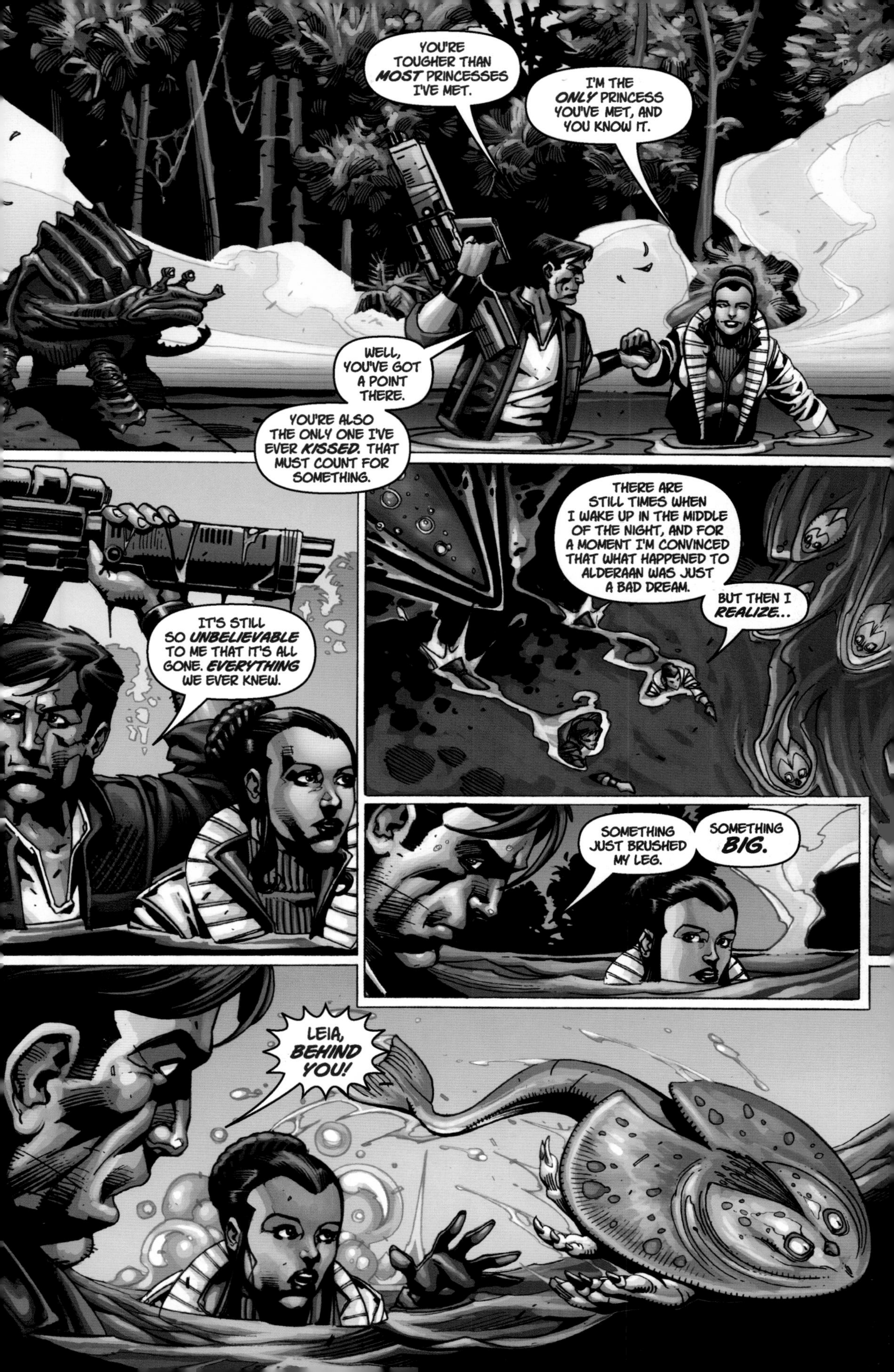
YOU'RE TOUGHER THAN MOST PRINCESSES I'VE MET.
I'M THE ONLY PRINCESS YOU'VE MET, AND YOU KNOW IT.
WELL, YOU'VE GOT A POINT THERE.
YOU'RE ALSO THE ONLY ONE I'VE EVER KISSED. THAT MUST COUNT FOR SOMETHING.
IT'S STILL SO UNBELIEVABLE TO ME THAT IT'S ALL GONE. EVERYTHING WE EVER KNEW.
THERE ARE STILL TIMES WHEN I WAKE UP IN THE MIDDLE OF THE NIGHT, AND FOR A MOMENT I'M CONVINCED THAT WHAT HAPPENED TO ALDERAAN WAS JUST A BAD DREAM.
BUT THEN I REALIZE...
SOMETHING JUST BRUSHED MY LEG.
SOMETHING BIG.
LEIA, BEHIND YOU!

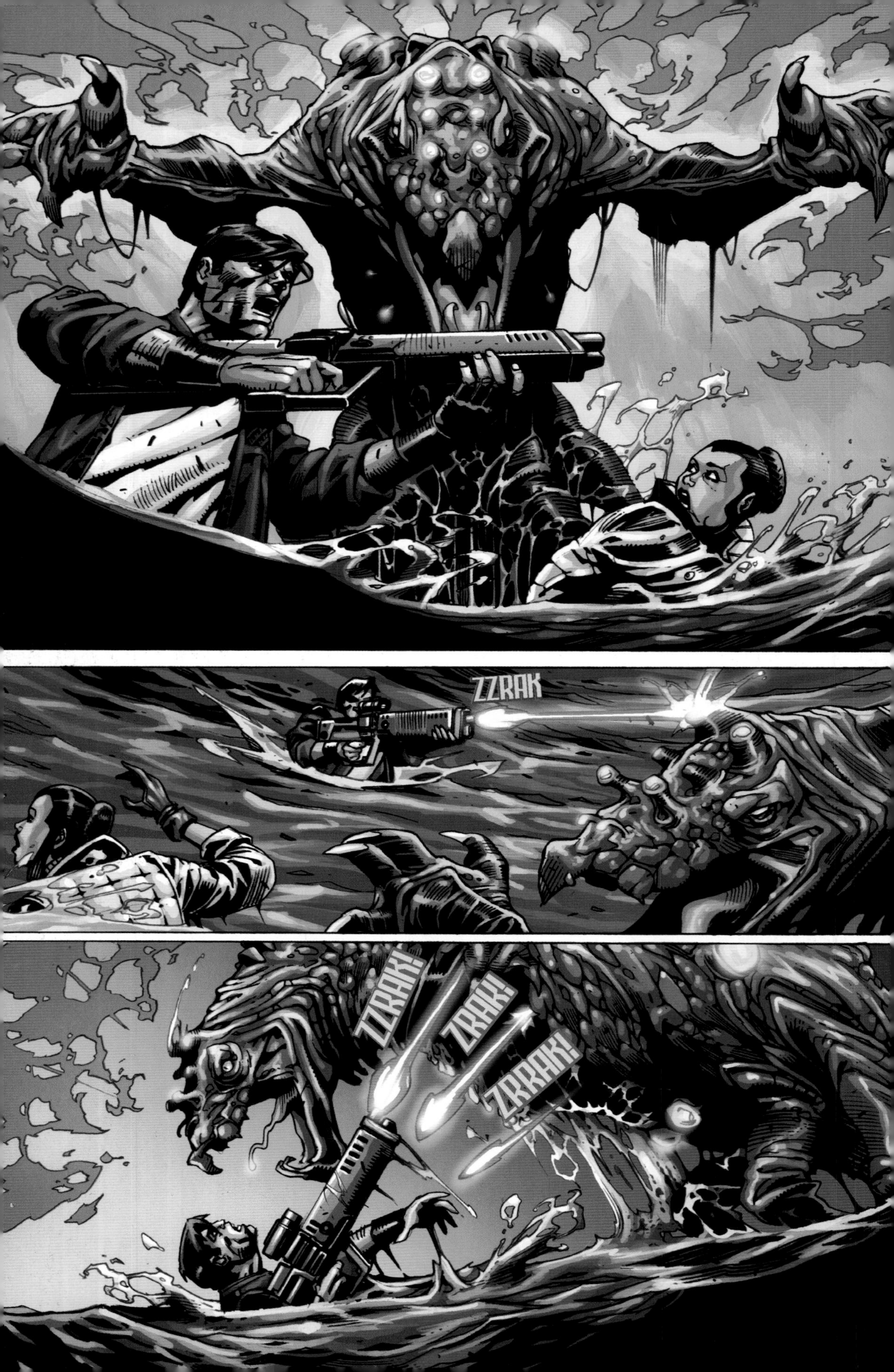
ZZRAK
ZZRAK!
ZRAK!
ZRRAK!

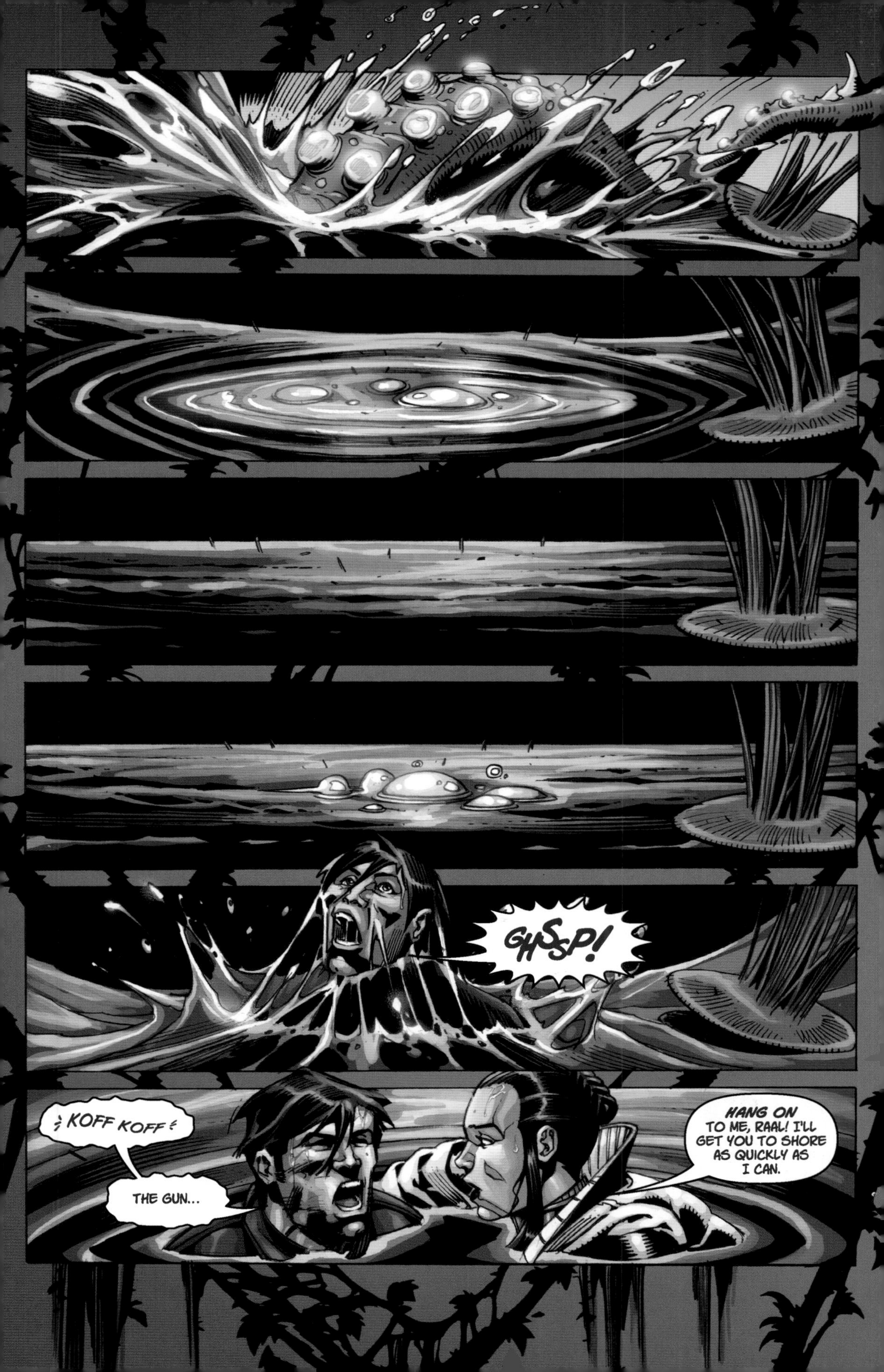
GHSSP!
KOFF KOFF
THE GUN...
HANG ON TO ME, RAAL! I'LL GET YOU TO SHORE AS QUICKLY AS I CAN.

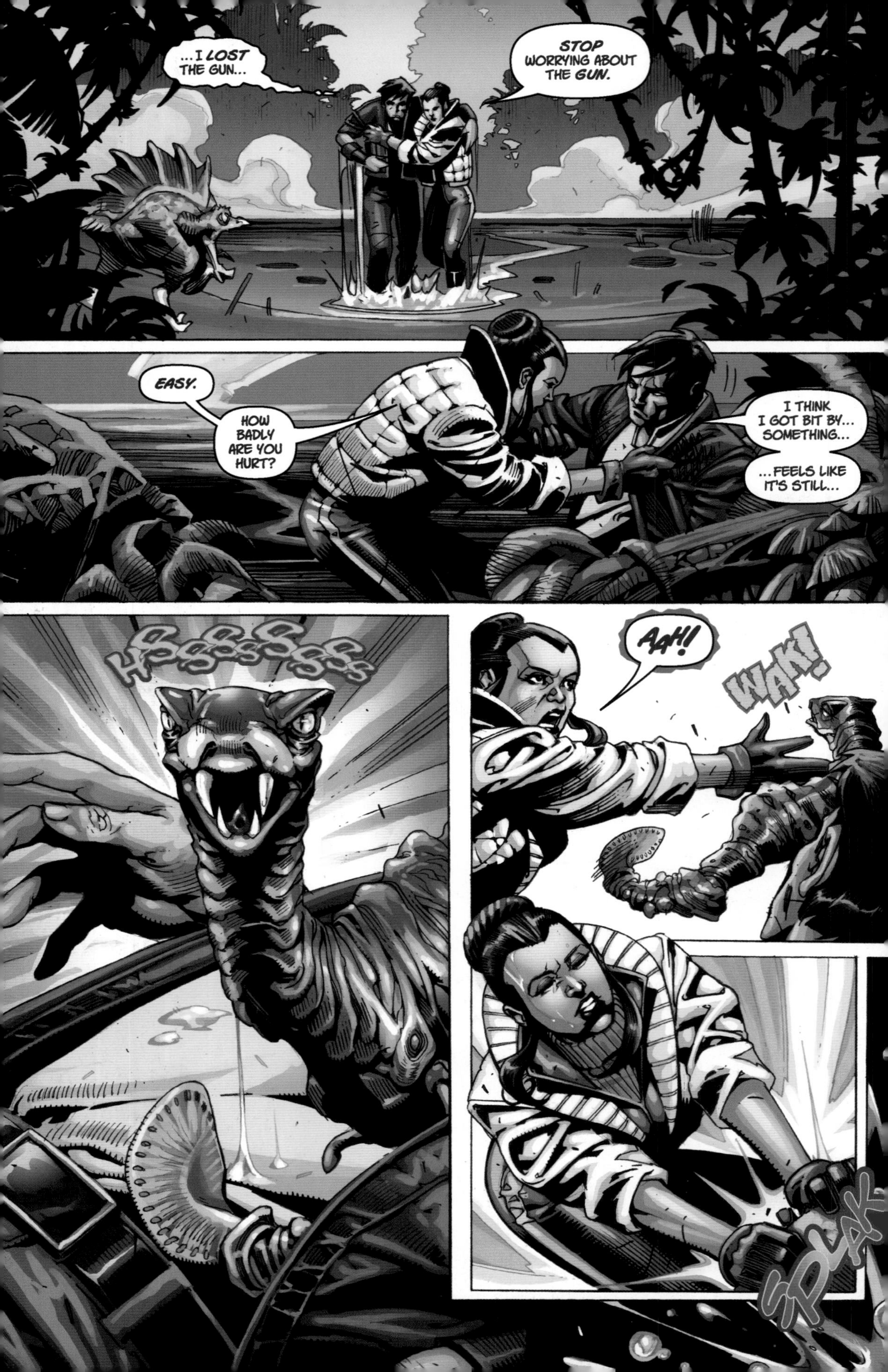
...I LOST THE GUN...
STOP WORRYING ABOUT THE GUN.
EASY.
HOW BADLY ARE YOU HURT?
I THINK I GOT BIT BY... SOMETHING...
...FEELS LIKE IT'S STILL...
AAH!
WAK!
SPLAK

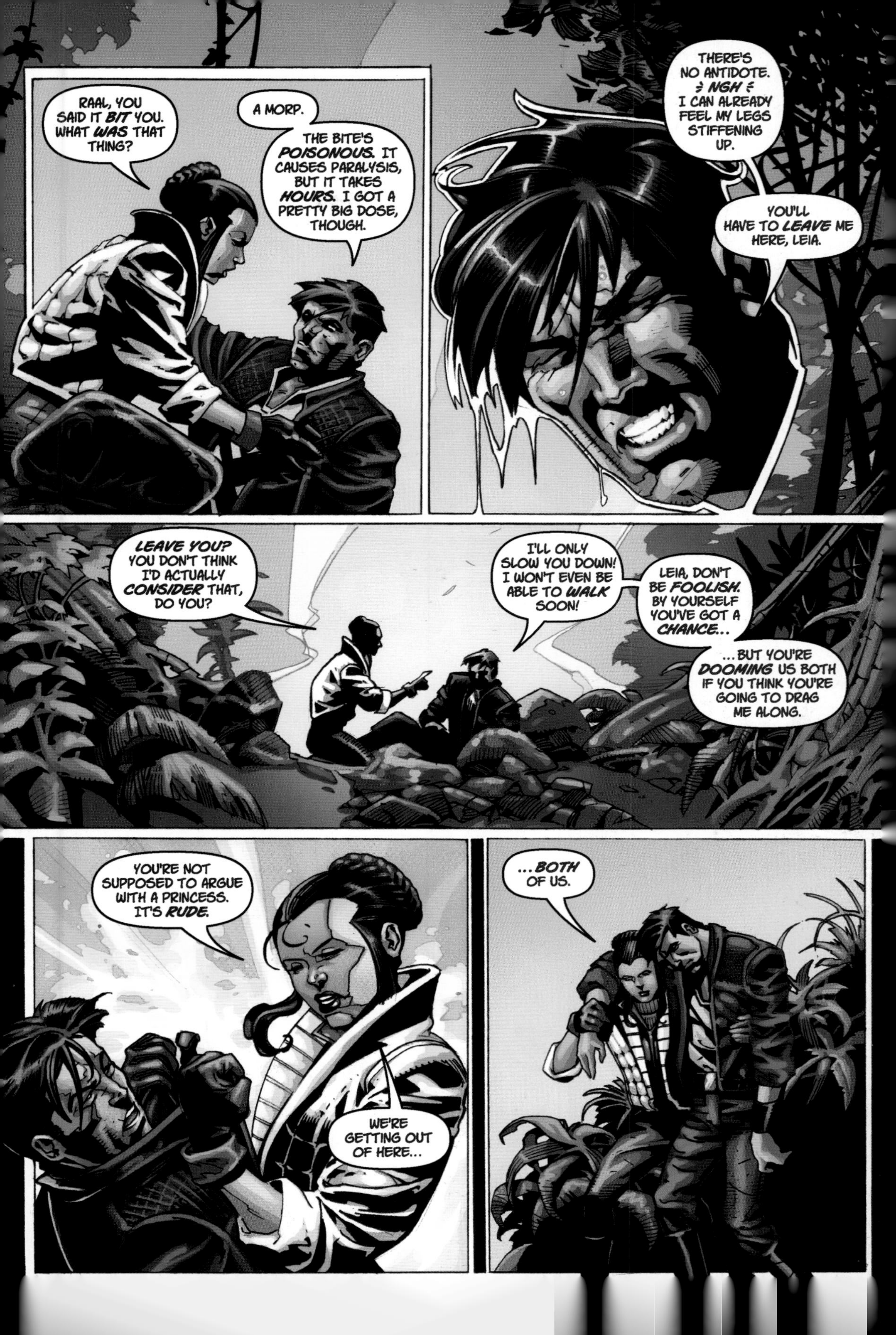
RAAL, YOU SAID IT BIT YOU. WHAT WAS THAT THING?
A MORP.
THE BITE'S POISONOUS. IT CAUSES PARALYSIS, BUT IT TAKES HOURS. I GOT A PRETTY BIG DOSE, THOUGH.
THERE'S NO ANTIDOTE. NGH I CAN ALREADY FEEL MY LEGS STIFFENING UP.
YOU'LL HAVE TO LEAVE ME HERE, LEIA.
LEAVE YOU? YOU DON'T THINK I'D ACTUALLY CONSIDER THAT, DO YOU?
I'LL ONLY SLOW YOU DOWN! I WON'T EVEN BE ABLE TO WALK SOON!
LEIA, DON'T BE FOOLISH. BY YOURSELF YOU'VE GOT A CHANCE...
...BUT YOU'RE DOOMING US BOTH IF YOU THINK YOU'RE GOING TO DRAG ME ALONG.
YOU'RE NOT SUPPOSED TO ARGUE WITH A PRINCESS. IT'S RUDE.
WE'RE GETTING OUT OF HERE...
...BOTH OF US.

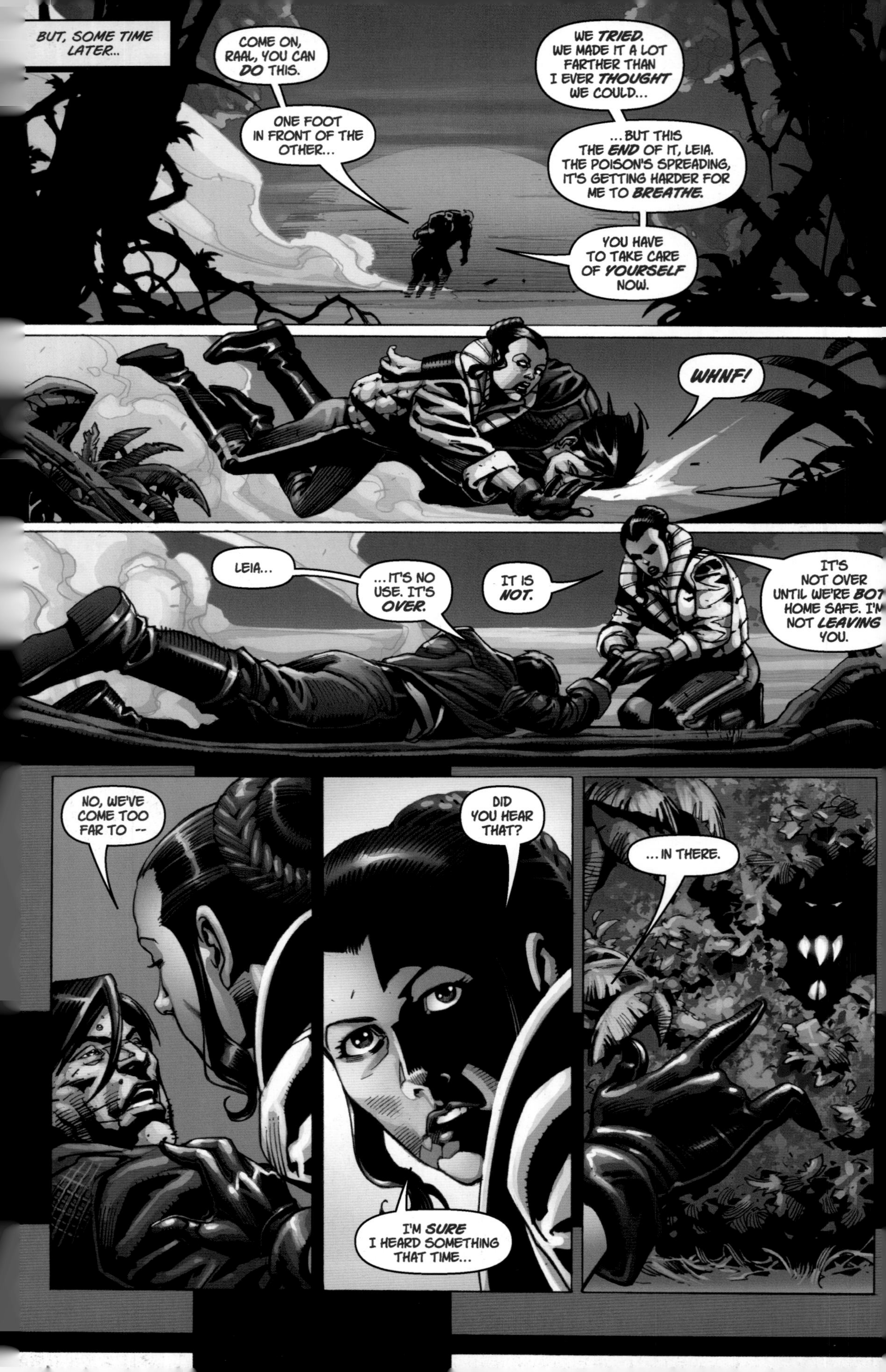

BUT, SOME TIME LATER...
COME ON, RAAL, YOU CAN DO THIS.
ONE FOOT IN FRONT OF THE OTHER...
WE TRIED. WE MADE IT A LOT FARTHER THAN I EVER THOUGHT WE COULD...
...BUT THIS THE END OF IT, LEIA. THE POISON'S SPREADING, IT'S GETTING HARDER FOR ME TO BREATHE.
YOU HAVE TO TAKE CARE OF YOURSELF NOW.
WHNF!
LEIA...
...IT'S NO USE. IT'S OVER.
IT IS NOT.
IT'S NOT OVER UNTIL WE'RE BOT HOME SAFE. I'M NOT LEAVING YOU.
NO, WE'VE COME TOO FAR TO --
DID YOU HEAR THAT?
I'M SURE I HEARD SOMETHING THAT TIME...
...IN THERE.

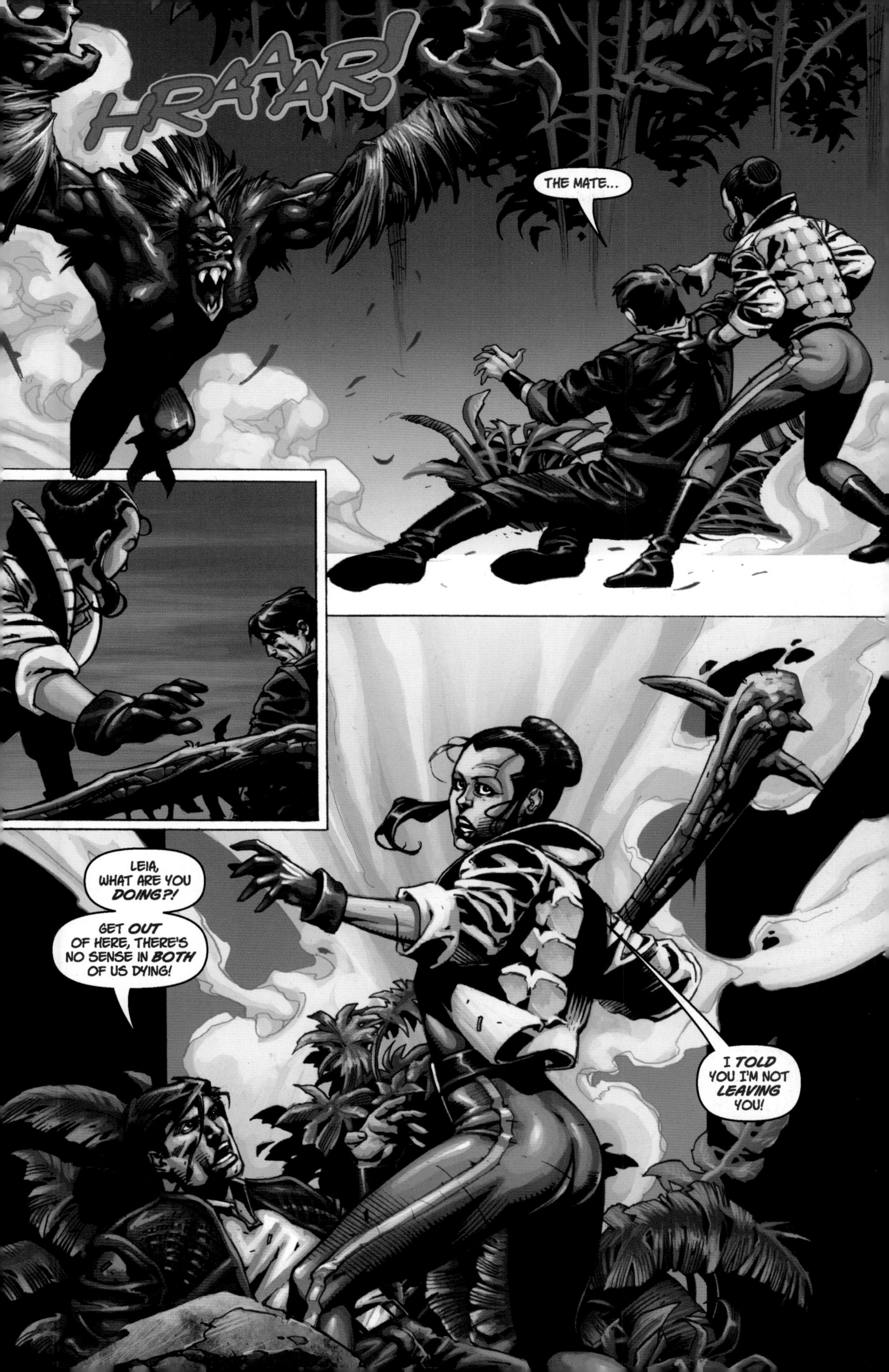
HRAAAR!
THE MATE...
LEIA, WHAT ARE YOU *DOING?!*
GET *OUT* OF HERE, THERE'S NO SENSE IN *BOTH* OF US DYING!
I *TOLD* YOU I'M NOT *LEAVING* YOU!

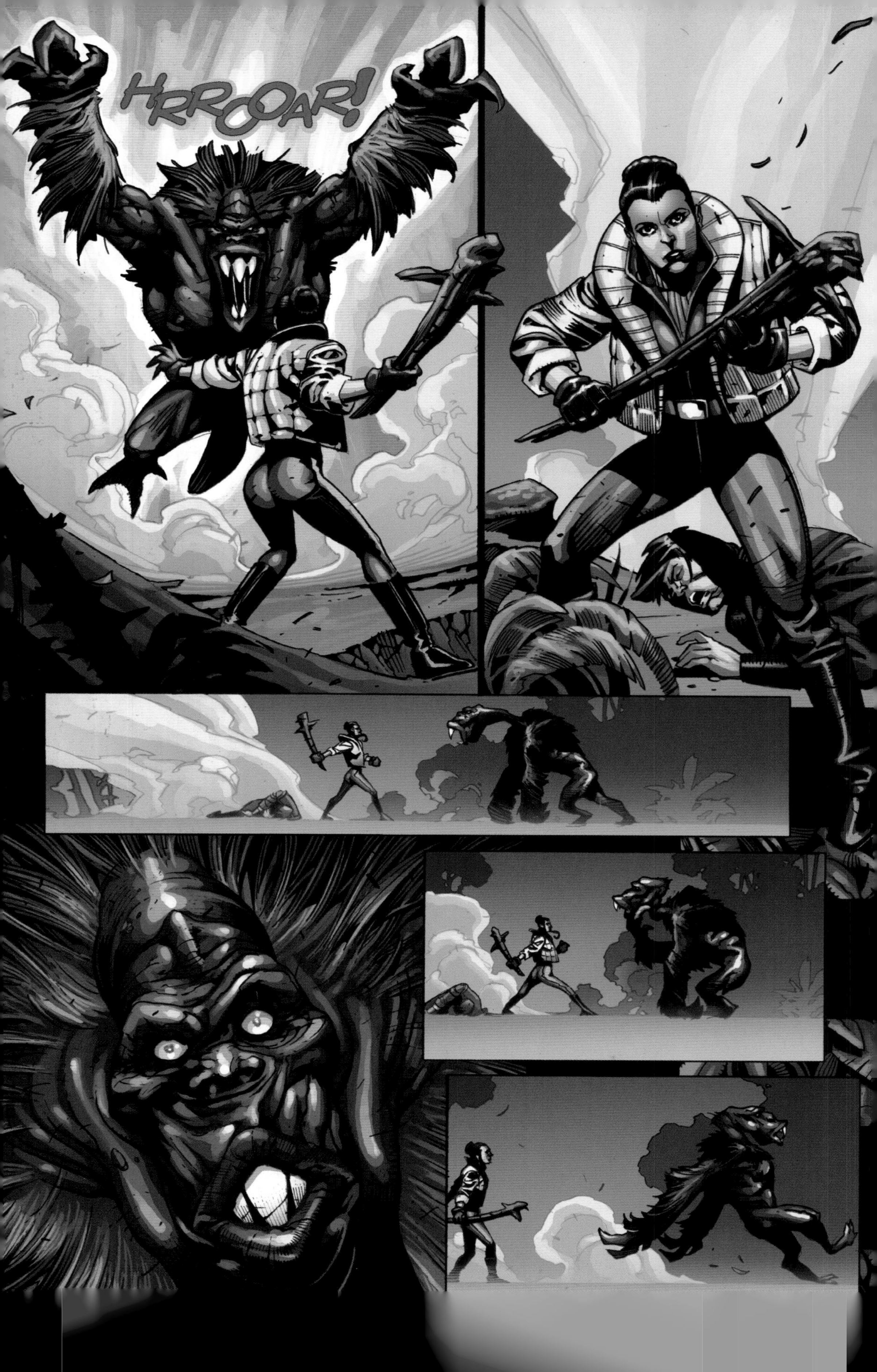
HRRROOAR!

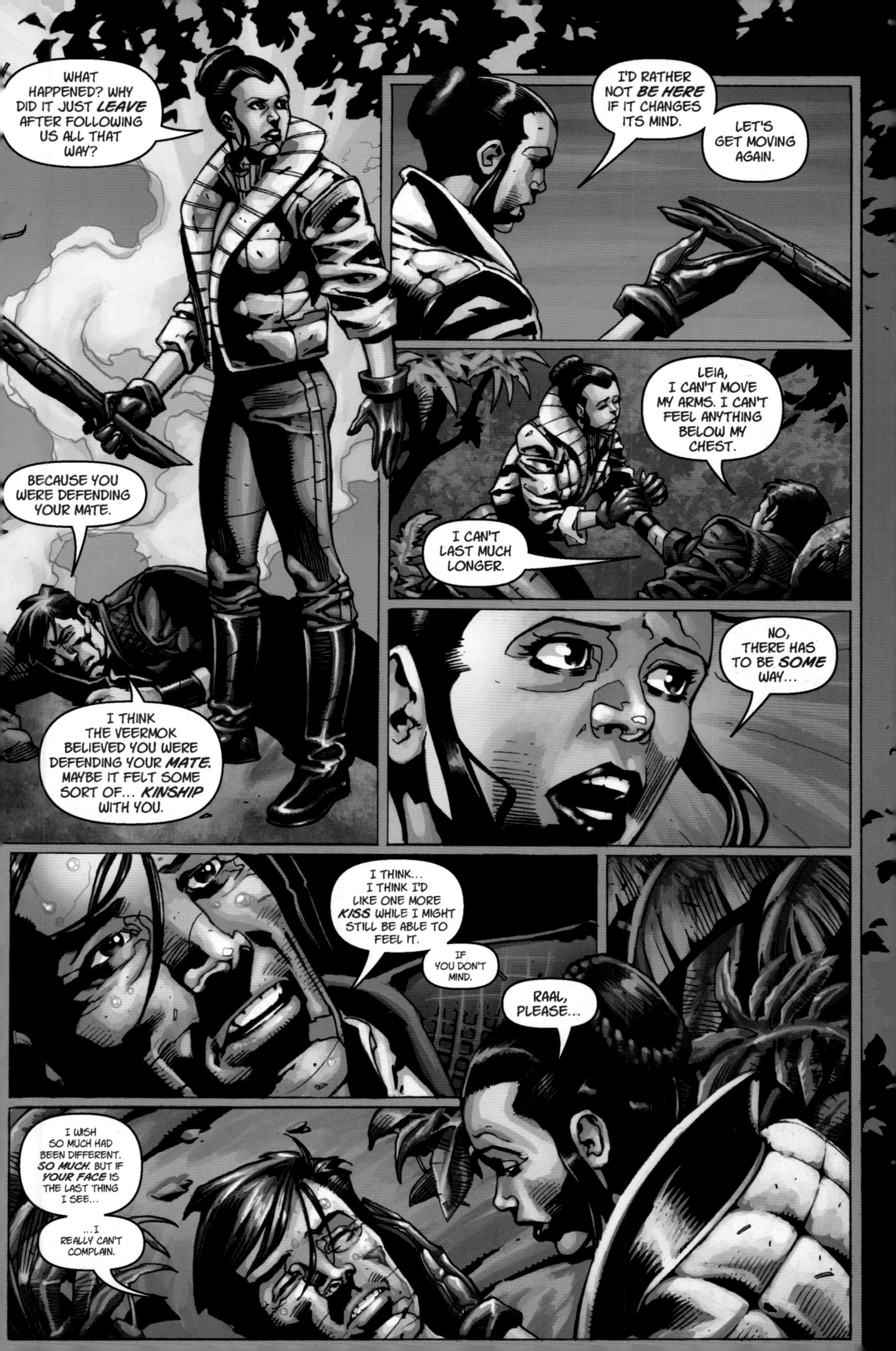
WHAT HAPPENED? WHY DID IT JUST LEAVE AFTER FOLLOWING US ALL THAT WAY?
I'D RATHER NOT BE HERE IF IT CHANGES ITS MIND.
LET'S GET MOVING AGAIN.
BECAUSE YOU WERE DEFENDING YOUR MATE.
I THINK THE VEERMOK BELIEVED YOU WERE DEFENDING YOUR MATE. MAYBE IT FELT SOME SORT OF... KINSHIP WITH YOU.
LEIA, I CAN'T MOVE MY ARMS. I CAN'T FEEL ANYTHING BELOW MY CHEST.
I CAN'T LAST MUCH LONGER.
NO, THERE HAS TO BE SOME WAY...
I THINK... I THINK I'D LIKE ONE MORE KISS WHILE I MIGHT STILL BE ABLE TO FEEL IT.
IF YOU DON'T MIND.
RAAL, PLEASE...
I WISH SO MUCH HAD BEEN DIFFERENT. SO MUCH. BUT IF YOUR FACE IS THE LAST THING I SEE...
...I REALLY CAN'T COMPLAIN.

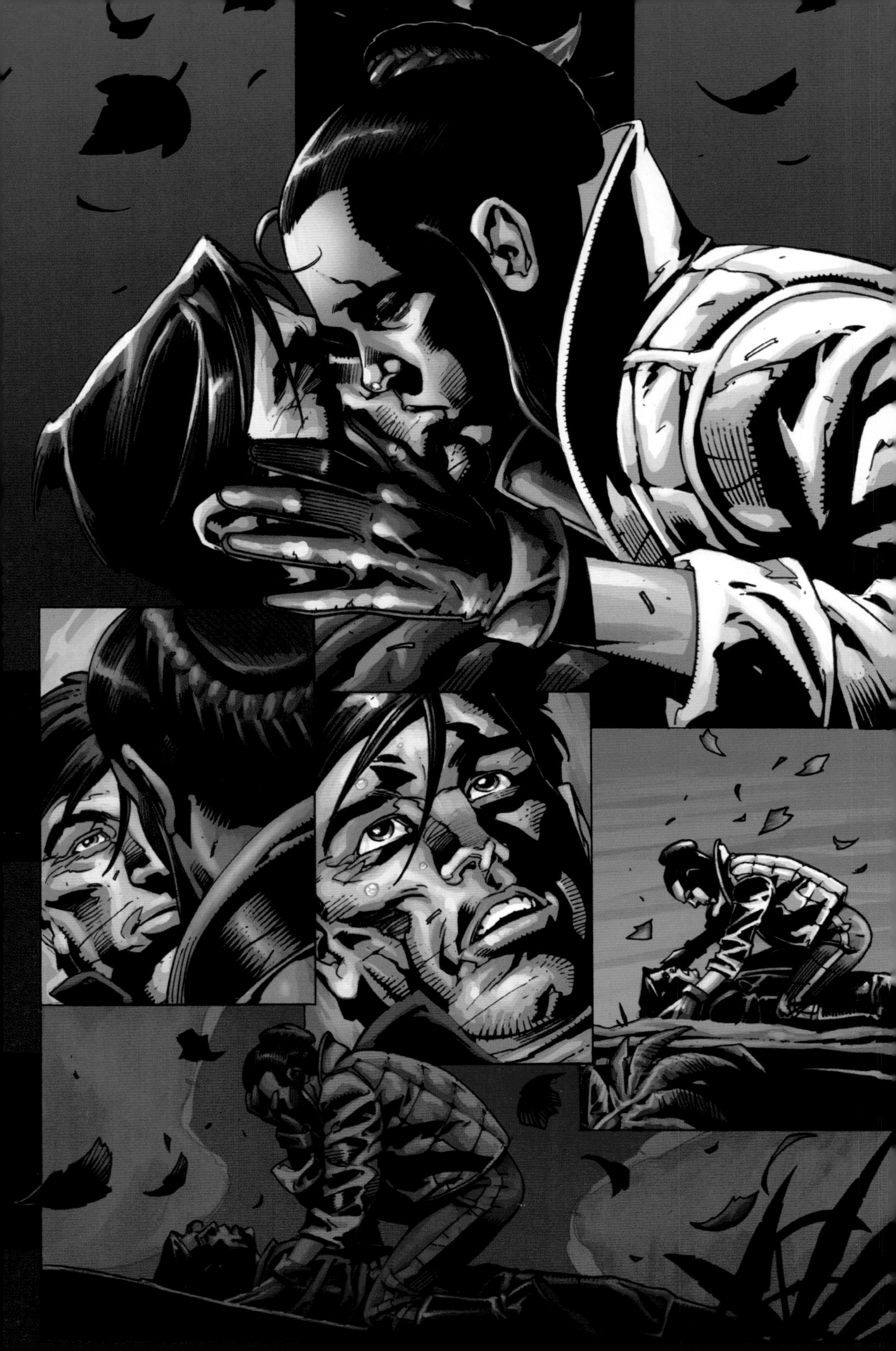

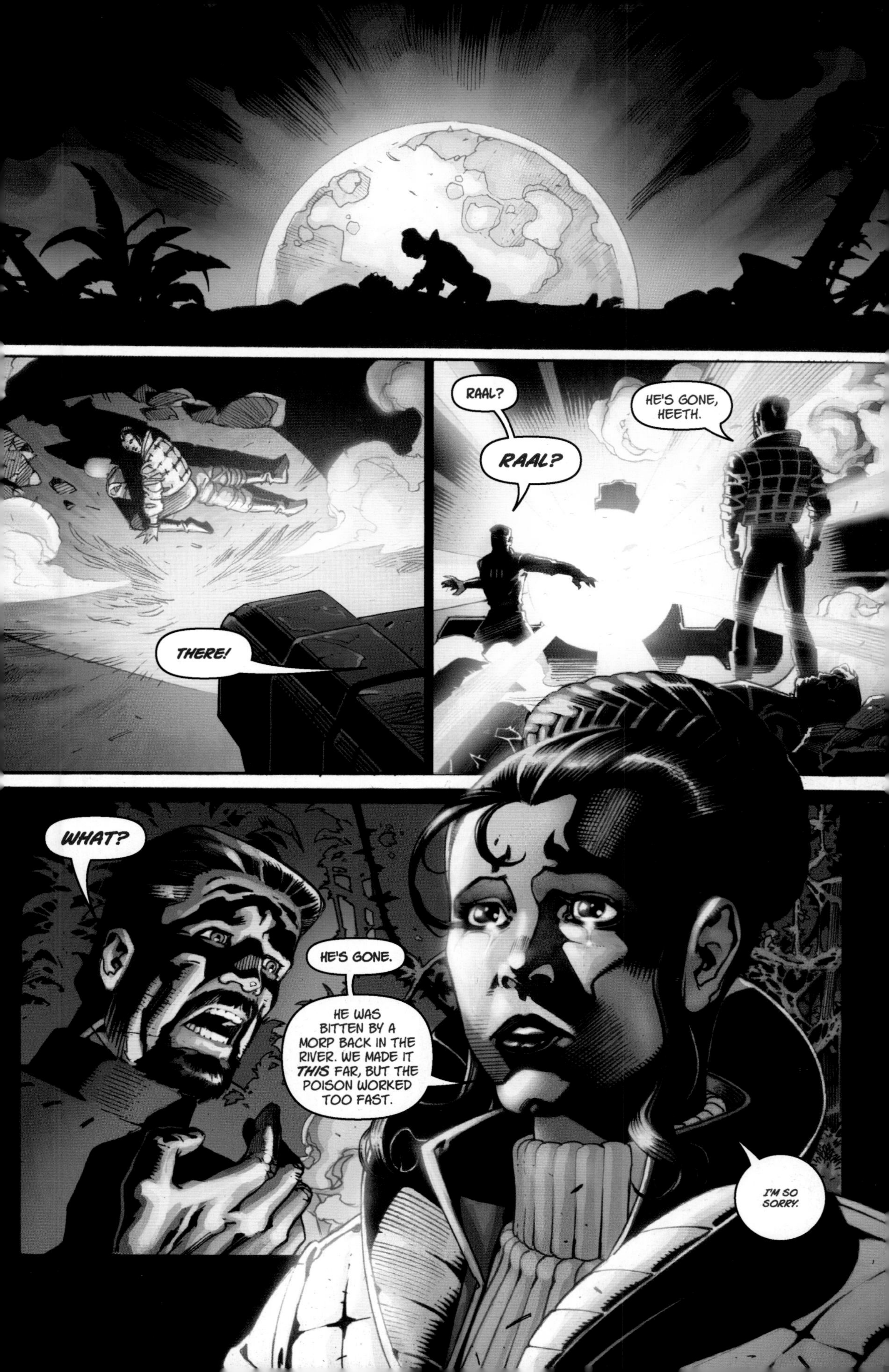
THERE!
RAAL?
RAAL?
HE'S GONE, HEETH.
WHAT?
HE'S GONE.
HE WAS BITTEN BY A MORP BACK IN THE RIVER. WE MADE IT THIS FAR, BUT THE POISON WORKED TOO FAST.
I'M SO SORRY.

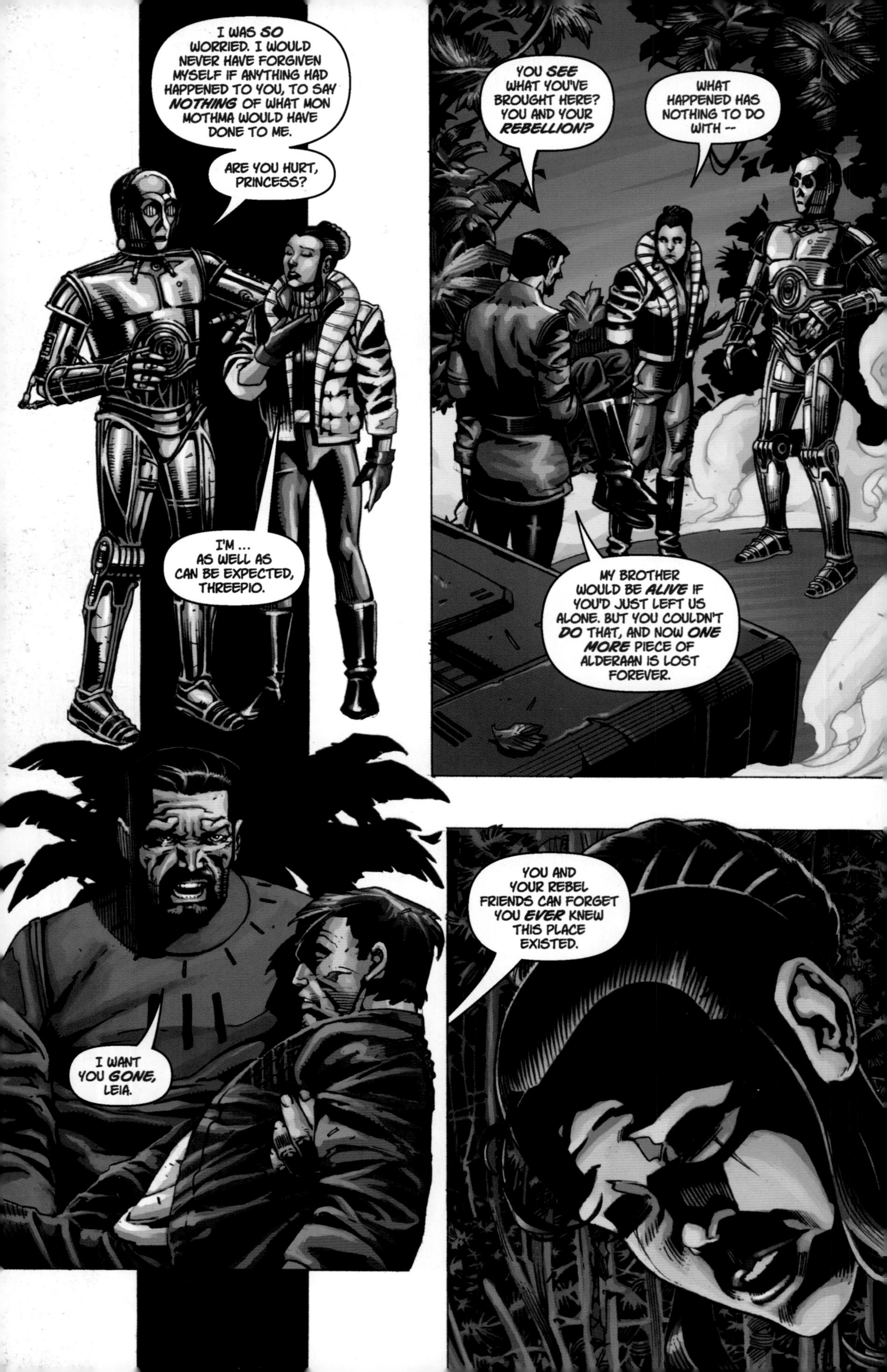
I WAS *SO* WORRIED. I WOULD NEVER HAVE FORGIVEN MYSELF IF ANYTHING HAD HAPPENED TO YOU, TO SAY *NOTHING* OF WHAT MON MOTHMA WOULD HAVE DONE TO ME.
ARE YOU HURT, PRINCESS?
I'M ... AS WELL AS CAN BE EXPECTED, THREEPIO.
YOU *SEE* WHAT YOU'VE BROUGHT HERE? YOU AND YOUR *REBELLION?*
WHAT HAPPENED HAS NOTHING TO DO WITH --
MY BROTHER WOULD BE *ALIVE* IF YOU'D JUST LEFT US ALONE. BUT YOU COULDN'T *DO* THAT, AND NOW *ONE MORE* PIECE OF ALDERAAN IS LOST FOREVER.
I WANT YOU *GONE,* LEIA.
YOU AND YOUR REBEL FRIENDS CAN FORGET YOU *EVER* KNEW THIS PLACE EXISTED.

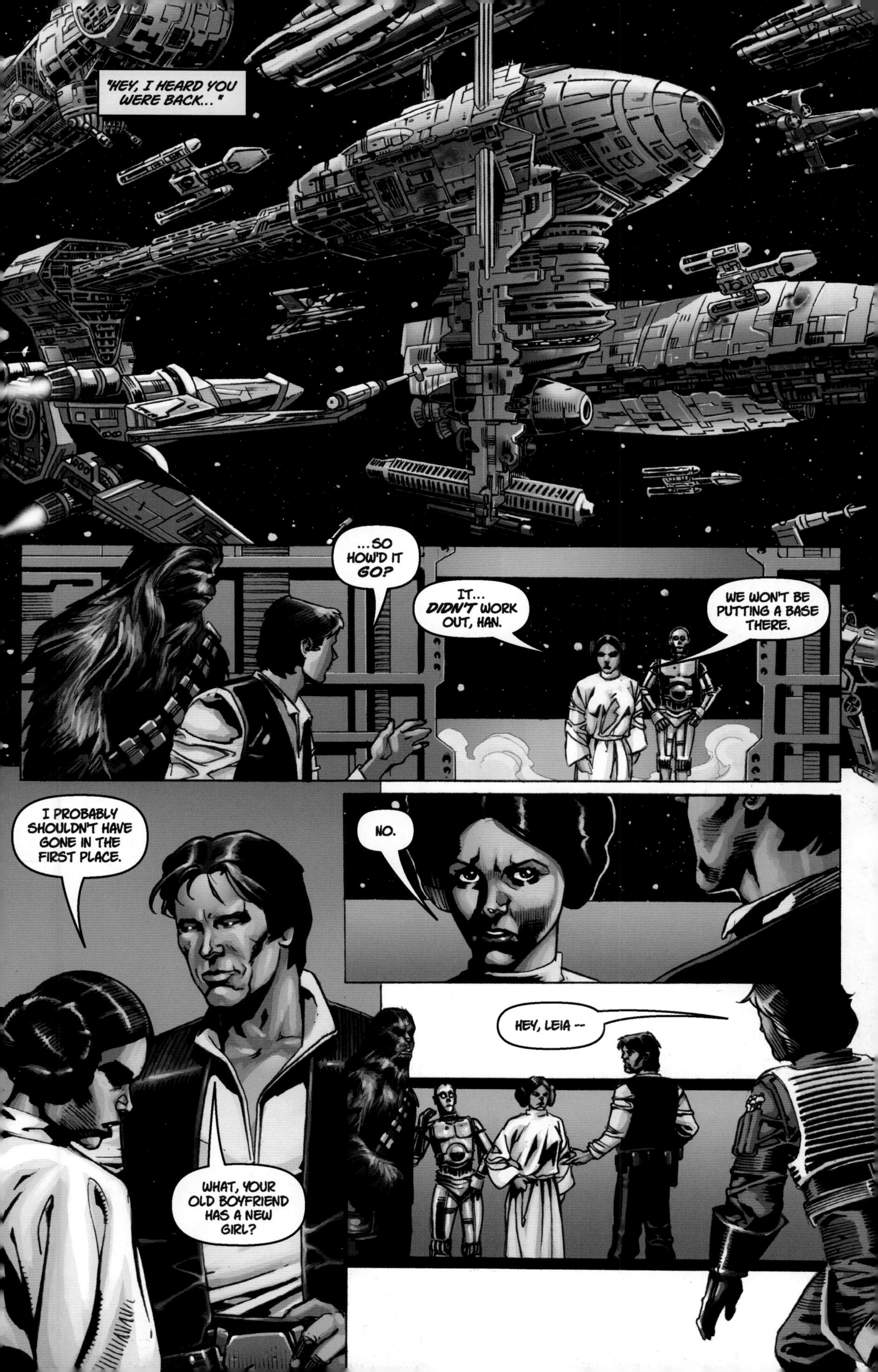
"HEY, I HEARD YOU WERE BACK..."
...SO HOW'D IT GO?
IT... DIDN'T WORK OUT, HAN.
WE WON'T BE PUTTING A BASE THERE.
I PROBABLY SHOULDN'T HAVE GONE IN THE FIRST PLACE.
WHAT, YOUR OLD BOYFRIEND HAS A NEW GIRL?
NO.
HEY, LEIA --

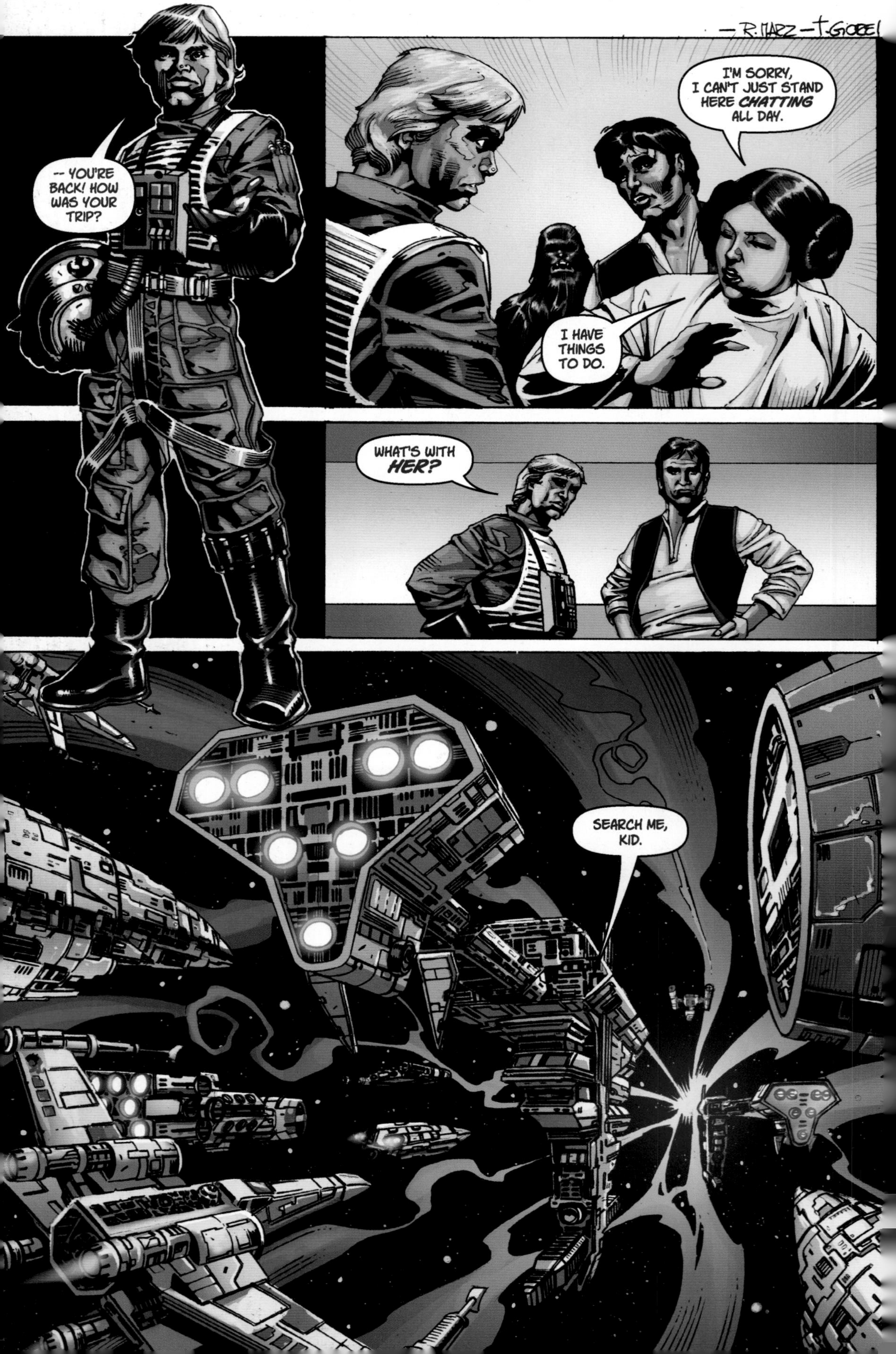
— R. MARZ — T. GIORELLO
-- YOU'RE BACK! HOW WAS YOUR TRIP?
I'M SORRY, I CAN'T JUST STAND HERE CHATTING ALL DAY.
I HAVE THINGS TO DO.
WHAT'S WITH HER?
SEARCH ME, KID.

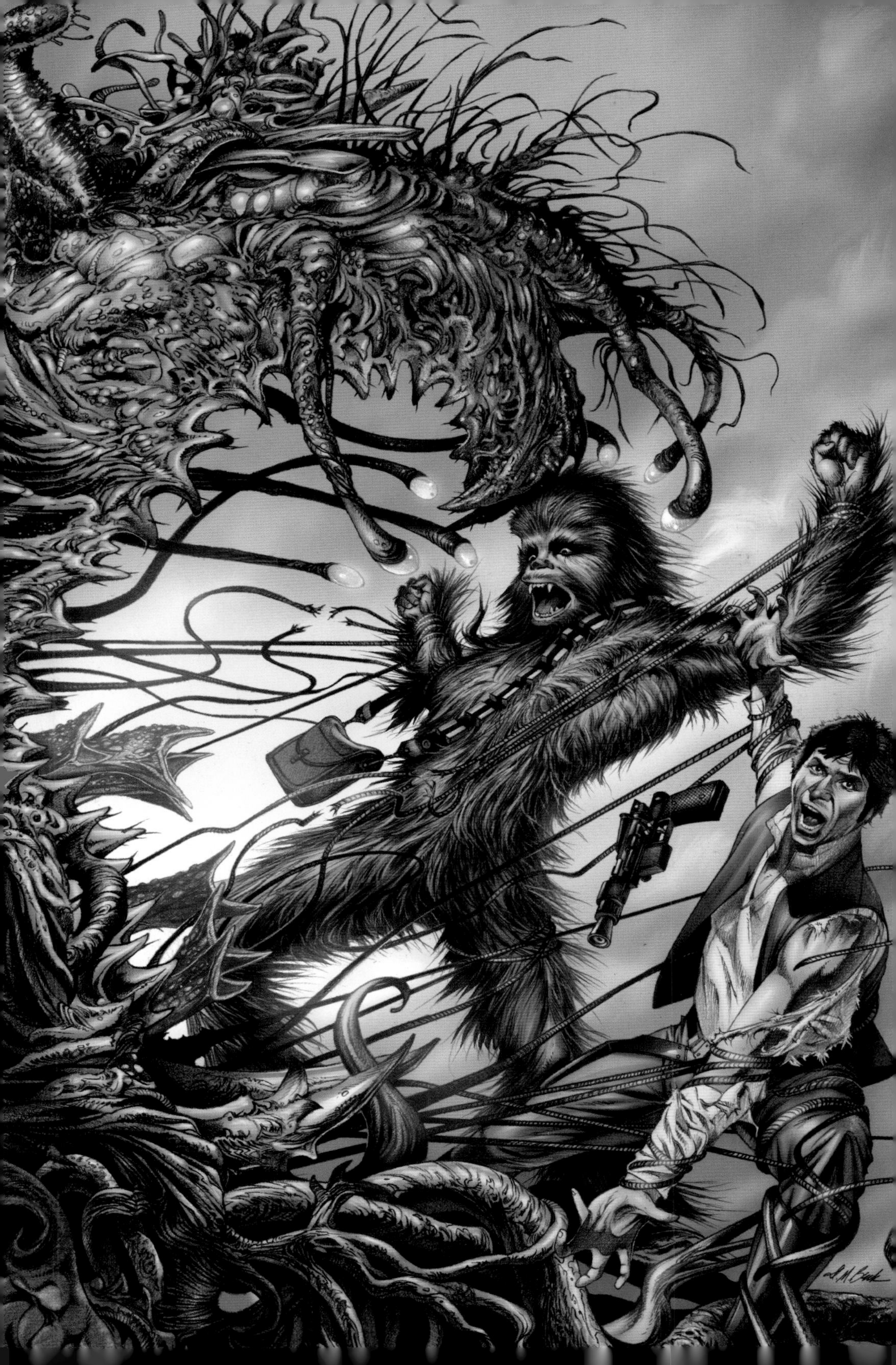

ALONE TOGETHER

Script WELLES HARTLEY
Art ADRIANA MELO
Colors MICHAEL ATIYEH

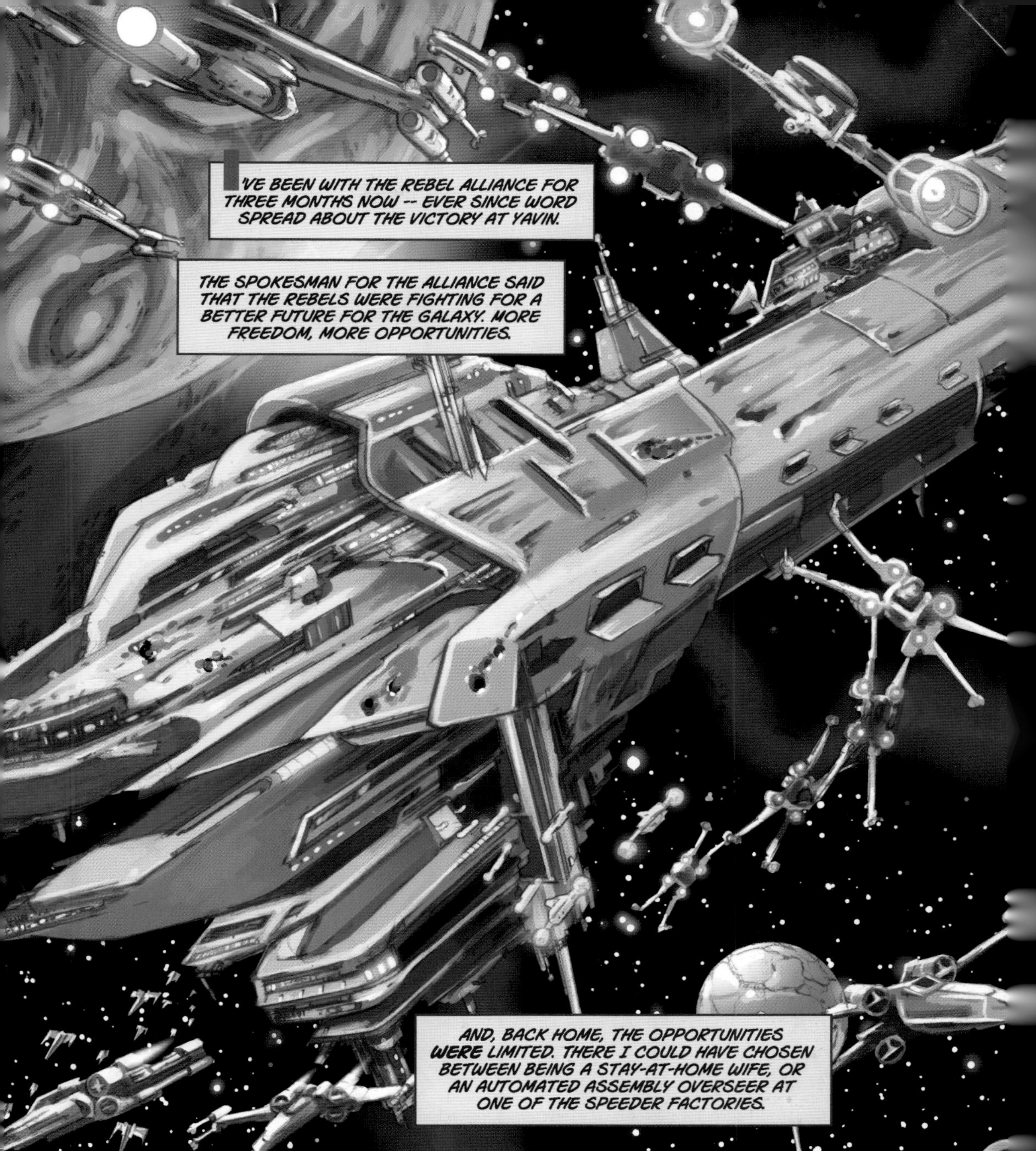
I'VE BEEN WITH THE REBEL ALLIANCE FOR THREE MONTHS NOW -- EVER SINCE WORD SPREAD ABOUT THE VICTORY AT YAVIN.
THE SPOKESMAN FOR THE ALLIANCE SAID THAT THE REBELS WERE FIGHTING FOR A BETTER FUTURE FOR THE GALAXY. MORE FREEDOM, MORE OPPORTUNITIES.
AND, BACK HOME, THE OPPORTUNITIES WERE LIMITED. THERE I COULD HAVE CHOSEN BETWEEN BEING A STAY-AT-HOME WIFE, OR AN AUTOMATED ASSEMBLY OVERSEER AT ONE OF THE SPEEDER FACTORIES.
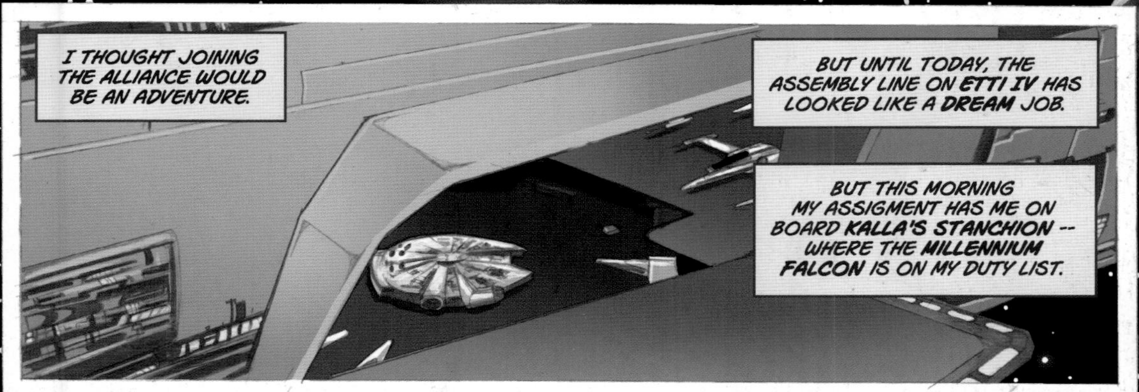
I THOUGHT JOINING THE ALLIANCE WOULD BE AN ADVENTURE.
BUT UNTIL TODAY, THE ASSEMBLY LINE ON ETTI IV HAS LOOKED LIKE A DREAM JOB.
BUT THIS MORNING MY ASSIGMENT HAS ME ON BOARD KALLA'S STANCHION -- WHERE THE MILLENNIUM FALCON IS ON MY DUTY LIST.

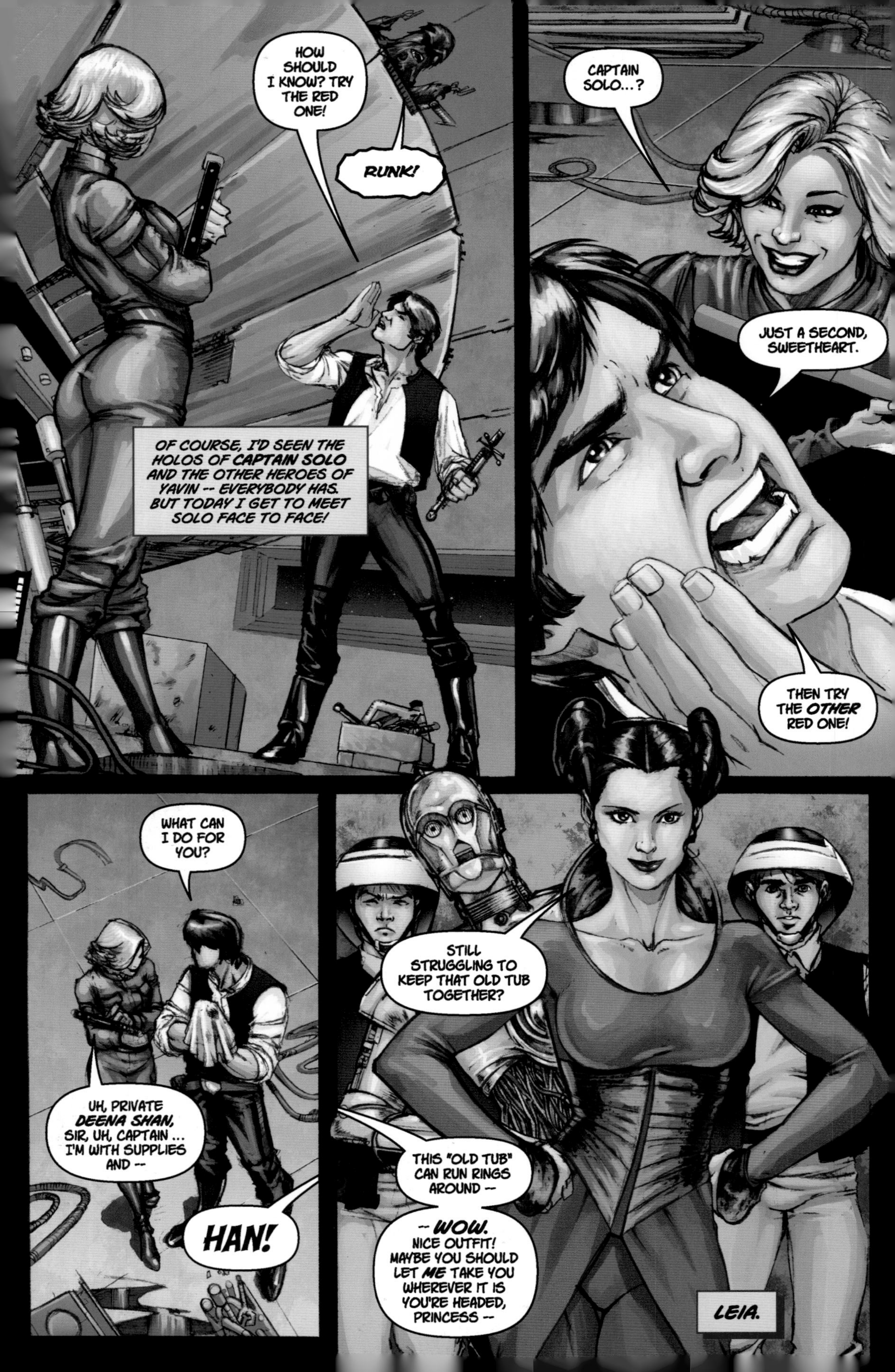
HOW SHOULD I KNOW? TRY THE RED ONE!
RUNK!
OF COURSE, I'D SEEN THE HOLOS OF CAPTAIN SOLO AND THE OTHER HEROES OF YAVIN -- EVERYBODY HAS. BUT TODAY I GET TO MEET SOLO FACE TO FACE!
CAPTAIN SOLO...?
JUST A SECOND, SWEETHEART.
THEN TRY THE OTHER RED ONE!
WHAT CAN I DO FOR YOU?
UH, PRIVATE DEENA SHAN, SIR, UH, CAPTAIN ... I'M WITH SUPPLIES AND --
HAN!
STILL STRUGGLING TO KEEP THAT OLD TUB TOGETHER?
THIS "OLD TUB" CAN RUN RINGS AROUND --
-- WOW. NICE OUTFIT! MAYBE YOU SHOULD LET ME TAKE YOU WHEREVER IT IS YOU'RE HEADED, PRINCESS --
LEIA.

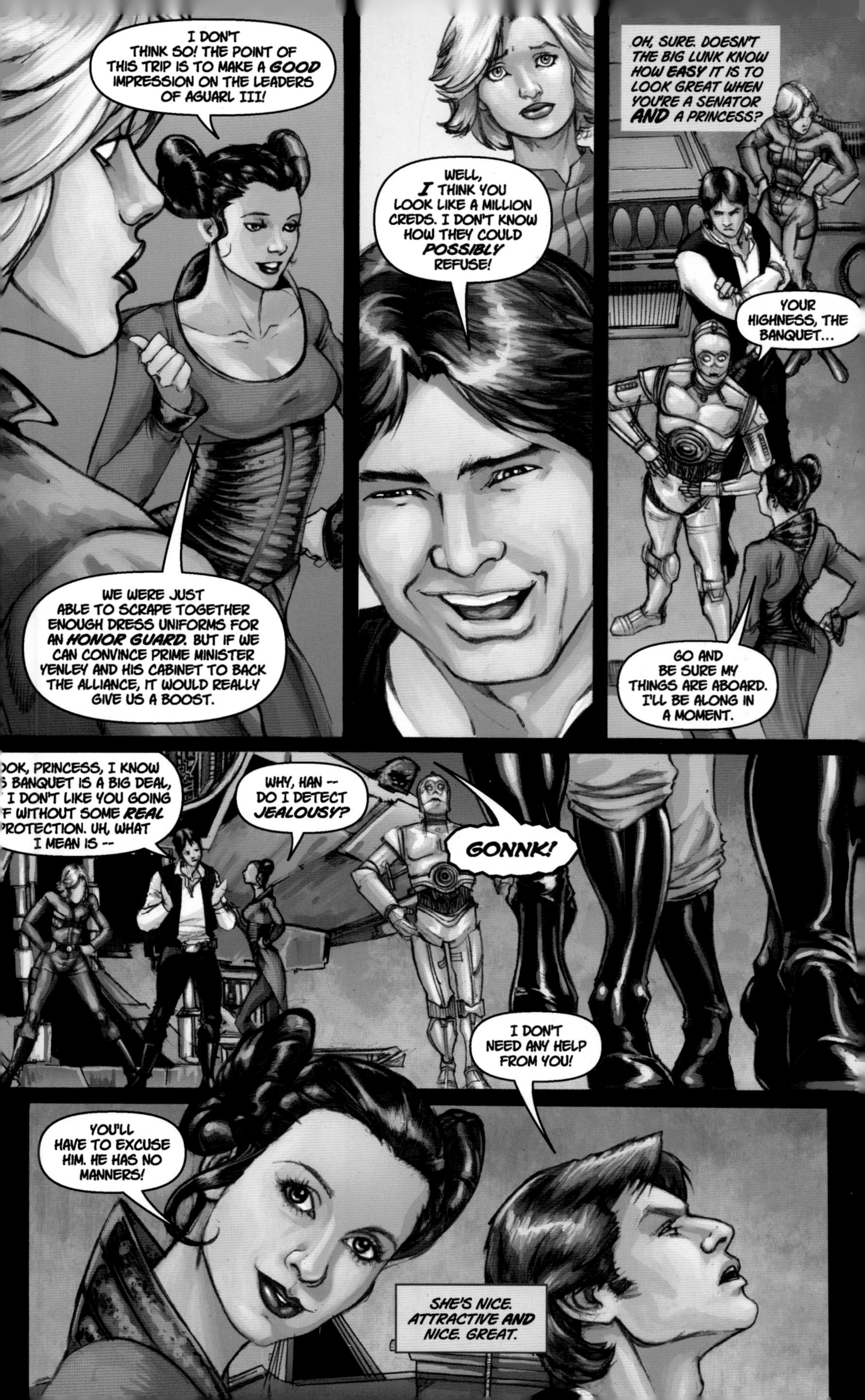
I DON'T THINK SO! THE POINT OF THIS TRIP IS TO MAKE A GOOD IMPRESSION ON THE LEADERS OF AGUARL III!
WE WERE JUST ABLE TO SCRAPE TOGETHER ENOUGH DRESS UNIFORMS FOR AN HONOR GUARD. BUT IF WE CAN CONVINCE PRIME MINISTER YENLEY AND HIS CABINET TO BACK THE ALLIANCE, IT WOULD REALLY GIVE US A BOOST.
WELL, I THINK YOU LOOK LIKE A MILLION CREDS. I DON'T KNOW HOW THEY COULD POSSIBLY REFUSE!
OH, SURE. DOESN'T THE BIG LUNK KNOW HOW EASY IT IS TO LOOK GREAT WHEN YOU'RE A SENATOR AND A PRINCESS?
YOUR HIGHNESS, THE BANQUET...
GO AND BE SURE MY THINGS ARE ABOARD. I'LL BE ALONG IN A MOMENT.
OOK, PRINCESS, I KNOW S BANQUET IS A BIG DEAL, I DON'T LIKE YOU GOING F WITHOUT SOME REAL PROTECTION. UH, WHAT I MEAN IS --
WHY, HAN -- DO I DETECT JEALOUSY?
GONNK!
I DON'T NEED ANY HELP FROM YOU!
YOU'LL HAVE TO EXCUSE HIM. HE HAS NO MANNERS!
SHE'S NICE. ATTRACTIVE AND NICE. GREAT.

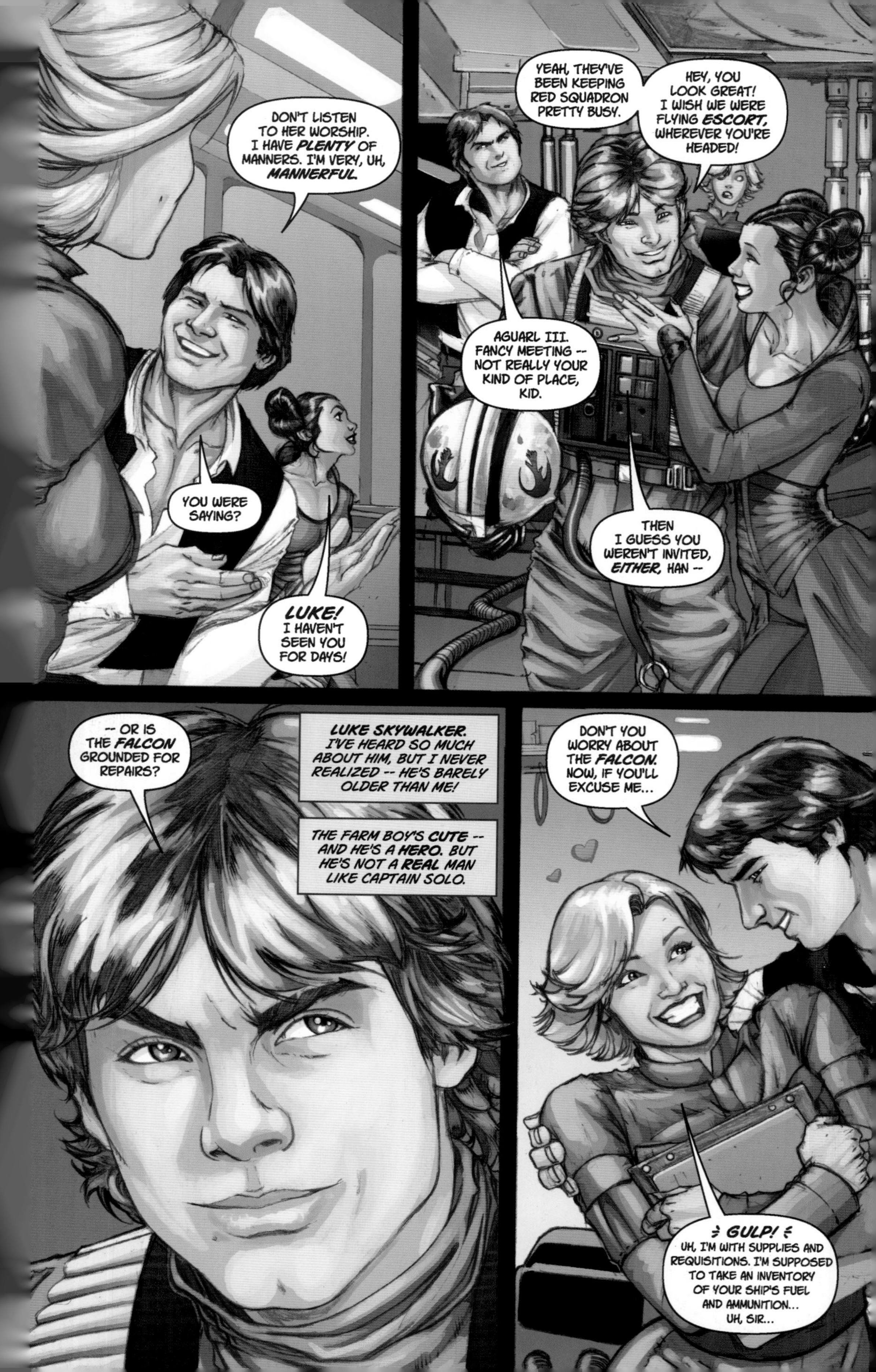
DON'T LISTEN TO HER WORSHIP. I HAVE PLENTY OF MANNERS. I'M VERY, UH, MANNERFUL.
YOU WERE SAYING?
LUKE! I HAVEN'T SEEN YOU FOR DAYS!
YEAH, THEY'VE BEEN KEEPING RED SQUADRON PRETTY BUSY.
HEY, YOU LOOK GREAT! I WISH WE WERE FLYING ESCORT, WHEREVER YOU'RE HEADED!
AGUARL III. FANCY MEETING -- NOT REALLY YOUR KIND OF PLACE, KID.
THEN I GUESS YOU WEREN'T INVITED, EITHER, HAN --
-- OR IS THE FALCON GROUNDED FOR REPAIRS?
LUKE SKYWALKER. I'VE HEARD SO MUCH ABOUT HIM, BUT I NEVER REALIZED -- HE'S BARELY OLDER THAN ME!
THE FARM BOY'S CUTE -- AND HE'S A HERO. BUT HE'S NOT A REAL MAN LIKE CAPTAIN SOLO.
DON'T YOU WORRY ABOUT THE FALCON. NOW, IF YOU'LL EXCUSE ME...
GULP!
UH, I'M WITH SUPPLIES AND REQUISITIONS. I'M SUPPOSED TO TAKE AN INVENTORY OF YOUR SHIP'S FUEL AND AMMUNITION... UH, SIR...

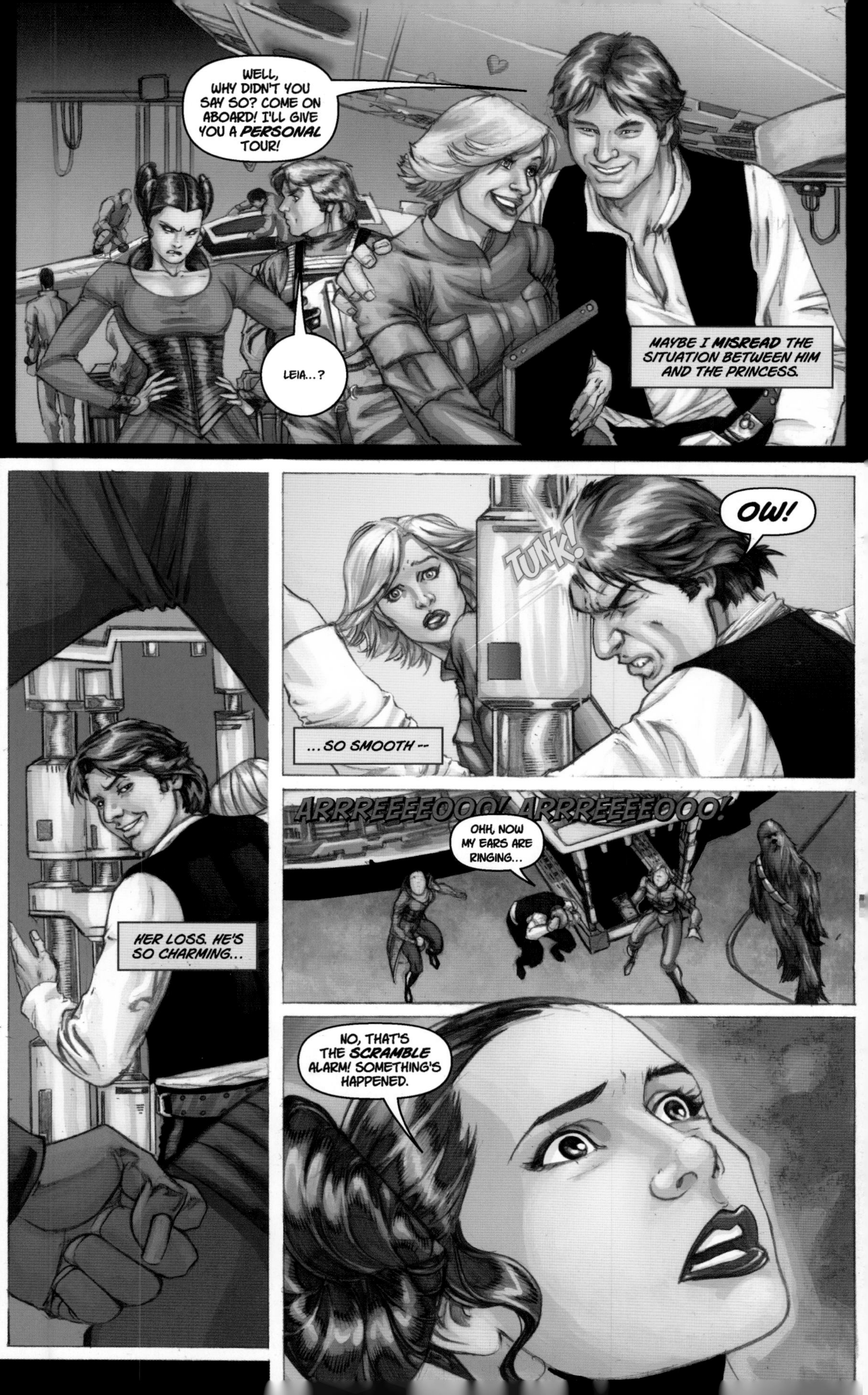
WELL, WHY DIDN'T YOU SAY SO? COME ON ABOARD! I'LL GIVE YOU A *PERSONAL* TOUR!
LEIA...?
MAYBE I **MISREAD** THE SITUATION BETWEEN HIM AND THE PRINCESS.
HER LOSS. HE'S SO CHARMING...
...SO SMOOTH --
TUNK!
OW!
ARRREEEEOOO! ARRREEEEOOO!
OHH, NOW MY EARS ARE RINGING...
NO, THAT'S THE *SCRAMBLE* ALARM! SOMETHING'S HAPPENED.

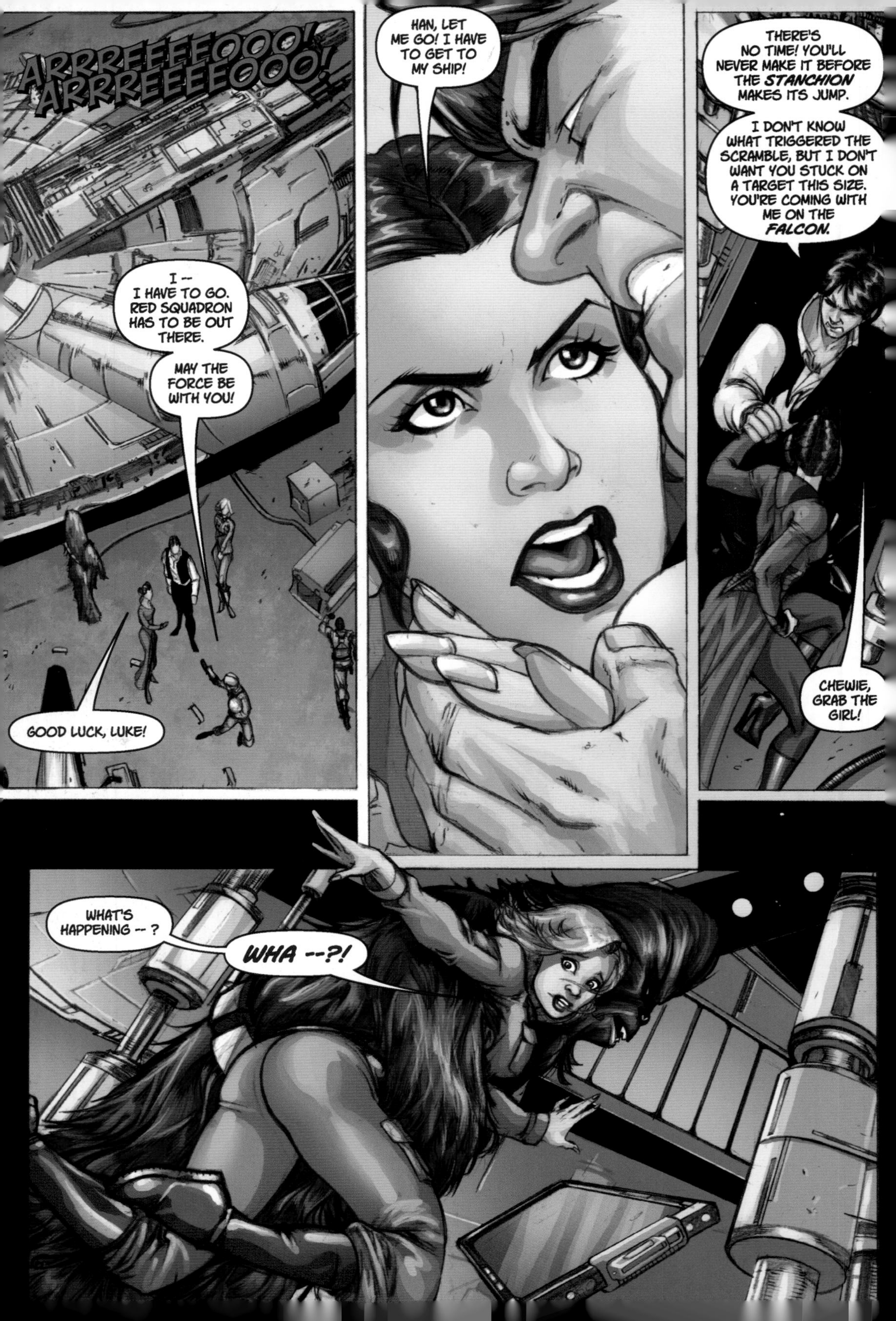
ARRRFFFFOOO! ARRRREEEEOOO!
I -- I HAVE TO GO. RED SQUADRON HAS TO BE OUT THERE.
MAY THE FORCE BE WITH YOU!
GOOD LUCK, LUKE!
HAN, LET ME GO! I HAVE TO GET TO MY SHIP!
THERE'S NO TIME! YOU'LL NEVER MAKE IT BEFORE THE STANCHION MAKES ITS JUMP.
I DON'T KNOW WHAT TRIGGERED THE SCRAMBLE, BUT I DON'T WANT YOU STUCK ON A TARGET THIS SIZE. YOU'RE COMING WITH ME ON THE FALCON.
CHEWIE, GRAB THE GIRL!
WHAT'S HAPPENING -- ?
WHA --?!

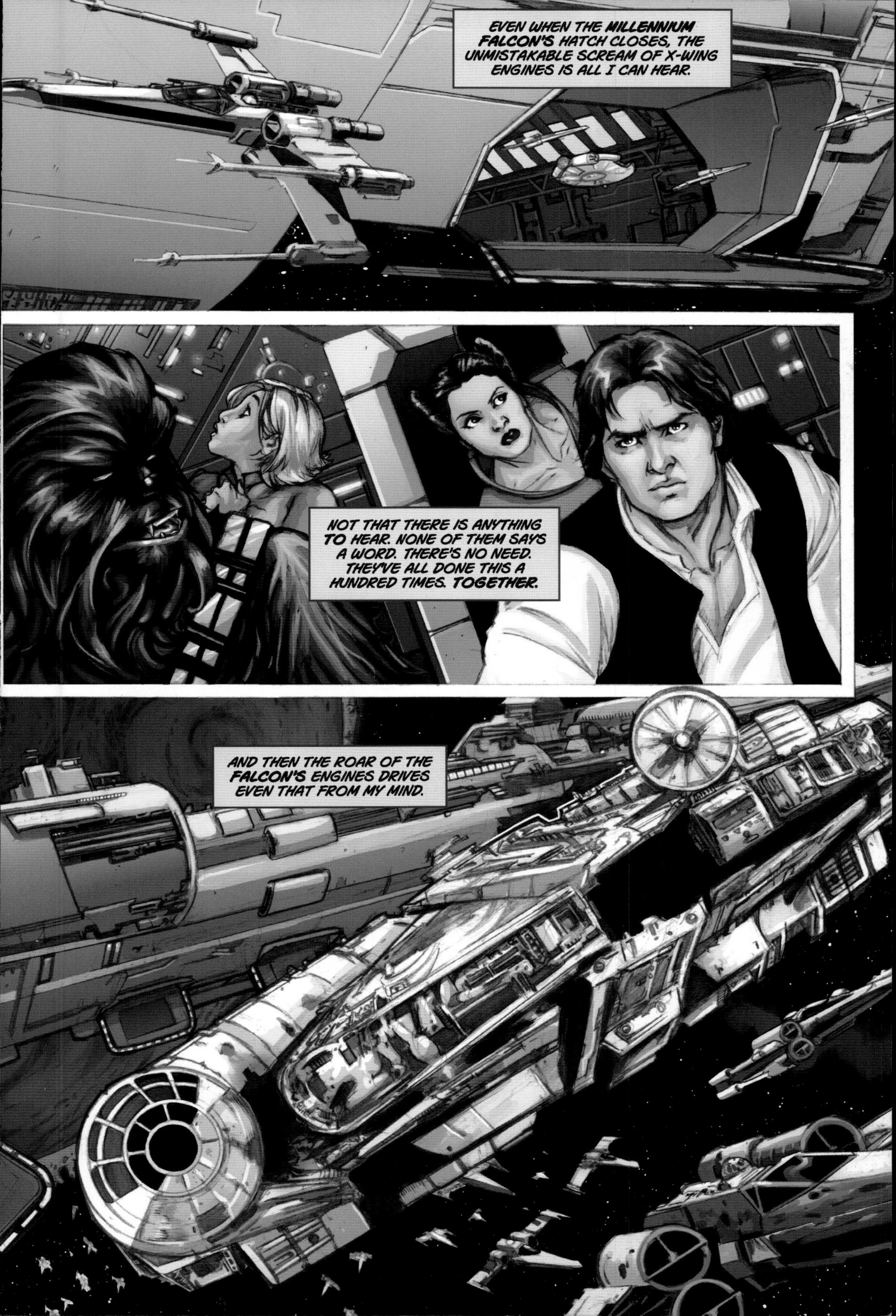
EVEN WHEN THE MILLENNIUM FALCON'S HATCH CLOSES, THE UNMISTAKABLE SCREAM OF X-WING ENGINES IS ALL I CAN HEAR.
NOT THAT THERE IS ANYTHING TO HEAR. NONE OF THEM SAYS A WORD. THERE'S NO NEED. THEY'VE ALL DONE THIS A HUNDRED TIMES. TOGETHER.
AND THEN THE ROAR OF THE FALCON'S ENGINES DRIVES EVEN THAT FROM MY MIND.

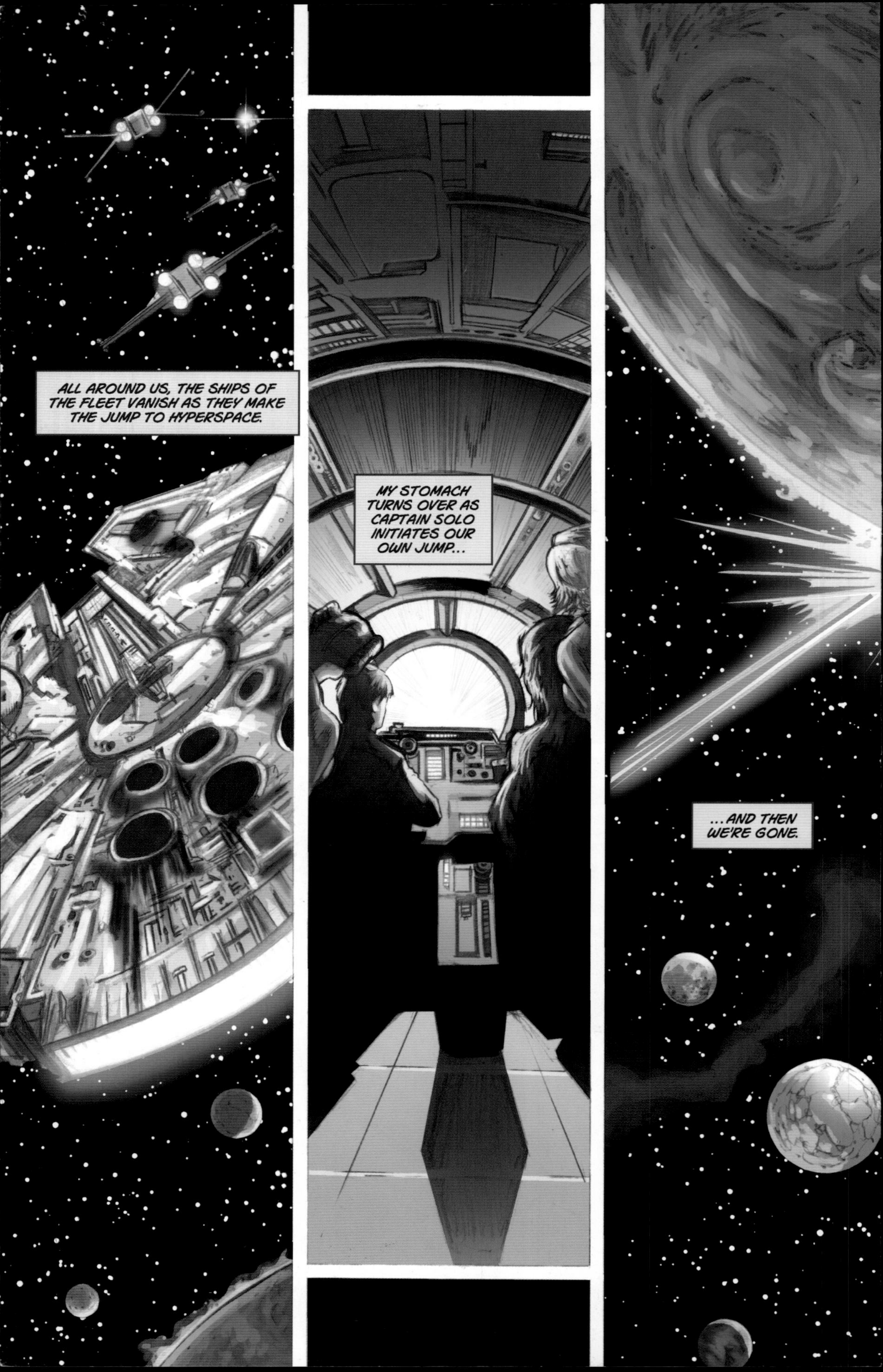
ALL AROUND US, THE SHIPS OF THE FLEET VANISH AS THEY MAKE THE JUMP TO HYPERSPACE.
MY STOMACH TURNS OVER AS CAPTAIN SOLO INITIATES OUR OWN JUMP...
...AND THEN WE'RE GONE.

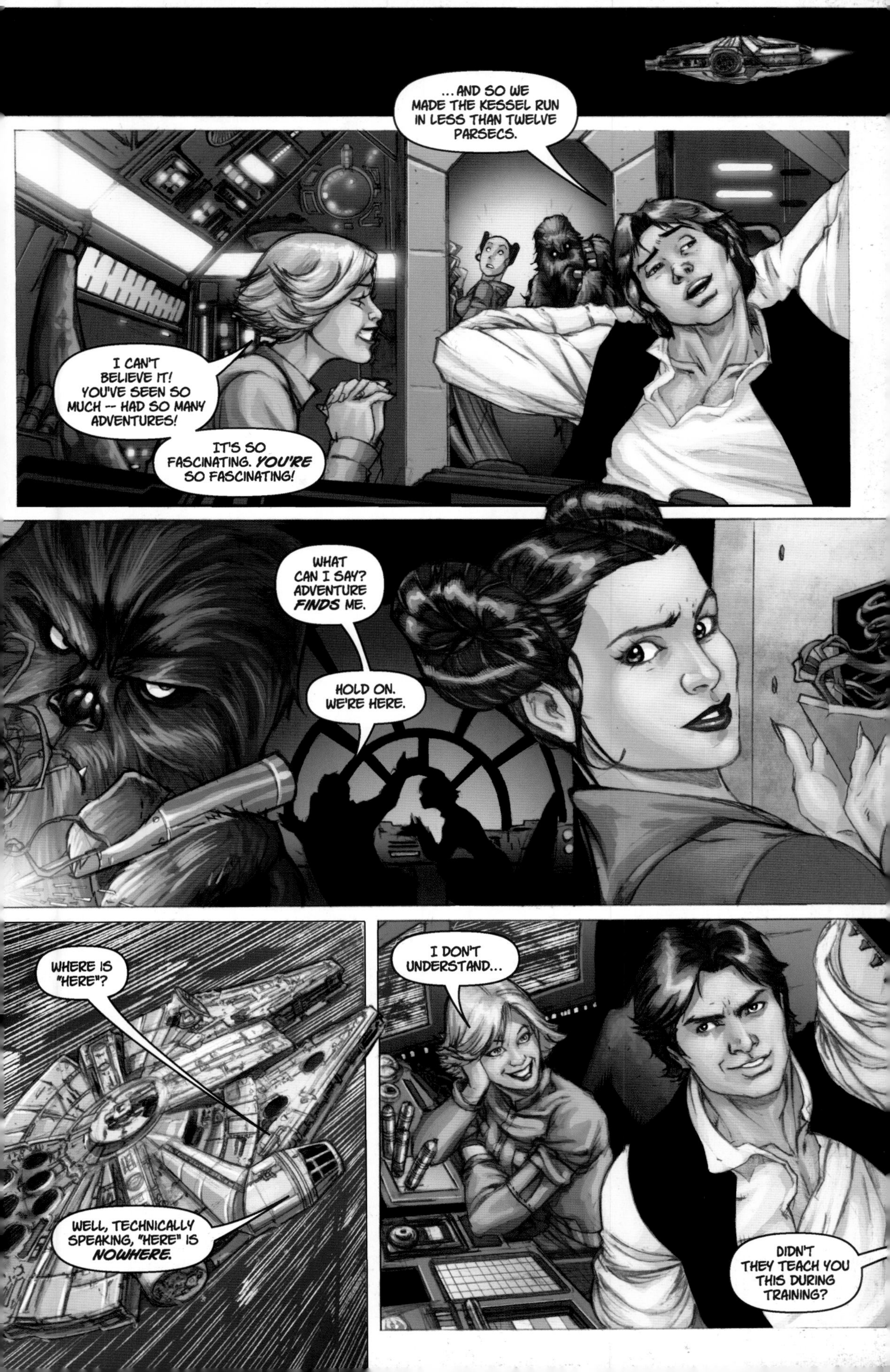
...AND SO WE MADE THE KESSEL RUN IN LESS THAN TWELVE PARSECS.
I CAN'T BELIEVE IT! YOU'VE SEEN SO MUCH -- HAD SO MANY ADVENTURES!
IT'S SO FASCINATING. *YOU'RE* SO FASCINATING!
WHAT CAN I SAY? ADVENTURE *FINDS* ME.
HOLD ON. WE'RE HERE.
WHERE IS "HERE"?
WELL, TECHNICALLY SPEAKING, "HERE" IS *NOWHERE*.
I DON'T UNDERSTAND...
DIDN'T THEY TEACH YOU THIS DURING TRAINING?

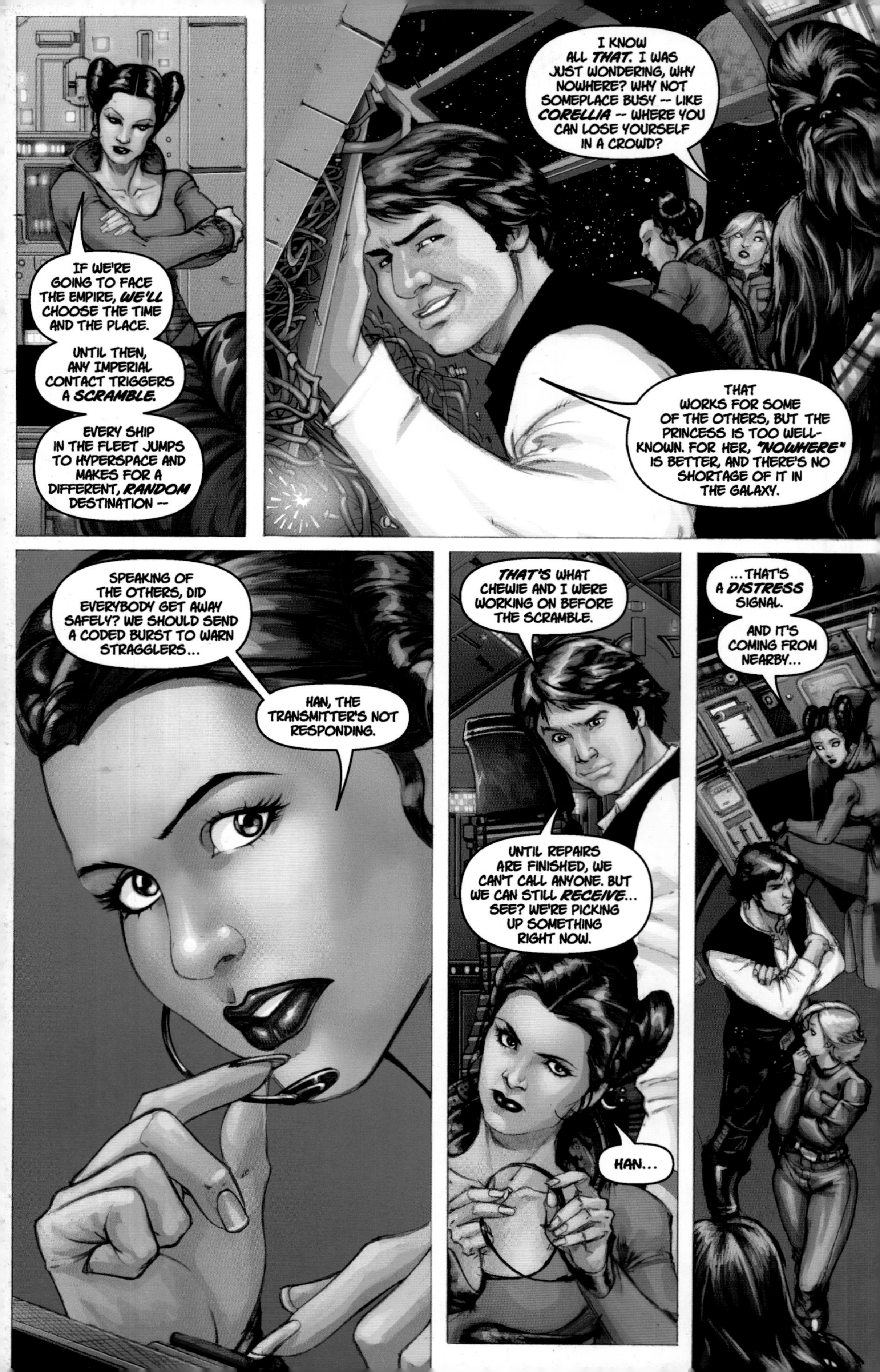
IF WE'RE GOING TO FACE THE EMPIRE, WE'LL CHOOSE THE TIME AND THE PLACE.
UNTIL THEN, ANY IMPERIAL CONTACT TRIGGERS A SCRAMBLE.
EVERY SHIP IN THE FLEET JUMPS TO HYPERSPACE AND MAKES FOR A DIFFERENT, RANDOM DESTINATION --
I KNOW ALL THAT. I WAS JUST WONDERING, WHY NOWHERE? WHY NOT SOMEPLACE BUSY -- LIKE CORELLIA -- WHERE YOU CAN LOSE YOURSELF IN A CROWD?
THAT WORKS FOR SOME OF THE OTHERS, BUT THE PRINCESS IS TOO WELL-KNOWN. FOR HER, "NOWHERE" IS BETTER, AND THERE'S NO SHORTAGE OF IT IN THE GALAXY.
SPEAKING OF THE OTHERS, DID EVERYBODY GET AWAY SAFELY? WE SHOULD SEND A CODED BURST TO WARN STRAGGLERS...
HAN, THE TRANSMITTER'S NOT RESPONDING.
THAT'S WHAT CHEWIE AND I WERE WORKING ON BEFORE THE SCRAMBLE.
UNTIL REPAIRS ARE FINISHED, WE CAN'T CALL ANYONE. BUT WE CAN STILL RECEIVE... SEE? WE'RE PICKING UP SOMETHING RIGHT NOW.
HAN...
...THAT'S A DISTRESS SIGNAL.
AND IT'S COMING FROM NEARBY...

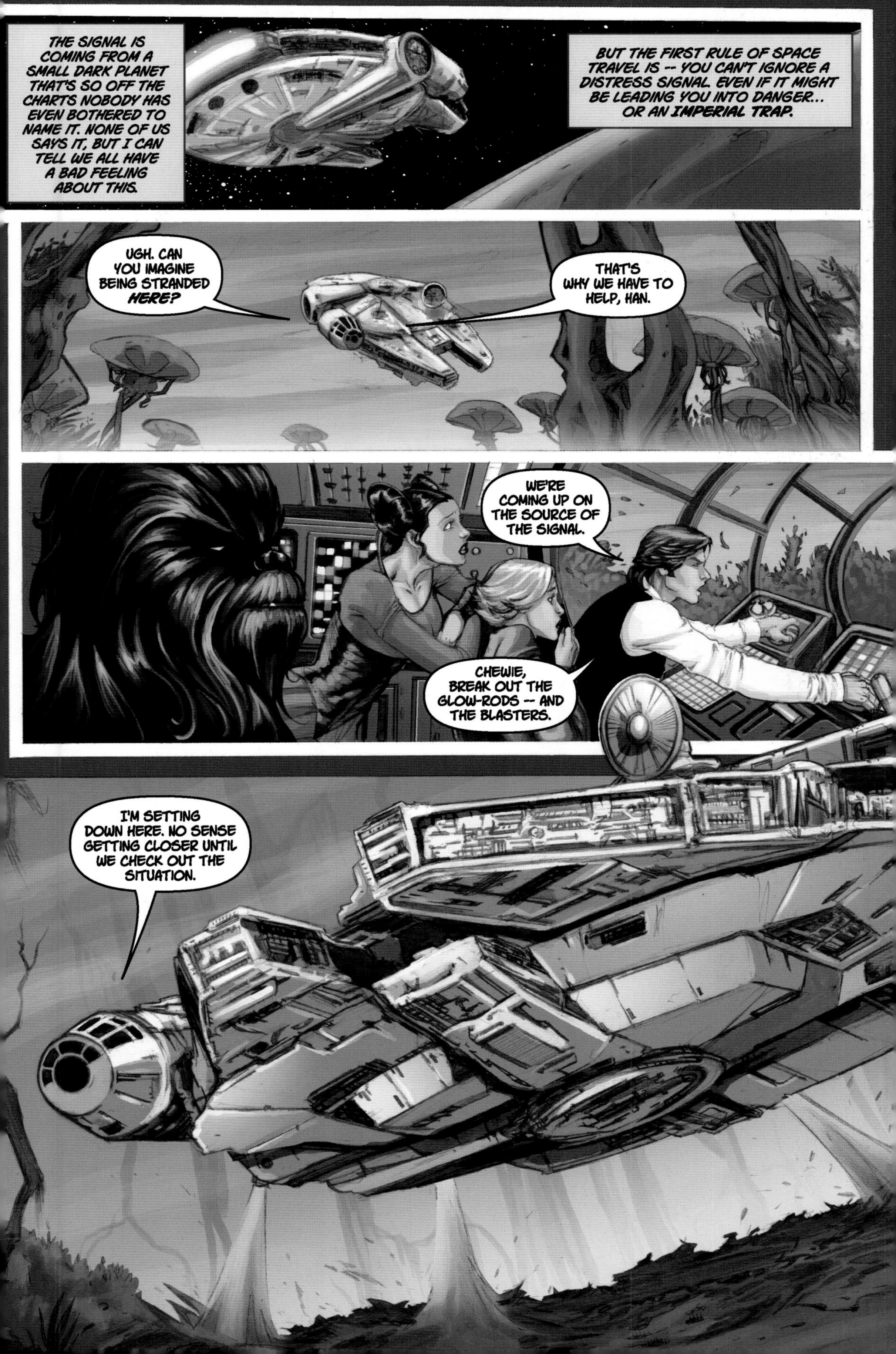
THE SIGNAL IS COMING FROM A SMALL DARK PLANET THAT'S SO OFF THE CHARTS NOBODY HAS EVEN BOTHERED TO NAME IT. NONE OF US SAYS IT, BUT I CAN TELL WE ALL HAVE A BAD FEELING ABOUT THIS.
BUT THE FIRST RULE OF SPACE TRAVEL IS -- YOU CAN'T IGNORE A DISTRESS SIGNAL. EVEN IF IT MIGHT BE LEADING YOU INTO DANGER... OR AN IMPERIAL TRAP.
UGH. CAN YOU IMAGINE BEING STRANDED HERE?
THAT'S WHY WE HAVE TO HELP, HAN.
WE'RE COMING UP ON THE SOURCE OF THE SIGNAL.
CHEWIE, BREAK OUT THE GLOW-RODS -- AND THE BLASTERS.
I'M SETTING DOWN HERE. NO SENSE GETTING CLOSER UNTIL WE CHECK OUT THE SITUATION.

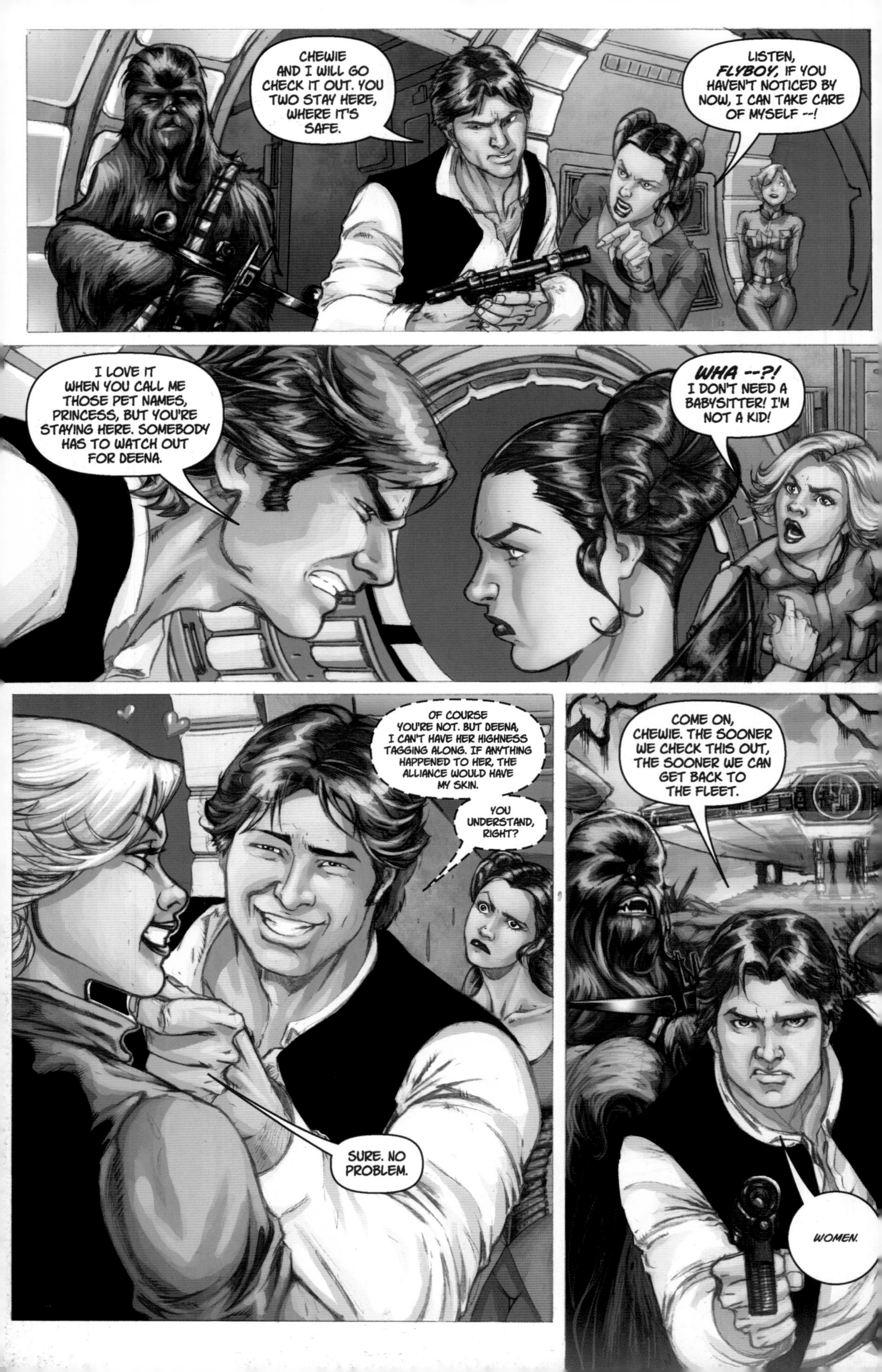
CHEWIE AND I WILL GO CHECK IT OUT. YOU TWO STAY HERE, WHERE IT'S SAFE.
LISTEN, FLYBOY, IF YOU HAVEN'T NOTICED BY NOW, I CAN TAKE CARE OF MYSELF --!
I LOVE IT WHEN YOU CALL ME THOSE PET NAMES, PRINCESS, BUT YOU'RE STAYING HERE. SOMEBODY HAS TO WATCH OUT FOR DEENA.
WHA --?! I DON'T NEED A BABYSITTER! I'M NOT A KID!
OF COURSE YOU'RE NOT. BUT DEENA, I CAN'T HAVE HER HIGHNESS TAGGING ALONG. IF ANYTHING HAPPENED TO HER, THE ALLIANCE WOULD HAVE MY SKIN.
YOU UNDERSTAND, RIGHT?
SURE. NO PROBLEM.
COME ON, CHEWIE. THE SOONER WE CHECK THIS OUT, THE SOONER WE CAN GET BACK TO THE FLEET.
WOMEN.

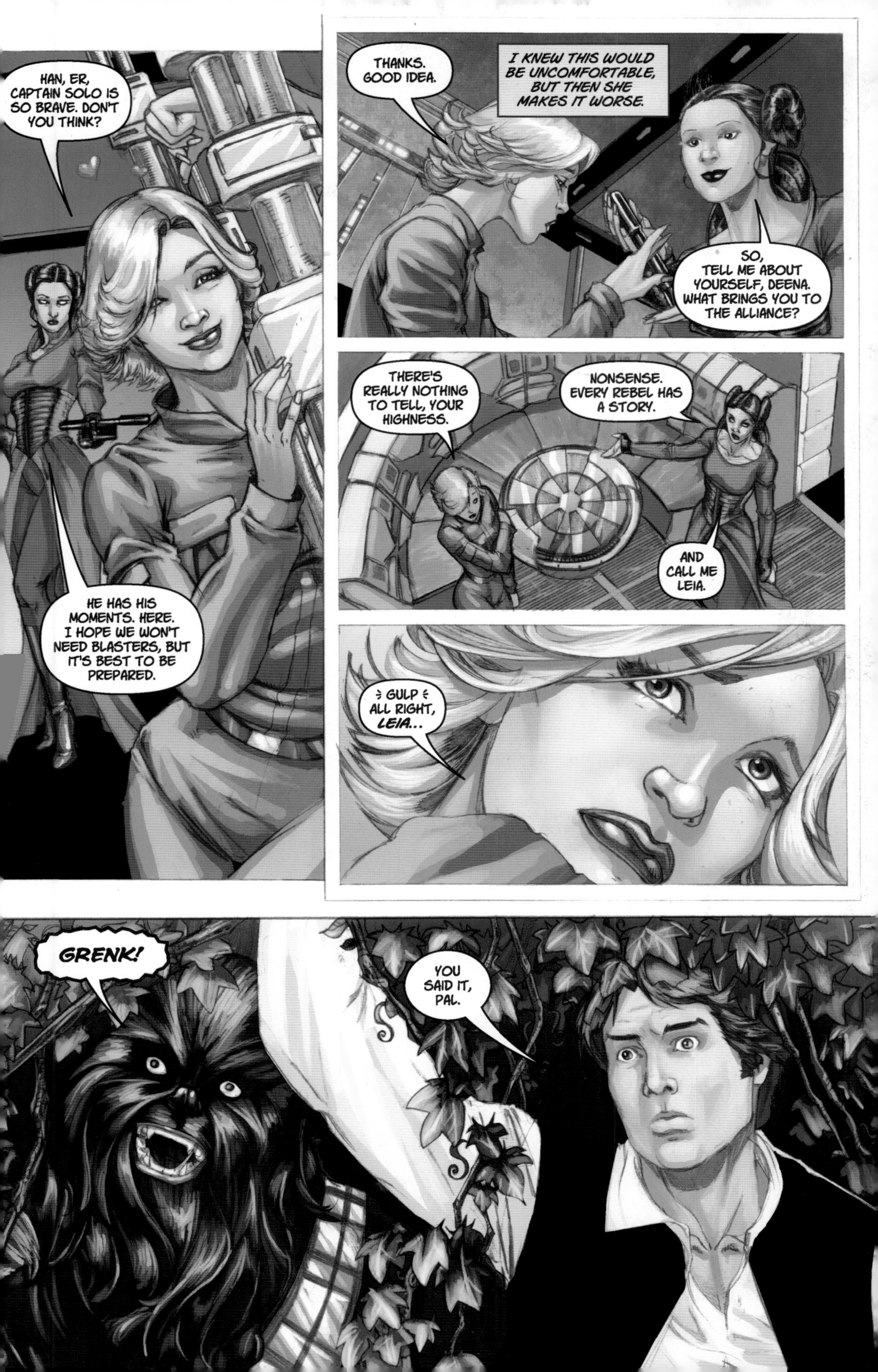
HAN, ER, CAPTAIN SOLO IS SO BRAVE. DON'T YOU THINK?
HE HAS HIS MOMENTS. HERE. I HOPE WE WON'T NEED BLASTERS, BUT IT'S BEST TO BE PREPARED.
THANKS. GOOD IDEA.
I KNEW THIS WOULD BE UNCOMFORTABLE, BUT THEN SHE MAKES IT WORSE.
SO, TELL ME ABOUT YOURSELF, DEENA. WHAT BRINGS YOU TO THE ALLIANCE?
THERE'S REALLY NOTHING TO TELL, YOUR HIGHNESS.
NONSENSE. EVERY REBEL HAS A STORY.
AND CALL ME LEIA.
GULP ALL RIGHT, LEIA...
GRENK!
YOU SAID IT, PAL.

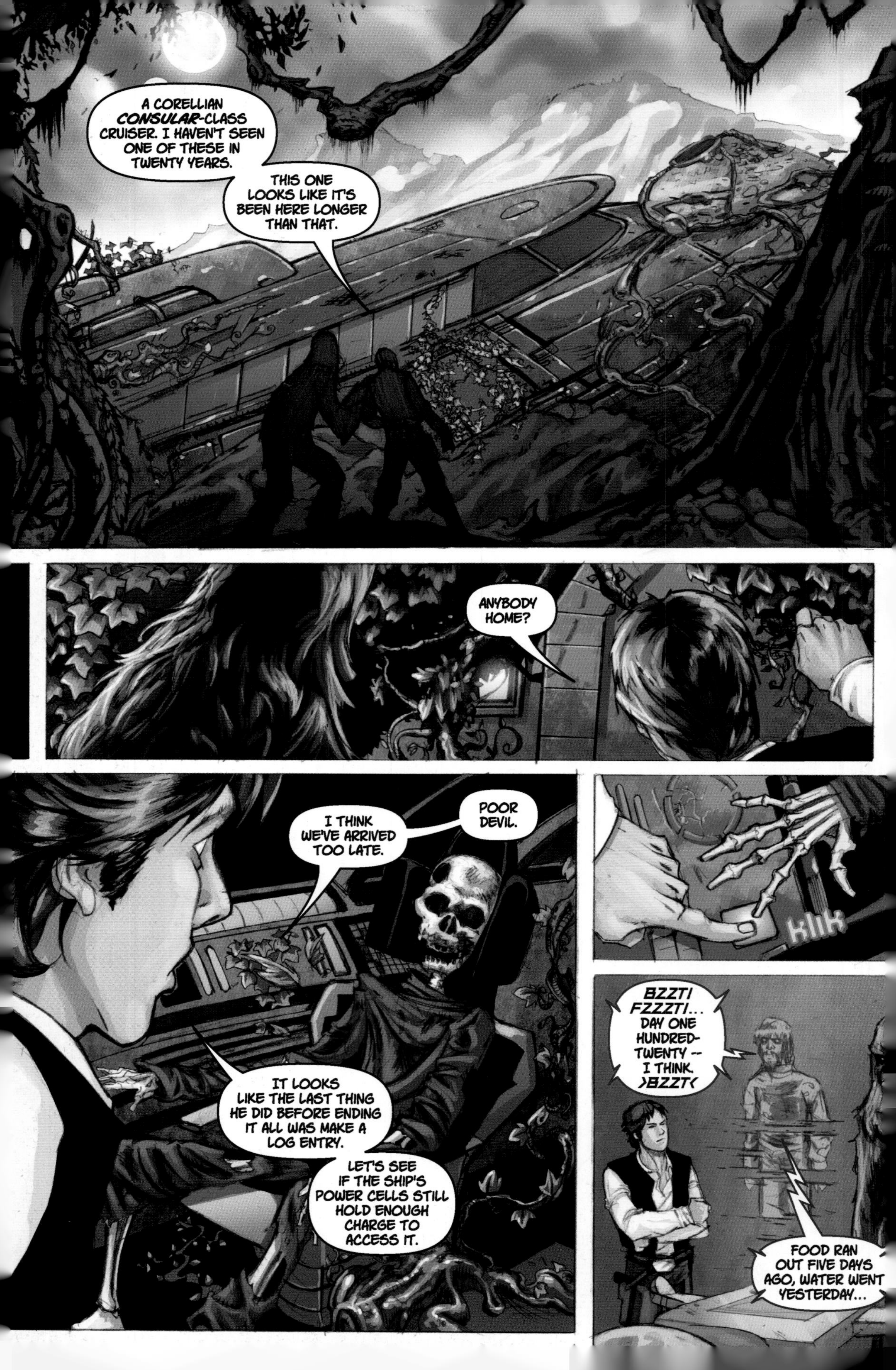

A CORELLIAN CONSULAR-CLASS CRUISER. I HAVEN'T SEEN ONE OF THESE IN TWENTY YEARS.
THIS ONE LOOKS LIKE IT'S BEEN HERE LONGER THAN THAT.
ANYBODY HOME?
I THINK WE'VE ARRIVED TOO LATE.
POOR DEVIL.
IT LOOKS LIKE THE LAST THING HE DID BEFORE ENDING IT ALL WAS MAKE A LOG ENTRY.
LET'S SEE IF THE SHIP'S POWER CELLS STILL HOLD ENOUGH CHARGE TO ACCESS IT.
KLIK
BZZT! FZZZT!... DAY ONE HUNDRED-TWENTY -- I THINK. >BZZT<
FOOD RAN OUT FIVE DAYS AGO, WATER WENT YESTERDAY...

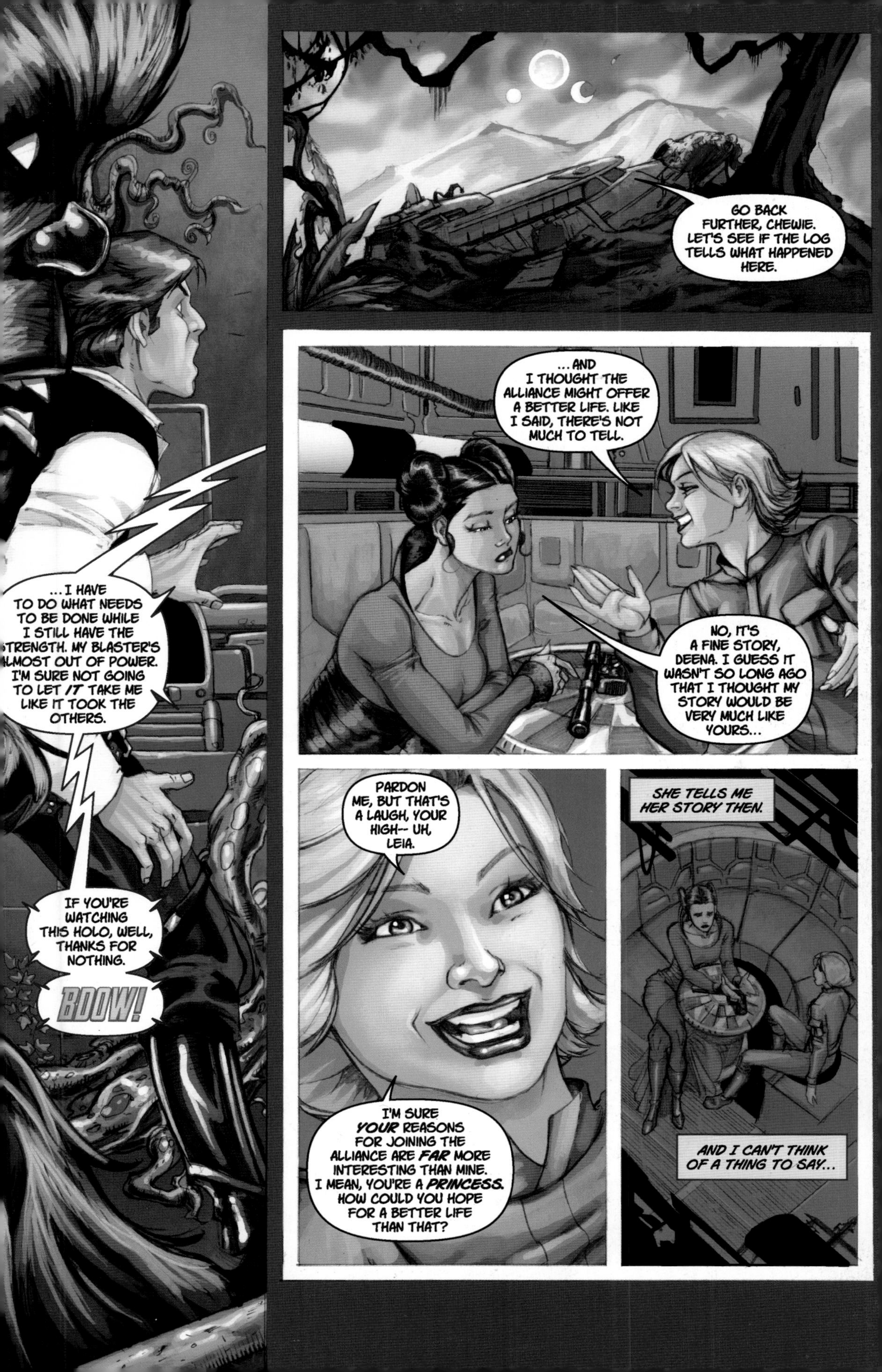

...I HAVE TO DO WHAT NEEDS TO BE DONE WHILE I STILL HAVE THE STRENGTH. MY BLASTER'S ALMOST OUT OF POWER. I'M SURE NOT GOING TO LET *IT* TAKE ME LIKE IT TOOK THE OTHERS.
IF YOU'RE WATCHING THIS HOLO, WELL, THANKS FOR NOTHING.
BDOW!
GO BACK FURTHER, CHEWIE. LET'S SEE IF THE LOG TELLS WHAT HAPPENED HERE.
...AND I THOUGHT THE ALLIANCE MIGHT OFFER A BETTER LIFE. LIKE I SAID, THERE'S NOT MUCH TO TELL.
NO, IT'S A FINE STORY, DEENA. I GUESS IT WASN'T SO LONG AGO THAT I THOUGHT MY STORY WOULD BE VERY MUCH LIKE YOURS...
PARDON ME, BUT THAT'S A LAUGH, YOUR HIGH-- UH, LEIA.
I'M SURE **YOUR** REASONS FOR JOINING THE ALLIANCE ARE **FAR** MORE INTERESTING THAN MINE. I MEAN, YOU'RE A **PRINCESS.** HOW COULD YOU HOPE FOR A BETTER LIFE THAN THAT?
SHE TELLS ME HER STORY THEN.
AND I CAN'T THINK OF A THING TO SAY...

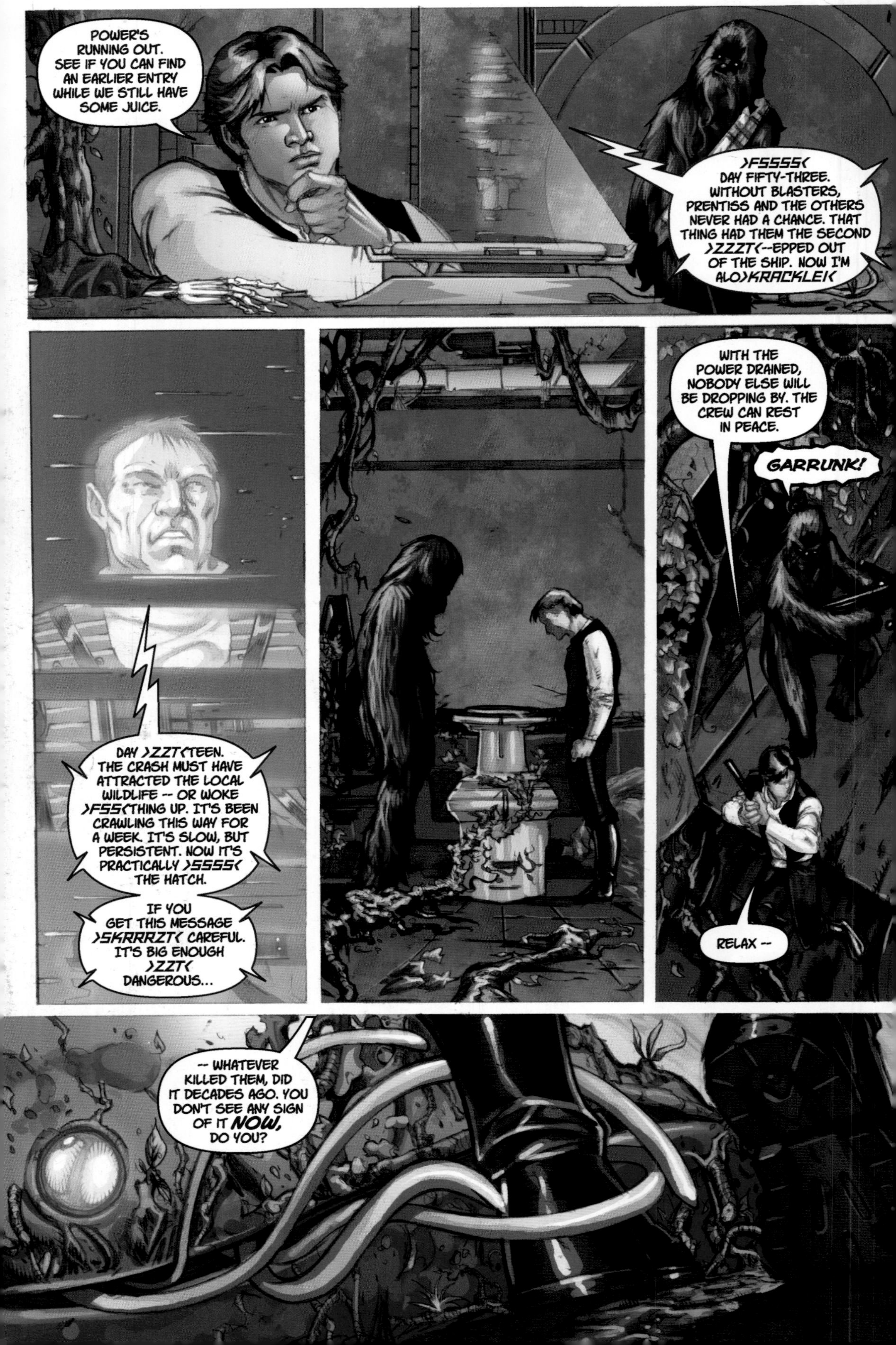
POWER'S RUNNING OUT. SEE IF YOU CAN FIND AN EARLIER ENTRY WHILE WE STILL HAVE SOME JUICE.
>FSSSS< DAY FIFTY-THREE. WITHOUT BLASTERS, PRENTISS AND THE OTHERS NEVER HAD A CHANCE. THAT THING HAD THEM THE SECOND >ZZZT<--EPPED OUT OF THE SHIP. NOW I'M ALO>KRACKLE!<
DAY >ZZT<TEEN. THE CRASH MUST HAVE ATTRACTED THE LOCAL WILDLIFE -- OR WOKE >FSS<THING UP. IT'S BEEN CRAWLING THIS WAY FOR A WEEK. IT'S SLOW, BUT PERSISTENT. NOW IT'S PRACTICALLY >SSSS< THE HATCH.
IF YOU GET THIS MESSAGE >SKRRRZT< CAREFUL. IT'S BIG ENOUGH >ZZT< DANGEROUS...
WITH THE POWER DRAINED, NOBODY ELSE WILL BE DROPPING BY. THE CREW CAN REST IN PEACE.
GARRUNK!
RELAX --
-- WHATEVER KILLED THEM, DID IT DECADES AGO. YOU DON'T SEE ANY SIGN OF IT NOW, DO YOU?

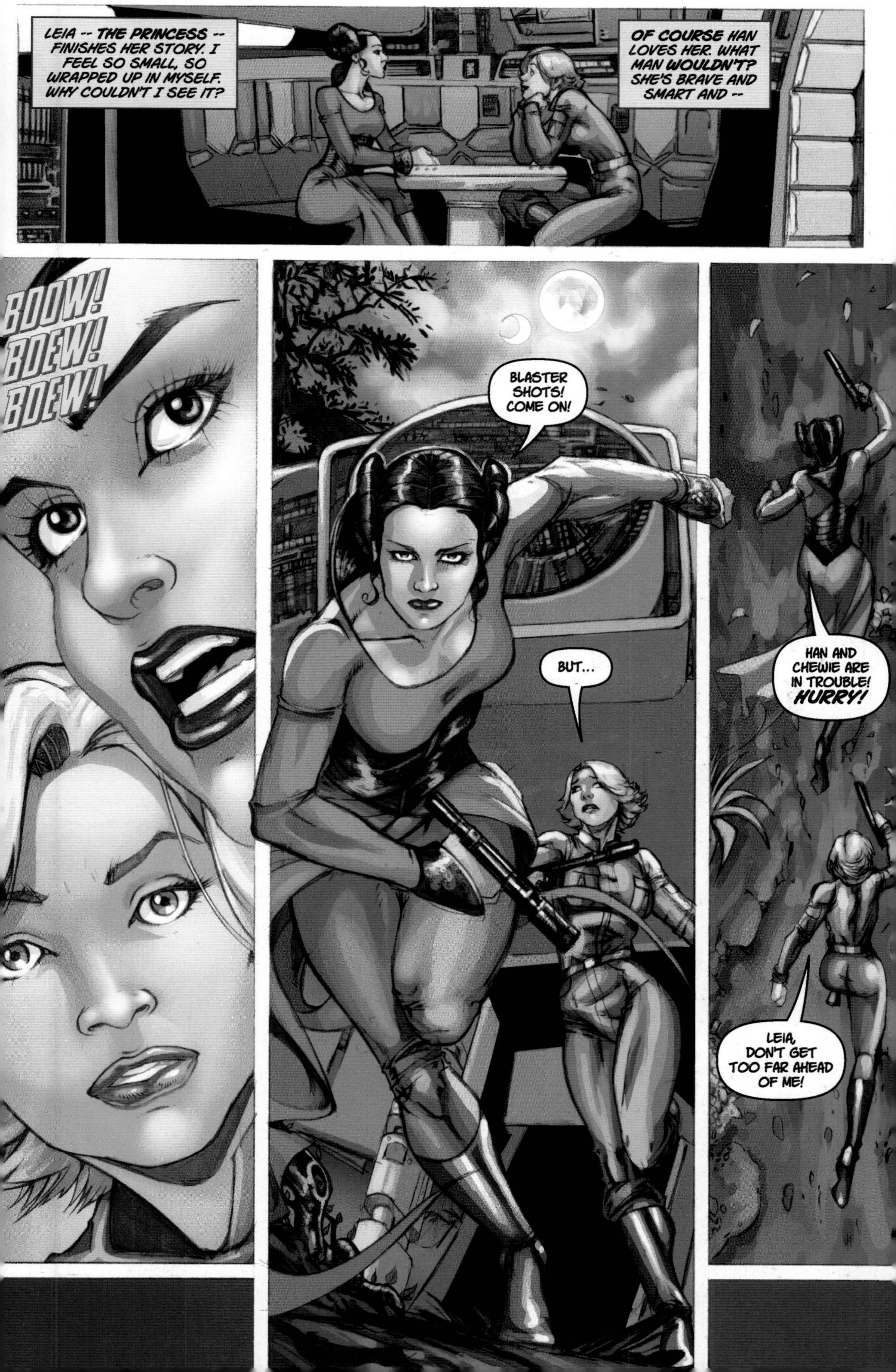
LEIA -- THE PRINCESS -- FINISHES HER STORY. I FEEL SO SMALL, SO WRAPPED UP IN MYSELF. WHY COULDN'T I SEE IT?
OF COURSE HAN LOVES HER. WHAT MAN WOULDN'T? SHE'S BRAVE AND SMART AND --
BDOW! BDEW! BDEW!
BLASTER SHOTS! COME ON!
BUT...
HAN AND CHEWIE ARE IN TROUBLE! HURRY!
LEIA, DON'T GET TOO FAR AHEAD OF ME!

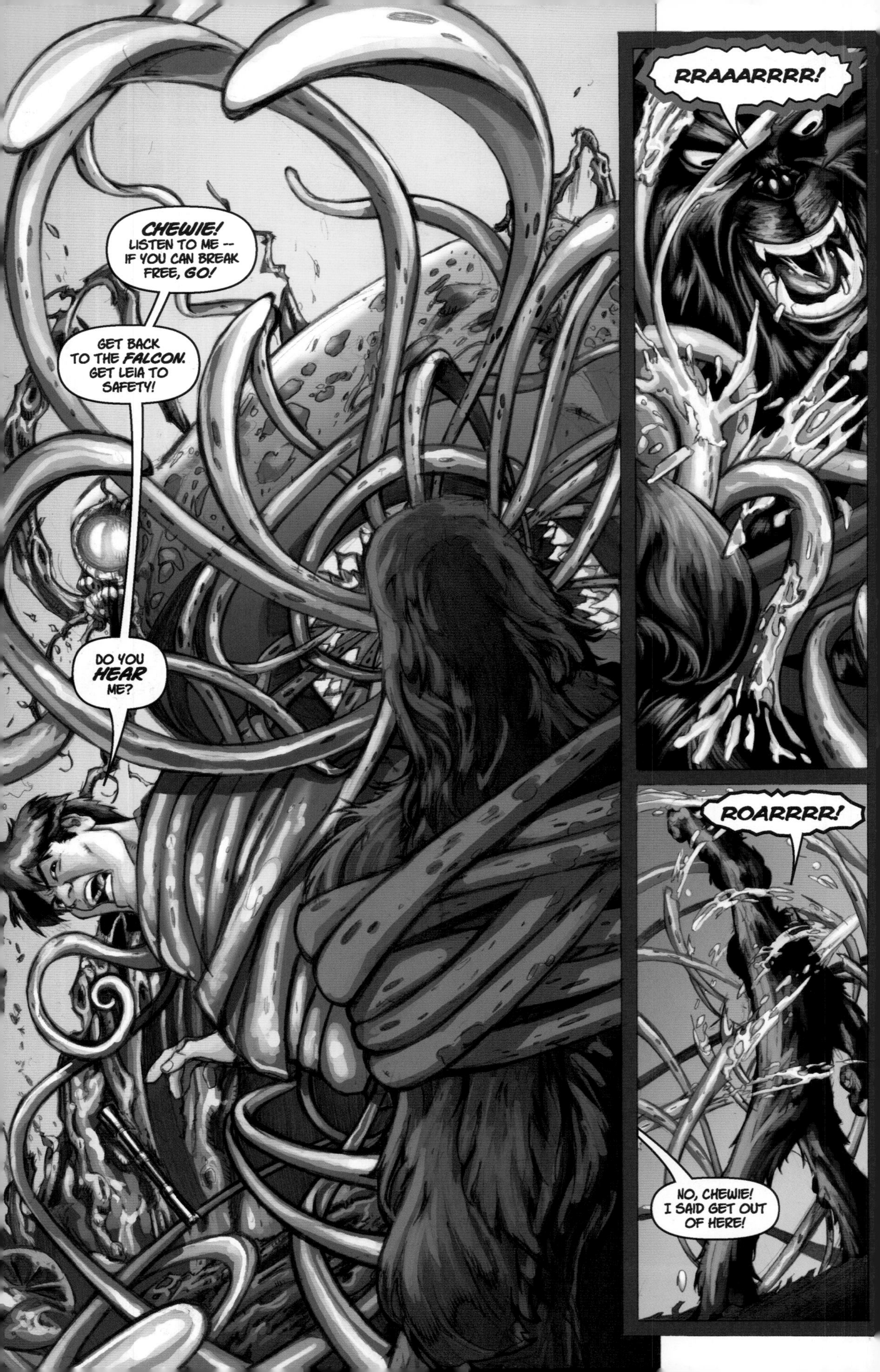
CHEWIE! LISTEN TO ME -- IF YOU CAN BREAK FREE, GO!
GET BACK TO THE FALCON. GET LEIA TO SAFETY!
DO YOU HEAR ME?
RRAAARRRR!
ROARRRR!
NO, CHEWIE! I SAID GET OUT OF HERE!

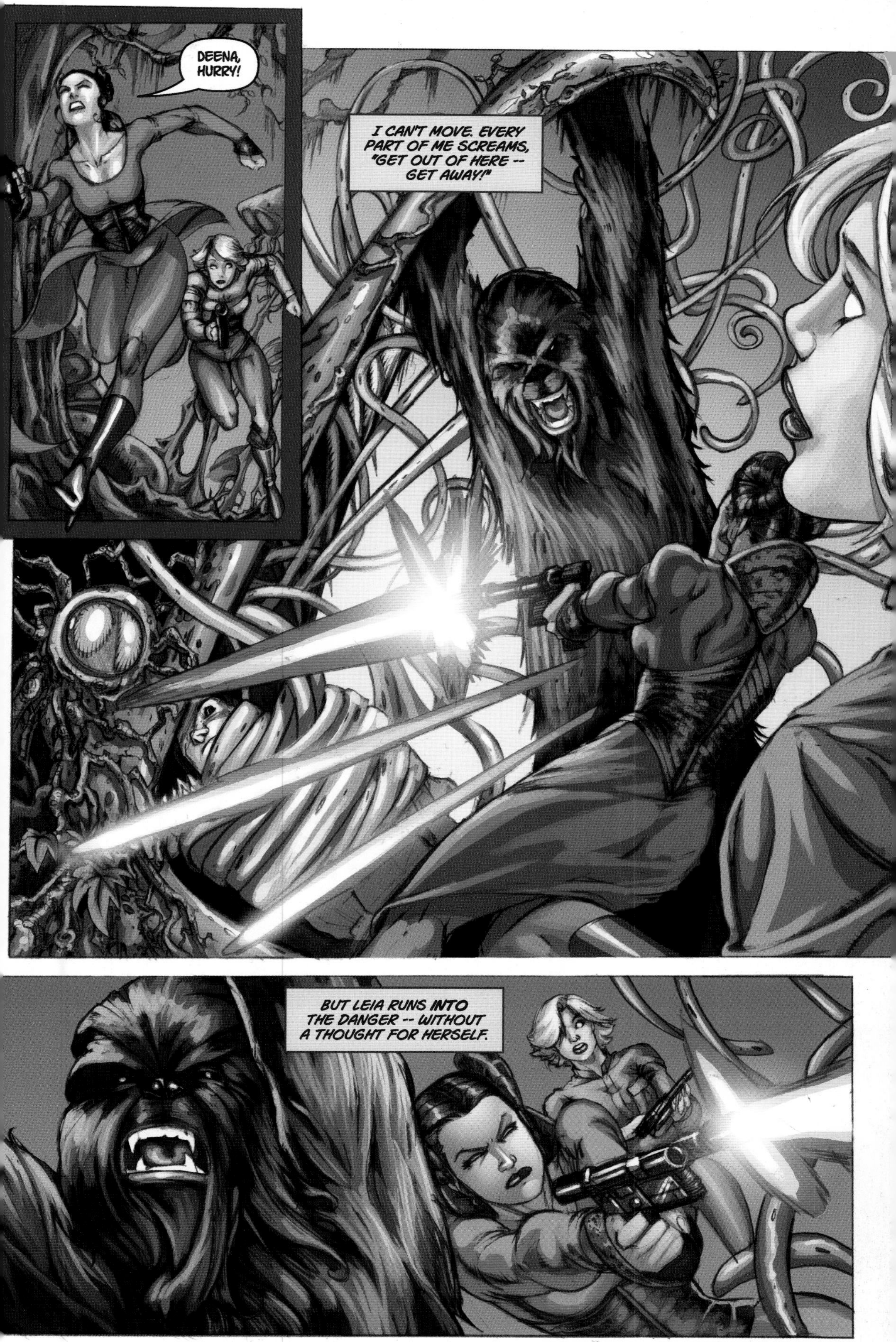
DEENA, HURRY!
I CAN'T MOVE. EVERY PART OF ME SCREAMS, "GET OUT OF HERE -- GET AWAY!"
BUT LEIA RUNS INTO THE DANGER -- WITHOUT A THOUGHT FOR HERSELF.

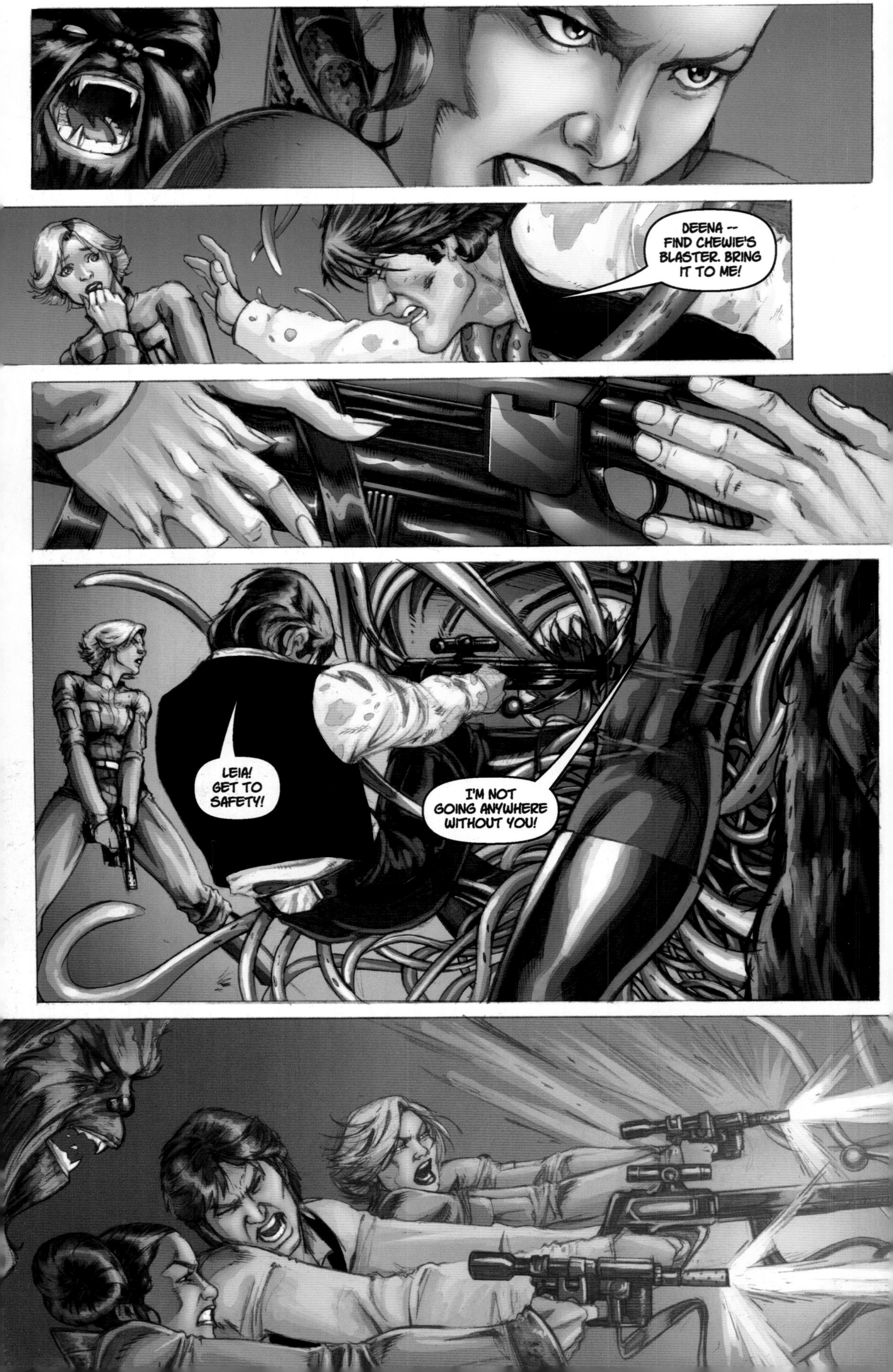
DEENA -- FIND CHEWIE'S BLASTER. BRING IT TO ME!
LEIA! GET TO SAFETY!
I'M NOT GOING ANYWHERE WITHOUT YOU!

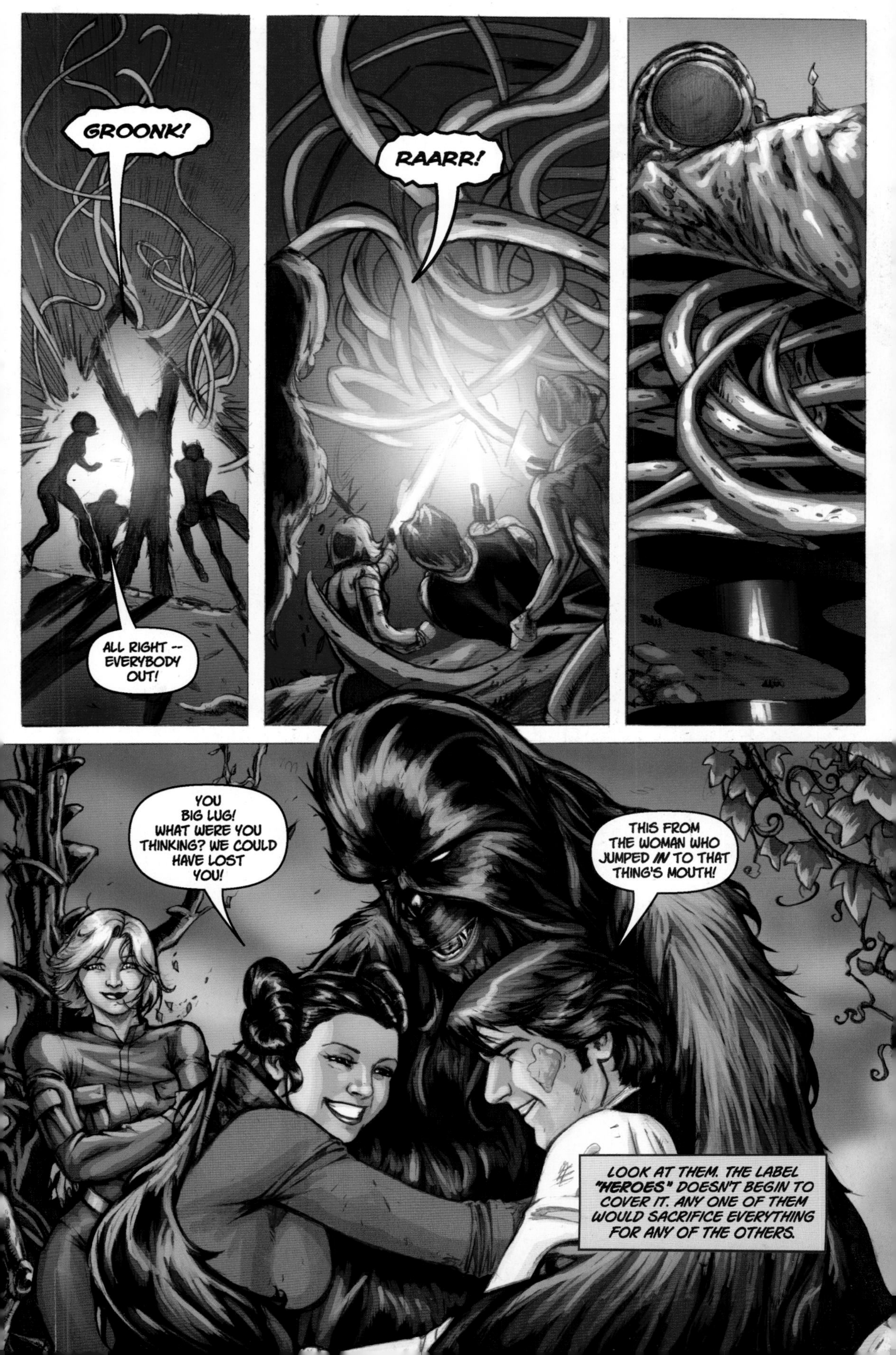
GROONK!
ALL RIGHT -- EVERYBODY OUT!
RAARR!
YOU BIG LUG! WHAT WERE YOU THINKING? WE COULD HAVE LOST YOU!
THIS FROM THE WOMAN WHO JUMPED IN TO THAT THING'S MOUTH!
LOOK AT THEM. THE LABEL "HEROES" DOESN'T BEGIN TO COVER IT. ANY ONE OF THEM WOULD SACRIFICE EVERYTHING FOR ANY OF THE OTHERS.

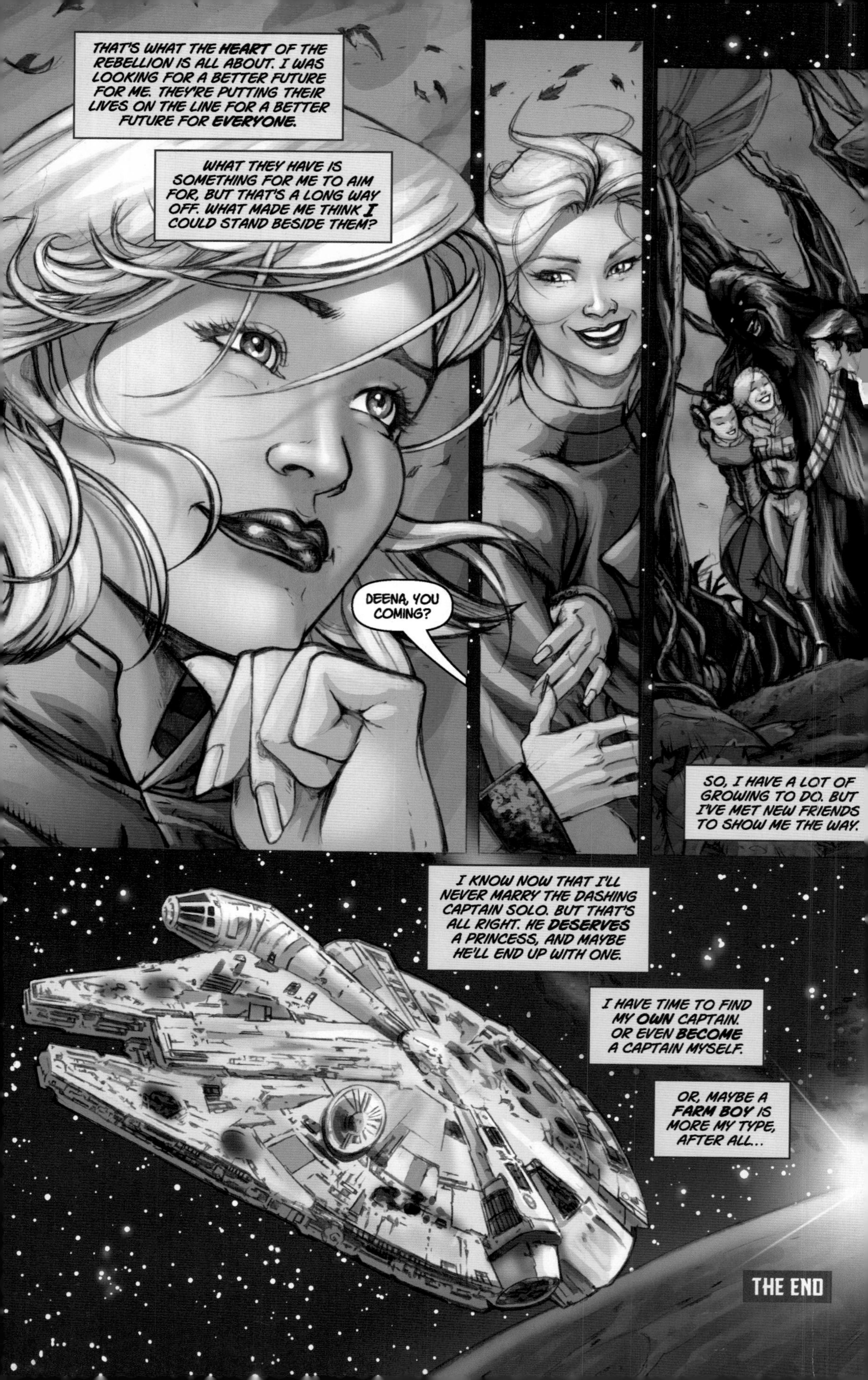
THAT'S WHAT THE HEART OF THE REBELLION IS ALL ABOUT. I WAS LOOKING FOR A BETTER FUTURE FOR ME. THEY'RE PUTTING THEIR LIVES ON THE LINE FOR A BETTER FUTURE FOR EVERYONE.
WHAT THEY HAVE IS SOMETHING FOR ME TO AIM FOR, BUT THAT'S A LONG WAY OFF. WHAT MADE ME THINK I COULD STAND BESIDE THEM?
DEENA, YOU COMING?
SO, I HAVE A LOT OF GROWING TO DO. BUT I'VE MET NEW FRIENDS TO SHOW ME THE WAY.
I KNOW NOW THAT I'LL NEVER MARRY THE DASHING CAPTAIN SOLO. BUT THAT'S ALL RIGHT. HE DESERVES A PRINCESS, AND MAYBE HE'LL END UP WITH ONE.
I HAVE TIME TO FIND MY OWN CAPTAIN. OR EVEN BECOME A CAPTAIN MYSELF.
OR, MAYBE A FARM BOY IS MORE MY TYPE, AFTER ALL...
THE END

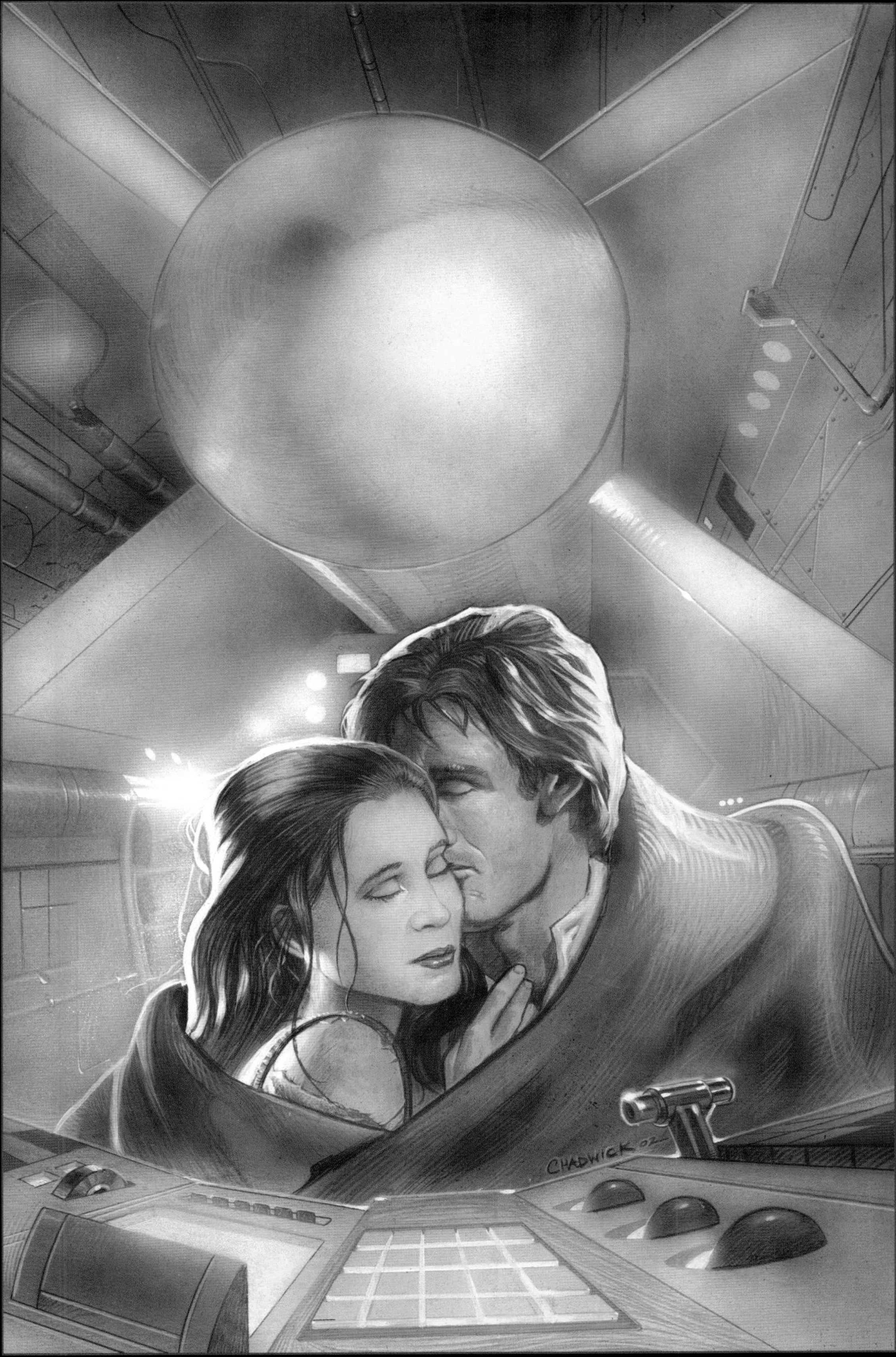
CHADWICK '02

PAUL CHADWICK

BREAKING THE ICE

SCRIPT JUDD WINICK
ART PAUL CHADWICK
COLORS KEN STEACY

A LONG TIME AGO, IN A GALAXY FAR, FAR AWAY...

THERE WERE FOUR HEROES.

THE YOUNG KNIGHT.

THE BRAVE WARRIOR.

HIS FAITHFUL COMPANION.

A SOVEREIGN LEADER.

THEY HAD DEALT A CRUSHING BLOW TO THE *EMPIRE* THAT WAS STIFLING THEIR GROWING REBELLION.

TOGETHER WITH THEIR SMALL ARMY, THEY DISPATCHED THEIR DARK ENEMY'S *GREATEST* WEAPON.

THEY SUCCEEDED WHEN ALL HOPE WAS LOST.

THEY FOUND STRENGTH IN THEIR RESOLVE.

THE *POWER* OF THEIR *WILL.*

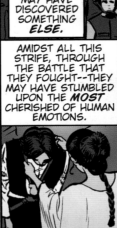

BUT *TWO* OF OUR HEROES MAY HAVE DISCOVERED SOMETHING *ELSE.*

AMIDST ALL THIS STRIFE, THROUGH THE BATTLE THAT THEY FOUGHT--THEY MAY HAVE STUMBLED UPON THE *MOST* CHERISHED OF HUMAN EMOTIONS.

PERHAPS, DESPITE THE WAR THAT WAGES AROUND THEM ...

...THIS PAIR MAY HAVE FOUND THE BEGINNINGS OF *LOVE.*

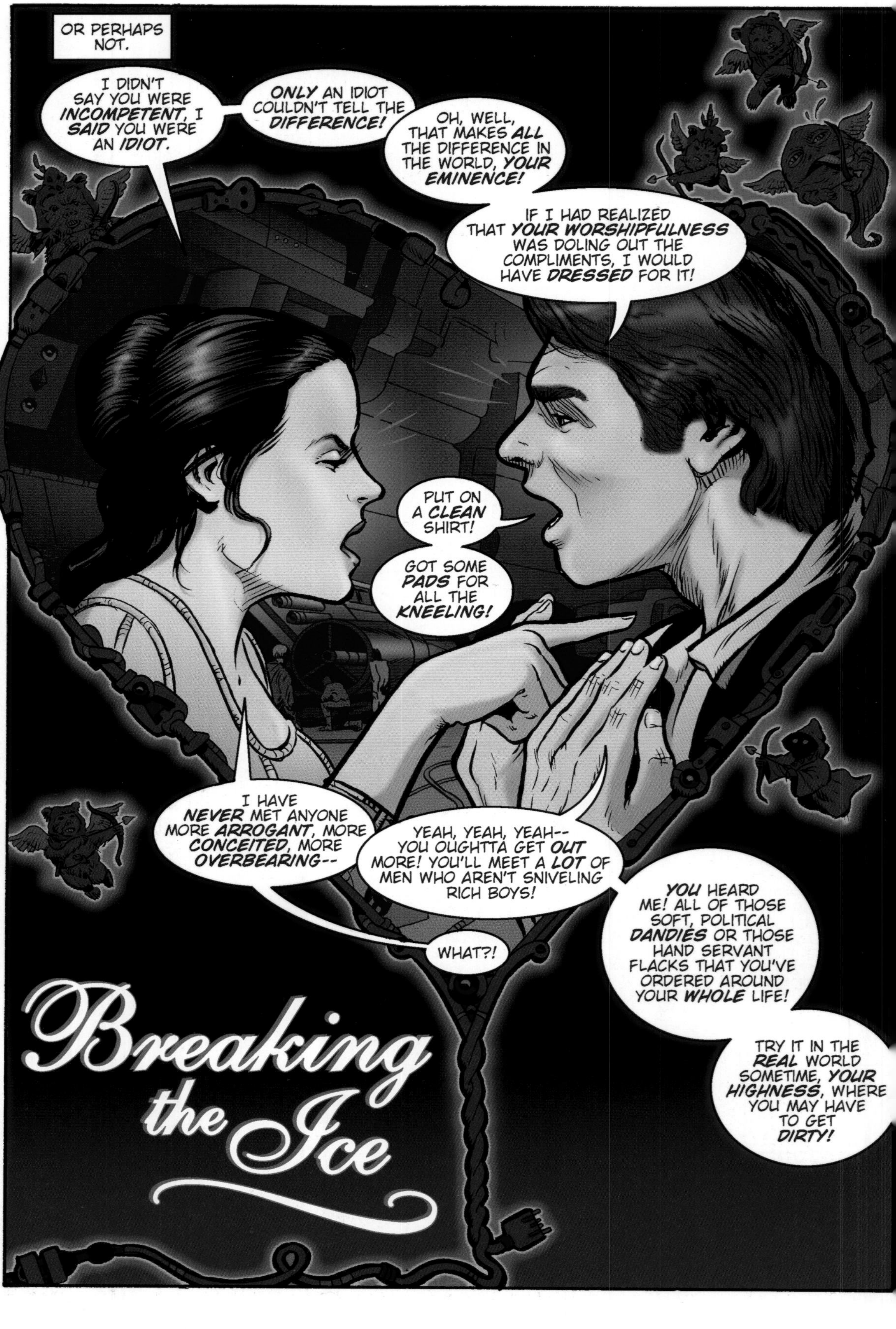
OR PERHAPS NOT.
I DIDN'T SAY YOU WERE INCOMPETENT, I SAID YOU WERE AN IDIOT.
ONLY AN IDIOT COULDN'T TELL THE DIFFERENCE!
OH, WELL, THAT MAKES ALL THE DIFFERENCE IN THE WORLD, YOUR EMINENCE!
IF I HAD REALIZED THAT YOUR WORSHIPFULNESS WAS DOLING OUT THE COMPLIMENTS, I WOULD HAVE DRESSED FOR IT!
PUT ON A CLEAN SHIRT!
GOT SOME PADS FOR ALL THE KNEELING!
I HAVE NEVER MET ANYONE MORE ARROGANT, MORE CONCEITED, MORE OVERBEARING--
YEAH, YEAH, YEAH-- YOU OUGHTTA GET OUT MORE! YOU'LL MEET A LOT OF MEN WHO AREN'T SNIVELING RICH BOYS!
WHAT?!
YOU HEARD ME! ALL OF THOSE SOFT, POLITICAL DANDIES OR THOSE HAND SERVANT FLACKS THAT YOU'VE ORDERED AROUND YOUR WHOLE LIFE!
TRY IT IN THE REAL WORLD SOMETIME, YOUR HIGHNESS, WHERE YOU MAY HAVE TO GET DIRTY!
Breaking the Ice

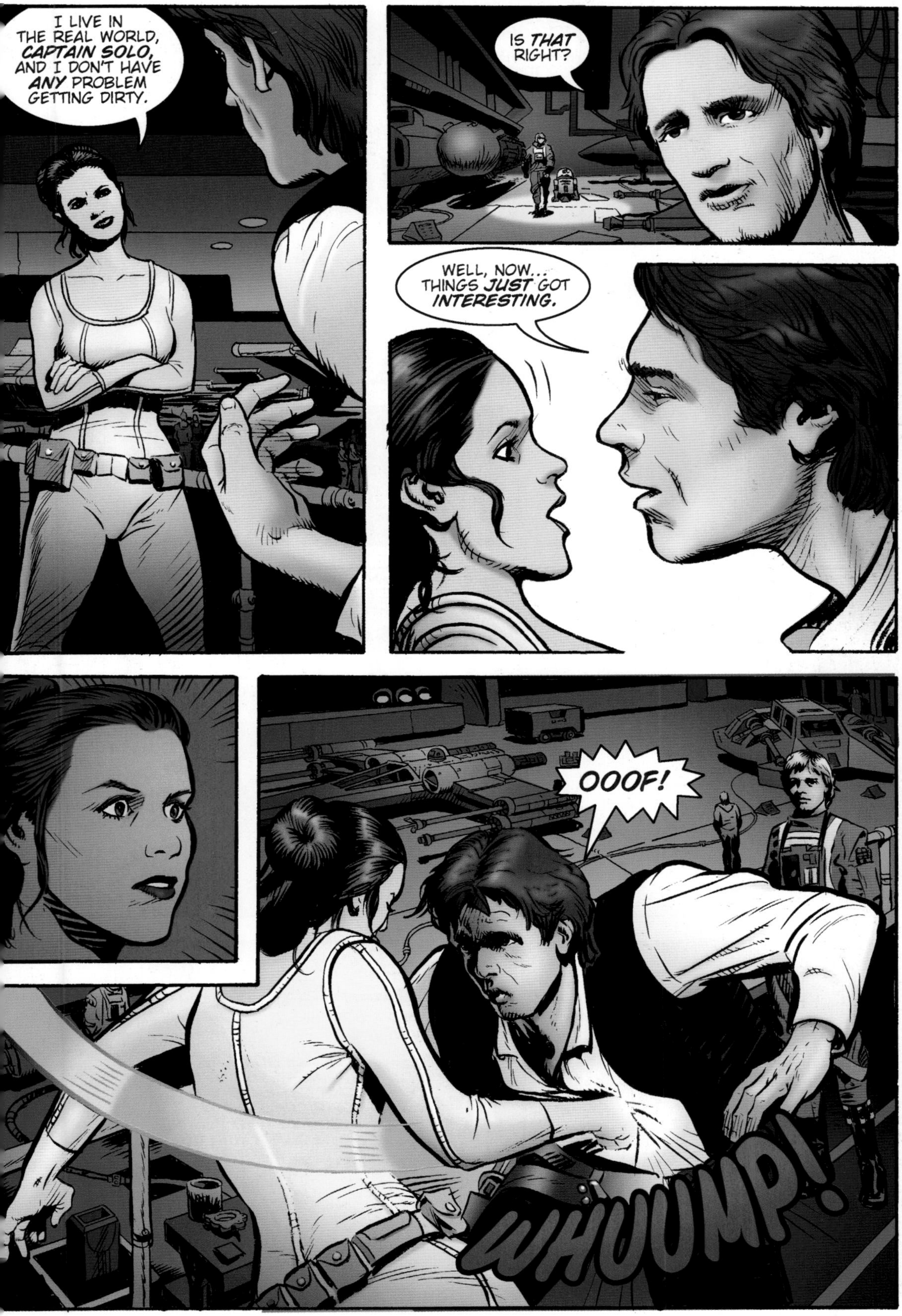
I LIVE IN THE REAL WORLD, CAPTAIN SOLO, AND I DON'T HAVE ANY PROBLEM GETTING DIRTY.
IS THAT RIGHT?
WELL, NOW... THINGS JUST GOT INTERESTING.
OOOF!
WHUUMP!

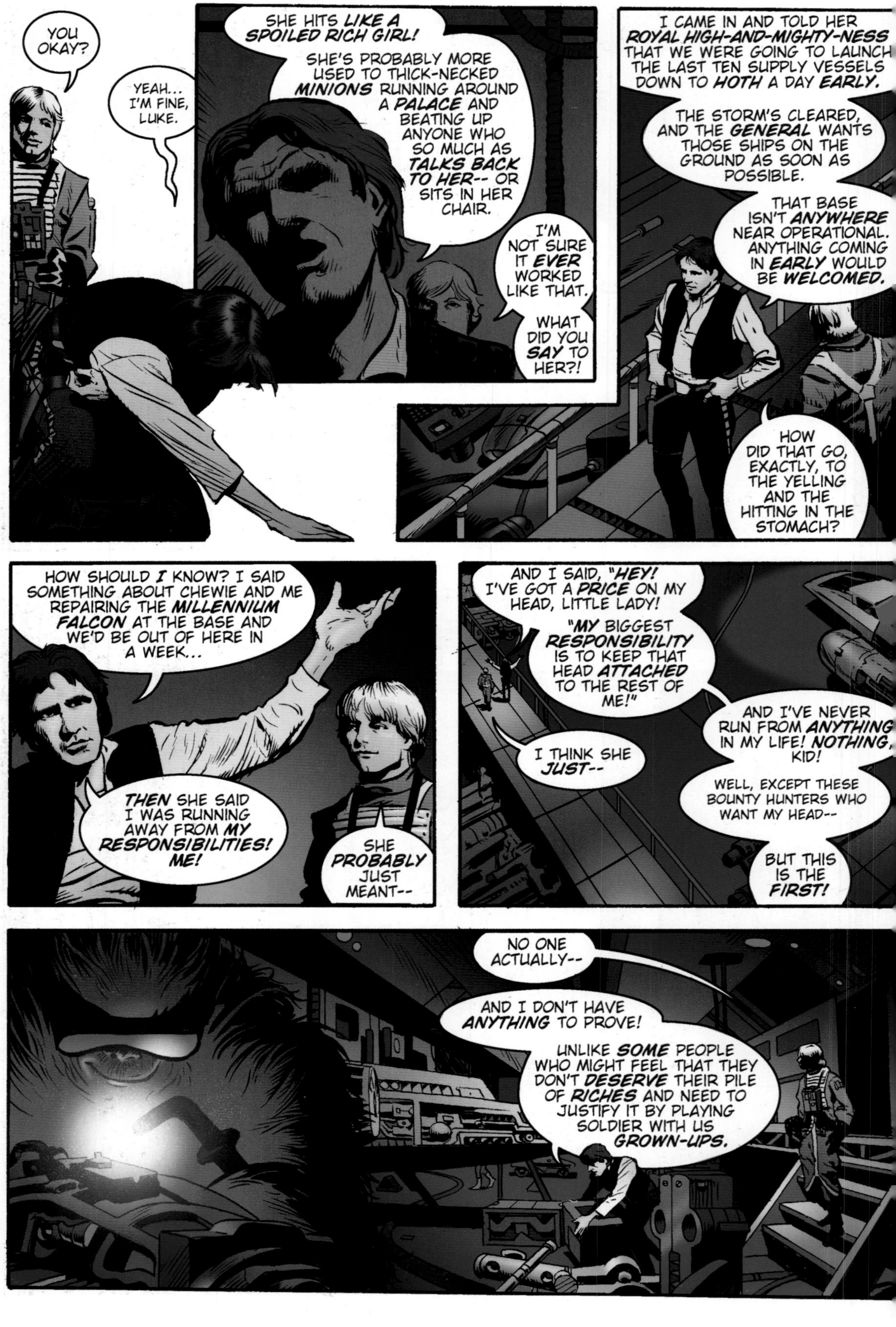
YOU OKAY?
YEAH... I'M FINE, LUKE.
SHE HITS LIKE A SPOILED RICH GIRL!
SHE'S PROBABLY MORE USED TO THICK-NECKED MINIONS RUNNING AROUND A PALACE AND BEATING UP ANYONE WHO SO MUCH AS TALKS BACK TO HER-- OR SITS IN HER CHAIR.
I'M NOT SURE IT EVER WORKED LIKE THAT.
WHAT DID YOU SAY TO HER?!
I CAME IN AND TOLD HER ROYAL HIGH-AND-MIGHTY-NESS THAT WE WERE GOING TO LAUNCH THE LAST TEN SUPPLY VESSELS DOWN TO HOTH A DAY EARLY.
THE STORM'S CLEARED, AND THE GENERAL WANTS THOSE SHIPS ON THE GROUND AS SOON AS POSSIBLE.
THAT BASE ISN'T ANYWHERE NEAR OPERATIONAL. ANYTHING COMING IN EARLY WOULD BE WELCOMED.
HOW DID THAT GO, EXACTLY, TO THE YELLING AND THE HITTING IN THE STOMACH?
HOW SHOULD I KNOW? I SAID SOMETHING ABOUT CHEWIE AND ME REPAIRING THE MILLENNIUM FALCON AT THE BASE AND WE'D BE OUT OF HERE IN A WEEK...
THEN SHE SAID I WAS RUNNING AWAY FROM MY RESPONSIBILITIES! ME!
SHE PROBABLY JUST MEANT--
AND I SAID, "HEY! I'VE GOT A PRICE ON MY HEAD, LITTLE LADY!
"MY BIGGEST RESPONSIBILITY IS TO KEEP THAT HEAD ATTACHED TO THE REST OF ME!"
I THINK SHE JUST--
AND I'VE NEVER RUN FROM ANYTHING IN MY LIFE! NOTHING, KID!
WELL, EXCEPT THESE BOUNTY HUNTERS WHO WANT MY HEAD--
BUT THIS IS THE FIRST!
NO ONE ACTUALLY--
AND I DON'T HAVE ANYTHING TO PROVE!
UNLIKE SOME PEOPLE WHO MIGHT FEEL THAT THEY DON'T DESERVE THEIR PILE OF RICHES AND NEED TO JUSTIFY IT BY PLAYING SOLDIER WITH US GROWN-UPS.

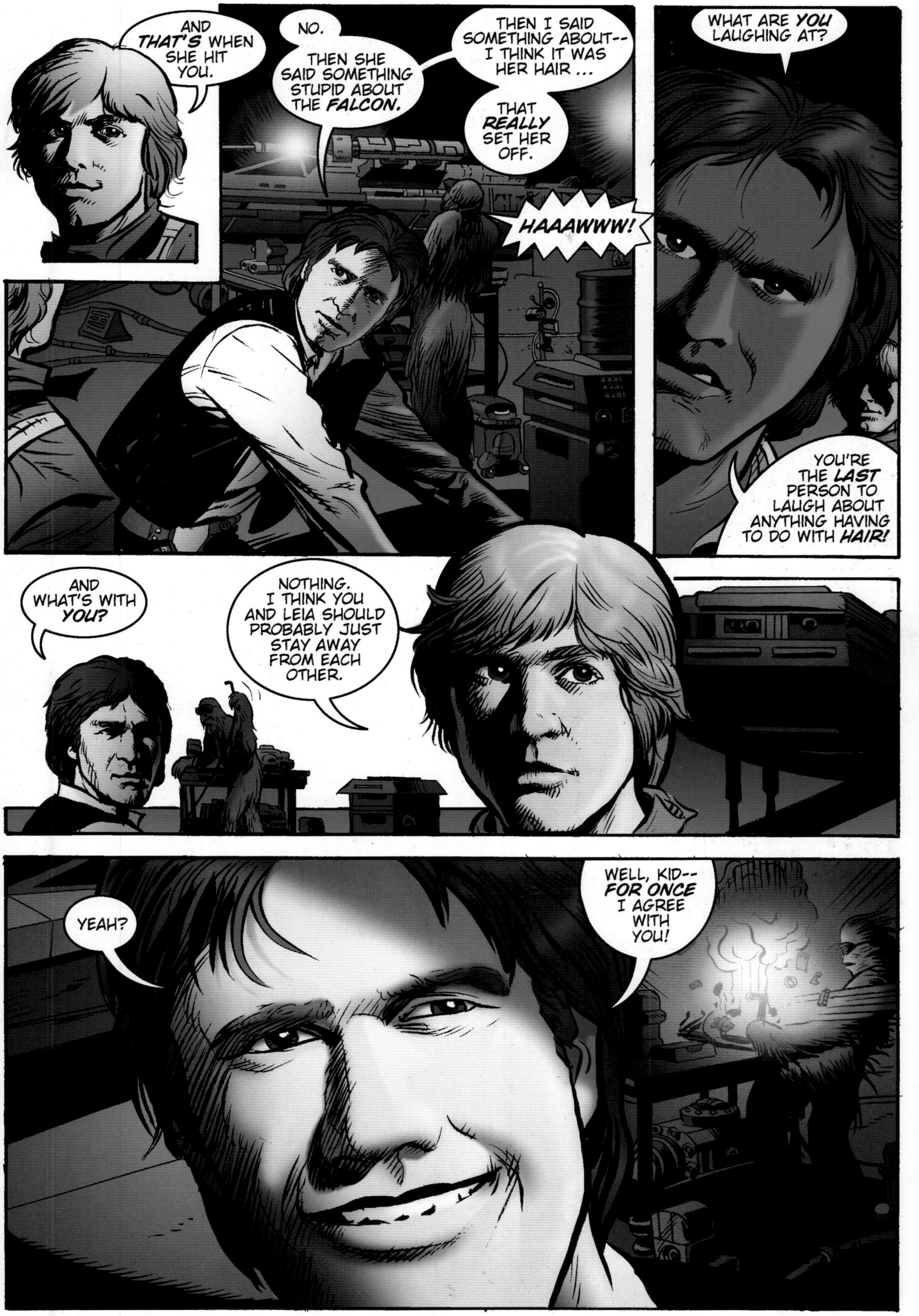
AND THAT'S WHEN SHE HIT YOU.
NO.
THEN SHE SAID SOMETHING STUPID ABOUT THE FALCON.
THEN I SAID SOMETHING ABOUT-- I THINK IT WAS HER HAIR ...
THAT REALLY SET HER OFF.
HAAAWWW!
WHAT ARE YOU LAUGHING AT?
YOU'RE THE LAST PERSON TO LAUGH ABOUT ANYTHING HAVING TO DO WITH HAIR!
AND WHAT'S WITH YOU?
NOTHING. I THINK YOU AND LEIA SHOULD PROBABLY JUST STAY AWAY FROM EACH OTHER.
YEAH?
WELL, KID-- FOR ONCE I AGREE WITH YOU!

NO, SIR, IT'S COMPLETELY *OFFLINE*.

WE WON'T BE ABLE TO GET THESE OUT UNTIL TOMORROW.

WE WERE PLANNING ON RIDING ALONG IN *ONE* OF THESE *CARRIERS*.

WE SHOULD *REALLY* GET DOWN ON THE SURFACE BY *TONIGHT*.

SINCE THE *FALCON'S* OUT OF COMMISSION UNTIL REPAIRS ARE DONE, WHAT SHIP *CAN* I FLY OUT OF HERE IN?

WELL, WE *DO* NEED TWO TWIN *M-CLASS FIGHTERS* DOWN THERE.

BUT ONE OF THEM HAS A BUSTED *NAVICOM*, AND THE *HYDROBOOSTERS* AREN'T ON AUTO. IT NEEDS A *CO-PILOT*.

I'D SEND ONE OF THE FLIGHT CREW, BUT WE CAN'T SPARE THE PILOTS, SIR.

THAT'S FINE. CHEWIE AND I WILL TAKE JUST THE *ONE*.

NO. IT'S A WASTE TO SEND JUST THE SINGLE SHIP.

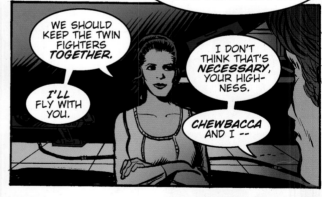

WE SHOULD KEEP THE TWIN FIGHTERS *TOGETHER*.

I'LL FLY WITH YOU.

I DON'T THINK THAT'S *NECESSARY*, YOUR HIGH-NESS.

CHEWBACCA AND I --

YOU'RE NOT THE *ONLY* ONES WHO NEED TO BE DOWN ON THE SURFACE, CAPTAIN.

AND I WASN'T *ASKING*.

I'LL SEE YOU IN LAUNCH BAY 81 IN TEN MINUTES.

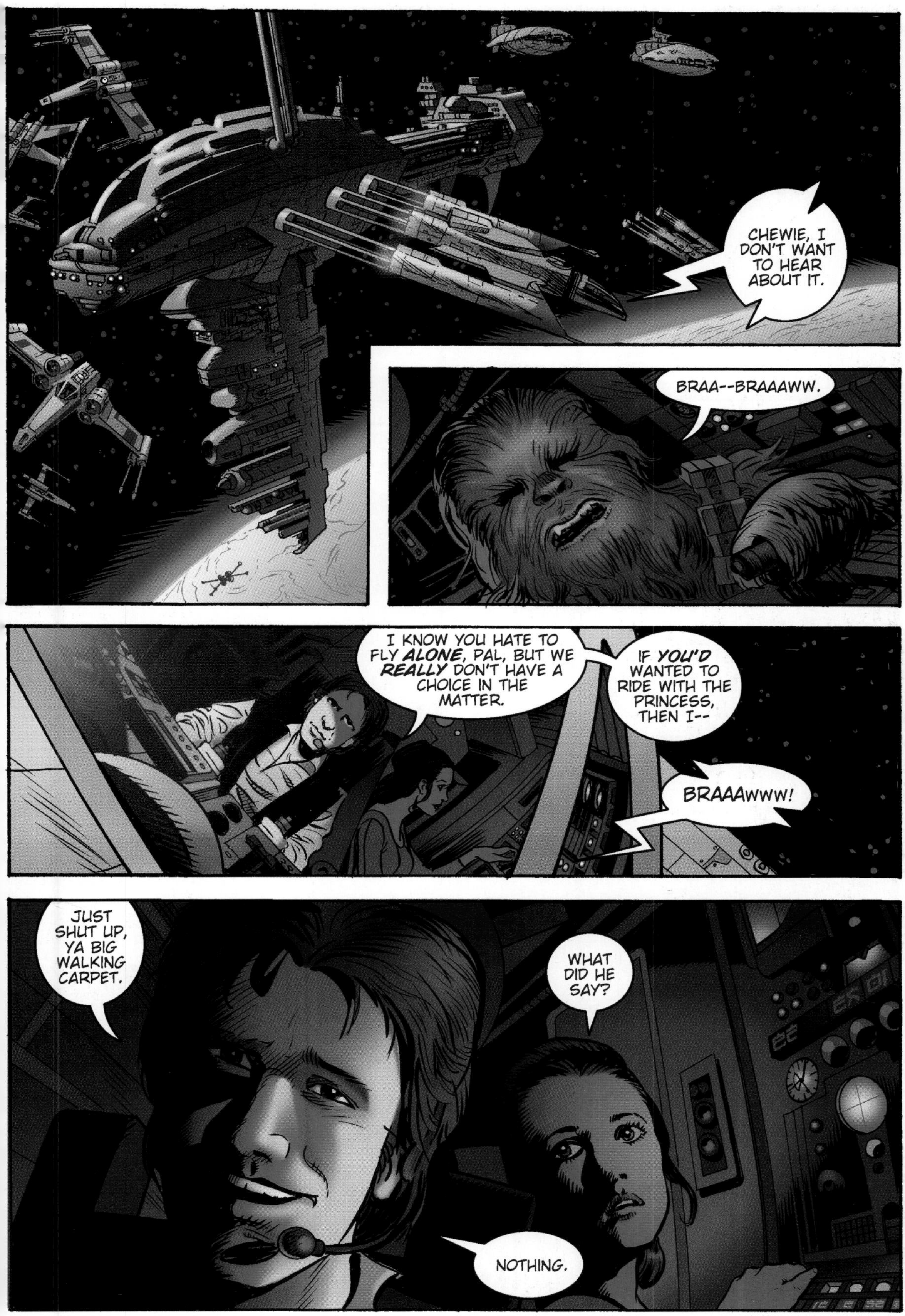
CHEWIE, I DON'T WANT TO HEAR ABOUT IT.
BRAA--BRAAAWW.
I KNOW YOU HATE TO FLY ALONE, PAL, BUT WE REALLY DON'T HAVE A CHOICE IN THE MATTER.
IF YOU'D WANTED TO RIDE WITH THE PRINCESS, THEN I--
BRAAAWWW!
JUST SHUT UP, YA BIG WALKING CARPET.
WHAT DID HE SAY?
NOTHING.

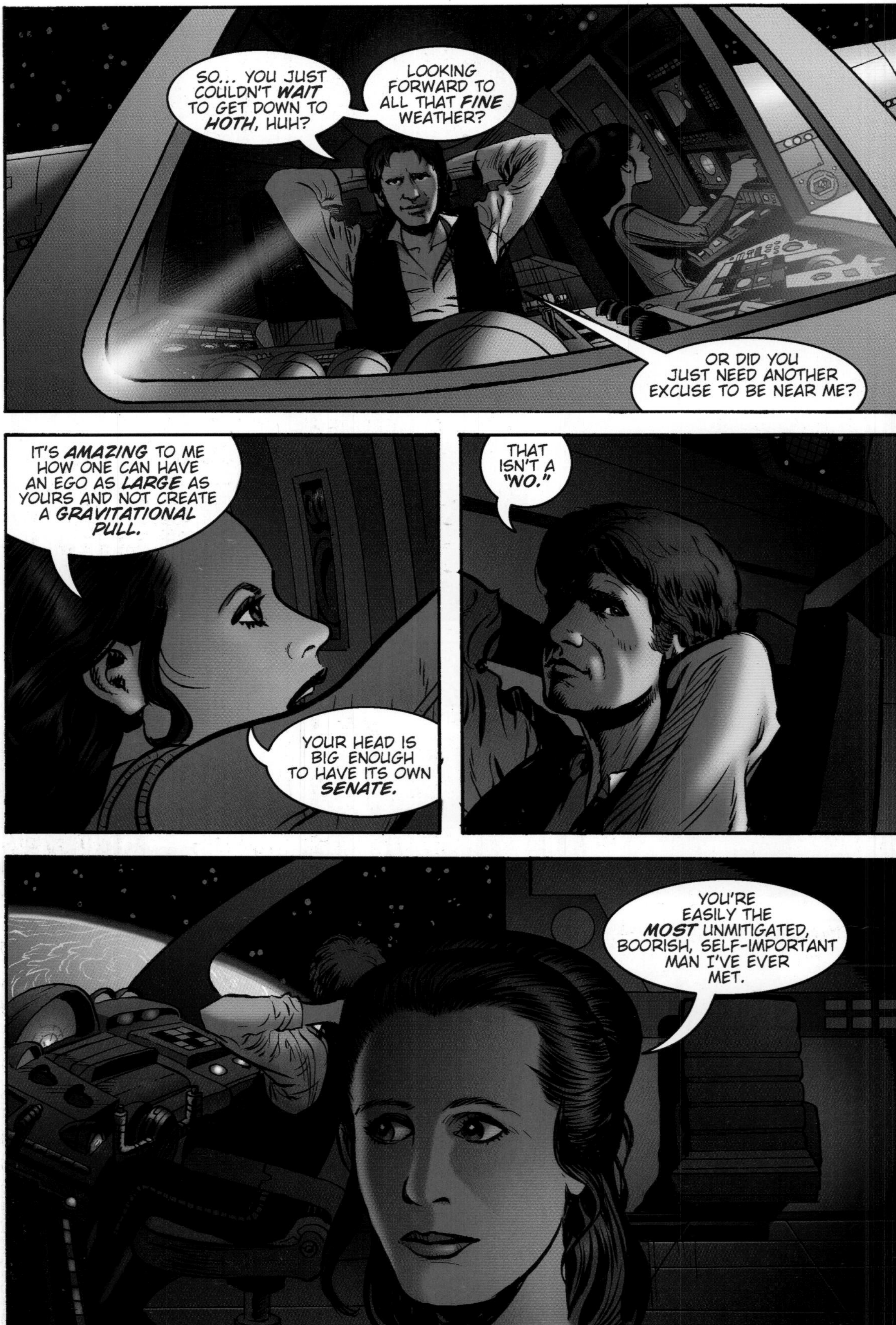
SO... YOU JUST COULDN'T WAIT TO GET DOWN TO HOTH, HUH?
LOOKING FORWARD TO ALL THAT FINE WEATHER?
OR DID YOU JUST NEED ANOTHER EXCUSE TO BE NEAR ME?
IT'S AMAZING TO ME HOW ONE CAN HAVE AN EGO AS LARGE AS YOURS AND NOT CREATE A GRAVITATIONAL PULL.
YOUR HEAD IS BIG ENOUGH TO HAVE ITS OWN SENATE.
THAT ISN'T A "NO."
YOU'RE EASILY THE MOST UNMITIGATED, BOORISH, SELF-IMPORTANT MAN I'VE EVER MET.

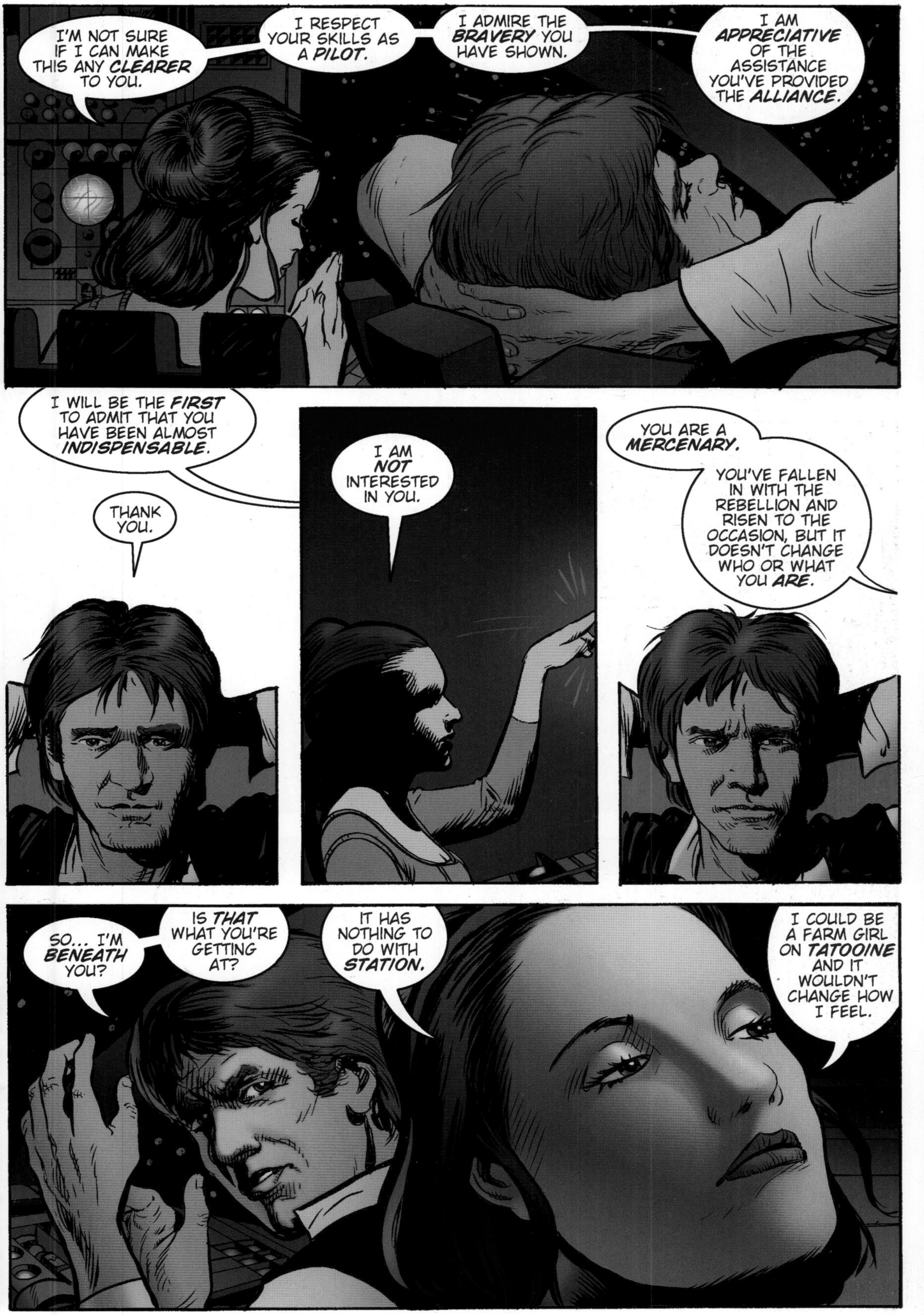
I'M NOT SURE IF I CAN MAKE THIS ANY CLEARER TO YOU.
I RESPECT YOUR SKILLS AS A PILOT.
I ADMIRE THE BRAVERY YOU HAVE SHOWN.
I AM APPRECIATIVE OF THE ASSISTANCE YOU'VE PROVIDED THE ALLIANCE.
I WILL BE THE FIRST TO ADMIT THAT YOU HAVE BEEN ALMOST INDISPENSABLE.
THANK YOU.
I AM NOT INTERESTED IN YOU.
YOU ARE A MERCENARY.
YOU'VE FALLEN IN WITH THE REBELLION AND RISEN TO THE OCCASION, BUT IT DOESN'T CHANGE WHO OR WHAT YOU ARE.
SO... I'M BENEATH YOU?
IS THAT WHAT YOU'RE GETTING AT?
IT HAS NOTHING TO DO WITH STATION.
I COULD BE A FARM GIRL ON TATOOINE AND IT WOULDN'T CHANGE HOW I FEEL.

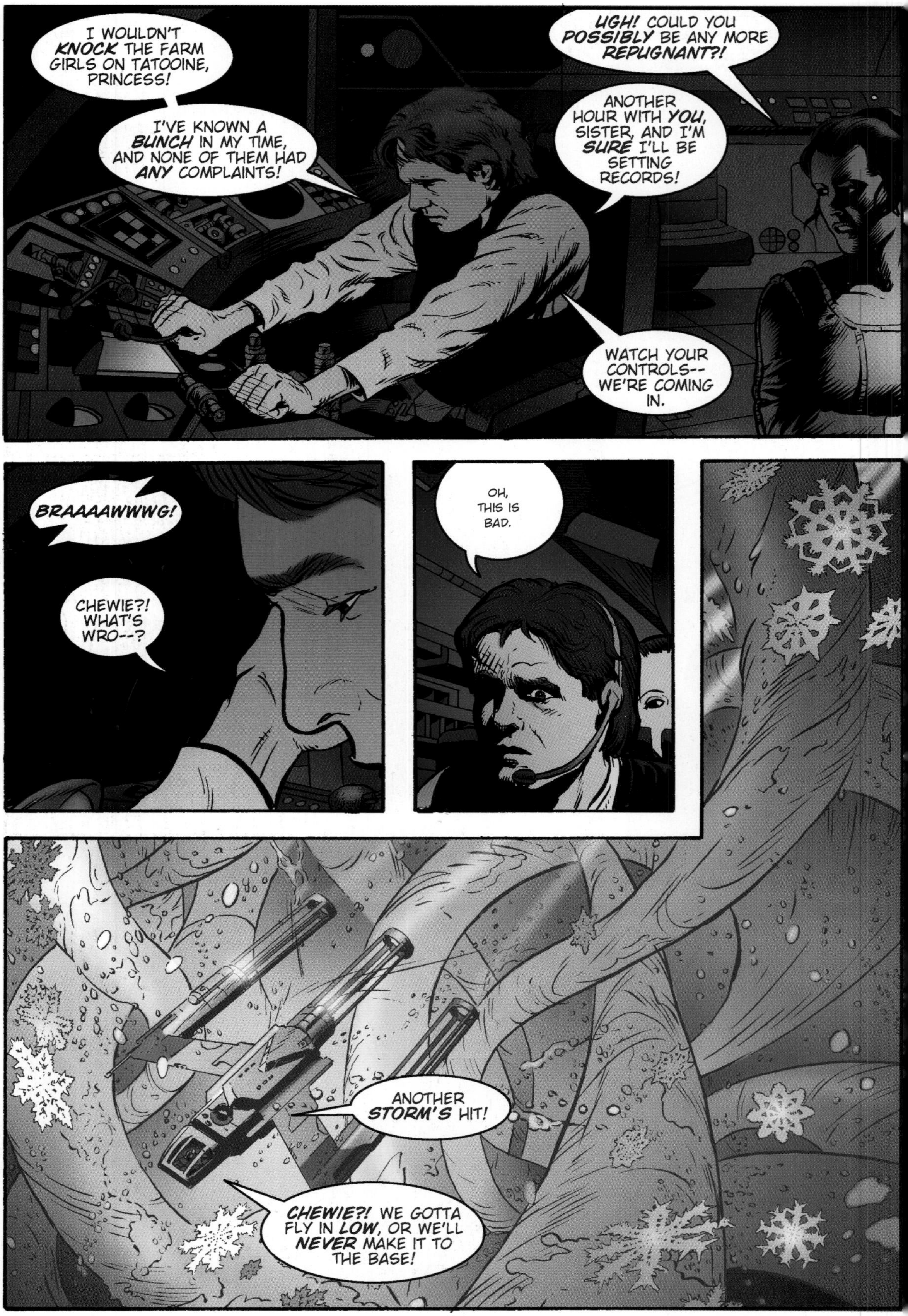
I WOULDN'T KNOCK THE FARM GIRLS ON TATOOINE, PRINCESS!
I'VE KNOWN A BUNCH IN MY TIME, AND NONE OF THEM HAD ANY COMPLAINTS!
UGH! COULD YOU POSSIBLY BE ANY MORE REPUGNANT?!
ANOTHER HOUR WITH YOU, SISTER, AND I'M SURE I'LL BE SETTING RECORDS!
WATCH YOUR CONTROLS-- WE'RE COMING IN.
BRAAAAWWWG!
CHEWIE?! WHAT'S WRO--?
OH, THIS IS BAD.
ANOTHER STORM'S HIT!
CHEWIE?! WE GOTTA FLY IN LOW, OR WE'LL NEVER MAKE IT TO THE BASE!

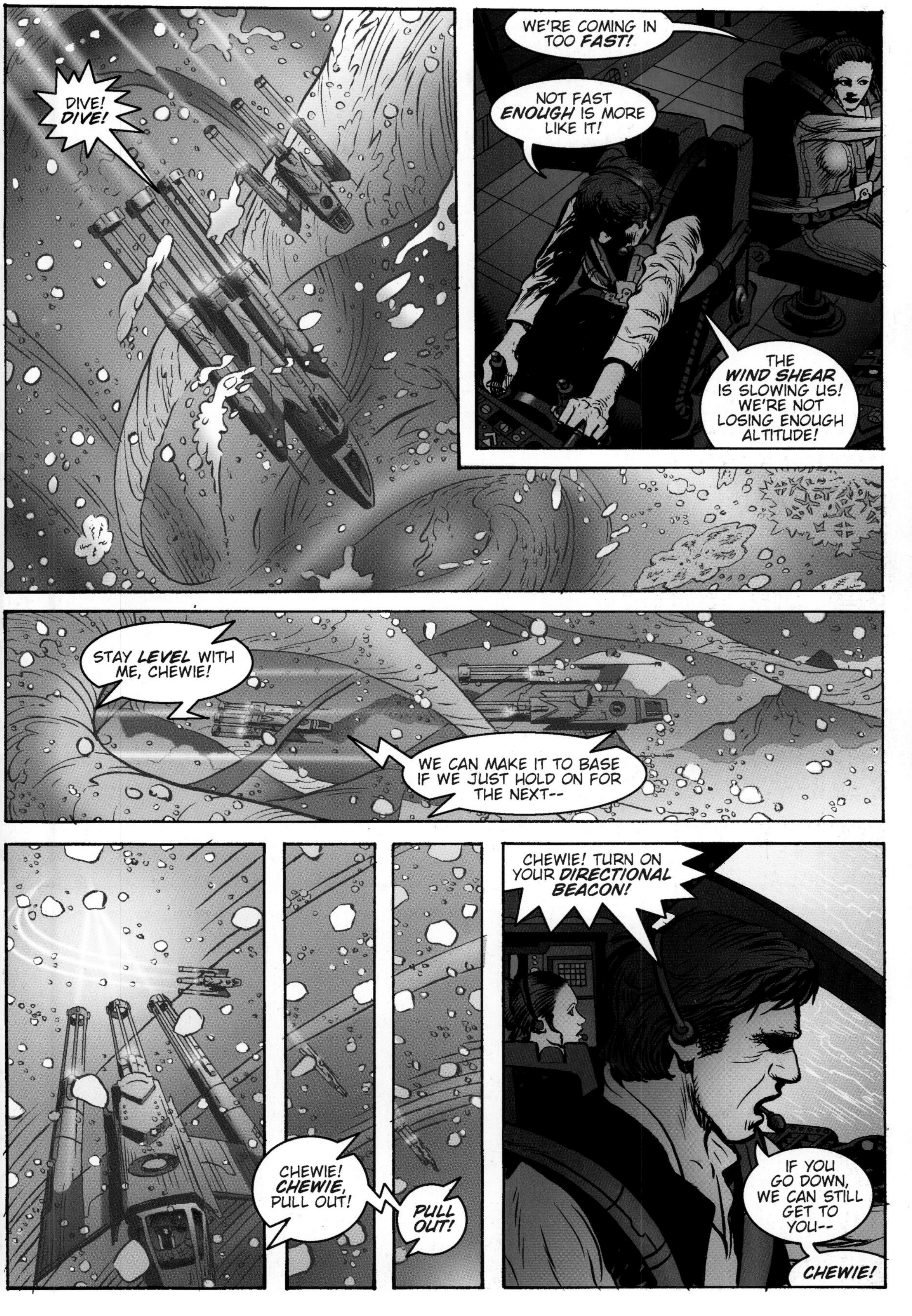
DIVE! DIVE!
WE'RE COMING IN TOO FAST!
NOT FAST ENOUGH IS MORE LIKE IT!
THE WIND SHEAR IS SLOWING US! WE'RE NOT LOSING ENOUGH ALTITUDE!
STAY LEVEL WITH ME, CHEWIE!
WE CAN MAKE IT TO BASE IF WE JUST HOLD ON FOR THE NEXT--
CHEWIE! CHEWIE, PULL OUT!
PULL OUT!
CHEWIE! TURN ON YOUR DIRECTIONAL BEACON!
IF YOU GO DOWN, WE CAN STILL GET TO YOU--
CHEWIE!

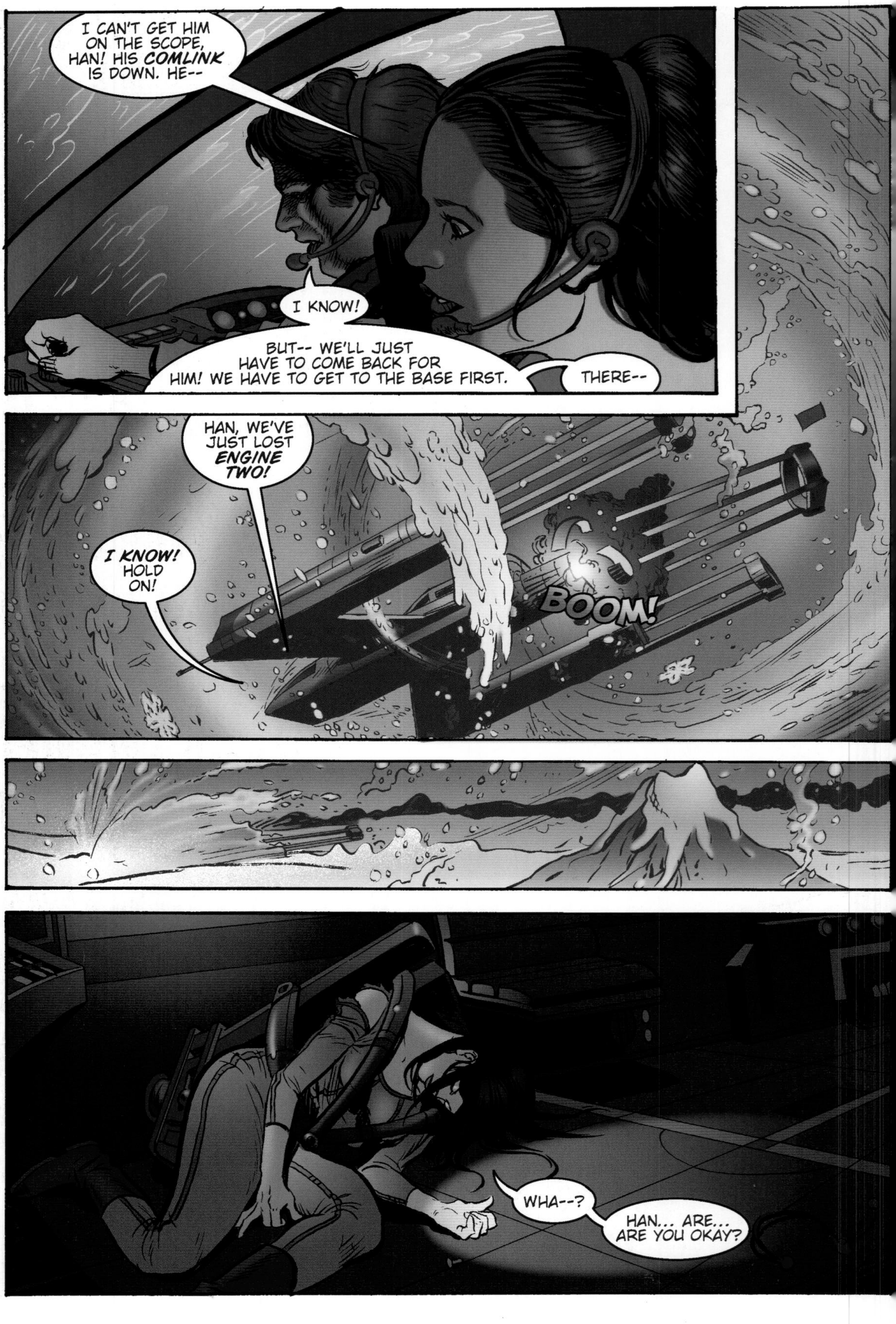
I CAN'T GET HIM ON THE SCOPE, HAN! HIS COMLINK IS DOWN. HE--
I KNOW!
BUT-- WE'LL JUST HAVE TO COME BACK FOR HIM! WE HAVE TO GET TO THE BASE FIRST.
THERE--
HAN, WE'VE JUST LOST ENGINE TWO!
I KNOW! HOLD ON!
BOOM!
WHA--?
HAN... ARE... ARE YOU OKAY?

I'M FINE.

I GOTTA GO GET CHEWIE.

HE'S ALONE OUT THERE.

ARE YOU *INSANE?!*

HE'S AT LEAST SEVERAL *KILOMETERS* AWAY!

WE HAVE TO WAIT UNTIL THE STORM LIFTS!

YOU'LL *NEVER* MAKE --

HWOOOOOOAR!

CHEWIE!

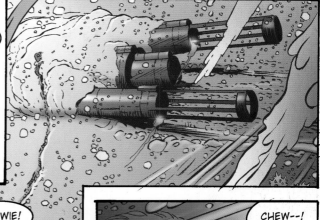

CHEWIE!

WHERE ARE YOU?!

CHEWIE!

CHEW--! CHEWIE!

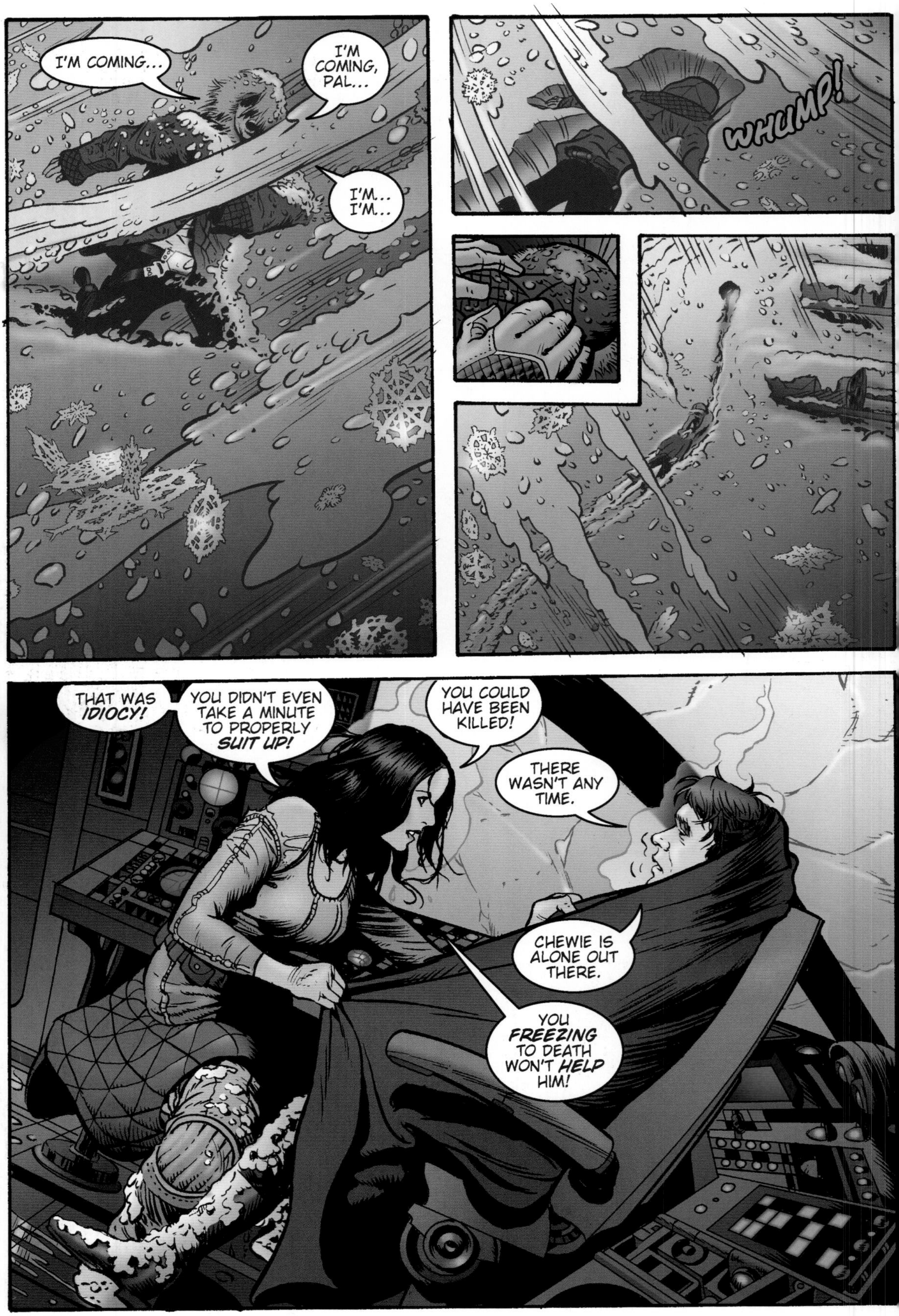

I'M COMING...
I'M COMING, PAL...
I'M... I'M...
WHLUMP!
THAT WAS IDIOCY!
YOU DIDN'T EVEN TAKE A MINUTE TO PROPERLY SUIT UP!
YOU COULD HAVE BEEN KILLED!
THERE WASN'T ANY TIME.
CHEWIE IS ALONE OUT THERE.
YOU FREEZING TO DEATH WON'T HELP HIM!

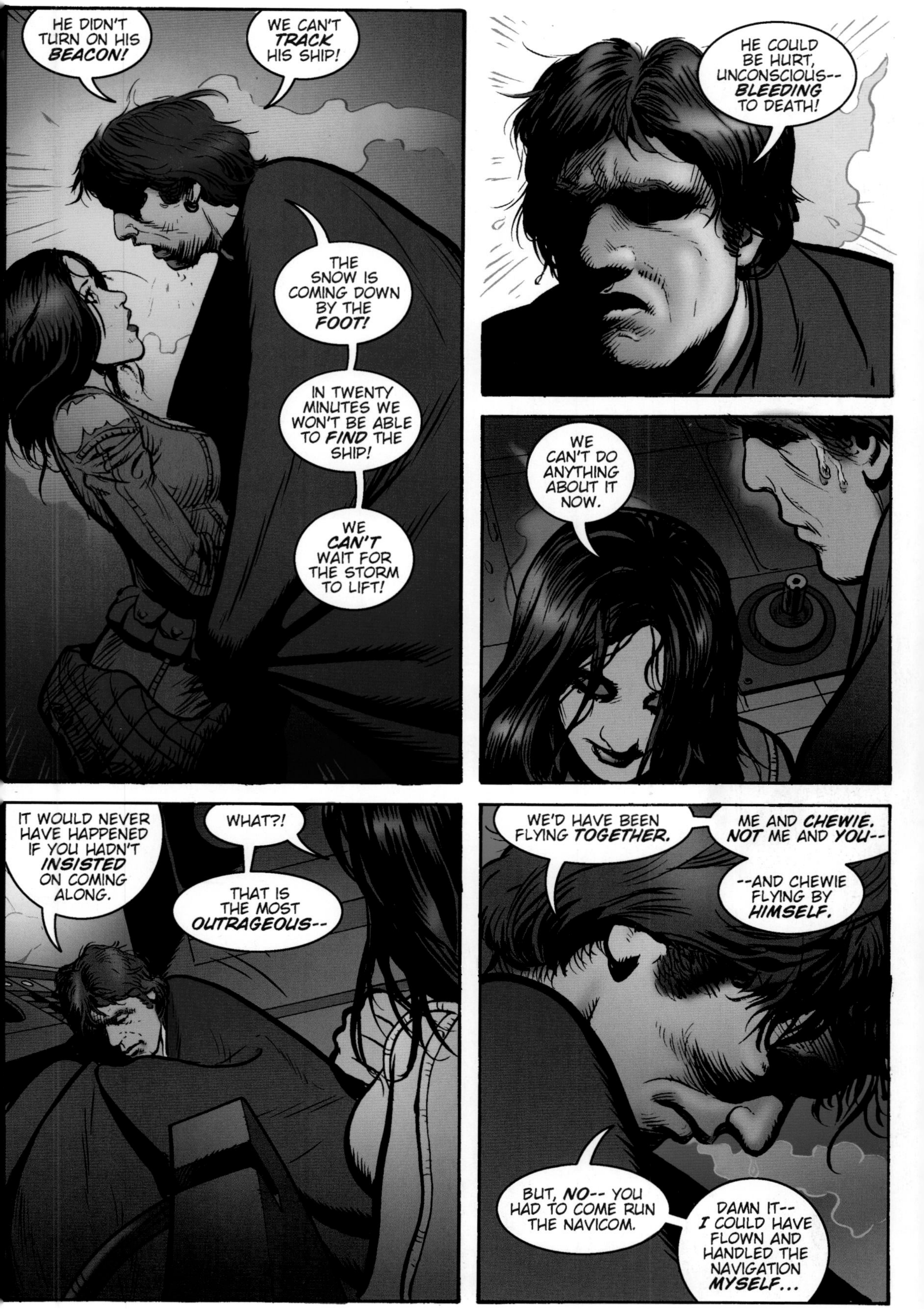
HE DIDN'T TURN ON HIS **BEACON!**
WE CAN'T **TRACK** HIS SHIP!
THE SNOW IS COMING DOWN BY THE **FOOT!**
IN TWENTY MINUTES WE WON'T BE ABLE TO **FIND** THE SHIP!
WE **CAN'T** WAIT FOR THE STORM TO LIFT!
HE COULD BE HURT, UNCONSCIOUS-- **BLEEDING** TO DEATH!
WE CAN'T DO ANYTHING ABOUT IT NOW.
IT WOULD NEVER HAVE HAPPENED IF YOU HADN'T **INSISTED** ON COMING ALONG.
WHAT?!
THAT IS THE MOST **OUTRAGEOUS--**
WE'D HAVE BEEN FLYING **TOGETHER.**
ME AND **CHEWIE. NOT** ME AND **YOU--**
--AND CHEWIE FLYING BY **HIMSELF.**
BUT, **NO--** YOU HAD TO COME RUN THE NAVICOM.
DAMN IT-- **I** COULD HAVE FLOWN AND HANDLED THE NAVIGATION **MYSELF...**

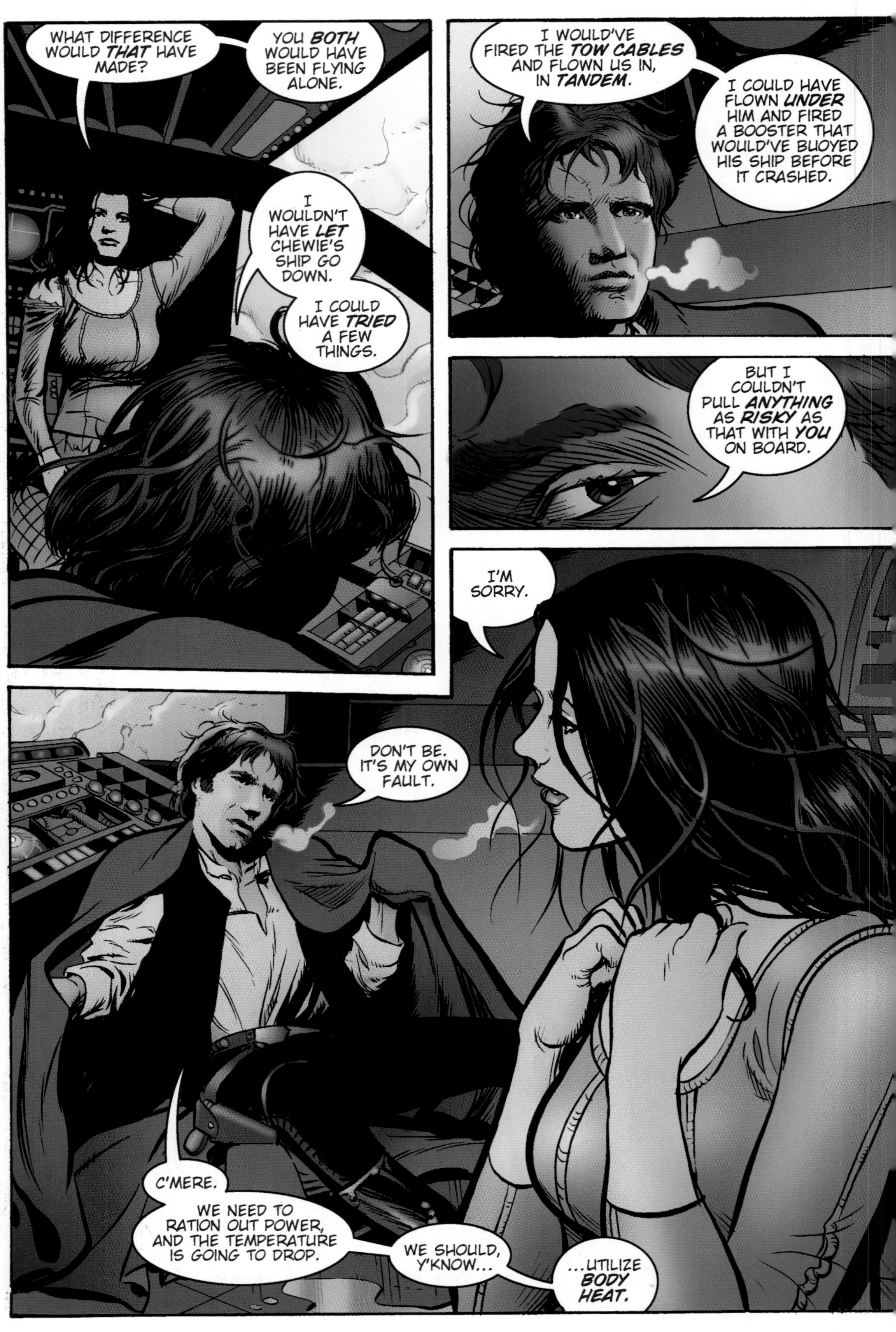

WHAT DIFFERENCE WOULD THAT HAVE MADE?
YOU BOTH WOULD HAVE BEEN FLYING ALONE.
I WOULDN'T HAVE LET CHEWIE'S SHIP GO DOWN.
I COULD HAVE TRIED A FEW THINGS.
I WOULD'VE FIRED THE TOW CABLES AND FLOWN US IN, IN TANDEM.
I COULD HAVE FLOWN UNDER HIM AND FIRED A BOOSTER THAT WOULD'VE BUOYED HIS SHIP BEFORE IT CRASHED.
BUT I COULDN'T PULL ANYTHING AS RISKY AS THAT WITH YOU ON BOARD.
I'M SORRY.
DON'T BE. IT'S MY OWN FAULT.
C'MERE.
WE NEED TO RATION OUT POWER, AND THE TEMPERATURE IS GOING TO DROP.
WE SHOULD, Y'KNOW...
...UTILIZE BODY HEAT.

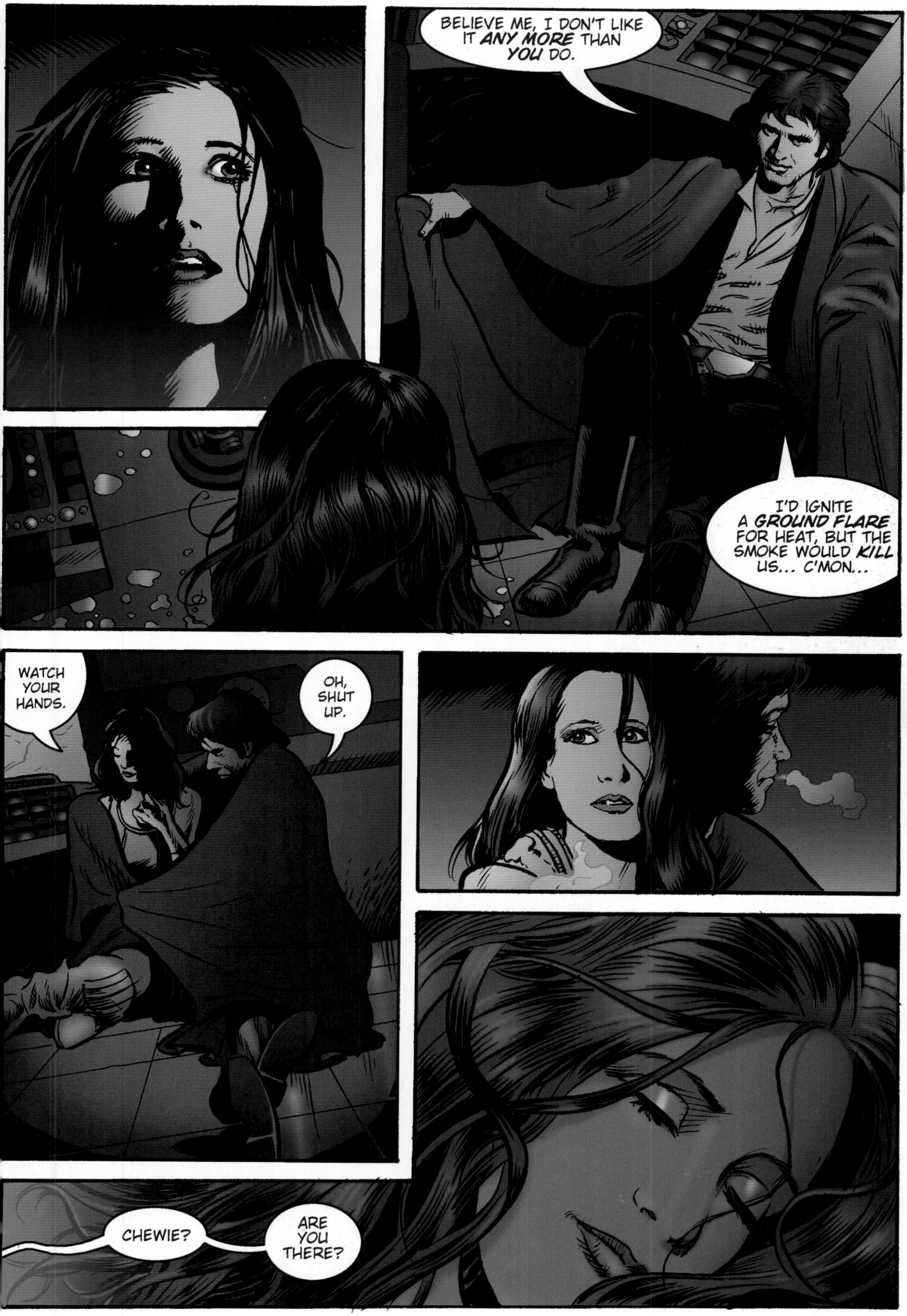
BELIEVE ME, I DON'T LIKE IT ANY MORE THAN YOU DO.
I'D IGNITE A GROUND FLARE FOR HEAT, BUT THE SMOKE WOULD KILL US... C'MON...
WATCH YOUR HANDS.
OH, SHUT UP.
CHEWIE?
ARE YOU THERE?

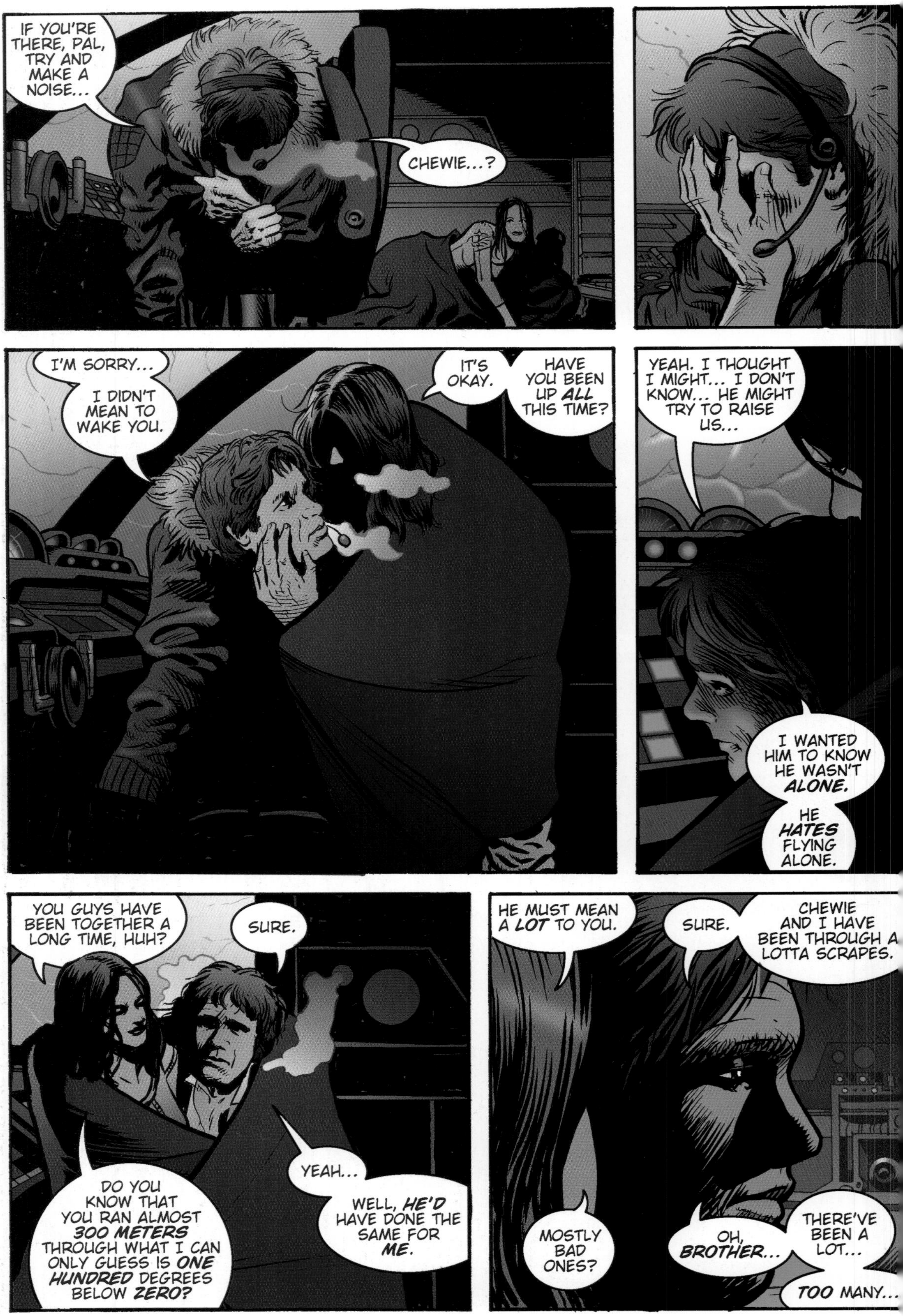
IF YOU'RE THERE, PAL, TRY AND MAKE A NOISE...
CHEWIE...?
I'M SORRY...
I DIDN'T MEAN TO WAKE YOU.
IT'S OKAY.
HAVE YOU BEEN UP **ALL** THIS TIME?
YEAH. I THOUGHT I MIGHT... I DON'T KNOW... HE MIGHT TRY TO RAISE US...
I WANTED HIM TO KNOW HE WASN'T **ALONE.**
HE **HATES** FLYING ALONE.
YOU GUYS HAVE BEEN TOGETHER A LONG TIME, HUH?
SURE.
DO YOU KNOW THAT YOU RAN ALMOST **300 METERS** THROUGH WHAT I CAN ONLY GUESS IS **ONE HUNDRED** DEGREES BELOW **ZERO?**
YEAH...
WELL, **HE'D** HAVE DONE THE SAME FOR **ME**.
HE MUST MEAN A **LOT** TO YOU.
SURE.
CHEWIE AND I HAVE BEEN THROUGH A LOTTA SCRAPES.
MOSTLY BAD ONES?
OH, **BROTHER...**
THERE'VE BEEN A LOT...
TOO MANY...

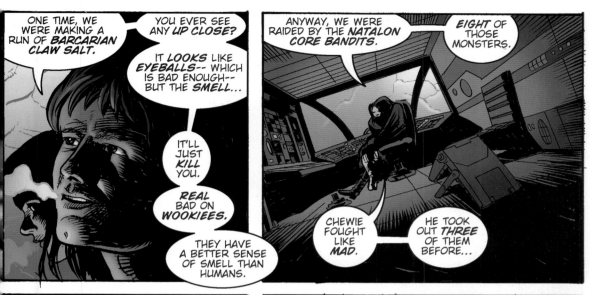

ONE TIME, WE WERE MAKING A RUN OF *BARCARIAN CLAW SALT.*

YOU EVER SEE ANY *UP CLOSE?*

IT *LOOKS* LIKE *EYEBALLS*-- WHICH IS BAD ENOUGH-- BUT THE *SMELL...*

IT'LL JUST *KILL* YOU.

REAL BAD ON *WOOKIEES.*

THEY HAVE A BETTER SENSE OF SMELL THAN HUMANS.

ANYWAY, WE WERE RAIDED BY THE *NATALON CORE BANDITS.*

EIGHT OF THOSE MONSTERS.

CHEWIE FOUGHT LIKE *MAD.*

HE TOOK OUT *THREE* OF THEM BEFORE...

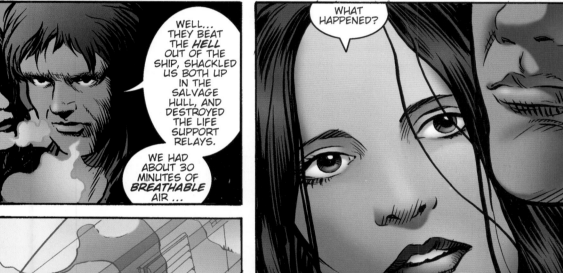

WELL... THEY BEAT THE *HELL* OUT OF THE SHIP, SHACKLED US BOTH UP IN THE SALVAGE HULL, AND DESTROYED THE LIFE SUPPORT RELAYS.

WE HAD ABOUT 30 MINUTES OF *BREATHABLE* AIR ...

WHAT HAPPENED?

HAN...?

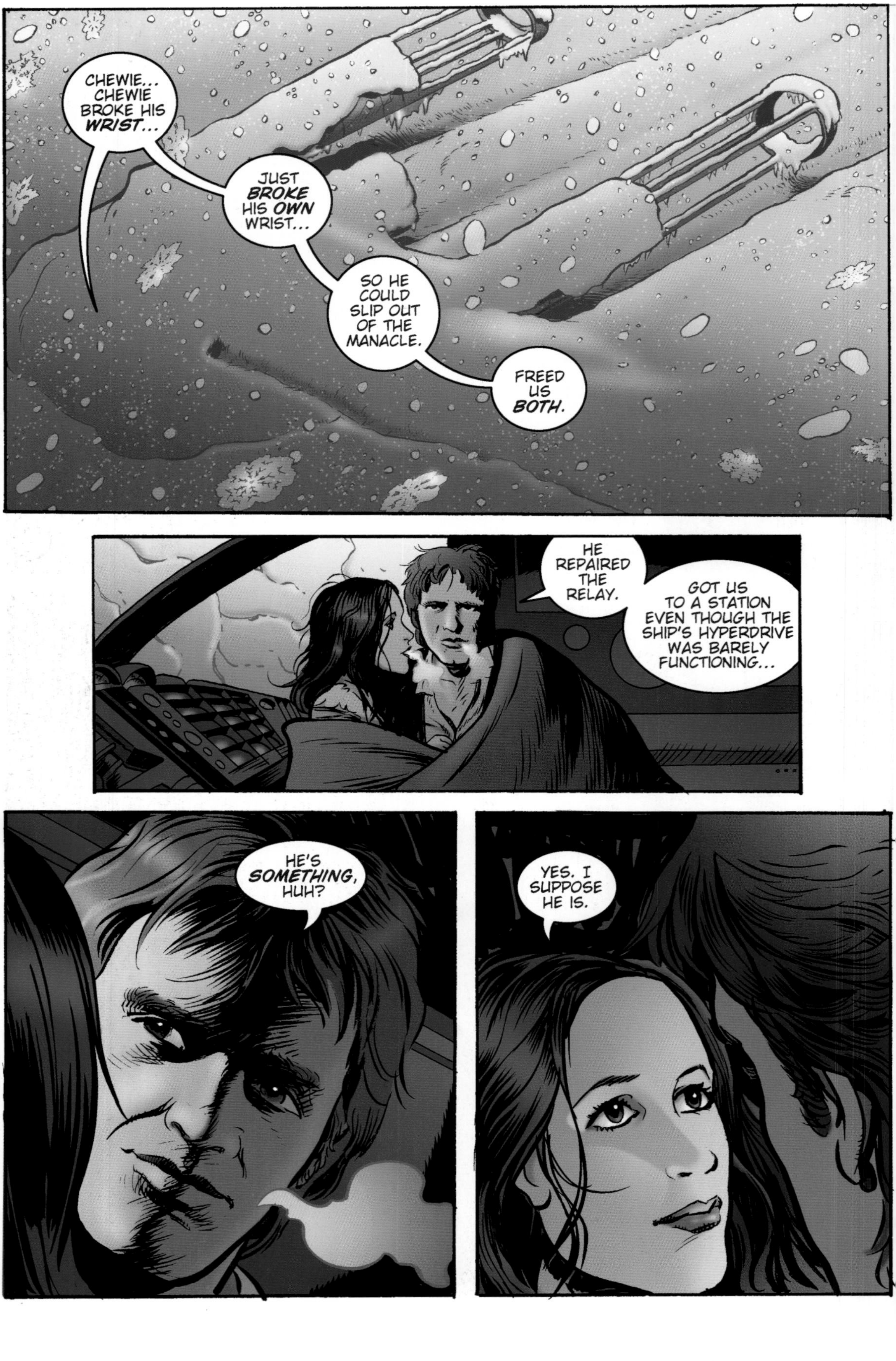
CHEWIE... CHEWIE BROKE HIS WRIST...
JUST BROKE HIS OWN WRIST...
SO HE COULD SLIP OUT OF THE MANACLE.
FREED US BOTH.
HE REPAIRED THE RELAY.
GOT US TO A STATION EVEN THOUGH THE SHIP'S HYPERDRIVE WAS BARELY FUNCTIONING...
HE'S SOMETHING, HUH?
YES. I SUPPOSE HE IS.

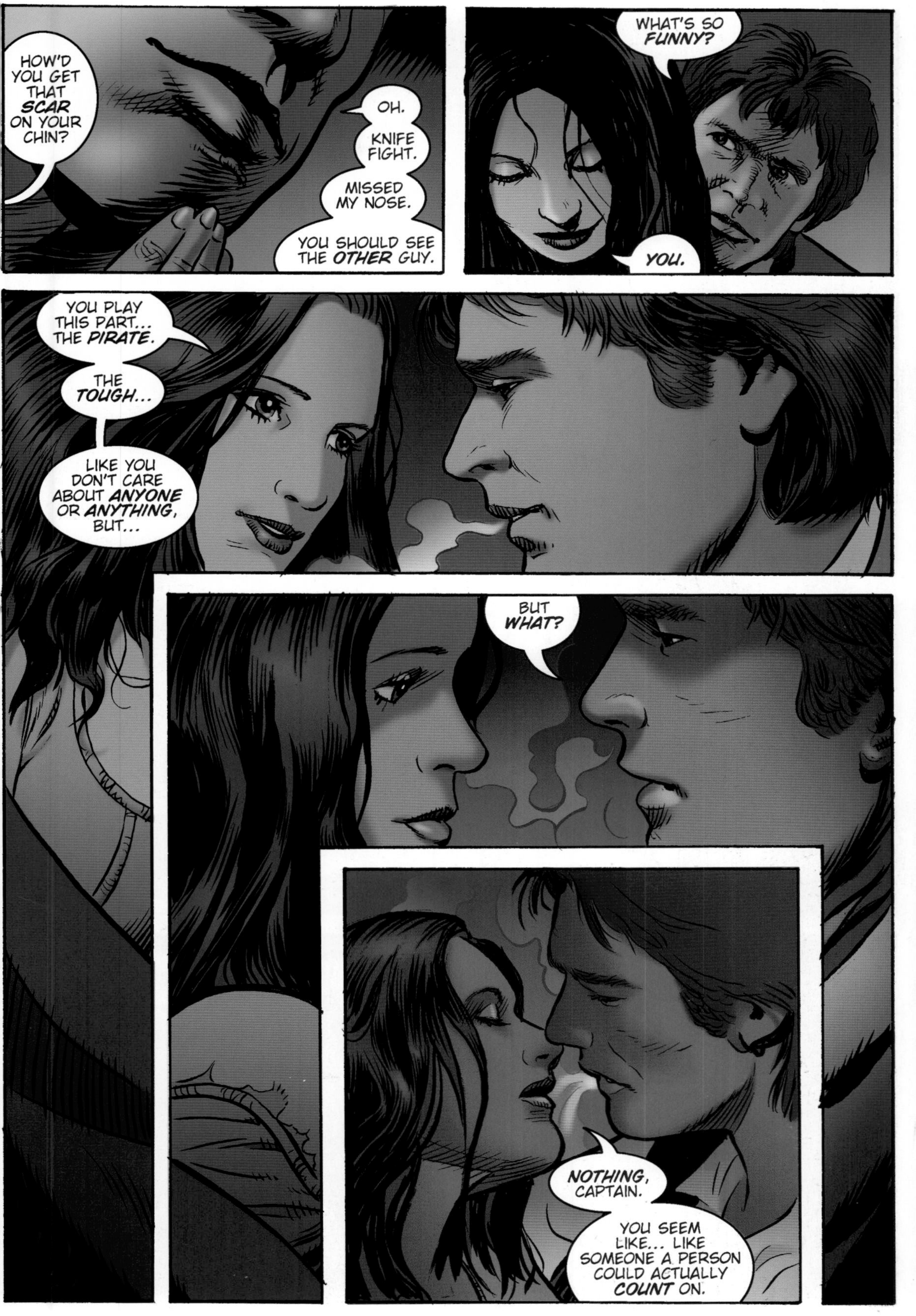
HOW'D YOU GET THAT SCAR ON YOUR CHIN?
OH.
KNIFE FIGHT.
MISSED MY NOSE.
YOU SHOULD SEE THE OTHER GUY.
WHAT'S SO FUNNY?
YOU.
YOU PLAY THIS PART... THE PIRATE.
THE TOUGH...
LIKE YOU DON'T CARE ABOUT ANYONE OR ANYTHING, BUT...
BUT WHAT?
NOTHING, CAPTAIN.
YOU SEEM LIKE... LIKE SOMEONE A PERSON COULD ACTUALLY COUNT ON.

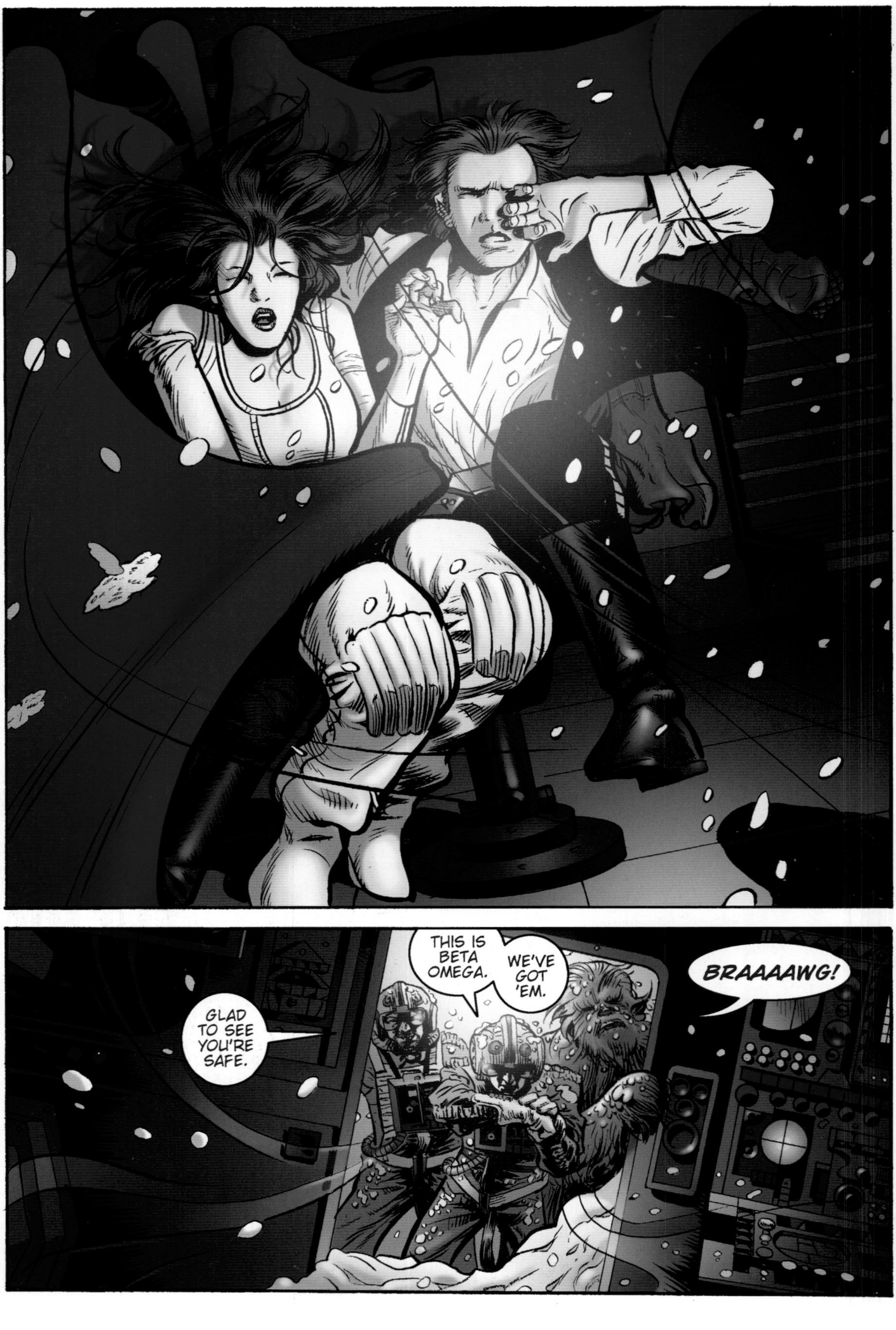

GLAD TO SEE YOU'RE SAFE.
THIS IS BETA OMEGA.
WE'VE GOT 'EM.
BRAAAAWG!

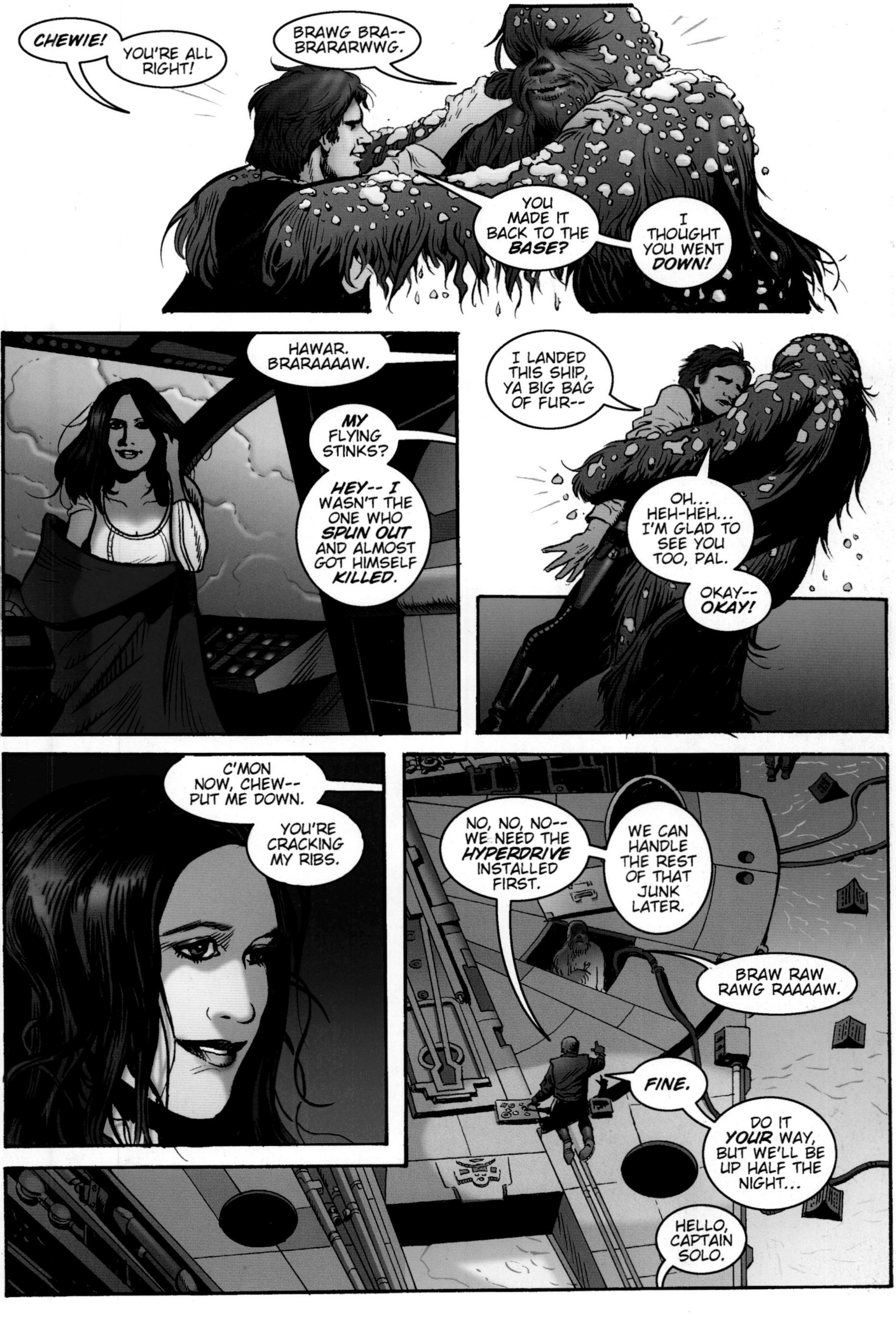
CHEWIE!
YOU'RE ALL RIGHT!
BRAWG BRA-- BRARARWWG.
YOU MADE IT BACK TO THE BASE?
I THOUGHT YOU WENT DOWN!
HAWAR. BRARAAAAW.
MY FLYING STINKS?
HEY-- I WASN'T THE ONE WHO SPUN OUT AND ALMOST GOT HIMSELF KILLED.
I LANDED THIS SHIP, YA BIG BAG OF FUR--
OH... HEH-HEH... I'M GLAD TO SEE YOU TOO, PAL.
OKAY-- OKAY!
C'MON NOW, CHEW-- PUT ME DOWN.
YOU'RE CRACKING MY RIBS.
NO, NO, NO-- WE NEED THE HYPERDRIVE INSTALLED FIRST.
WE CAN HANDLE THE REST OF THAT JUNK LATER.
BRAW RAW RAWG RAAAAW.
FINE.
DO IT YOUR WAY, BUT WE'LL BE UP HALF THE NIGHT...
HELLO, CAPTAIN SOLO.

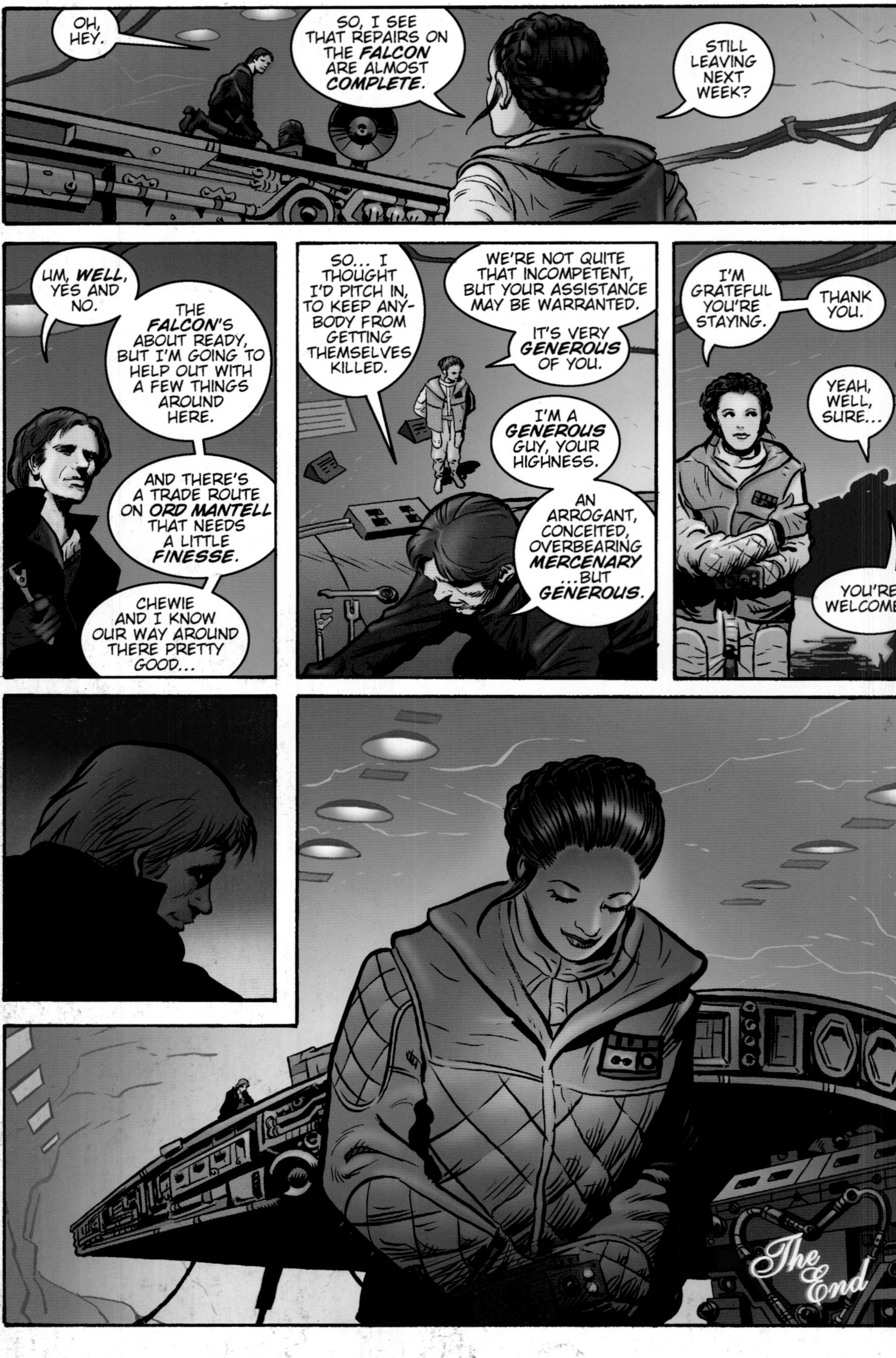
OH, HEY.
SO, I SEE THAT REPAIRS ON THE FALCON ARE ALMOST COMPLETE.
STILL LEAVING NEXT WEEK?
UM, WELL, YES AND NO.
THE FALCON'S ABOUT READY, BUT I'M GOING TO HELP OUT WITH A FEW THINGS AROUND HERE.
AND THERE'S A TRADE ROUTE ON ORD MANTELL THAT NEEDS A LITTLE FINESSE.
CHEWIE AND I KNOW OUR WAY AROUND THERE PRETTY GOOD...
SO... I THOUGHT I'D PITCH IN, TO KEEP ANY-BODY FROM GETTING THEMSELVES KILLED.
WE'RE NOT QUITE THAT INCOMPETENT, BUT YOUR ASSISTANCE MAY BE WARRANTED.
IT'S VERY GENEROUS OF YOU.
I'M A GENEROUS GUY, YOUR HIGHNESS.
AN ARROGANT, CONCEITED, OVERBEARING MERCENARY ...BUT GENEROUS.
I'M GRATEFUL YOU'RE STAYING.
THANK YOU.
YEAH, WELL, SURE...
YOU'RE WELCOME.
The End

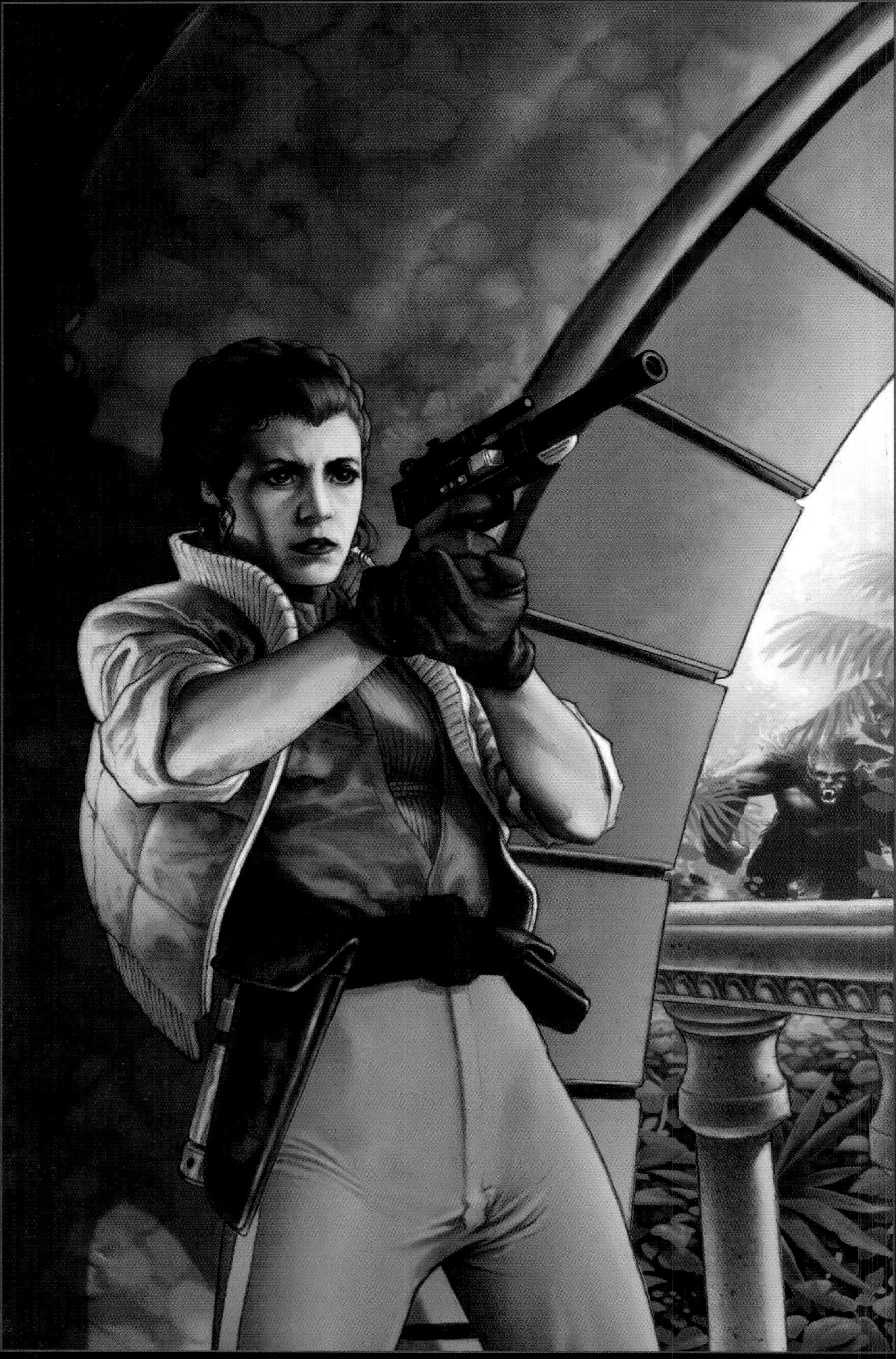

DOUG WHEATLEY

STAR WARS®

TIMELINE OF TRADE PAPERBACKS AND GRAPHIC NOVELS!

OLD REPUBLIC ERA:
25,000-1000 YEARS BEFORE
STAR WARS: A NEW HOPE

Tales of the Jedi—
Knights of the Old Republic
ISBN: 1-56971-020-1 $14.95

Dark Lords of the Sith
ISBN: 1-56971-095-3 $17.95

The Sith War
ISBN: 1-56971-173-9 $17.95

The Golden Age of the Sith
ISBN: 1-56971-229-8 $16.95

The Freedon Nadd Uprising
ISBN: 1-56971-307-3 $5.95

The Fall of the Sith Empire
ISBN: 1-56971-320-0 $15.95

Redemption
ISBN: 1-56971-535-1 $14.95

Jedi vs. Sith
ISBN: 1-56971-649-8 $17.95

RISE OF THE EMPIRE ERA:
1000-0 YEARS BEFORE
STAR WARS: A NEW HOPE

The Stark Hyperspace War
ISBN: 1-56971-985-3 $12.95

Prelude to Rebellion
ISBN: 1-56971-448-7 $14.95

Jedi Council—Acts of War
ISBN: 1-56971-539-4 $12.95

Darth Maul
ISBN: 1-56971-542-4 $12.95

Jedi Council—
Emissaries to Malastare
ISBN: 1-56971-545-9 $15.95

Episode I—
The Phantom Menace
ISBN: 1-56971-359-6 $12.95

Episode I—
The Phantom Menace Adventures
ISBN: 1-56971-443-6 $12.95

Outlander
ISBN: 1-56971-514-9 $14.95

Star Wars: Jango Fett—
Open Seasons
ISBN: 1-56971-671-4 $12.95

The Bounty Hunters
ISBN: 1-56971-467-3 $12.95

Twilight
ISBN: 1-56971-558-0 $12.95

The Hunt for Aurra Sing
ISBN: 1-56971-651-X $12.95

Darkness
ISBN: 1-56971-659-5 $12.95

The Rite of Passage
ISBN: 1-59307-042-X $12.95

Episode II—Attack of the Clones
ISBN: 1-56971-609-9 $17.95

Clone Wars Volume 1:
The Defense of Kamino
ISBN: 1-56971-962-4 $14.95

Clone Wars Volume 2:
Victories and Sacrifices
ISBN: 1-56971-969-1 $14.95

Clone Wars Adventures Volume 1
ISBN: 1-59307-243-0 $6.95

Clone Wars Volume 3:
Last Stand on Jabiim
ISBN: 1-59307-006-3 $14.95

Clone Wars Volume 4: Light and Dark
ISBN: 1-59307-195-7 $16.95

Droids—The Kalarba Adventures
ISBN: 1-56971-064-3 $17.95

Droids—Rebellion
ISBN: 1-56971-224-7 $14.95

Classic Star Wars—
Han Solo At Stars' End
ISBN: 1-56971-254-9 $6.95

Boba Fett—Enemy of The Empire
ISBN: 1-56971-407-X $12.95

Dark Forces—
Soldier for the Empire GSA
ISBN: 1-56971-348-0 $14.95

Mara Jade—By the Emperor's Hand
ISBN: 1-56971-401-0 $15.95

Underworld
ISBN: 1-56971-618-8 $15.95

Empire Volume 1: Betrayal
ISBN: 1-56971-964-0 $12.95

Empire Volume 2: Darklighter
ISBN: 1-56971-975-6 $17.95

REBELLION ERA:
0-5 YEARS AFTER
STAR WARS: A NEW HOPE

Classic Star Wars, Volume 1:
In Deadly Pursuit
ISBN: 1-56971-109-7 $16.95

Classic Star Wars, Volume 2:
The Rebel Storm
ISBN: 1-56971-106-2 $16.95

Classic Star Wars, Volume 3:
Escape to Hoth
ISBN: 1-56971-093-7 $16.95

Classic Star Wars—
The Early Adventures
ISBN: 1-56971-178-X $19.95

Jabba the Hutt—The Art of the Deal
ISBN: 1-56971-310-3 $9.95

Vader's Quest
ISBN: 1-56971-415-0 $11.95

Splinter of the Mind's Eye
ISBN: 1-56971-223-9 $14.95

A Long Time Ago... Volume 1:
Doomworld
ISBN: 1-56971-754-0 $29.95

A Long Time Ago... Volume 2:
Dark Encounters
ISBN: 1-56971-785-0 $29.95

A Long Time Ago... Volume 3:
Resurrection of Evil
ISBN: 1-56971-786-9 $29.95

A Long Time Ago... Volume 4:
Screams in the Void
ISBN: 1-56971-787-7 $29.95

A Long Time Ago... Volume 5:
Fool's Bounty
ISBN: 1-56971-906-3 $29.95

A Long Time Ago... Volume 6:
Wookiee World
ISBN: 1-56971-907-1 $29.95

A Long Time Ago... Volume 7:
Far, Far Away
ISBN: 1-56971-908-X $29.95

**Battle of the Bounty Hunters
Pop-Up Book**
ISBN: 1-56971-129-1 $17.95

Shadows of the Empire
ISBN: 1-56971-183-6 $17.95

**The Empire Strikes Back—
The Special Edition**
ISBN: 1-56971-234-4 $9.95

Return of the Jedi—The Special Edition
ISBN: 1-56971-235-2 $9.95

NEW REPUBLIC ERA:
5-25 YEARS AFTER
STAR WARS: A NEW HOPE

**X-Wing Rouge Squadron
The Phantom Affair**
ISBN: 1-56971-251-4 $12.95

Battleground Tatooine
ISBN: 1-56971-276-X $12.95

The Warrior Princess
ISBN: 1-56971-330-8 $12.95

Requiem for a Rogue
ISBN: 1-56971-331-6 $12.95

In the Empire's Service
ISBN: 1-56971-383-9 $12.95

Blood and Honor
ISBN: 1-56971-387-1 $12.95

Masquerade
ISBN: 1-56971-487-8 $12.95

Mandatory Retirement
ISBN: 1-56971-492-4 $12.95

**Shadows of the Empire
Evolution**
ISBN: 1-56971-441-X $14.95

Heir to the Empire
ISBN: 1-56971-202-6 $19.95

Dark Force Rising
ISBN: 1-56971-269-7 $17.95

The Last Command
ISBN: 1-56971-378-2 $17.95

Dark Empire
ISBN: 1-59307-039-X $16.95

Dark Empire II
ISBN: 1-56971-119-4 $17.95

Empire's End
ISBN: 1-56971-306-5 $5.95

Boba Fett—Death, Lies, & Treachery
ISBN: 1-56971-311-1 $12.95

Crimson Empire
ISBN: 1-56971-355-3 $17.95

Crimson Empire II—Council of Blood
ISBN: 1-56971-410-X $17.95

Jedi Academy—Leviathan
ISBN: 1-56971-456-8 $11.95

Union
ISBN: 1-56971-464-9 $12.95

NEW JEDI ORDER ERA:
25+ YEARS AFTER
STAR WARS: A NEW HOPE

Chewbacca
ISBN: 1-56971-515-7 $12.95

**INFINITIES:
DOES NOT APPLY TO TIMELINE**

Infinities — A New Hope
ISBN: 1-56971-648-X $12.95

Infinities—The Empire Strikes Back
ISBN: 1-56971-904-7 $12.95

Infinities—Return of the Jedi
ISBN: 1-59307-206-6 $12.95

Star Wars Tales Volume 1
ISBN: 1-56971-619-6 $19.95

Star Wars Tales Volume 2
ISBN: 1-56971-757-5 $19.95

Star Wars Tales Volume 3
ISBN: 1-56971-836-9 $19.95

Star Wars Tales Volume 4
ISBN: 1-56971-989-6 $19.95

AVAILABLE AT YOUR LOCAL COMICS SHOP OR BOOKSTORE
To find a comics shop in your area, call **1-888-266-4226**
For more information or to order direct: • On the web: www.darkhorse.com • E-mail: mailorder@darkhorse.com
• Phone: 1-800-862-0052 or (503) 652-9701 Mon.-Sat. 9 A.M. to 5 P.M. Pacific Time